Stumbling Thru

Book Two:
Keepin' On Keepin' On

Stumbling Thru

Book Two:
Keepin' On Keepin' On

by
A. Digger Stolz

Follyworks Publishing, LLC
Copyright 2013

Published in the United States of America by
Follyworks Publishing, LLC.

Printed in the United States of America.

Library of Congress Control Number: 22013952063

Stolz, A. Digger
Stumbling Thru: Keepin' On Keepin' On: a novel / A. Digger Stolz
ISBN 978-0615897585

Follyworks Publishing, LLC, Niantic, Connecticut

First Edition

Book design by Stewart A. Williams

For Mops

I'm glad I got some of your crazy.

Acknowledgements

I would be remiss in thinking I could have written this book without the special help of some special people:

Bird—for being the boss of me and otherwise snapping the whip.

B-Bop—for insisting we go to, what felt like, a thousand book readings and author talks.

Hibs—for yet another classic commando-style read through.

The Spike—for being a good field doctor and a terrible trail scientist.

Frizzle—for being the dippiest hipster I know…and a great faceman.

Bonnie—for an unexpected PR push throughout the greater Erieville area.

Finally, I'd like to thank all the hikers, volunteers and maintainers who tirelessly help to promote and protect the Appalachian Trail experience.

PART TWO:

KEEPIN' ON KEEPIN' ON

Something was different. Something had changed.

On the surface, it was all the same. Strikingly similar really, but still curiously, not. By this time, the motions and the terrain, the sights and sounds had become familiar friends, background noise, little more than smooth-worn parts of an old routine.

Left, right. Left, right.

Up, over and down. Up. Over. Down.

With a certain clockwork regularity, the trail disappeared into the woods, it wandered through the woods and climbed above the woods before finally slipping down and out of the woods, just in time to head back into the woods once more.

Wetlands became pasturelands became woodlands became bare rocky summits became woodlands became pasturelands became wetlands.

Sleep. Wake. Eat. Walk. Eat. Walk. Eat. Walk. Eat. Eat. Sleep.

Generally, the changes in flora and fauna were so glacially slow, they didn't register. Sure Virginia was different than Georgia, but not so much different as to make an impression. It wasn't Balinese beaches and Alaskan mountain ranges different. There were still big trees and little birds overhead, brown rodents and black snakes underfoot, wildflowers swaying and dead leaves skittering before a similarly gentle breeze.

Maybe the something different was with the trail. Maybe it was with Bartleby. Maybe it was the quiet that had temporarily settled itself over them both. Maybe it was something else entirely, the alignment of the stars or the earth wobbling momentarily on its axis. Bartleby didn't know and he didn't much care to solve the mystery if that meant analyzing it all to death.

Besides, he wasn't complaining.

Different felt good. Something felt good. Feeling felt good.

Close on the heels of that last thought, Sweet Jane came galumphing out of the woods and gave Bartleby a perfunctory little sniff-snort. She'd already moved on, snuffling at the firepit before he got his pack off.

Partnership Shelter.

"Hiya, Bumblebee."

Mad Chatter stood by the picnic table, barefoot and bare chested. He appeared to have recently scrubbed himself to a healthy pink glow. The little old man's pointed beard dripped water, his hair looked towel-dried wild. Although he hadn't shaved, he was in the middle of applying Old Spice aftershave; gently patting too much of the stuff around his face and neck. Bartleby instantly recognized the faux ivory bottle, his father had used the same brand.

Chatter paused his ministrations long enough to gesture at the shelter's far side, "See? I wasn't fooling about there being a shower. Even left some hot water for ya."

After dropping his pack, Bartleby lurched over to investigate. He'd grown so accustomed to the extra weight and odd balance that came with wearing a backpack, his mind was momentarily confused and his legs strangely uncertain without it. Like how a sailor's sea legs can betray him on that first pier walk from ship to shore.

And sure enough, the old man had been right—the shelter did come equipped with a working shower. To keep from being disappointed, Bartleby hadn't let himself believe Chatter's unlikely story that Partnership Shelter was equipped with shower facilities. But now that he had set eyes on the place, Bartleby saw the truth of Chatter's claims. A bit beyond the shelter was a permanent privy and a paved road not fifty yards beyond that. Partnership wasn't the biggest or the newest shelter Bartleby had seen, but it was big and new and easily the nicest. Because of the easy access to this shelter, the construction volunteers had been able to soup it up special with thick wooden shingles, a poured concrete foundation, the plumbing for hot and cold running water and a rung ladder leading up to an enclosed second floor. The place even had a garbage can.

Once he'd pulled his shirt on, Chatter snugged his hat back into place. It was wide brimmed and made of forest green felt. A lighter green hat band circled the crown and a matching green ostrich feather plumed out to the rear. On the hat's left side, the brim was turned up at a jaunty angle. The thing looked like something nobody but a renaissance reenactor or an honest-to-god musketeer would dare wear. But to give the man his due, Chatter mostly pulled it off. It had taken Bartleby a full day of hiking to figure out that the hat's connection to Virginia was through the University of Virginia's mascot. A cavalier.

"I got her straight?"

"Ish."

"Book says there's a payphone a hundred yards up the way. What say we order pizza?"

"Go ahead," Bartleby grinned ruefully. "No room in my budget for pizza parties."

He was officially the poorest he'd ever been. As a swaddled infant, Bartleby had access to more money than he did currently. Only $191 left from the $850 Angie'd given him in Georgia.

The money had gone quick. There were those first gear expenditures at Neels Gap, a night in Hiawassee, new socks and hiking shoes in Hot Springs and a thirty-four dollar dinner splurge in Erwin. Not to mention Aquamira, denatured alcohol and the other unavoidable costs incurred during weekly resupplies. The occasional luxury grocery items: fruit, cold cuts and nuts added up quickly. There hadn't been any postage, phone calls or motel rooms, and unlike many hikers, Bartleby had avoided blowing his wad on fancy new gear or drinking in trail town bars. Still, the simple fact of it was, he was quickly running out of money.

"Listen, son," Chatter pointed a trembling finger at him, "it must be fifteen, twenty years since I've successfully used a payphone. I'll happily put up for the pizza, if you can see your way to working the phone and getting it delivered."

"Back in school we used to call that 'I buy, you fly'."

"Yeah, that's it then. Fly, Bumblebee, fly. Heh-heh. You're lucky, pizza delivery hadn't been invented yet when I was in school."

As much as for Chatter's generosity, Bartleby was grateful for the attempt at masking the charity with the pretense of shared responsibility. At this point in his life, Bartleby would have taken just about anything that was offered to him from just about anyone, but he didn't feel good about it.

❦

There was no soap in the shower and the water was lukewarm at best. The pizza place didn't even pretend to be a purveyor of appetizing food and the delivery guy arrived almost thirty minutes late. The two pies were cool and already congealing. As evening crept on, the clouds of mosquitoes took on an almost solid appearance.

"Don't get much better than this, huh?"

Bartleby grunted wholehearted agreement around an extended mouthful of pepperoni and cheese.

"Might be the best pizza I ever had."

Bartleby nodded along, wolfing down the crust on his third slice and holding the fourth in his hand, poised and ready to go.

While Bartleby had gone to wait for the pizza delivery, Chatter collected a pile of branches and started a small fire. Theoretically, the smoke helped to keep the bugs away. Turned out, this was one of those little tricks of the woodcraft trade that had been forwarded and CC'd and emailed to just about everyone that mattered. Except the mosquitoes. At least, they were acting like they hadn't received that particular memo.

"I figure we'll start seeing other hikers again pretty soon. Whoever hasn't quit, has got to be about whooped out by now. I know I would be."

It was Sunday night and officially the end of Trail Days. Any hikers that hadn't already left Damascus and returned to trail would be doing so shortly.

"Shame, eh? Been awful peaceful out here. Closer to what I imagined the whole trail would be like. Course, it might of been lonesome if you didn't show up," Chatter shook his head. "I mean, except for those two day hikers we passed in the Highlands, do you remember seeing anyone else out here?"

"Just them two and all those ponies," Bartleby said.

At the mention of ponies, Sweet Jane's ears perked up. Grayson Highlands was known for, among other things, its strangely fearless population of wild ponies. They had seen a small herd at a distance and Jane had wanted very much to cozy over for a better look. It had taken Chatter and Bartleby both pulling on her leash to convince her otherwise.

"Oh, you," Chatter tossed her a crust, "what would you have done, we let you go play with the ponies? Gonna eat 'em? They'd kick you right in your big ol' snout. Or maybe you wanna make friends and leave this old man before he leaves you, huh? Ever think they might not a liked you as much as I do?"

Jane waited and nobly suffered this chastisement before scapping up the crust, and slinking off to eat it in peace.

When he was done with dinner, Chatter got out the whiskey bottle and his baggie of pills. It took him forever to hunt and peck his way through the assorted hodgepodge and find his "nightlies." He kept up a constant stream of murmured mumbling the whole time, "Where's that blue one? Here you are. But you're not the right blue are you? Tricky, tricky. Yeppers. Okay, I got a yellow, I got two yellows, now I got three yellows, but I don't need yellows. White pill...white pill...big white pill, need one of these, not one of those..."

With his pills swallowed and his whiskey sipped, Chatter disappeared into his tent. Bartleby spread out his sleeping bag in the empty shelter. He climbed in and watched the last bits of fire die down.

The old man was right—the trail would fill up with hikers again soon. Generally, that was fine, probably even a good thing, but

Bartleby had grown spoiled these last few nights. Prior to Damascus, he'd rarely slept in a shelter that wasn't sardined full, and he hadn't dreamed of having one to himself. Without all the snoring, the farting, the swishing of synthetic fabrics, the zippers and whatever else, Bartleby slept better than he had in years. Nobody stepped on him, nobody elbowed him, nobody kicked him or otherwise crowded into his sleeping area. Nobody hung dripping wet clothes over his head. Nobody got up to take a whiz, stubbed a toe and made such a caterwauling cry as to wake all shelter occupants and surrounding tenters. Nobody talked in their sleep, nobody talked too loudly, nobody talked ad nauseam. Nobody did nothing but sleep.

Register: Partnership Shelter

5/13 I wanna be one
   of those wobbling Weebles
   who never wipes out.

   High-Ku

It was a misty, moisty morning. Wafting wisps of fog curled close and perched weightlessly in the air; they came in shades of gray ranging from silvery white to a dark, pewtery purple.

Beneath Bartleby's feet, the grass was slick with a heavy dew. His breath steamed as he trod forward with a stiff lurching stride and dark eyes—evidence that neither his legs nor his mind had yet fully warmed to the day's work before him.

Out of the tumbling mists appeared a starkly imposing tree, a lone crow perched on its lowest limb. As Bartleby passed, the crow called; a single, cawing croak. He spared it a long glance, but otherwise kept on trudging through the shifting shadows of this murky world.

And then, so suddenly it seemed more a function of magic than nature, the heavy fog parted and the gray haze lifted like the curtain on opening night. Bartleby couldn't rightly have said if the swirling clouds dissolved or evaporated or just went back to wherever it was that wispy mists came from.

An unbroken dome of blue appeared overhead and the surrounding pastureland flooded with sunlight. The grass shone Technicolor green against the contrasting black and white of Holsteins, a whole grazing herd of them, some no more than twenty yards away. While he walked through this newly bright world, Bartleby couldn't help but marvel at the wonder of it all.

🍁 🍁 🍁

When Bartleby arrived, Jane was barking and pulling on the end of her snagged leash. Chatter was tangled and tied up maybe a yard further in.

"That you, Bumblebee?" The old guy's pack was hooked so that he couldn't turn to look south.

"Uh-huh."

"Think I got caught on something."

"Looks like you've been stuck in a giant spider web."

"Eh. Well, you gonna get us down, or do I gotta wait for all them Trail Days yahoos to catch up?"

A tree, its branches still heavy with buds and young leaves, had blown over and crashed across trail. It lay in such a way that there wasn't any good option for getting around it. A freshly trampled footpath led off far to the west, along the length of the trunk and around the skeletal spread of roots that had lost their hold on things. At more than a hundred steps, this was an unusually long walk-around.

A shorter path circled eastward around the tree's lollipop top. This trail traversed boggy, sloping terrain and a number of rutted trenches and fresh skid marks implied the difficulties inherent in this route.

Not liking either of his options very much, Chatter had gone with door number three. Straight up the gut. Without a dog, a squirrellier hiker might've slipped out of their pack and, pulling it behind, successfully climbed through the monkey-bar tangle of branches.

Nutty as he was, there was nothing squirrelly about Mad Chatter. Between not bothering to remove his pack and the additional encumbrance of being leashed to a big dog, he really had had no chance of climbing through the snarl of branches.

Which is why when Bartleby lumbered around the last bend, Chatter and Jane were snagged up in the blowdown and doing a passable imitation of Charlie Brown's kite.

It was nice not having anything better to do than sit back and watch the mouse. It wanted into his food bag, but first had to navigate the upside down tuna can hanging from the rafters by a length of twine. Apparently, the mouse had no problem climbing straight down the twine, but things got more interesting when it reached the tin can obstacle. The little bugger put one tentative paw out, and then the other. Bartleby held his breath. The precariously tipping can seemed to prompt a moment's thoughtful hesitation from the mouse, but then, as it had done at least a dozen times already, it went ahead and shifted its full weight off the twine and onto the can.

As per its design by some clever hiker, the tin can see-sawed sharply beneath this new passenger. Unable to find any purchase on the smooth metal, the mouse tumbled free and fell four feet to the shelter floor with a heavy thrud.

It took a long second for the mouse to collect itself and scurry into a dark corner. When it reappeared on the rafters a few minutes later, Bartleby could only shake his head in wonder. He was dreaming of his wife's lasagna long before the mouse gave up.

Register: Chestnut Knob Shelter

5/23 Looks like my original blisters actually got blisters and now that everything is on the mend, my scabs have scabs.
Bartleby

As Chatter and Bartleby were sitting, recuperating from the last few miles of toil, Sweet Jane went tearing off trail. She'd been lying nearby, tongue lolling in the dirt when suddenly, with no warning, she was up and bounding through the woods. Twenty yards away, in a sunbeam, an orange-winged butterfly wafted along on some worthy purpose.

Jane reached the circle of light, leapt, snapped and missed all in one grand motion. She thudded to the ground in a heavy jumble of limbs.

"Heh-heh," Chatter chortled, "she do like herself some flappers."

Bartleby nodded, "She's a regular ol' flying flapper trapper."

Bartleby was a little surprised that he didn't lose Mad Chatter. He He wasn't trying to, exactly, but kind of expected it would happen anyway. The guy was eighty easy, maybe eighty-five, and he hiked along like a wounded goose. Instead of full strides and a steady pace, Chatter doddered forward with shaky half steps and frequent breaks. If it weren't for Sweet Jane pulling him on the uphills, Bartleby doubted the old man would've even made it this far. He kept the dog's leash in one hand, a thick blackwood walking staff in the other. Each morning, Chatter started hiking at least a full hour before Bartleby woke and generally showed up at the evening's shelter just in time to sip his nightly splash of whiskey and watch dusk turn to dark while waiting for dinner to cook.

Sometimes on the straightaways, Chatter let Jane off her leash. There wasn't much of anyone to get pissy about her running free and she never went far. If Bartleby were in sight, she might gallop ahead for a visit, but otherwise kept protectively close to Chatter and sniffed out their way.

And their way was noisy.

Bartleby could always hear Chatter coming. It was impossible not to. The old guy rattletrapped his way along, virtually enveloped in a personal clamor. His kit consisted of odds and ends kludged together and haphazardly stowed to all but guarantee a steady, swinging, swishing, jingling-jangle.

And it sounded like Chatter's thumping thick boot soles kicked and caught against every little rock or twisty root in his path. Without his hat, the guy wasn't more than a hundred and thirty pounds, but somehow his thudding footfalls made him sound like an armored stormtrooper.

One noise, though, rose above the rest. An almost constant mumbling murmur, an indistinct but unending string of nonsense words, private encouragements and unthunk thoughts, bubbling and babbling and spilling from Chatter's mouth like springtime snow melt rushing down a mountainside gulley.

None of which seemed to bother his partner in crime, Sweet Jane the Greatest Dane. In fact, she moved along with her own noisy clatter of interrogative whuffs, exertive huffs, friendly sniffs and the occasional wet sneeze. She didn't bark much, but when she did it was dauntingly deep and loud. And because Chatter packed her saddlebags with the same whimsical laxity that he packed his own ruck, more often than not, Jane moseyed along accompanied by the dice-cup shaking of hard dog food. Also, the single tin bell attached to her collar had, somewhere along the way, been partially crushed and now instead of tinkling merrily, it tonked discordantly as she bounded up trail.

Register: Jenkins Shelter

5/24 All but tripped over a tortoise this morning. Poor Jane
       didn't know what to make of it. Nice to see something out
       here moving slower than me.
                              —Sweet Jane & Mad (c)Hatter

Nothing against Pony Express or JoJo or anyone else that Bartleby
had spent time hiking around, but he now realized how nice it could
be to hike alone. No one hurried you through a rest break, held you
back from your preferred hiking pace or trailed so close behind that
it became awkward when you didn't do your part to help maintain a
rambling conversation throughout the long hiking day. Out there,
mostly alone in the woods, Bartleby couldn't help but find himself
enveloped in a peaceful quietude. Nothing much more than bird-
calls, bickering squirrels and wind-rustled branches.

The downside to all this newfound solitude was all the time it gave
Bartleby to think. Rusty as they were, the cogs in his mind had broken free and started turning again. They didn't produce anything
world shattering, no fourth law of thermodynamics or an equitable
proposal for peace in the Middle East, but still.

Bartleby thought about the future. He thought about Angie and
the kids, how they might be managing without him and when he
might see them again. He thought about returning home; both how
that might go down if he ever actually reached Mt. Katahdin or if he
went home sooner: unsuccessful and unwanted. About going home
broken and going home fixed. Wondered too, what it might actually
mean to be "fixed." He thought about not returning home at all and
the possibility that home wasn't waiting for him if he did manage to
return. About Angie moving on, taking a lover or otherwise becom-

ing unknown and unavailable.

He thought about running out of money. What he'd do, how he'd eat and where he might be when it happened. Considered strategies to forestall this inevitability—skimp on this, avoid purchasing that or maybe stopping long enough to pick up a few days' work in some trail town. He even contemplated getting a real job off trail and who might hire him. Which led to pondering what he was good at or, at least, what he was qualified to do.

When Bartleby circled around to the current problem of his diminishing financial resources, it wasn't too long before this led him to thinking about the past. He hated to admit it, but there were obvious and uncomfortable similarities between his current fiscal crisis and the one that had overwhelmed him a few years earlier. Bartleby thought about his dad back when he was alive, when he was dead, and that horribly hectic time in the hospital when he hadn't been much of either.

Bartleby thought about managing the family business. How he hadn't wanted to get involved, but immediately understood that he had to. How it had started out so well, but had somehow collapsed like a house of cards on his watch. Thought that what had happened hadn't really been his fault, but then who's fault could it have been? It was Bartleby who'd been caught carrying five properties in varying stages of development when the housing market stalled out. The market had spun faster and hotter until it seized up, like an engine without oil and suddenly no one was buying anything. He remembered selling off one cleared lot for half what he'd sunk into it, and how that money did surprisingly little to delay the inevitable foreclosures on the remaining properties.

He remembered how in its death throes, the business had been such a hungry suckhole—draining away the business accounts, the life insurance payout, Bartleby's own 401k from the pharmacy, ten grand Angie's parents lent him, even the meager college funds they'd started for the kids.

More than anything else though, Bartleby thought about the

strange path in the woods on which he'd suddenly found himself, and where, if anywhere, it might be leading him.

The trail wasn't so much muddy as sodden from the heavy dew. Each step he took, Bartleby's shoes left a print in the wet ground. At heel and toe, the soles were worn smooth, but along the edges, remnants of the rubber treads remained.

If he'd cared to turn back and study these prints, he'd have noticed that despite being cast from the same mold, each print differed slightly from the others. Like snowflakes, no two exactly alike.

"So…how have you been? Good? Feet holding up? Guess you got enough of them, huh? Hey, drink your water already and stop looking at me like that. Sorry, girl, but I'm fresh out of whatever it is that you're looking for."

Sitting on her haunches, Jane was eye level with Bartleby, who himself sat on a log. She inched closer.

"Seriously. I got nothing for you. No food in my pockets, no butterflies up my sleeve. Don't even have sleeves."

Trembling with anticipation now, Jane crowded in close.

"Chatter's in the privy. You gotta wait, he'll take care of you."

The anticipation was clearly too much for her. She closed what little distance remained between them and bulled her head in under Bartleby's chin. She left him no real choice but to start scratching behind her ears.

Big and awkward as she was, it was still difficult for Bartleby to think of Sweet Jane as anything but dainty. She trotted along trail with a resigned grace that seemed to convey her belief that this whole thru-hiking venture was a bad idea. She waited with saintly patience while Chatter went about setting up camp each night. Sometimes he forgot to give her a snack or put her water down right away. All she did was wrinkle her brow, rest her chin on her crossed front paws and sigh. Jane liked people, but she was tolerably discerning and gravitated toward a select few. She liked Bartleby and Pony Express just fine, didn't much care for Poohbah. Had actually seemed to be a little scared of Lazy JoJo.

If Sweet Jane had any one defining characteristic, it was her maternal instinct. She watched over Chatter like he was the runt of her litter: kept him warm at night, licked his face clean each morning and nosed him along whenever he needed it. Which was more often than not. For the most part, Sweet Jane entirely ignored squirrels, rabbits and birds. She wouldn't have batted an eye if a chipmunk curled up and took a nap in the crook of her neck when she laid on her side. But as soon as one of those little critters happened too close to Chatter, Jane wouldn't take her eyes off them. If they persisted, she'd give off a low rumbling growl. If that didn't do the trick, Jane bared teeth, flattened ears and otherwise readied herself to pounce. Bartleby had only actually witnessed her attack pounce once—it was about as graceless and ungainly a motion as he guessed any predator ever made—but ninety-five pounds of lurchingly uncoordinated canine was still enough to send the local herbivores sprinting for cover.

She wasn't the only dog out hiking the trail, but Sweet Jane was, far and away, the best of the bunch. Wounded Knees' dog, Shunka, was one ugly-assed Rottweiler mix; a hellhound half-breed with the territorial instincts of a grizzly. Once Shunka worked himself up into a fervor defending his plot of land (which happened *every* time Wounded tied the dog up), he'd go after anyone crazy enough to come close. One time, Shunka caught and quartered a rabbit not more than six feet from where Flutterby was standing. She had to wait three days to machine-wash the blood spatter out of her shorts.

The tight-fisted Canadian thru-hiker, Nickleback, had a German shepherd named Lancelot. Lancelot was an unrepentant and incurable humper. Would happily mount up and hump on other dogs, unsuspecting civilians and unguarded backpacks.

GoingGoingGone's canine compadre, Wily, liked to eat socks. She could render a single Smartwool midweight hiking sock unusable in fifteen seconds, disappear it entirely in less than ninety. Needless to say, this was a skillset that did not make Wily popular around shelters.

The trail loped gently along a wooded ridge.

"Got any family, Bumblebee?"

"Yep."

Except for labored breathing and occasional birdsong, there ensued a half mile of relative quiet.

Chatter stopped and turned back, "You're good company, Bumblebee, don't get me wrong. Great having you around, but I'm buggered if you aren't about the worst conversationalist I ever did meet."

Bartleby's new beard couldn't quite hide a sheepish smile.

"Not the first time you've heard that particular complaint, is it?"

They started moving again.

"Least I'm listening now. Used to be I couldn't even do that. Bet my wife would call it an improvement."

"So you're married?"

"Yeah, I guess I probably still am."

"Strained?"

"Shouldn't be. Angie's great. We used to be pretty great together."

"So?"

"So...I'm not so great."

"That why you're out here?"

Bartleby's shrug went unseen by the old man.

"Not much of my family left," Chatter said. "And except for Jane, everyone still alive thinks I'm a kooky old geezer who talks about three times more than he should. Don't want anything to do with me. But what're you gonna do? Life's a funny business. No choice but to shuffle along and hope for a sunny someday."

❦ ❦ ❦

Something like fifty miles south of Pearisburg, Bartleby came up on a trailside art installation. Someone had carried old furniture out into the woods and arrayed it in an open area, not fifteen feet off the AT. This artiste had positioned the furniture as you might traditionally find in an apartment. The couch and coffee table faced a wood-paneled TV. A non-matching toilet and sink stood off to one side in a "bathroom area." The "kitchen" held a table and chairs. Empty picture frames hung from tree limbs and a braided oval rug covered the ground between couch and TV. It was incongruous, curious and, Bartleby quickly concluded, a massive waste of time and effort.

There was a plaque bursting full of small print which explained the artist's inspiration, intentions and methodology. Bartleby didn't bother reading it. Instead he thought how Bawdy was going to have a grand old time dissecting and deconstructing it all when he passed through.

Only after approaching the couch, did Bartleby realize it was occupied. A lanky, bald-headed character was curled up and drowsing peaceful as a dog in the sun. Bartleby cleared his throat and shuffled his feet. When this didn't provoke any response, he dropped his pack from waist height. It landed with a good thrunking cronk. The man's eyes popped open.

He sat up, yawned, scratched.

"Sorry," Bartleby said, "I, ah…didn't see you there."

"It's okay," he mumbled sheepishly, "I couldn't resist." He patted the cushion on the far end of the couch. "Here sit, take a seat. She's a bit damp and earthy, but otherwise a sweet ride. Name's Bindle Stiff."

Bartleby sat, pulled out food and started on lunch. Bindle Stiff set to rolling a thick joint. He was just licking it closed when Jane came bounding into the living room. When he arrived, Mad Chatter dropped unceremoniously into the armchair, and set exposed springs spronging in complaint.

Bindle Stiff lit up, inhaled, held it. He offered the joint over to Chatter. Bartleby figured the old guy was going to pass, but Chatter took the joint and toked like he'd just spent a wet weekend at Woodstock. He passed it over to Bartleby. It was good stuff.

"That's a nice hat," Bindle Stiff complimented Chatter. "Damn nice."

A daddy longlegs went traipsing across the top of the coffee table. It moved with grotesque grace on impossibly delicate legs. A breeze picked up, rustled through the leaves overhead and knocked a flurry of seedpods twirling down. A yellow-winged butterfly came flickering and flapping along. Whimsically rising and falling on invisible air currents, floating effortlessly and worry free. Until, in one surging snap, Sweet Jane scoffed it away.

Bindle Stiff absentmindedly rubbed an open palm against his hairless head. Back and forth, back and forth, back and forth.

While he did so, Bartleby took a good long look at him. There was no denying it, Bindle Stiff was one funky looking homo sapien. He wasn't just bald or balding, he was slash-and-burn, scorched earth bald. The hair was long gone and never coming back. It left him with a perfectly round hemisphere (at least to Bartleby's eye), bronzed over and sun-freckled, without even a single stray wisp remaining in residence. Bindle's eyebrows were Einstein bushy. His oversized ears were lumpy and misshapen. How they stuck off his head, poised to catch the next strong wind reminded Bartleby of some Seuss-like creature. Below these elephantine ears grew a great brush pile of a beard, a thick jumble of gray and brown and black hairs, seeded through with what had to be a week's worth of food crumbs. This unruly thicket kept on and disappeared down into the collar of his shirt without showing any signs of letting up.

"You know, I been bald so long, it'd seem strange to have hair now," Bindle Stiff admitted.

Bartleby realized he must've made some of these last observations aloud.

"Was partying this one time. Like thirty years ago now," Bindle Stiff continued, "and someone wanted to know when I'd lost my hair. They all got to talking about what I might've looked like with hair. This one girl asked, 'You wanna see what you look like with hair, cuz I can show you,' and everyone was like yeah, and I was like sure, so she gave me this little compact mirror to hold. Then she shimmies her skirt up. The dang girl didn't have nothing on underneath and she, well, she straddled my head and plopped herself right down. 'There you go,' she said, 'that's about what you'd look like with hair.'"

Chatter and Bartleby were stunned silent.

"Can tell you this," Bindle Stiff concluded ruefully, "my wife don't like that photo one bit."

🍁 🍁 🍁

Register: Jenny Knob Shelter

5/27 Sweet Jane scared up a whole field of flappers. Never seen her so excited. Jumping and barking like she was a danged pup again. Musta ate a couple dozen. Guess she gives a whole new meaning to having "butterflies in your belly."

—Sweet Jane & Mad (c)Hatter

🍁 🍁 🍁

At the water source for Doc's Knob Shelter, Bartleby washed scabby crusts of mud from his inner calves. It had rained for most of the last day and a half. It had rained for most of the last day and a half. After a particularly nasty wipeout, he'd reached the conclusion it was sloppier but much safer to wade straight through the puddles that accumulated along trail. Leaping from raised rock to wet root in an effort to try and keep his (already wet) feet dry was all risk and no reward. It was just asking to get waylaid with a twisted knee or a sprained ankle. So he walked through puddles, across streams and straight into muddy quagmires without attempting to avoid them anymore.

Took him some scrubbing, but he got most of the mud off.

Back at the shelter, he shucked his socks and squeezed out every drop of muddy water he could, before hanging them to dry. Which, he knew, they wouldn't. He was already dreading that cold shock of soggy socks on his dry feet first thing in the bright and early, but he hadn't been able to figure a way around it.

❧

Sometime later, Bartleby dreamed he was back building homes again.

On the various jobsites, Bartleby's role had been simple. Maintain a presence and "encourage progress." This was his father's catchall term for everything from keeping an eye on the contractors, fielding questions, solving problems, gophering material and generally running interference with angry neighbors and bored building inspectors. When he wasn't actively engaged in any of that, Bartleby took it upon himself to keep the building sites clean. He swept up scrap wood and empty coffee cups. He filled dumpsters with cardboard, styrofoam packaging and wooden pallets. Vacuumed away sawdust, bent framing nails and an unending supply of cigarette butts.

Bartleby spent way more time holding the nozzle of a shop-vac in his hand than he did any hammer. He had a three wheeled jobber with 6.0 horsepowers of suck, a twelve gallon stainless steel drum and a hose that was too backbreakingly short for him to use while standing upright. The vacuum was the size and shape of R2-D2, but it had way more sass. Always snagging on this, catching on that, tripping and tipping over most everything else. But for all its shortcomings, that vac could suck. Scarfed down nuts, bolts, rocks, broken glass and more without a hiccup.

In his dream, Bartleby was running this vacuum through an unfamiliar house. At first the rooms were rough framed with bare plywood subfloors. He sucked up piles of sawdust, colorful snips of wire, copper pipe ends and yellow wire nuts. His back ached, his hands were numb from the vibration, but he kept on. It was a dream, he couldn't stop. The vac pulled him along like Jane pulled Chatter.

On the house's second floor, the rooms had been drywalled and taped. He vacuumed black drywall screws, dried globs of joint compound and and sanded grit that had collected in the floor joints. It kicked out clouds of white dust that Bartleby felt on his teeth, up his nose, in his eyes. He kept on: sucking up door shims, end bits of wood trim and tile spacers. The next rooms were primed, painted and carpeted. He vacuumed blue crumples of painter's tape, scraps of foam padding, loose fuzzies where the carpets had been cut to fit and dusty footprints off gleaming hardwood floors.

The last room in the house was an expansive master bedroom. The room already looked clean, but just the same, he vacuumed every inch of it. When he finished the walk-in closet, he thought he was done, but there was a little crawlspace door at the back of the closet. He got down on his knees and crawled blindly into the dark attic. Couldn't find a light switch, couldn't see to work, but the vacuum insisted. It was still hungry.

He knelt there in the cramped darkness, powerlessly watching as the vacuum swallowed away his dad's legacy, his mom's comfortable retirement, his wife, his children. But still, the vacuum wasn't full. There in the dark, it turned on Bartleby and gobbled down his self-respect, his happiness, his well-being, his entire life. Last to go was his soul. Frayed and tattered as it was, his soul still had enough kick left to shriek bloody murder as the nozzle came in close—

🍁

Bartleby woke in the shelter, drenched in sweat and totally discombobulated. He lay there, breathing hard in the cool dark.

A horrific screeching keen broke the night's stillness. This was so gut-wrenchingly primal, Bartleby scrambled for his headlamp and unzipped his bag. Up and out of the shelter, he followed the noise to a nearby tree. In a high limb, he could faintly discern a dark form. Two glass-bright eyes looked down into the light. It was hard to know for sure, but he guessed they belonged to a raccoon.

Back at the shelter, Jane started barking.

The raccoon was wedging itself into a knothole, working to get at some unlucky inhabitant. A bird or squirrel probably, though Bartleby wouldn't have thought either capable of producing such a cat-dying-in-a-gutter shriek. The raccoon alternated between sticking its face and a forearm deep into the knothole.

Another cry. This one woeful and low, but no less visceral.

During the last years of lying about, Bartleby had watched enough Nature Channel to understand about letting nature run its course, not getting involved, not upsetting the circle of life. But he couldn't sit back and ignore that shrieking lament.

So Bartleby picked up a stone, hurled it overhand. It winged high over the branch and disappeared into darkness. A second stone hit the branch, clattered harmlessly away. This, at least, got the raccoon's attention. When he missed with a third stone, he picked up a tree branch and whump-cracked it against the trunk.

The raccoon hissed down a challenge. Overcome by the moment, Bartleby responded with his own growled frustration. He battered at the trunk until he was left holding little more than splinters.

At some point during this barrage, Bartleby must've convinced the raccoon that there were easier dinners to be had elsewhere. It came stalking down the tree, head first and hissing the whole way. With surprisingly long legs and a bristly shag of fur, the raccoon looked big and burly; it was easy to see how one might get the best of a dog.

Back on solid ground, the raccoon gave Bartleby a surly glare before skulking away into the underbrush.

They hit Pearisburg midmorning. Chatter checked in at a run-down motel. It was the type of place with weeds growing up through the parking lot asphalt, scratchy linens and plastic lawn chairs set outside each room. The sink was cracked and the bathroom tile grout was black with mildew. Bartleby had never wanted to stay anywhere so grimy, so badly.

The motel was holding one of Chatter's maildrops. Bartleby bummed a shower, appropriated a role of thin, sandpapery toilet paper from atop the toilet tank, and jealously watched Chatter sift through all the goodies he'd sent himself. It was like watching someone else tear through a stuffed Christmas stocking when you knew there wasn't a single present anywhere with your name on it.

The old guy had sent himself more cashews, pistachios and jerky than he'd be able to eat in a week. He got new hiking shoes and two pair of wool socks. Got whiskey, ziplocs and a whole confusion of pills; more Werther's, batteries, Q-tips and a roll of toilet paper that was so soft and thick Bartleby would've happily used it as a pillow. Chatter also got another envelope containing another hundred dollar bill.

"Bumblebee," Chatter said, "you gotta help me eat some of this. I can't carry it all." He set out watercress crackers, summer sausage and an expensive chunk of cave-aged cheddar. "Eat up. This cheese is something like seven years old."

There were even special cans of wet dog food for Jane. Took her all of two minutes to unearth one and nose it over for Bartleby to open.

Bartleby ate some of the spiced meat and old cheese, the lion's share probably, but still couldn't help feel miserable and mean. He didn't want to go back out into the woods so soon after arriving in town. His shoes were squishy wet and his clothes reeked. He didn't want to spend the night in a shelter, eat old pasta for dinner or wake up with a stiff neck and sore shoulders from sleeping on a hardwood floor. And he definitely didn't want to walk any further. But staying a night in town cost money he could ill-afford.

Of course, Chatter invited him to stay the night and share the motel room. Nice as the offer was, Bartleby declined. First, it bruised his ego to have Chatter pay his way. An "I buy, you fly" pizza run was one thing, but straight up charity just felt wrong. Course, bruises heal, and he probably would've sheepishly accepted the offer but for the simplest fact of civilization: Everything cost money. Even if he stayed in town for "free," he'd still end up spending far beyond his means. No way he wouldn't treat himself to dinner, an after-dinner snack and then, come morning, a big breakfast too. Town would snap up thirty or forty bucks quick as Jane snapped butterflies. If he wanted to keep on, to give himself at least a fighting chance of reaching Maine, to maybe feel better about life, the world and his little place in it, Bartleby knew he needed to do without such creature comforts as a shabby motel room and greasy hot calories. So he made lame excuses and slipped off before Chatter could press him and break his resolve.

Bartleby ducked into the motel's front office and got directions to the nearest grocery store. On the walk there, he finished off some flattened old bread and peanut butter from his food bag. Figured if he stuffed himself before shopping, he'd buy less. Still, he somehow spent nineteen precious dollars on four pounds of pasta, three pounds of peanut butter, a sleeve of bagels, a tray of Hydrox cookies and a plastic looking block of yellow cheddar. He stood drooling over an Entenmann's All Butter French Crumb Cake for long minutes before pulling himself away. He knew he could eat the entire thing in one sitting. There was a salad bar/deli section with free packets of ketchup, yellow mustard, mayonnaise and sweet relish. Hit by sudden inspiration, Bartleby grabbed handfuls of each and jammed them into his pack.

He scuttled back to trail with a newly heavy pack and a heavier heart.

Turned out the first shelter north of town was only a few miles in. When Bartleby arrived, the sky was nearly as dark as his mood. Bindle Stiff was laid out in the shelter with earplugs snugged in tight. Having already smoked some after-dinner dope, he was contentedly zonked and offered up very little in the way of conversation. Which was just fine with Bartleby.

Before Bartleby coaxed water to a boil, Bindle Stiff started up snoring. Low and easy, with a comfortable rhythm; as such, these snores were far preferable than the tumults Bartleby had come to expect from hikers like Blitz and JoJo.

Bindle Stiff's farting, on the other hand, was another matter entirely. The first blast came soon after Bartleby got himself tucked down for the night. Sounded like a Bismarck-sized battleship firing off random salvos from the main guns; thunderously sharp retorts booming out into the dark of night. Each one sudden and shocking and certain to shake Bartleby awake. Concussions echoed off the shelter walls and reverberated through the wooden floor all through the night.

❦

Bartleby woke to something heavy pressing into his sleeping bag. It was big and wet and momentarily confusing. When a sandpapery tongue set to work on his forehead, he knew Sweet Jane had found him.

"Heh-heh. Still asleep?"

"Go away," Bartleby grumbled from the dank depths of his sleeping bag.

"Gotta be almost ten by now."

Bartleby squinted into daylight.

"Better get moving, it's gonna be a hot one."

It was a hot one. First day over ninety. And late May at that. Up in Connecticut, Bartleby wouldn't have expected to see the red side of ninety degrees until late July or August. But come noontime, the Virginian air was already sticky with humidity.

Oppressively so.

Under the relentless heat, Bartleby's motivation wilted like old lettuce. It became a great struggle to simply keep hydrated. He found it physically unpleasant to try and drink water on pace with what came sweating out of him. Back home at least, heat and humidity had always killed his appetite, but now he couldn't eat enough. Except for a thirty minute reprieve directly on the heels of a meal, he was constantly hungry.

To avoid the worst of the sun's heavy heat, they began taking long, shaded siestas. Jane and Chatter napped, Chatter with his floppy hat tilted over his eyes. Try as he might, Bartleby rarely managed sleep.

Instead, he idled the hours away by reading from random books left in shelters or writing long rambling letters to Angie. These were sometimes passionate, sometimes angry and sometimes apologetic, but they were never mailed.

More and more, Bartleby contented himself with drafting along behind Chatter and Jane. Chatter was happy for the company. He proceeded to bombard Bartleby with suspicious floral and vegetative factoids, partial stories and disjointed anecdotes from his life. Bartleby found all of this difficult to follow. In the blink of an eye, even the simplest story could become a kinked spiderweb of tangents and digressions. Chatter glossed over details, regularly confused the names of major characters and a surprising amount of these narratives stopped dead when Chatter simply couldn't recall what happened next. For all that, Bartleby enjoyed the challenge of trying to make sense of these seemingly infinite and nonsensical monologues. Where he could, Bartleby gave helpful prompts and asked questions, endeavoring to herd the stories back on course whenever it seemed they'd gone wandering. Ultimately, it didn't matter too much if the stories made sense, because linear, logical or not, they sure helped the miles pass.

Even with Jane pulling him, Chatter lagged behind on the ups. At the top of a climb, Bartleby would take a seat and wait the ten or fifteen minutes for Chatter to appear. The old man would sit, catch his breath and start up talking again. For all the things that did slip his mind, his desire to talk wasn't one of them.

Topographically, Virginia settled down some. It wasn't flat exactly, but definitely not an ass kicking state in terms of elevation change. The hills and valleys were more rolling than sharp. The state still had its share of decent climbs, and some spectacular views, but all in all it was good ground for long hauling. The AT crossed many a grassy field rich with jumping ticks and cow paddies. More often than not, helping Sweet Jane to climb over or otherwise navigate the numerous fence stiles was a two-man operation with Bartleby doing most of the heavy lifting.

***

Register: Sarver Hollow Shelter

5/20 rip-stop silnylon,
        fleece, cordura, quallofill,
        spandex and smartwool

                                    High-Ku

***

Slumping along, traversing the length of yet another of Virginia's rolling ridgelines. It was still an hour or two before the day's heat peaked.

Because his head was down and his eyes were scanning oncoming trail for safe footing, Bartleby didn't see the goats until he was surrounded.

Swarmed would be a more accurate term.

They weren't exotic or even particularly attractive. Just domesticated livestock gone feral. An audacious mob, the largest of which reached to Jane's shoulder. The goats had yellow slit eyes and short, bristly hair. They pressed close and licked at his bare legs with probing tongues that were simultaneously slimy and rough.

"Must want the salt in our sweat," Chatter suggested.

The goats jostled past Sweet Jane as if she weren't there. She ignored their overwhelming presence after one halfhearted and entirely unheeded "whuff." With her head held high and her eyes averted, Jane waded through the goats with all the poise she could muster.

Things took a turn for the serious when one of the bigger nannies took a nibble at Bartleby's shorts.

"These are my only shorts," he growled and put a hand on the nanny's head and pushed her back. Or at least tried to. The goat didn't budge. A second goat went low, chewed on the cuff of his sock. He shoved at this second goat with no better result.

In a rising panic, Bartleby looked over at Chatter. The old guy was holding them off with his walking stick. Any goats that slipped close, he grabbed by the ear and gave a good tug.

"You can't push goats," Chatter called. "Gotta pull 'em."

Bartleby didn't have time to wonder how Chatter came by this little bit of knowledge, but it worked. By shielding himself with his hiking poles and pulling on any goats that slipped in close, Bartleby extricated himself from the crowd. Once the way was open for him, he hurried himself along and quickly caught up to Chatter.

Safe now from the madding crowd, Chatter started up belly laughing.

"What's so funny?"

"Did you see that one nanny with the beard and them droopy teats?"

"Yeah?"

"Bears a striking resemblance to my late wife."

Dragon's Tooth was a single rocky spire jutting up and above the summit of Cove Mountain. The climb was a gut-wrenching bit of hand-over-hand scramble, but Bartleby managed to crab his way up to the peak and lay himself down out of the wind.

Unpredictable gusts buffeted the black silhouettes of turkey buzzards circling overhead. Below him, the indistinct green of a million treetops swayed in unison. Bartleby lay watching the hypnotic movement until he heard the telltale tap-tap-tapping of Chatter's walking stick.

"Hope there's room for me up there," the old guy called.

"Maybe don't come all the way up," Bartleby answered. "It's sort of sketchy."

Either Chatter didn't hear or he chose not to listen, because he clambered all the way out to the pointed tip-top of the rocky tooth formation. It was a bit of a squeeze for both of them to fit on the limited real estate.

This last little ascent was obviously too steep and treacherous for

Jane. She whined from the Tooth's base, fifteen yards below.

When he got settled, Mad Chatter gave Bartleby a you-aren't-the-boss-of-me-I-can-do-anything-you-can-do grin. It was the same look toddlers give parents as they fearlessly insist on crawl-climbing any stairs in sight.

The grin hadn't quite faded from Chatter's face when a gust caught at the floppy brim of his cavalier hat and sent it spiraling away and out of reach, like a pinwheel slipped free from its stick. The old man made an earnest but incompetently wild lunge after the departing hat, promptly lost his balance and looked poised to follow in its wake.

Except Bartleby had been braced for something bad to happen. He hooked three fingers into Chatter's belt and single-handedly hauled him back from the brink.

Close as he was to Chatter, Bartleby couldn't help but catch a noseful of Old Spice. It sent him for a quick trip in the wayback machine. Kneeling there on the rocky precipice of Dragon's Tooth in southern Virginia, Bartleby's mind unexpectedly flooded with images of his father.

Of his father humorously slapping his freshly shaved face with far too much Old Spice. Of a trip to the beach on the Fourth of July, when a young, barefoot Bartleby had stepped on a hot sparkler stick and his father carried him back the car to bandage the blistering burn. Of his father laying in his casket, gray and unmoving, looking nothing like himself, but still smelling the same as always.

Register: Catawba Mountain Shelter

6/1 Passed the Audie Murphy Monument today. I can remember watching his movies way back a hundred years ago.
> —Sweet Jane & Mad (c)Hatter

6/1 If anyone stumbles across a floppy green hat, please hurry it up trail to one Mr. Mad Chatter. He's been sulking ever since it flew away.   - Bartleby

❧ ❧ ❧

When they arrived on top of Tinker Cliffs, there was already a day hiker enjoying the broad western view. "I'm Lightning Rod," he said. "Y'all thru-hiking?"

"I'm gonna take a sit down for a bit," a hatless Chatter huffed, "but I'm not through hiking. Got a long way to go still, sonny."

As advertised, Chatter plopped himself down and proceeded to unlace his boots. It took him a while to work them free, but when he did, a handful of sand and stones poured out of each one. This accounted for maybe a third of the sour mood he'd been in all morning. The remaining two-thirds were a direct result of his missing hat—both that it was gone from his possession and that he now had to soldier on with the sun searing at the pale skin of his scalp.

The summer sun was high and bright and the bare stone cliffs throbbed with its heat. A pesky breeze wafted in from the west.

"I'm Bartleby, the grump is Sad Chatter and the one trying to jam her nose into your crotch, that's Sweet Jane."

Lightning Rod had tubs of peanut butter and jelly out and open with a loaf of bread standing by. "Well, listen, I got plenty of water and y'all are welcome to make yourselves sandwiches."

Bartleby's eyes lit up, "You serious?"

"Sure am. Only got a three mile walk back to my car. Y'all got a long way to go still. Eat up."

Jane sat watching as Bartleby mortared two drippy sandwiches together. When finished, he handed one to Chatter and tore into the other.

Lightning Rod nodded at Jane, "She's a pretty good dog, huh?"

"She's a great dog," Chatter corrected him around a mouthful of PB&J.

When Chatter finished eating, he made his way toward the cliff edge. He had his baggy of ashes clutched in one hand.

"Not *too* close," Bartleby warned. He was using the last of the bread to make his third sandwich, a super sloppy triple-decker, and couldn't easily break away to lifeguard the old guy.

Mad Chatter waved him off and inched forward. When he'd gotten close, but not *too* close, he cast a handful of ashes over the edge.

Except the ashes of his late wife didn't go over the edge. They were caught by that pesky westward breeze and billowed up into Chatter's face. Particles of fine white ash clung to his eyebrows, his cheeks, his greasy Gandalf beard; they were in his eyes, his open mouth and caught in the dark tufts of hair sprouting from his ears.

Chatter moved back from the cliff edge, sputtering and coughing. Lightning Rod was up and pounding Chatter's back as quick as his name implied. Bartleby had been about to close his monster PB&J as these events unraveled. His gaze returned to the open sandwich, now liberally sprinkled with white ash.

Bartleby stole a glance over to see that Chatter and Lightning weren't looking his way. He shared a guilty look with Sweet Jane and quick clapped the sandwich together before anyone came close.

As far as Bartleby could tell, Chatter was all wrong about his wife. She wasn't the least bit bitter.

❋ ❋ ❋

Register: Wilson Creek Shelter

5/22 Behold, pilgrim friends:
        tinker, tinker, waterfall.
        Sister Dillard rocks!
                                High-Ku

❋ ❋ ❋

While Bindle Stiff was the first new thru-hiker Bartleby had met since leaving Damascus, he wasn't the last. Shifting four or five days forward had plopped Bartleby down amidst a whole new cast of northbound characters. These included Grandma Deuce and Scraping By, the caffeine-addicted Cowboy Coffee and the babbling Jabberwalky; Fast Eddie, Lumbering Jack, Blue Merle and Goodtimes Charlie; the gangly Jive Turkey, Mister Blister Rump, a heavyset Virginian going by V.A. Moose (pronounced: vamoose), Overdrawn (printed on a recent ATM receipt), Past Time, Nowadays, Getting There (he wasn't—a bum knee was threatening to end his hike early) and High Noon, who maintained a strict policy of lighting up by lunchtime.

Another of these new hikers was a girl named Longlegged Lemming. She had a nose ring, a lip ring, a toe ring, six or seven earrings and a high wattage smile that more than made up for the hazy dimness lingering in her brown eyes.

"Bet she's got a few more rings we can't see," the Original Grand Poohbah speculated. He'd been cruising big miles; caught up to and passed Bartleby a day earlier, but as soon as he bumped into Lemming, Poohbah hit the brakes and tossed his hat into the ring.

As the first part of her name implied, Lemming had long, shapely legs. An ugly mound of reddish scar tissue across the inside of her left wrist may well have explained the second part of Lemming's name. Bartleby didn't ask.

Around the shelter, Lemming wore sandals, a short hemp skirt and a tie-dye tank top that did very little to cover or contain her pendulous breasts. The unsupported and unruly duo swung to and fro, jiggled and jounced with what some would call commendable vivacity. During the hiking day, she wore short-short running shorts, an overworked sports bra and running shoes.

By any normal standards, Lemming wasn't much to look at. Course, with a gender imbalance of something like fifteen to one, the AT wasn't anywhere close to normal. She'd quickly become a hot commodity out there in the woods. And she seemed to take a certain wicked pleasure from all the attention.

Five unattached male hikers, dopey boys really, tumbled along in Lemming's wake. A harem, Bartleby decided after a few hours observation, there was really no other word for it. They were a friendly enough bunch, but all were quite obviously vying for her favor. Like a squirming pile of puppies, each stepping on the others to suckle at a heavy teat. The shelter air was thick with brinksmanship, put downs and pranks. All of which Lemming, tacitly, at least, encouraged. Through private conversations, playful looks and other flirtations, she had each of the five convinced they were about to clinch the nomination.

With all of his previous trail experience to brag about, it took Poohbah little time to establish himself as a serious contender. Easily mistaken for confidence, his natural haughtiness served him well in this arena. He dusted off and displayed a certain greasy charm. Poohbah complimented Lemming, asked enough questions to show interest, but not enough to make himself seem *too* interested. He talked knowingly of trail matters and upcoming towns. Also, he spent long hours brushing a fine shine into his long hair.

One of the harem boys, Thunk, appeared to have all but given up the chase. At twenty-five, he was balding and had beady eyes and a weak chin that even his new facial scruff couldn't entirely hide. Rightly figuring the cause already lost, Thunk took a certain sour grapes enjoyment out of making the other harem members look as bad as possible. He'd turned the "take my ball and go home" philosophy on its ear. Since Lemming wasn't and wouldn't be Thunk's, he couldn't take her (i.e. "the ball") and go home; instead he endeavored to take all the other players away from the ball. It was the oddest and one of the most entertaining approaches to courtship that Bartleby had ever seen put into action.

Thunk had gone ahead and re-trail-named the brawniest guy in their group Buttercup. At some earlier point, Buttercup had been traveling under the moniker Hiking Viking. How Thunk had gotten the name Buttercup to stick was beyond Bartleby, but there was no denying the emasculating effect. Despite Buttercup's better than average looks, his manly physique and a fine head of yellow hair, everyone (but Buttercup) understood that he'd fallen from favor. DanK (his actual name was Danny Kloot), Grog and Bigfeets filled out the squad of suitors.

On the first night that Bartleby shared a shelter with Lemming and her harem, it became implicitly understood, through winks and smirking grins, that Thunk had snuck a large rock into DanK's pack earlier in the day. On discovering that he'd carried a full five pounds of rock for a dozen miles, DanK unleashed a Donald Trumpesque tantrum. He ranted, raved and generally acted badly, particularly when Bigfeets tried to mollify him.

"You gotta admit, it's funny," Bigfeets said. "I mean, five pounds is like almost twenty percent of your pack weight. How do you not notice that kinda difference, especially coming over that last big climb?"

"Really? Really?" DanK seethed. "But, yeah, I guess that actually makes sense."

"What does?"

"That the guy with the tiny ballerina feet, the guy who came out to hike the AT because he'd heard that all the walking would make his feet grow a size or two, that that guy would be the final authority on funny, wouldn't he, *Bigfeets*?"

DanK stormed off in a sulky huff and hid in his tent for the rest of the night. Thunk was still chuckling to himself when he went to sleep.

The green hillside pasture was bordered by two rickety stiles and countless old hickory posts, weathered down to smooth nubbins. The trail gently switchbacked its way up and across the hill, eventually disappearing over a humped crest. Hundreds of cow paddies littered the ground, some desiccated and old, some pungently fresh and others playing host to clusters of red-capped mushrooms. The guilty parties, a dozen glassy-eyed dairy cows, were spread across the field. Each with their heads down, studiously intent on filling four stomachs.

Halfway up the rise, Thunk stalled out. He preferred hiking shirtless, so he globbed sunscreen onto his neck and shoulders while waiting for Bartleby and Chatter.

"Would you look at them," he called. "Just chewing and crapping, crapping and chewing. You gotta admit—it's a sweet setup."

"Until they end up on a menu."

"Look at that one, he's really stupid looking."

"Which one?"

"That one."

Chatter said, "She's got *udders*." Without the shade his hat had provided, his face and forehead were newly pink and peeling.

"Partly why he looks so stupid. I'm telling you, they are like *the* dumbest mammals. Seriously. Eating all day long, pooping anywhere they please. They aren't worried about melting icecaps or oil spills. No rat race, no road rage, no worries about losing their jobs. For a bunch of certified dummies, they've got it made."

With megaphoned hands, Thunk imitated a lowing bovine. The call was filled with long and low guttural grunts. To Bartleby's unschooled ear, it sounded like an argument between a Beluga whale and a broken printer, recorded live and played back in slow motion. Even Jane seemed to cringe.

"What are you doing?"

"Giving them a cow call. See? Not one looked over."

"So?"

"So that's how stupid they are." Thunk picked up a rock and flung it at the nearest cow. After missing by a wide margin, he started up hiking again, "Good-bye, you great big dumb dummies."

Chatter gave Bartleby a look, plainly asking if he could do any better. Bartleby shrugged, raised his hands and gave it a go.

"MMMMOOOOOOOOOOOOOOOOOOOOOOOOOOOO."

Every cow on the hillside looked over. Two dozen unblinkingly curious eyes turned to see what all the commotion was about.

❦ ❦ ❦

Lemming and her harem were fast movers. Or, at least, Long-legged Lemming was a fast mover and the boys had to keep up or lose their chance with her. There was this constant pressure to keep with the pack and not get left behind. In the morning, the sound of DanK breaking his tent down wasn't any different than the unwelcome buzz of an alarm clock for Bigfeets and the rest of the crew. Like it or not, it meant it was time for them to get up and out. When the harem hiked, they pushed long miles, covered lots of ground with improbable bursts of cheetahesque speed. And when they weren't racing along trail, they were recuperating in trail towns or lounging around hostels or anywhere else that would have them.

There was a definitive start and stop mentality to their advancement. Often, it seemed like Lemming & Co. were only hiking to get to the next town as quickly as was humanly possible. Once the hard work was behind them and they'd arrived at their destination, they pampered themselves with some lazy combination of nearo and zero days.

For Bartleby and Chatter, there were no fits and starts. There were no big miles and there was certainly no sprinting. There was also no prolonged town visits or hostel stays. Bartleby couldn't afford such luxuries and Chatter's canine sidekick severely hampered his lodging options.

Instead, they were slow and steady. They weren't sluggards, they didn't slack off. They cruised along at an average of fifteen miles a day. Each day. Every day. Rain or shine. Come hell or high water.

As it turned out, both groups covered roughly the same amount of ground in the same timeframe. Spent almost every other night sharing a shelter.

As Bartleby stepped across the trickling waters of an unnamed stream, a silvery glint caught his eye. The stepping stones, slicked over and mossy, made for precarious footing, hence he was looking down more than he might've been otherwise.

At first, he assumed he'd simply seen the quick flash of a fish but a second glance revealed the silvery glint to be an aluminum can. Half a dozen of them, actually.

He almost kept on, but he'd heard people talk about this type of thing. Figured it couldn't be true, was probably just trash, but what the hell, and reached into the water.

From which Bartleby pulled four Bud Lights and two Pepsis. An honest, happy-to-be-in-the-moment smile stretched across his face as he sat and waited for Chatter.

"Heya, Bumblebee."

"Interest you in a cold beverage?"

Chatter squinted, "What now?"

"Looks like somebody left us a little trail magic."

"Did they? Heh-heh. Don't mind if I do." Chatter popped the top on a Pepsi and took a swallow. "Wow, that's something, huh? It always this good?"

"I never thought so before."

Before they finished, Thunk came rambling along, "Please tell me there's at least one more cold soda."

"Only the two, sorry."

He groaned with disappointment.

"Couple Bud Lights though."

"Seriously? You shitting me? Not funny if you are. Come on— really? Are you joking? Better not be."

❧

Thunk drank the first of the beers on the spot and sipped the second as they hiked. Since Bartleby and Chatter weren't interested, he saved the remaining two for later at the shelter.

The shelter wasn't much further along and Thunk still had a bit of a buzz when they arrived. He started up playing fetch with Jane. Bartleby absently sucked on his mustache. Chatter went hunting after morel mushrooms.

"She won't ever get tired and quit," Bartleby said. "Just put the stick down when you've had enough."

"It's cool," Thunk said. "Nice to be playing fetch with an actual stick instead of a frozen bird."

Before this comment fully registered, Bartleby nodded along as if he'd had the same thought a thousand times himself. Then, "Eh—what's that, Thunk?"

"After my father split, my mother felt it was important that me and my sister had a male role model. Made us spend a lot of time around her brother, Uncle Jack. He was a big time hunter. Ducks, turkeys, deer, it didn't matter, whatever was in season. He always kept Labradors around the house. We didn't have a dog, so it was cool to go play with the labs. Except he wouldn't let us throw sticks to them. Guess that can confuse hunting dogs. Sends them the wrong signals about what they should be retrieving when he shoots a duck, you know?

"Not really."

"At Christmas, Uncle Jack always had these frozen doves waiting in his freezer. Made a big deal of singing 'Two turtle doves' when he presented them to us. They were frozen solid and duct taped around so they wouldn't fall apart too quickly as they thawed. Made us throw them with the dogs."

Thunk wrestled the stick from Jane, launched it end-over-end, "With feathers coming loose, their heads wobbling around and falling off, you can imagine—it sucked some of the fun out of the holidays."

❦

Poohbah arrived at the shelter in both a foul mood and wet boots. "Couple of day hikers said they saw cold drinks in the stream past that last road. I spent twenty minutes wading around," he chuffed.

"Couldn't find anything."

Thunk slugged off his beer, "Guess we got the last of them. Want the rest of this one? I didn't backwash too much."

Poohbah tried to ignore this offer, but Thunk's insistence wore him down.

"No, seriously, here, take it. It's all good." Smiling, Thunk handed the beer over.

Poohbah drank off the last swallow in a single pull and nodded. "Thanks, Thunk."

"Really, it's nothing," Thunk said, fighting to keep his face straight. He reached into his pack, pulled out the fourth and final can of Bud Light, "I got another one, anyway."

Register: Bobblets Gap Shelter

6/2 My sleeping bag is slimy with sweat, sprinkled with
      dandruff and smells like old farts. Home sweet home.
                                    -Bigfeets

After a long, lazy lunch, Mad Chatter went to shoulder his ruck. He'd just topped off his water at a sweet burbling spring. Those three liters combined with a full week's worth of food made hoisting the pack into place more difficult than usual.

Chatter had learned to use a two-part lifting motion to get his pack up where he needed it. Wasn't so different from the clean and jerk of Olympic weight lifters. He used all of his body mass and some little momentum to heave the pack up to a resting position on his knee. From there, he slipped his left arm through the left pack strap, swung the pack right and twisted into it.

This time, though, something went wrong.

Instead of two distinct motions, Chatter's jerk came too closely on the heels of his clean. The pack hadn't entirely lost its upward momentum and when Chatter swung it around, it sailed past his waiting back. And since one of his arms was already looped through a shoulder strap, he got pulled along in the pack's wake. The two of them, man and pack, kicked up a billowy cloud of dust when they hit the ground.

As the only witnesses to this scene, Bartleby and Jane shared a look of disbelief as they waited for the dust to settle.

There was an inviting shady spot beneath a stand of tall oaks. It was about time for a break, so Bartleby leaned back against a wide trunk and zonked out like Johnny Appleseed after a hard day's planting. Or he tried to. Almost immediately a squirrel took offense at his presence, kept up a steady barrage of chittering chastisements. Bartleby ignored this at first, but the scolding squirrel got louder and closer and increasingly insistent.

When Thunk arrived, he immediately cut to the heart of the matter, "Is it me, or is that squirrel trying to chase you off?"

Bartleby was just levering himself upright, getting ready to move on.

"That's crazy," Thunk said. "Don't get up. Rodents need to learn their place." He chucked a pinecone that missed by less than a foot.

"That's right you bushy-tailed rat, I'll knock you right outta that—"

With a lightning burst of rodent speed, the squirrel squirted from limb to limb and raced headlong down a nearby trunk. On reaching the ground, it charged straight at Thunk.

"Ohshitohshitohshitohshitohshit," Thunk backpedaled, tripped over his feet and went sprawling flat on his pack like a turtle flipped on its shell.

With its domination complete, the squirrel scampered back up into the high branches, where it continued to chirp triumphantly and chitter rodent-sized smack.

In the course of about three seconds, Thunk's face traveled from overconfident to shocked and awed to sheepishly shamefaced.

It was easily five years since Bartleby had last laughed so hard. Tears streamed down into his beard. His throat actually hurt and he couldn't catch his breath. He kept on like that for the rest of the day.

As the trail slogged through a low, boggy area, Chatter pointed out some skunk cabbage to Bartleby. "You see the purple bulb there at the bottom? That right there is where all the stink happens. Trust me—I found out the hard way."

One moment, Bartleby and Thunk were hiking along by themselves. The next moment, a kid appeared in line behind them.

"Hey," the kid said by way of making his presence known, "any chance you guys met Dragonfly?"

"Don't think so," Thunk said.

This kid was college-aged and whip-thin with bouncy black hair. Also, he talked with the willingness of one who was lonely or trail-crazed, "She's moving fast. Would've went through a couple of days ago."

"Definitely not," Thunk confirmed.

"I'm Tanuki No-Tail. Been trying to catch her since Damascus," he offered. "Humping thirties for over a week."

"You banged out seven thirties in a row?"

"Yeah or maybe more. Eight or nine, I think probably."

"She owe you money?"

"Nah."

"Kill your family?"

"No."

Thunk wasn't one to let a diversion slip away easily, "So?"

"So she's Asian."

"Yeah?"

"And so am I."

"So?"

"I think I'm in love."

"She super hot?"

"Someone showed me a picture they had on their camera...."

"But?"

"She was mostly hidden behind a branch."

"You've never even laid eyes on this Dragonfly chick?"

"Uh-uh."

"Am I missing something here?"

"She hikes fast."

"And?"

"Far as I know, she's the only other Asian on trail."

"Seriously?"

"Yeah. I been asking—"

No," Thunk said, "I meant—seriously, that's your reason for chasing after a woman you've never even laid eyes on?"

"Have you noticed how it's only white people out here?"

"Uh-uh."

"Well, I'm not surprised you didn't notice, but it is. How many Asians have you seen out here? How many brown people? Many? Any?"

"There was a Spanish guy back in Georgia," Bartleby said.

"Spanish like from Spain or South America?"

"He said he was Spanish, so Spain I guess."

"Europeans don't count as brown people."

They labored along a rising slope and paused for a drink at the top.

"Okay, Tanuki-dookie," Thunk said, "you've obviously got your racism radar turned on and pinging away, right?"

"I guess. Maybe a little."

"Well, listen. I'm a dickhead. Everything I've ever heard about my father indicates he was too, so it might be a hereditary defect. Either way, I've got this big mouth that spews all sorts of obnoxiousness. I was like knee high when my father left and ever since my little sister hit puberty, I've taken it on myself to harass any boys following her home. Didn't matter if they were good guys or not, I made sure to give them a tough time of it. Pick on them, scare them, let them know someone's watching them. Classic big brother, right?

"So, this past fall, my sister starts dating a black dude. Guess they had a couple engineering classes together at Geneseo. He's nice enough, a little geeky maybe, but whatever. When she finally brought him around, I froze up. Instead of pulling all the usual shit, I shook his hand, I offered him a beer and made pleasant small talk. I did everything *but* make him uncomfortable."

"Sounds okay so far."

"Yeah," Thunk continued, "but is it? I mean, I didn't want him to think I was racist, so I was way nicer than I would've been to any random white kid."

"But that's okay, because you treated him *better*," Tanuki said.

"Really? Feels wrong not to have busted his balls, especially when I didn't only because of the color of his skin."

"Nah, it don't work that way—"

"I don't know if it was racist exactly," Bartleby said, "but if you wanna protect your sister, let boys know someone's watching them, you gotta do it to every boy comes in range, not just this boy or that one."

"Right? That's what I was thinking. Remind me—next time we got service, I gotta send that kid an intimidating text message."

Register: Thunder Hill Shelter

6/3 Happy Birthday to ME. Love and Kisses,
                                    Longlegged Lemming

Thunder Hill Shelter was a ratty but otherwise non-descript shelter somewhere deep in the Virginian hinterlands. The harem was celebrating Longlegged Lemming's birthday in style.

DanK and Bigfeets had been carrying Jiffy Pop and marshmallows since Troutville. They'd collected a bunch of dead wood, but it was still wet from an afternoon rain shower and not burning very well.

Buttercup gave Lemming a nip bottle of rum and a can of Coke. He'd cooled the can in the stream for an hour beforehand. Grog gave her a travel size bottle of shampoo.

"What am I supposed to do with this?"

"Wash your hair, what do you think?"

Buttercup snorted.

"Seriously," Grog said. "Follow me."

Lemming followed Grog and the rest of the boys trailed along behind. Some distance away from the shelter by the creek, Grog had strung his tarp between two trees and created a privacy screen of sorts.

"You stand on this side. I'll stand over here with my eyes closed. Tell me when and I'll pour the water."

Lemming's face lit up, "That's so sweet, Grog. You sure you don't mind?"

"It'll be fun."

"Well, only if you let me pour water for you too then."

Thunk elbowed Bartleby and they moseyed back towards the shelter, "Turns out Grog is an evil genius, huh? I mean, it's the perfect gift—he barely had to carry anything, he gets to cut her away from the pack *and* he gets to "help" her take a shower. No way he won't be sneaking and peeking either. Brilliant."

"Here," Thunk tossed a packet of Jell-O Cheesecake pudding to Bartleby. "Mix this up, if you want to. I remembered she said once that she liked cheesecake, so I got this for her, but shit, cheesecake pudding can't compete with shampoo and a shower."

Bartleby and Thunk sat back against the picnic table. Bartleby spooned a dripping glob of yellow colored sludge from his pot. His beard was sprinkled with drying drops of cheesecake-flavored pudding.

He held the pot over for Thunk to take a spoonful.

Thunk spooned and swallowed, "It's not bad."

"It's not good."

"No. It's not good. But it's not exactly bad though."

"Not pudding really."

"No, not quite pudding either. More like wet icing."

"Almost."

"Yeah." Pause. "And you know the worst part?"

From where they sat, they had a distant view of the birthday shower. From this range, they couldn't hear much more than the occasional laugh from Lemming. She and Grog appeared to be having a grand time soaping up and pouring water over each other.

"Uh-uh," Bartleby said distractedly. He was watching a June bug march the length of his forearm.

"I'm sitting here and I'm absolutely riddled with jealousy."

"Yeah? Well—she does have a certain last-girl-in-the-world appeal."

"I'm not jealous of him and her—I'm jealous of that shower setup. I mean, I got me an industrial case of itchy-itchy bung-bung. A few minutes of hard scrubbing behind that privacy screen with a little soap and water—I'd be a new man."

Register: Highcock Knob Shelter

6/4 Best shelter name ever!   Bigfeets

6/4 I want whatever they were on when they decided naming
   this shelter after a big throbbing stiffy was a good idea.
                                                    – Grog

6/4 The Original Grand Poohbah's definitely pitching a tent
   tonight!

6/4 They musta seen me coming.   Buttercup

6/4 Then you're lucky they didn't call it "Tiny Hairless Balls
   Shelter"   Thunk

6/4 Gonna have some sweet dreams tonight!
                                    Longlegged Lemming

From out of the corner of his eye, Bartleby caught a flash of orange. It vanished behind a large boulder almost before he saw it.

Curious, he leaned against a nearby trunk; waited and watched. Wasn't too long before the orange reappeared on the boulder's far side.

A fox.

Not so much orange as russet, he could see now. Bigger than a big tomcat, but not by much. Black ears listened and twitched as sharp yellow eyes panned the forest scrub ahead.

When the way seemed safe, the fox picked something up in its mouth and spurted across trail. The long, limp body of a snake dangled from its jaws as it vanished into the woods without a sound.

Much like driftwood bobs before the will of tides and currents, so too are thru-hikers helplessly swept along on the cycles and rhythms of the natural world. When it was sunny and hot, there was no escape to air conditioning or even the temporary relief afforded by ice cubes. There was nothing for it but to hi-broil under direct sun, to slow bake in the shade, to spend the long nights steaming in puddles of sweat. Likewise when it rained, there was no choice but to get wet. But since available drinking water was largely dependent on that same rain, getting wet wasn't all too bad. Without rain the creeks and springs ran low and lower until they didn't—which was pretty bad and yet just another part of the natural cycle.

As the season began to twist toward summer, morning came both earlier and louder. Earlier because of the lengthening days and louder because of the birds. As much as an hour and a half before the sun was squinting over the closest horizon, the earliest of them had begun to chirp gossipy news of the coming day. It was always a single rumormonger starting this conversation, but it quickly grew as many feathered friends joined in.

Bartleby had never been a morning person, but now he regularly woke with the rising sun. There were no shades to pull down and block the light, no pillow to muffle nature's early bird alarm. Often, by six o'clock, he was already packed and setting off. The system couldn't have been simpler: he slept while the sun was down and woke when it returned. On trail, surrounded and submersed in the natural environment, nothing could've felt more normal.

Register: Punchbowl Shelter

6/6 The bullfrogs were going good when I got here last night. Was after dark when I finally dipped my water bottles in the mudhole for which this shelter was named. Found a crayfish sitting in the bottom of my nalgene this morning. Little bugger's lucky I didn't make crayfish coffee.

Thunk

*   *   *

The grassy summit expanse of Cold Mountain.

"Got any service?" Thunk wanted to know. He stood near the summit sign with his phone held over his head.

Bartleby didn't answer right away. He was too busy using his lungs to oxygenate his blood. After the climb, it felt like there was nothing but lactic acid left in his legs.

"Seriously, dude, can you check for a signal?"

"No phone."

"Shut up. Come on."

"Honest."

Thunk paused long enough to give Bartleby a once over, "Can't tell if you're just kidding or crazy." He shook his head and continued circling.

"Something wrong?"

"I gotta make a call. Forgot to do it from back at that last road. Now I'm five miles deep in the bush and I got no bars."

"Pretty up here, huh?"

"I don't got time for pretty," Thunk grated. "Gotta call into unemployment by close of business or they're not gonna send me my check. That's two hundred eighty-nine dollar, dollar bills y'all, but only if I don't fuck it up."

They could hear someone whistling nearby. Thunk pounced as soon as the whistler got close.

"Lemme borrow your cell, Chatter."

"What now?"

"Your phone. I need to make a call."

"Think I saw a payphone back in Buena Vista."

"Just great," Thunk growled. "I'm stuck hiking around the only two guys on the whole AT who aren't carrying phones." He hooked a pack strap over his shoulder and stormed off.

Chatter wiped sweat from his face.

"Oh-wee boy," he said, "sure is pretty up here, huh?"

"Peaceful now, too."

❋ ❋ ❋

Register: Seeley-Woodworth Shelter

5/30 Dearest Virginia:
    Been together far too long.
    It's not you, it's me.

                    High-Ku

❋ ❋ ❋

The car swerved wide without slowing and honked as it sped past. It was the seventh to drive by.

Thunk sent it on its way with what had become his customary rear window salute—two raised middle fingers.

"They had an empty backseat," he muttered. "Coulda fit us easy."

Despite there not being a car in sight, Bartleby still held his thumb out. "You ever in your life actually picked up a hitchhiker?"

"Uh-uh. In Syracuse, hitchhiker roughly translates to homeless bum."

"Me neither. Seems kinda funny now standing here, expecting someone to pick us up."

"Yeah, but we're thru-hikers. It's totally different."

"Bet we smell as bad as most homeless people."

"Worse probably."

❋ ❋ ❋

It was an easy ninety-five degrees across the rolling lowlands of Virginia. It felt at least fifteen degrees warmer than that as Bartleby clomped his way up The Priest.

The four thousand foot ascent seemed particularly brutal. Rivulets of sweat streamed down Bartleby's arms and legs; his shirt and socks sponged up what they could, but still drips fell from his nose, his chin and his elbows. The sky was that special sharp shade of blue it gets when the UV index creeps up out of the red and into the purple. Whenever he stopped to take a breather, Bartleby imagined he could feel his skin crisping over like burnt bacon.

Bacon skin.

Perverse as it was, the idea of eating a bacon skin sandwich with lettuce, tomato and a liberal smear of mayo was unavoidably appetizing. His mouth watered thinking about it.

The top quarter of the mountain was completely enveloped in wispy white clouds. This wasn't any kind of incoming weather system, but a stationary cloudbank encircling the mountaintop. One moment he was out sizzling under direct sunlight and then, two strides further, he was cloaked in a silvery moistness. The moisture was so thick, he couldn't see more than a few yards in any direction. The temperature dropped drastically, like walking into the lobby of an air conditioned building during a heat wave.

This standing mist blocked any views from the summit, but still, it was so refreshingly cool, Bartleby stopped for an early lunch. He broke out the stove and cooked up his last mac and cheese. With Waynesboro looming so close, there was little point in carrying extra food back into town.

Bartleby was draining the water from his pasta as Chatter and Jane arrived. Chatter was flushed white and breathing harder than normal. Jane was curious about the doings in Bartleby's cook pot.

"Some climb, huh?"

Chatter could only nod.

Bartleby reached out to touch a drifting cloud, "Got to be twenty degrees cooler up here."

Chatter grimaced, and, when he'd sufficiently caught his breath, set to work chewing jerky.

Then Longlegged Lemming came strolling along and stopped to

be social.

"So I can't tell," Chatter asked, "which a them boys you sweet on, Lemming?"

Lemming shrugged and rolled her eyes, "I don't know. It's problematical. See, I've got this boyfriend back home."

"He must be some nice guy, eh?"

Lemming shrugged again.

"Funny? Smart? He like hiking?"

She thought for a bit, "I don't know."

"Well, what'd'ya like about him?" Chatter said.

"That's easy," she brightened, "he's got a really nice bike."

"So he does like to hike," Chatter said.

"Uh-uh."

Chatter looked to Bartleby for explanation.

"She said 'bike'."

"Bike? Like a bicycle? What bicycle?"

Bartleby shrugged. They looked back to Lemming.

"A motorcycle," she explained. "Kawasaki Ninja. So fast, it's like you're flying."

"Oh, botheration."

To Lemming's credit, she blushed a little. "This is all such a nice change of pace. Back home, it's like I'm a minnow in a mud puddle, right? Out here, I mean, sure it's a little pond, but who cares? For once in my life, maybe the only time ever, I get to be the big fish."

In Waynesboro, Bartleby slept out on the YMCA's back lawn. Was supposed to pay for the privilege but he cheesed out on the fee. Had he money to spend, the shower alone would've been worth twenty bucks to him. He spent a good while sifting through the hiker box. It was a gold mine of unwanted couscous and corn pasta, dried figs, powdered milk and instant oatmeal packets. He also scored half a roll of duct tape. Still had some, but figured you couldn't ever have too much of the stuff.

In exchange for Bartleby agreeing to babysit Sweet Jane so he could grocery shop and flit about town on various errands, Mad Chatter took Bartleby to breakfast at Weasie's Kitchen.

Weasie's was an old school diner and a minor trail institution. Bartleby ordered coffee and orange juice, a bacon and tomato omelet with hash browns and buttered toast, a stack of pancakes and then, at the last minute, he panicked and added a sausage, egg and cheese biscuit on top of everything else.

He didn't realize how ridiculously gluttonous the order was until it all came out and the waitress had to puzzle all the plates together to make them fit on the table. Figuring that he'd maybe overstepped the bounds of Chatter's generosity, Bartleby offered to pay his share. A chuckling Chatter waved him off, "You think you can eat it, you should quick order something else, Bumblebee. Don't want anyone hitting trail hungry."

Bartleby took his time, savored every bite and when it was gone, he still had room to help with the last of Chatter's potatoes.

❧ ❧ ❧

Register: Blackrock Hut

6/12 Long live the Skyline Drive! Yogi'd my way into two
       sandwiches, a Yoo-Hoo and half a watermelon. — Poohbah

❧ ❧ ❧

In many ways, Shenandoah National Park was similar to the Smokies. Both parks enforced similar camping rules and restrictions on overnight hikers. Both parks hosted dense populations of black bears. Both places were easily accessed and overrun by auto-tourists.

The hiking terrain throughout Shenandoah was considerably

easier than what the AT covered in the Smokies. Wide and level straightaways rolled on for miles and miles. Any elevation changes were relatively nominal though, when compared to the sharp saw-teeth of the Smokies. Also they were gradual and smooth, as if they'd been engineered. The AT paralleled and frequently crossed Skyline Drive, a paved and scenic auto road that wiggled its way through the park. This meant traffic noise was audible along much of the hundred mile stretch of trail.

Within the park there were three big lodges, each offering up fine dining and faux-rustic hotel rooms, the cheapest of which cost more than Bartleby had left in his bankroll. Also, every so often along Skyline Drive, there were gas stations that sold pretty much anything a hungry thru-hiker might want, including dollar bottles of Yuengling beer.

Because they were so plentiful and accustomed to people, Shenandoah's black bears were particularly problematic for hikers. The abundant park literature posted at all shelters and trailheads advised hikers not to leave packs unattended, even for a few minutes. An unconfirmed rumor went around about how Lumbering Jack had left food in his tent while strolling off to one of the gas stations. He came back to the campsite with cold beers in hand, to find his tent shredded, his pack gutted, his food eaten and his gear mostly mangled. When a ranger showed up, she gave him a ticket for improper food storage.

There were awesome vistas throughout Shenandoah and there was a parking pull-off at each and every one of them. If you wanted to look out at the rounded shoulders of the Blue Ridge Mountains in all their hazy, summertime glory, you did it surrounded by RV-tourists, civilian sightseers and miserable family vacationers.

Between the hungry bears, the endless traffic and the restricted camping, Shenandoah was a place that many thru-hikers endeavored to blow through as quickly as possible. They did this by hiking twenty-five, thirty, even thirty-five miles a day; by carrying next to no food and by zooming past all the vistas without even pausing for a quick look-see.

* * *

Bartleby and Thunk and Jane and Chatter were humping along in a line. The level terrain made for easy conversation. Chatter had spent the better part of the last two hours telling them all about his hat shop. Where he got the merchandise, how the hat game had changed over the fifty-some-odd years he'd been playing it and all the celebrity clients that he serviced. This last was a surprising list of top-tier actors, athletes and rappers. It was all very interesting in an after-the-first-few-days-of-novelty-long-distance-hiking-can-be-ass-numbingly-boring-and-absolutely-any-topic-is-better-than-lis-tening-to-the-heavy-clump-of-feet-for-the-next-however-many-more-miles sort of way.

Thunk snorted. "You're honestly trying to tell me P. Diddy used to come and buy lids from your shop? Sorry, Chatter, but I can't quite swallow that one."

"Eh? Who's this P. Diddy?"

"P. Diddy. Puff Daddy. You said you sold hats to Sean Combs."

"Many, many. And let me tell you something about him, Sonny."

"By all means."

"Mr. Combs has a keen eye for fine headwear. A real aficionado. Our world would be a better place if everyone had just a tenth of his style sense and taste. Starting right here with you. It looks like an old abandoned sand lot you're carrying around up top."

"Getting bad up there, isn't it? I tell you, I haven't missed mirrors one bit out here. Makes it nice and easy to forget about little stuff like premature hair loss."

"With those ears of yours, I could see you in a flat cap. Maybe a dark gray tweed to set off your eyes. Give you a nice sharp, confident man-about-town look. Takes a certain chutzpah for a man to really carry off a hat these days, but you get the right one, and the ladies will line up around the block.'"

"Seriously?" And, "What's a flat cap?"

"Like a newsboy hat."

"Is that anything like a Kangol?"

Chatter's mouth puckered like he'd just taken a bite of bad fish, "That's the general idea, but Kangol isn't a cut, it's a brand name. Trust me, my hats are a whole lot better than any off-the-rack Kangol."

"You really are a nutty old hat guy, huh?"

"Ayup."

"Funny thing to be into."

"Seems to me it doesn't matter what line we get into, long as we approach it with the necessary passion, we're going to find success. I liked hats, I got into hats, I did well with hats. What do you do, Thunk?"

"Nothing."

"Must do something."

"Well, yeah," Thunk said. "Sure. I used to sell cars for General Motors. But that was a job, not a career. I was a Junior Associate until GM ran out of money and our dealership got shuttered. No warning either. Like 9:15 on a Tuesday morning and this SWAT team of suits suddenly shows up. They spread out across the sales floor, the service center, even the car lot. Had the whole place locked down in five minutes flat. Made an announcement for everyone to collect their shit and vacate the premises within fifteen minutes."

"That sounds rough," Bartleby said.

"Personally, I hadn't made a sale in over a month. Between that and the nightly news going on about how the economy was shitting the bed—we shouldn't have been surprised.

"I was lucky—no kids and no home to be under water with. I broke my apartment lease and moved back in with my mom. My cousin has his own moving company. He paid me under the table so I could still collect unemployment.

"That's a nice hook-up."

"It was. I mean, he was totally a hard-on, but it was cool until the prick fired me. He wanted me to wear a shirt. I was like 'fuck you,

Cuz.' I mean, he was working in the office, dealing with customers. I was carrying fifty pound boxes of books up six flights in August. That's some hard, hot work. Regularly soaked through my shirt in the first ten minutes on the job. No way was I spending the next ten hours squelching around in a wet shirt.

"After that, I figured I'd sneak out here, hike the trail while still collecting. Mostly it's worked like a charm. I mean, you saw me freaking out the other day about putting the call in, but usually I've got it planned out better."

"Don't they make you come down to the unemployment office? Meet with someone?"

"Yeah. When I got to Hot Springs, I quick hitched into Asheville and caught a flight home. Put in a grand total of thirteen minutes face time with my rep. She'll probably want me to come in again sometime soon, but I think I'll generally have a week to figure out a way home. I'm from New York, so we're getting closer every day."

Register: Bearfence Mountain Hut

6/14 Today, I stopped and watched this big brown toad get all animal kingdom on an earthworm. He sucked it down like wet spaghetti. Yet another reason thru-hiking is way better than a desk job.   Thunk

It was somewhere in Shenandoah that Bartleby first started wrapping his hiking shoes with duct tape. He'd put almost six hundred miles on them since Hot Springs and they were all done. The soles were peeling off the front like rotten banana skins. They should've been retired out to the shoe farm, but Bartleby couldn't afford a new pair. Course, walking on rocks and whatnot, it didn't take too terribly long to wear through the mummy-wrapped duct tape. Depending on his mileage, the terrain and local weather conditions, he stopped and reapplied tape sometimes as often as three times a day. Because Bartleby didn't bother removing the old tape before applying a fresh wrap, his sneakers gradually began to look like awkwardly oversized clown shoes.

And these weren't the only things threatening to give out on him. Of the clothes Bartleby purchased at Neels Gap, only the shorts were still fully functioning—and they were stained with sap, sun-weathered and now a size too large. He'd chewed through six pairs of socks and walked his wicking underwear into shreds. No choice left, but to go without.

The t-shirt he'd been wearing was threadbare under his pack straps. Just at the summit of his shoulders, what individual threads remained couldn't be expected to last long. When it got so he was afraid to pull the thing over his head, he started duct taping the shirt as well. Inside and out. Didn't feel very comfortable, particularly with the pack straps pressing the tape edges down into his skin, and it might've actually looked sillier than his shoes.

Even by using only two or three drops of Aquamira to purify a liter of water (the instructions called for seven drops per) he ran out between towns. He started boiling his dinner water a little longer and hoping like hell the rest of the time. Last thing he needed was a ripe case of giardia.

Still had ziplocs with him that he'd been using since Hiawassee. Many of these had gotten so that they no longer zipped or locked. Some sported little holes and leaked food into the depths of his food bag. In Waynesboro, Chatter donated some used baggies and Bartleby retired his holiest offenders.

Angie had sent Bartleby off with half a bottle of aspirin, but they'd run out somewhere before Fontana Dam. He'd hiked most of the last seven hundred miles without even temporary medicinal relief for the aching muscles of his legs and feet. In the morning, his knees and ankles were so throbbingly stiff, his thighs and calves were strung so tight, he couldn't help but hobble about camp. Bartleby's feet bottoms felt bruised from heel to big toe. Before he warmed them up, the balls of his hips creaked rustily with each step. Even once he got going and worked his leg muscles loose, they still cooled and contracted surprisingly quick during rest breaks. Then he'd have to go through all the tightness and pain of working them awake again.

All of this, though, was a part of the process. It was the AT doing what it did. Forget cold sodas in a stream or a memorable hitch into town, this was the real magic of the Appalachian Trail. Weathering and wearing at body and mind; whittling away the excess and unnecessary, the rotten and warped, until there was nothing left but a solid indispensable core. Then, when nothing more could be shaved off and discarded, the trail set to strengthening and sharpening whatever remained.

Thunk pulled up in the middle of trail to appreciate what had to be the largest gobbler he'd ever set eyes on. And with all the time he'd been dragged out hunting with his uncle, this was actually saying something. The turkey was beach ball-sized and about as ugly as they come. Its head and neck were covered over in wrinkly skin ranging from a fleshy pink to a veiny blue. Impossibly bizarre wattles hung down from the bird's beak and neck like melting silly putty.

Half-recalling badly taught lessons from an earlier decade, Thunk put his hands together and attempted to improvise a turkey call. This sounded like the sickly warbling of a dying Tauntaun.

"What is that thing?" Lemming whispered. Thunk hadn't heard her arrive.

"Tom Turkey."

"Really? Looks like some kinda evil alien."

Thunk called again to the gobbler. Aside from the occasional glance, the big bird scratched for food and otherwise ignored them.

"What are you doing?"

"Turkey call." He did it again to no better effect.

"Does it work?"

Poohbah came tramping up the trail, was still some ways back when he caught sight of Lemming and called out for her to wait up.

For the turkey, this was the last straw. It wandered away into deeper woods without so much as fanning its tail feathers.

"Not usually," Thunk said, as Poohbah hurried to catch them.

❦ ❦ ❦

In the deep shade beneath a high leafy canopy, rolling fields of hip-high ferns continued further than Bartleby could see in any direction. A feathery green blanket of fern fronds which worked to muffle the ambient noises of nature.

Despite the absence of a breeze, it was coolish in the shade. Individual fern stalks didn't so much as tremble in the still air. Which was why Bartleby took note when an outlying patch of ferns started swaying and shaking violently. This was accompanied by the rustling-crunch of some beast crashing through the undergrowth.

Curious and standing on tiptoe, he couldn't see anything more than ferns being savagely trampled. The obvious explanation was a bear. Which would've been cool with Bartleby, as he still hadn't laid eyes on one. Course it might've been something else: a small deer, a large rodent, a wild boar, a fisher cat or some other predator struggling to subdue lunch.

Bartleby watched for long moments, but still couldn't catch any glimpse of whatever was causing the commotion. So he clinked his poles together, a sort of here-I-am declaration.

The ferns went stock still and the clamor cut off in mid-crunch. Then, with an explosion of renewed motion, the invisible fern-flattening force came hurtling straight towards Bartleby.

Curiosity quickly turned sour in his mouth.

With little time to do anything else, Bartleby braced himself and held his hiking poles at the ready. The line of trampled ferns grew closer and closer and the rustling-swish of dead leaves and live ferns grew louder and louder.

His heart was thuddering against the confines of his ribcage when Sweet Jane bounded out of the ferns. She was all but crazy with delight and leapt at him with irrepressible joy.

She yipped and reared up, licked at his face.

"I'd be so mad at you," Bartleby told her when he'd sufficiently caught his breath, "if I wasn't so happy to see you."

Chatter bent low and filled his water bottles at a dribbling little streamlet. This task took longer than one might expect, as flat-footed water bugs kept getting sucked in with the flowing water. It was five or six tries before his bottles were full and bug free.

When Bartleby's headlamp gave out, he was standing a dozen steps from the shelter and letting loose with three pints of darkly yellow urine. Even in the dying orange glow of his headlamp's last moments, he could see that much. When his headlamp went dark, he thwumped it against his palm, but there just wasn't any juice left in the batteries for him to thwump free.

Heavy clouds blocked out any possible light from the night sky. The lightning bugs had called it quits hours ago. It was about as dark as dark got out in the woods.

Bartleby was able to alternately stumble and inch his way back to the shelter. This involved catching his shin on the edge of the picnic table, tripping over something that might've been a backpack and, when he got close, stubbing a toe on the shelter itself.

If possible, it was even darker inside the shelter. He couldn't see enough to find his sleeping spot.

"Thunk," Bartleby whispered. "Wake up."

"Whazzat?"

"Turn your light on. Mine died."

Thunk toggled his light on and waited while Bartleby settled back down.

When they were once again enveloped in darkness, Thunk sighed sleepily, "I was having this crazy dream. Carrying this big old wheel of cheese with me, you know, out on trail. Jammed a Leki through its center, turned it into a unicycle without pedals. Could coast on the downhills and every once in a while I would, you know, stop for a cheesy good snack."

❀ ❀ ❀

"I'll catch up," Thunk called. "Gotta see a tree about a pee."

Shortly after Thunk dropped behind, Mad Chatter cleared his throat, "I got a theory, Bumblebee."

After ducking beneath a low hanging branch, Bartleby held it for Chatter to pass under.

"Seems like there's two categories. People come out here to either get lost or find themselves. Sonny boy," Chatter gestured back towards Thunk, "represents the finding category. He probably didn't start hiking with any grand desire for reinvention, but I'm betting this little walk gives him perspective on his life and future."

"And I'm a poster child for the former, more selective 'get lost' category. I mean, frankly—I'm an old coot on my way out. Not planning on dying or anything, but I'm done 'living' in any forward looking sense of the word."

"Huh," Bartleby said warily.

"With those guidelines in mind, it's been easy to plop most everyone out here into one category or the other," Mad Chatter continued. "Lemming, Pony, even JoJo are all out here looking for themselves in some little way or another. Seems like maybe that pushy little Poohbah, wants to lose himself out here. I mean, this is his fourth go-round, isn't it?"

Bartleby groaned inwardly, he knew what was coming.

"But you aren't so easy, Bumblebee. I can't tell if you're getting lost or found."

Then for a long time there was nothing to be heard but the plod of feet and the flat tonk of Jane's broken bell. Bartleby had been wondering the same thing for weeks now, and he still hadn't come up with any kind of useful answer.

Register: Gravel Springs Hut

6/8 Slither, slither, hissss.
    Copperheads, rattlers and blacks:
    Jump back—heart attack!

                              High-Ku

Jim and Molly Denton Shelter had an attached wooden deck, built-in bench seats, a solar shower and a picnic table under a detached cooking pavilion. It was a great place for a break.

"Even got skylights," Thunk pointed out.

"Clerestory windows," Bartleby corrected.

"Really? Look like skylights to me."

"Skylights go in the roof. Windows go in walls."

"Huh."

Thunk poured his food bag out and poked through the accumulated wrappers in search of an exciting snack.

"Absolutely nothing fun about these fun-size bars. So small ya can't find them without dumping everything out. I swear it takes more work to eat one than they're worth."

"If you don't want them…."

"Ha."

"Got any spare p-cord?"

Thunk grunted negatively around a nougaty mouthful of chocolate.

Bartleby was trying to rig up his shoes again. One of the laces had broken a couple miles back and the remnants were so knotted as to make a fix next to impossible.

When he removed the broken lace entirely, the shoe's tongue came flapping loose.

"You need some new kicks, dude."

He glared over at Thunk, but the kid was impervious to such subtleties. Bartleby dumped out his pack, sifted through for some stray bit of string he could use as a replacement lace. He found four stale but otherwise edible peanut M&Ms and two ketchup packets that he'd tucked away for safe keeping, but nothing that came close to resembling a shoe lace.

"Could use the cinch string on your shorts," Thunk suggested.

"Then how am I going to keep my pants up?"

"Dunno. Maybe if you got some p-cord, you could make a belt."

"Why don't you go chase Lemming off a cliff?"

"I'm giving up on all that; officially quitting the gnat pack. Got caught up in all the excitement, ya know, but she's not even my type."

"Since when?"

"Since I wasn't getting nowhere. Good riddance."

Bartleby ripped a length of duct tape from his shrinking supply and set to rolling it up into a tight tube. The work wasn't easy but eventually he had something that would likely do the job. It took some patience threading the tube of tape through the eyelets of his shoes, but it was an improvement over the broken lace.

"That's good work and all, but I think you're still gonna need new shoes. Those ain't got nothing left."

"That what you think, Thunk?"

While Bartleby made a shoelace from duct tape, a line of gray clouds swept in from the west and blocked out the sun.

"Time you got?"

"It's on my pack."

Bartleby checked Thunk's watch. "We been here like two hours, huh?"

"Least."

"Chatter shoulda showed by now."

"Probably keeled over."

"Not funny."

"I know it's not. Dude's one rickety old geezer. No way is he gonna make it all the way to Maine. He's like your shoes—there just ain't nothing left."

Although Bartleby agreed with Thunk, he wasn't going to admit it out loud. Instead he pursed his lips and listened to the wind in the trees.

"And why's he always calling you Bumblebee?"

"Guess he thinks it's my name."

"Is it?"

Bartleby shrugged. "Just as much as Bartleby is, I guess."

"What's your real name?"

Bartleby hesitated, then, "Walter."

"What—didn't wanna tell me or something?"

"Couldn't remember for a sec there."

Bindle Stiff loped along a few minutes later.

"You see Chatter back there?" Bartleby asked him.

Before he could answer, Bindle Stiff sneezed. One of those painful looking full body contractions. "He'll be—" Bindle said. He paused, plugged a nostril with his finger and blew a thick gob of yellow phlegm onto the ground, "—along. Was picking flowers, I think."

The sky was growing darker by the minute.

"Next shelter's six miles," Thunk said. He was standing near his backpack, packed up and primed to resume hiking. "You going on or what?"

Bartleby had been planning to go on, hadn't done many miles yet today, what with shooting into Front Royal for a quick resupply. He gauged the sky but it showed no signs of lightening. He assessed the shelter area—this one was way better than most—and looked southward down the trail. There was still no sign of Jane or Chatter.

"Starting to look iffy."

Thunk stood there with a pack strap slung over one shoulder, "You worried about the old guy or you worried about rain?"

"Uh-huh."

Thunk's pack hit the ground with a crunking-clank, "Well, I'm not getting wet by myself."

❧

Chatter showed up just as the first fat raindrops came spitting down. Jane was hurrying him along fast as she could pull him. He had a red-spoked flower tucked behind one ear. It didn't entirely make up for his missing hat, but it did spruce him up a bit.

His eyesight and determination were such that he might've marched through the clearing, continued on northward if Bartleby hadn't whistled Jane over. She veered toward the shelter and dragged Chatter in her wake.

"If this is Manassas Gap Shelter, I just set a new speed record."

"Only Jim and Molly Denton Shelter, but I'm quitting early today, Chatter."

"Why's that? Because I wasn't following along quick enough? You're not coddling me are ya? I got half a mind to keep on to Manassas Gap. Trail's awaiting and I'm not getting any younger."

"Half a mind's about right," Thunk agreed.

After giving her ears a good scratch, Bartleby unhooked Jane's leash and removed her panniers. She wandered into the shelter and sniffed around before flopping down near Bartleby's pack.

"*I'm* staying here," Bartleby pointed at the sky, "because I don't wanna get wet."

"Huh," was all Chatter said. He stood there, chewing this over for a bit. The rain picked up enough, he couldn't help but scuttle under the roof with the rest of them.

Mumbled "traitor" at Jane as he unpacked.

Bartleby's dinner was pretty much the same as it had been for nine nights running. Half a pound of elbow pasta under five packets of ketchup and sweet relish and seasoned with garlic powder and pepper from Chatter's spice collection. There was nothing tasty or exciting about it, but it was the absolute cheapest meal Bartleby could devise. The elbow pasta was expired and had been on sale: two pounds for a dollar. He'd bought ten pounds worth. Coupled with stolen condiment packets, it turned into twenty meals at a quarter a piece. Figured it had enough calories to keep him going and he hoped the ketchup and sweet relish contained enough vitamins to at least keep him from getting scurvy.

His pot was still half-full, but for the first time in more than month, Bartleby didn't feel the least bit hungry. In fact, just looking at the remaining food in the pot turned his stomach. He forced a few more bites down, but it was clear that finishing the meal was somehow beyond his abilities. When Jane came sniffing around, he put the pot down for her. She took two long whiffs and walked away without touching it.

"You know you got some serious ghetto pasta going on," Thunk observed, "when even a big dumb dog won't eat it."

❦

The rain continued on into the morning. Bartleby slept straight through the night. With some effort he roused himself and put water on for instant oatmeal and tea. These seemed to be the only items he found in hiker boxes with anything close to regularity. Chatter and Jane were just starting off and Thunk was taking down his tent.

This last was puzzling for two reasons. First, no one tents in the rain if they can avoid it. Even Chatter, who usually tented to keep Jane from bothering the masses, had opted for the shelter last night. The reason being, if somehow, miraculously, your tent didn't leak and you actually slept dry, you still had to carry a wet tent away in the morning and risk soaking everything else in your pack. Second,

Bartleby distinctly remembered Thunk sleeping next to him in the shelter. Nearest to Bindle Stiff.

From under the shelter's roof, Thunk shook his tent out best as he could.

"How'd you end up tenting?" Bartleby asked.

"You must be kidding," Thunk rolled his eyes and jerked a thumb at Bindle Stiff's sleeping form. "You're not kidding? You didn't hear him?"

"What," Bartleby lowered his voice, "the farting?"

"Oh, there some of that, sure, but no. He was snoring. It was like a, a drowning grizzly bear. I yelled at him. I threw my shoes at him. I threw *your* shoes at him. I even went over and prodded him, tried to roll him with my foot. Didn't even slow him down." Thunk shook his head, "I've never heard anything like it."

⁂

When Bartleby ducked into Dick's Dome Shelter some four hours and ten miles later, the back of his throat felt raspy and his sinuses and lungs were leaking yellow phlegm. According to the shelter's register, Thunk had also lunched at Dick's Dome, but he was apparently moving faster and had already gone ahead. Bartleby didn't have any clue how much further the next shelter was, but after sitting around for an hour feeling like hell's dirty back end, he decided to find out.

Bartleby's progress could only have been called plodding. He moved well below his normal pace, but still the effort was unusually taxing. His muscles felt feeble and his bones felt fragile. It got so each step was a fight, simply standing an unwelcome labor. He wanted to stop, to lay down, to sleep for a week, but with no tent in his pack and no shelter in sight, he didn't have much of a choice. Couldn't do anything but keep on, following each step with another aching step, hacking and wheezing and sniffling his way slowly northward.

Out in the open, the raindrops were juicy as grapes. They came driving down heavy and cold. Under tree cover, the drops dripped off of leaves erratically, but with no less determination to wash him away. His bare head became tender from the pelting. Cold water trickled down between his shoulder blades with an annoyingly impish irregularity. Had it been a constant flow, it would've been easier to ignore. In short order his runny nose was rubbed Rudolph-red, his throat burned with postnasal drip, his head felt strangely heavy and his chest ached from violent fits of coughing.

When Bartleby's thoughts were conscious, he worried that his Hefty bag pack liner might not be keeping his gear dry; he worried that he'd somehow passed the shelter; he worried that the shelters might've all run out; he worried that the rollercoaster hills and the rain would go on and on interminably, until he collapsed and drowned right there beside trail. When his thoughts weren't conscious, images of Angie and the kids floated through his head like empty barrels bobbing down a running creek.

As the day wore on, the puddles fattened with slick mud. His skin turned white and wrinkled. Every couple hundred yards, Bartleby leaned up against a tree trunk, gathering himself for the next push. He hadn't eaten much all day, didn't feel hungry, but knew he needed calories. He tried a handful of peanuts, but they went down like a mouthful of glass, so he settled for sucking down a few mayonnaise packets.

Usually the trail was full of people—south-bound section hikers, random day hikers, weekender greenhorns and familiar thru-hiker colleagues wending their way northward. Today though, he didn't spot another soul. Not even Mad Chatter, whom Bartleby generally traded the lead with half a dozen times each day. Underfoot, the earthworms were all drowned and floating in mud puddles.

The terrain left next to no impression on him. If asked to describe a section, even ten or fifteen minutes after passing, Bartleby wouldn't have been able to get any closer than to say it had mud and water and the occasional tree trunk. Toward day's end, he couldn't focus more than four or five steps ahead and little further than a foot to either side of trail.

His feverish mind lost all objective ability to gauge time and distance. There were moments when it felt like he'd been hiking straight for forty days and nights. Somewhere in there, he started talking to himself, mumbling about "A&W Root Beer" and how his "keepin' on needed to keep on." There was all sorts of other gibberish including a jingle from an old McDonald's commercial he pulled from the dirtiest dustbin of his mind and then repeated a few thousand times:

We are Nippersinkers, We're in Luck
If it rains all week just pretend you're a duck!
Wack Wack Waddle Waddle Wack Wack Waddle Waddle.

Luckily for Bartleby, when he reached it, the trail sign for Rod Hollow Shelter was terribly obvious. If it had been set high in a tree or too far off to the side, the odds were good he would've missed it entirely.

Mad Chatter, Thunk and a woman unfamiliar to Bartleby were already at the shelter when he stumbled in. After removing his pack, he gave her a big friendly smile.

"Hey there. I'm Bartleby, what's your name?"

"Mudsucka."

"Mudsucka, huh? Mud-sucker. I like that. Muuuudsuckerrrr."

"Wondered if you were gonna make it, Pokey," Thunk said. "We been here for hours already."

Bartleby sniffled, then sneezed. Somehow this became a wet dredging cough that produced a mouthful of phlegm. With an aplomb that was both cavalier and uncharacteristic, Bartleby gripped the wall, leaned far off the shelter platform and spat a yellow-green gob in a high tumbling arc. Task accomplished to his satisfaction, he turned back and gave Mudsucka a warm, welcoming smile.

"Hey there," Bartleby said, "I'm Nippersinker, what's your name?"

"Er...Mudsucka."

"Mudsucka, huh? Mmmmud-suuuucker! That's a good one. Know what, Mudsucka? I think I might be a duck."

And then, without any more antics, Bartleby collapsed into a feverish pile of wrinkled wet flesh.

✤

They brought Bartleby around with smelling salts that looked as crusty old as Chatter himself.

"Who'zat," Bartleby declared.

By this time, Thunk and Mad Chatter had skinned his wet outer layer and stuffed him into his sleeping bag. If the bag wasn't officially damp before, it certainly was afterwards. Bartleby was sweating and shivering both. They sat him up against the back wall of the shelter and settled Jane into his lap.

While all this was going on, Mudsucka boiled water for tea.

Since Bartleby hadn't yet opened his eyes, Chatter hit him again with the salts.

"What's happening?" Bartleby said.

"Heh-heh. Told you they worked, Thunk."

Jane licked at Bartleby's face, and with his arms pinned into the depths of his sleeping bag and his head pressed against wood, he couldn't do anything but cringe before her slobbery onslaught.

"Gack. Where am I?"

"Rod Hollow Shelter."

"Figured I missed it."

"Safe and sound, sonny."

Mudsucka brought the steaming tea in close, "Here, this should warm you up."

Bartleby took a small sip and then another.

He looked at Mudsucka for the first time. "Thanks. I'm Bartleby, what's your name?"

✤

"A nasty summer flu, huh?" Thunk said. "Where you think it came from?"

"I don't know. Bindle Stiff, maybe."

"You totally got bindle-stiffed, huh? Classic. He coming along still today ya think?"

Bartleby shrugged, "He hadn't even moved yet when I left this morning."

"So let's hope he's not already dead or dying, right?"

Bartleby nodded absently. Then, "Wait—what?"

"We're out in the woods and don't know anything going on back in the world. What if there's been some crazy virus outbreak? Maybe that's actually brain jelly leaking out of your nose. I mean, this could be the beginning of the end of the—"

"Don't be an idiot," Mudsucka cut in with the no-nonsense tone she reserved for precocious children, "he's caught a twenty-four hour bug. Summer flus happen. Finish your tea and get some sleep. You'll feel better in the morning."

❦ ❦ ❦

Register: Gravel Springs Hut

5/31 I turn 70 yrs old today. B-Day celebrations include:
— 1 hr basking in sun
— a king-size Baby Ruth bar (mmmm)
— 7 miles of hiking (1 for each decade of my life)
— one pr clean underwear
— and one personal promise to never live in Bismarck
Thinking about turning around at Katahdin and hiking back south. They tell me it's called "yo-yoing". Happy birthday and long live a FREE me.
                                        The Knitty Biddy

❦ ❦ ❦

Come the morning, Bartleby didn't feel much better, but after drinking down a concoction of ginger tea infused with alka-seltzer cold tablets (Chatter's), three aspirin (Mudsucka's) and a packet of Vitamin C powder (Thunk's), he at least felt able to continue hiking. He moved slower and less steadily than normal, but anything seemed better than laying up alone and sick as a dog with a crusty buildup of snot growing on his mustache.

The rain and clouds had cleared, but until mid-afternoon, sunlight was sporadic at best. Every time Bartleby took a break at what looked like a cozy, sun-warmed spot, the sun promptly went away and he was left shivering in the shade. Which isn't to say it was cold out. Mid-to-high eighties in direct sun and dropping down only slightly in the shade.

He caught up to Mudsucka as she sat trail-side, nibbling Fig Newtons.

"You feeling better?"

"Uhn."

"Well, you really hit the lottery today," she said.

"Oh, yeah?" He sniffled, hacked up some goop and hawked it into the underbrush, "Doesn't feel like it."

She nodded over at a trail sign standing a few yards away.

WELCOME TO WEST VIRGINIA
A.T. CONFERENCE TR 16.8 MI.
HARPERS FERRY 17.4 MI.
MARYLAND BORDER 17.5 MI.

The gouged wooden plaque was bolted to an equally worn post.

Despite his health, Bartleby perked up, "Finally leaving Virginia, huh? How long's it been? Feels like a couple years."

"I don't know exactly. More than five hundred miles. Close to five-fifty, I think."

"Pretty much forever."

"Yeah, well. So, I have this thing going where I take a photo at each state line. Used to be able to attach my camera to my Leki pole, but I broke the stupid plastic attachment on McAfee's Knob."

"So what—you want me to take your picture?"

"Naked."

Bartleby grunted as if she'd said something moderately funny.

"Seriously. I send them to my husband. The dirty dog loves them. Could hardly wait for me to get out of Virginia already. Is that gonna freak you out?"

He shrugged, "No, I guess it won't."

No sooner had he said this than Mudsucka tossed him her smartphone and began peeling clothes off.

She was in her mid-forties, with sandy hair cut shaggy short. At five foot three, one hundred thirty pounds, she had the full, curvy figure of a woman tempered by a thousand miles of hiking. There was an almost glaring contrast between the bright white of her feet and midsection and the sun-bronzed brown of her arms, legs and face.

When she was wearing nothing but trail dust, Mudsucka posed behind the sign post so that only the curves of her hips showed around either side, her breasts were mostly hidden behind the sign itself.

Bartleby snapped a few shots.

"Is this sexy? The poor guy hasn't seen me in five hundred miles—don't want to come across as too formal. Should I show more? I could turn sideways or, or stand on tiptoe and let the girls rest on the sign. What'd'ya think?"

"I think those scouts are going to earn themselves a new merit badge, you don't put something on quick."

A string of boys were marching southward along the trail. They were far enough away they hadn't seen Mudsucka yet, but they would soon. She frantically pulled clothing on, "You gotta go stall them," she hissed, "or no, don't move, just keep standing in front of me."

Bartleby stood, blocking as best he could, any view of Mudsucka as she finished dressing. She was more or less covered as the scouts passed by. The scout leader gave them a suspicious once-over. Mudsucka burst out laughing once they'd gone.

"You really send those photos to your husband?"

She pixie-grinned, "Part of the agreement we made when I left. Been married twenty-two years now. Surprising what a few photos and a little abstinence can do to put some spice back in the relationship." She gave Bartleby a sly look, "You want to take one?"

"No, that's—"

"Seriously, I don't mind. It's only fair, really."

Bartleby was never quite sure if Mudsucka was offering him a copy of her picture or for her to take a shot of him posing naked. Either way, he didn't imagine that Angie would've been too thrilled.

Hunched as it was at the confluence of the Potomac and the Shenandoah rivers, Harpers Ferry had a certain craggy charm to it. The place was stony and steep; threaded through with worn cobble lanes, weathered rock walls, Civil War-era architecture and heaping mounds of historical character. But thinking back through every history class he'd ever taken in high school and college, Bartleby couldn't recall a single event that had taken place there.

After joining US-340 long enough to cross the rushing Shenandoah, the AT peeled right and climbed a low rise. It kept to a thin stretch of woods until breaking cover to cross the tiny historic downtown. While Bartleby knew next to nothing about the town or the services it might offer thru-hikers, he did know that budgetary restrictions largely limited him from taking advantage of any opportunities. Despite this, he couldn't help but feel a certain optimistic excitement on returning to civilization. His time on the AT had taught him that the most boring resupply was better than none at all. And even thinking about the remote possibility of a hot shower gave him an anticipatory thrill.

Just as Bartleby entered Harpers proper, he spotted Two-Speed Tortoise's straw cartwheel hat. He hadn't seen her since sometime before Trail Days and there she was sitting beneath it, alone on a bench, encircled by mounds of gear and food and cardboard boxes.

Bartleby wandered over, dropped to sit nearby, "Hiya."

She looked up and passed a long moment trying to place his face. When Tortoise did finally smile, he noticed it contained more than a little cringe.

"Bartleby! Haven't seen you for ages. How are you? How's it going?"

"Alright."

"Looks like maybe you've been having a rough time of it."

Bartleby tried for a nonchalant grin and failed badly, "What makes you say that?"

"I don't know. You've lost weight, the clothes and...are you sick? You look like a hobo ghoul."

This brought a genuine smile to his face, "That bad, huh?"

"Like, pretty bad."

"Going on my third day of a twenty-four hour summer flu. Might look terrible, but honestly, I'm feeling alright. Maybe good even. What about you, Tortoise? I don't know exactly, but you're glowing."

Bartleby wasn't just saying this. Tortoise looked to have burned off her freshman fifteen and her facial acne had cleared away. There was an aura of health and happiness radiating from her that even a blind man would've recognized.

Tortoise blushed, "Me and Hairbrained broke up like two days ago. Said he had to hike his own hike and went running off ahead. Guess I was cramping his style." Pause. "He was really a jerkwad, huh?"

Bartleby nodded, "One serious stinker."

She gestured at the packages and foodstuffs laying nearby, "I'm trying to get sorted, replace whatever gear he left with. Spent yesterday thinking. With the train station here, it'd be easy to go home, but we've already come more than a thousand miles. Pretty much halfway. Maybe I can't do it by myself, but I think I wanna try. And you know what else? I'm changing my name. Always hated Two-Speed Tortoise. What'd'ya think about...Fancy Pants?"

She popped up, modeled her yellow-stripped shorts for Bartleby, "I mean, aren't they awesome? My best friend sent them to me."

"It's a good name, Fancy Pants."

"Here, have some Thin Mints."

Bartleby took the proffered sleeve of cookies, popped one in his mouth and savored the chocolaty goodness.

"Better take them back before they disappear."

"Go ahead. My mom sent food for me and Brian both, so I got way too much and maybe they could do you some good."

Bartleby set to, polished off the entire sleeve in no time. After, he slouched his head back on his pack, closed his eyes and drowsed in the sun. Fancy Pants, humming some little tune to herself, continued sorting through the goodies and gear piled round her.

"You picky about what you eat?"

"Can't afford to be," he said.

"I'm going to have some extra stuff here when I'm done. You want?"

"Yes. Anything. Please."

"Okay, good. You staying here for a few days?"

"Gotta keep moving."

"Like today already?"

Bartleby nodded.

"Me too. Cool. When I'm done here, I'll take you over to the hostel—you can sneak a shower."

"They got a hiker box and some denatured alcohol?"

"Probably."

"Sounds good."

"We just gotta make one stop on the way, okay?"

❦

Harpers Ferry was home to the headquarters of the Appalachian

Trail Conservancy. The ATC was the administrative body overseeing the AT and one of their self-appointed duties was taking pictures of all thru-hikers walking into Harpers. They maintained dozens of Polaroid-stuffed albums going back for decades.

Bartleby wasn't too keen on having his picture taken, but Fancy Pants insisted. She even reached an arm up across his shoulders, pulled him down and hugged him in tight just before the flash went off.

"Think that was a good one," the woman said.

She was right, it was a good one. Fancy was smiling wide and virtually glowing with her newfound freedom. Her mood must've been powerfully infectious, as even Bartleby looked bright-eyed and eager for the next leg of their journey.

❧

It was midday and quiet at the hostel. Not much of anyone around. Turned out to be a perfect time for rummaging through the accumulated debris and castoffs that were the standard fare of AT hostels. Thru-hikers were like rolling stones. Gathering moss was against their nature. They swept into hostels, cleaned themselves up and rested their heads for a night or two before resuming the great quest to Katahdin. In their wake, they left half-eaten sandwiches and jugs of juice in the fridge, clothes hanging in the bunkroom, gear forgotten under beds and half-read books lying open on tabletops. At any given moment, some large percentage of the items in a hostel were unclaimed and up for grabs. This had been true as far back as Neels Gap, though Bartleby hadn't noticed the trend until later in Erwin.

From the hiker box, he pulled a few shrimp flavored ramen, another baggie of old raisins and one of white sugar. He also found a yellow t-shirt that looked to be in mint condition. The shirt wasn't just yellow though, it was banana yellow and it sported the Chiquita banana logo across its front—an oversized electric blue oval containing the familiar image of a woman wearing a ruffle-sleeved dress and a fruit basket on her head with the word 'Chiquita' written beneath her.

Bartleby held the shirt up for Fancy Pants' inspection, "What'd'ya think? Polyester. Size large."

"Worlds better than what you got now."

Even a month ago, the shirt would've been tight on him, but now it fit well enough. If he kept losing weight at the same pace, it wouldn't be long before the shirt was hanging off him.

He tossed his raggedy old shirt into the garbage and kept looking around, hoping to find something that might serve as a replacement for his current footwear. This was a long shot. Bartleby eventually settled for a pair of balled up socks he found in a dusty corner, half-hidden behind a stack of old *Backpacker* magazines. In the kitchen, he scapped up a few hot cocoa packets and a gallon-sized ziploc of what turned out to be potato flakes. Must've been almost three pounds of them.

More than anything else, hostel fridges traditionally overflow with condiments. This fridge was no different. Some condiments were fairly new, others obviously much older. Generally, condiments were fair game, and even if they weren't, Bartleby wasn't going to be around long enough to face any consequences. Right there on the spot, he finished off old olives, maraschino cherries and a jar of pickles (there was only half a dill pickle left, but he drank the juice). Packed away two bottles of A1 Steak Sauce, a squeeze bottle of yellow mustard, some apricot preserve, a green cylinder of grated parmesan and the last third of an undoubtedly stale loaf of sliced bread.

Between the food he walked into town with, the stuff Fancy Pants donated and now this new booty, Bartleby figured he was good for another week anyway. With this clandestine pillaging completed, he squashed everything down into his pack. At the sink, he filled water bottles and rinsed the accumulated crud of a month's meals from his cook pot and spoon. Lastly, he topped off his bottle of denatured alcohol.

With one chore left to complete, Bartleby ducked into the bathroom. A swampy dampness pervaded the cramped room, the shower stall was skuzzy and the soap sliver had two curly black hairs embedded in it. None of which bothered Bartleby in the least. He stood there with the steaming hot water raining down until he worried he might be parboiling himself.

❧ ❧ ❧

By late afternoon, Bartleby and Fancy Pants were heading down Washington Street toward the train station. Before slinking out of town, he'd hoped to tell Chatter to hurry along and catch up soon but didn't see him or Jane anywhere. So Bartleby settled for asking Thunk to convey the message. Thunk and Bigfeets were passing a brown paper bag back and forth, so Bartleby figured there was maybe a fifty percent chance of Thunk actually remembering, but it was better than nothing.

❧ ❧ ❧

Bartleby had already crossed the Potomac and walked four miles out of town when he realized he'd neglected to scrounge replacement shoelaces. There was nothing to do but keep on suffering through with the stopgap he'd rigged up. The tubed-tape was strong enough, but didn't cinch tight very well. It sufficed to keep his shoes on his feet, but if felt like he might go oozing out the front of them, particularly on the downhills.

He walked with his head down, alternatively berating himself and wondering if Fancy Pants might have some spare cordage, when she called to him from off trail. "I ducked off trail to pee and look—"

Fancy pointed to a low canopied tree at the edge of a small clearing whose branches sagged under the weight of purplish-maroon fruit clusters.

"What is it?"

"Cherry tree."

"Any good?"

Fancy Pants popped cherries into her mouth with both hands. Her fingers and lips were stained the color of dark welts. It wasn't long before his were too.

❧ ❧ ❧

Bartleby was still coughing and hawking and spitting like a congested camel. No tissues or anything extra to blow his nose into, but while he was upright and walking, it was easy enough to fall back on the old farmer's blow. He pushed a finger against one nostril and sent a snot rocket flying out the other.Whenever he laid down though, it felt like he was going to drown under a rising tide of mucus.

"What are you taking for that?" Fancy asked. She'd already boiled up her nightly chamomile tea and poured some into Bartleby's pot. After squeezing the still-steaming teabags, she held them to her eyes like warm compresses. Bartleby lay propped up on his back, making a wheezy, wet ruckus.

"You got some nasal decongestant or something?"

"Uh-uh."

"I got some stuff might make you feel better."

"Thanks, but this probably won't kill me and," he shrugged, "and the world might not mind so much if it actually did."

Fancy rolled her eyes, "You know, if I had my neti pot, I'd flush your sinuses out good. That and a couple ear candles and you'd be better than new. You know ear candles?"

Bartleby shook his head.

"These waxy tubes, you stick one end in your ear and light the other end on fire. Creates a vortex to suck the bad juju out of your head. Could really help you."

After plumbing the depths of her pack, Fancy produced a bag of health care products. "Still, though, I got tons of mainstream stuff. Echinacea, Nyquil, Vicks. Here, I even got a men's multi-vitamin. Meant to dump it in Harpers. Can't hurt, right? And—I'm carrying like six of Brian's bandanas so now you got a hanky too. Okay?"

"I guess."

"Good. All that sniffling is grossing me out."

The Nyquil had started to dry out Bartleby's congestion when Thunk arrived at the shelter. "There decent water here?"

Fancy Pants directed him down to the spring. Thunk took a long pull on his water bottle and poured the remainder over his head. The liquid had an unnaturally yellow tinge to it.

"Was that water?" she asked. "Looked like lemonade."

"Yeah, shit. Forgot I'd mixed in Kool Aid powder. Fuck it, I don't even care. It's too hot. Africa hot. Feels like my brain's gonna melt."

❦

Sometime during the night, Bartleby woke to muttered cursing. This was coming from Thunk's tent which was only a few yards from the shelter.

Bartleby lay there listening to Thunk thrashing, slapping and cussing. Effectively, it was just the two of them, Fancy was tenting off by herself.

When Thunk's headlamp snapped on, Bartleby sighed and raised his head, "What's happening?"

"Owwww! Shit. I'm being invaded. Ants. Thousands of ants. And Jesus, these little fuckers hurt."

Bartleby's stomach grumbled. He remembered reading somewhere that every known species of ant was safe for human consumption.

"Got a coupla little holes in my bug mesh," Thunk said. "They're trooping right in. Owwww!"

Thunk unzipped his tent door, jumped out and started frantically swatting at himself. The moon had been full a few days earlier, was still plenty bright in the sky. Bartleby could make out the ghostly gleam of torso and feet. The headlamp beam jerked madly as Thunk slapped at himself and spit empty threats. It was probably as close as Bartleby would ever come to witnessing a wild rumpus.

Eventually, Thunk stopped to catch his breath, "They getting you too?"

"Uh-uh," Bartleby said, "but then, I didn't lure them in with lemonade."

❦ ❦ ❦

As he hiked, Bartleby did the math. He had something like twenty-eight dollars left. They were only fifteen miles out of Harpers. Which mean it was at least eleven hundred miles still to Katahdin. Twenty-eight divided by eleven hundred.

He figured an answer quick enough, but still went ahead and triple-checked his work.

To his disappointment, he'd gotten it right on the first try. It worked out to just over 2.5 cents a mile.

He figured that was some bad math.

❦ ❦ ❦

June 21st. The Summer Solstice. This was the longest day of the year and, amongst the thru-hiking community, it was officially known as National Nude Hiking Day.

Without a watch, cell phone, wall calendar or a sundial by which to track the date, Bartleby didn't know any of this when he opened his eyes on that sunny Tuesday in June.

It was a few hours later when he pieced together that maybe something was up.

Thunk and Grog went trooping past during his midmorning rest break. They were in good spirits, whooping it up and having an unusually boisterous time. And as usual, Thunk wasn't wearing a shirt. It took Bartleby two quick blinks to realize he wasn't wearing any shorts either. Grog was similarly stitch-free.

"Fellas?"

"National Nude Hiking Day, bro."

"Ya gots to git nekid or git off!" Grog hooted. "Ya play ya cards right and maybe ya might git both."

Except for socks, hiking shoes, and Grog's customary headband, neither were wearing anything. They had their t-shirts arranged and hanging down over pack belts like makeshift loincloths. Made it so, if you weren't actively curious, you couldn't quite tell their religious leanings.

Bartleby wasn't even a little bit curious.

"You with us, B?"

"Thanks, guys. Go ahead. I'll catch-up."

"Seriously, B," Thunk called, "don't let shame make you lame."

As they marched away, Bartleby couldn't help think that his particular lameness had nothing to do with shame.

They marched ahead and out of sight. Bartleby was just thinking it might be safe for him to start up again when Mudsucka and Fancy Pants came bouncing around the bend.

Mudsucka was wearing nothing but her bright pixie smile. Fancy had tied some spare bandanas to cover most of what she wanted covered. They pulled to a stop, but Mudsucka kept on telling a story.

"—and it was my last one. I'd been holding off, looking forward to it for a day and a half. And there I went and dropped the stupid thing right in a mud puddle. Puddle isn't the right word. That implies water. This was just muddy slop. And my last jolly rancher had all but disappeared, only one little red corner still visible. If it was apple or peach, I woulda left it there easy, but no way was I losing a watermelon. I scooped it out, blew most of the yuck off and popped it into my mouth. Shaggy Bob and Wham-O were there with me. Wasn't five minutes before I'd been officially christened Mudsucka."

During this story, Bartleby kept staring at the ground. Couldn't quite look either woman in the eye and was struggling to keep his eyes from ranging over the rest of them.

"Hey," Mudsucka barked at him, "I already went through this with those two chuckleheads up ahead. Am I disgusting to you?" She gestured a hand at her various untanned bits, "Is something about this grossing you out?"

Seeing that Bartleby wasn't going to answer, she kept on, "I don't care if you get down to it with us today, but it's more than likely I'm only going to thru-hike the Appalachian Trail just this once in my lifetime. Today is National Nude Hiking Day and I don't want to look back in ten or twenty years and regret that I didn't hike naked. I'm not ashamed of my body and I'd prefer that you didn't make me feel weird about it by looking away. You wanna look, you better look. I get the chance, better believe I'm gonna be checking you out. I mean, isn't that the natural order of things?"

Mudsucka followed this with a wolfish smile and started up hiking.

Fancy Pants gave Bartleby an uncomfortable shrug, "In theory, I agree with everything she just said, but in reality...it's okay if you don't look at me so much."

🍁

After more than two months spent hiking the AT, the sight of nude hikers wasn't all that shocking. Compared to everyday life in these United States, thru-hiking imposed an intimacy of proximity, and it did so at warp speed. Bartleby figured that every hour spent with someone on trail was easily the equivalent of spending a full twenty-four hours together off trail in the regular world.

People talked. It was only natural. While hiking, there was nothing much else to do. Even the hikers carrying ipods could only listen for so long before their ears hurt, before their batteries died, before they came to hate whatever it was they were listening to.

Off came the earbuds and on came the conversation.

Even the world's most boring conversation went a long way in keeping hiker's minds off the next mile, the next mountain, the next day's march. Which isn't to say the conversations tended towards boring. Every single person had a story worth hearing and most had a few. The AT was a melting pot of people and ideas, a potluck of perspectives and experiences. Could be a retired humanities professor, an ex-convict and a militaristic born-again all sharing the same roof for a night. Each of them with vastly different opinions and points of view on most any topic under the sun. More than any other single thing, this mishmash mixing of people was the heart and soul of the AT.

And if you hiked around the same people for a while, became friendly and got bored enough, it wasn't long before they were telling you things they'd never told anyone else. Not all of it was juicy or even interesting, mostly it was banal, trivial and trite to boot, but it was all an open window into their lives.

After only a few days hiking around Fancy Pants, Bartleby was more familiar with her, her history and her habits than he was with any other woman, short of his own wife. He knew about Fancy's first kiss, her first pet, her first report card. How she felt about her father's job, her grandmother's quilting and her cousin's new baby. Without at all trying to, he'd caught glimpses of her as she changed clothes inside her sleeping bag. He'd seen her running off to water the nearest bush, balled up tight and fast asleep, teary-eyed tired at the end of a hard day's hike. He knew she didn't eat enough while on the go, and that this often resulted in crazy-shaky episodes of low blood sugar. He knew she was lazy about getting water and constantly running dry. He knew she could be tough and soft and funny and that she burped more loudly, more proudly than most teenage boys. He even knew that for hours after Fancy ate couscous, the shelter would smell like low tide at the mud flats.

He knew all of this and more, because trail time was quality time on steroids.

At its most basic, thru-hiking was a thousand challenges strung together from Springer to Katahdin. All these challenges were stressful in varying ways, they laid bare emotions and reactions that might not have been exposed in five years of normal friendship. It was more than a little like being tossed into a blender with a handful of random people. Everybody got a good look at all the bits and pieces that made up everybody else.

And so, when Bartleby caught up shortly before the trail crossed

I-70, he wasn't wearing any pants. A high footbridge spanned the six lane highway. Cars and trucks sped east and west on important business. A few honked, but they couldn't see so very much through the chain-link fencing.

Thunk tossed him a tube of sunscreen.

"Better lube up, bro. Keep the sun off them buns, right?"

"You say that to all the guys?"

"Nah, just the strong, silent types."

Register: Pine Knob Shelter

6/10 VA to PA.

Four state challenge: forty-three
fucking miles or bust.

High-Ku

Later that night at Ensign Cowall Shelter, Bartleby (once again wearing clothes) went to sleep with his bag unzipped and draped over top of him. The night was a particularly hot one. He stuck first one and then both bare legs out from under the covers. By morning, he'd entirely swapped places with his sleeping bag, was laying on it instead of the other way around. In and of itself, this really wasn't at all a surprising turn of events.

The erection threatening to escape the confines of his boxer shorts, though—that was totally unexpected.

First one in eighteen months easy. Probably longer. It felt way longer.

As people were already up and about, he quickly covered himself and vaguely worried who might've seen what. This first stage was short-lived. It quickly gave way to an almost boyish elation. It had been a full year at least since he'd last worried over the loss of this particular bodily function. And now, suddenly and without any pre-amble or symbolic portents, here was Lazarus risen up and returned from the dead. Bartleby suppressed a sudden urge to mount the pic-nic table and display himself for the world to see, or at least go and find someone to high-five. But since none of this would've been in character, he settled for eating breakfast, A1 flavored instant grits and ginger tea, in bed.

❦ ❦ ❦

Register: Ensign Cowall Shelter

6/21 Nude-hiked today. Unhappy to report bug bites, sunburn and trail dirt in places that weren't intended for such things.   Mudsucka

6/21 It was nice letting my dingle-dongle dangle in the dirt.
                    Hunka Hunka Burning Thunk

❦ ❦ ❦

Coming out of Harpers, it took a combination of cold medicines, mothering from Fancy Pants and some fortyish miles of hiking before Bartleby was feeling near to human again. When they walked into Pen-Mar State Park, they couldn't have timed it better if they'd tried. It was a beautiful Saturday afternoon. The park's rolling lawns were randomly splotched with blankets and lawn chairs, wheeled coolers and portable grills. The air was thick with the smells of cut grass, smoking charcoal and grilling meat. It was the height of sum-mer and they'd just walked into a picnicker's paradise.

Fancy Pants and Bartleby pulled up and surveyed the scene arrayed before them. "Lots of food here, huh?" she said. "I know I'm a veg-etarian and all, but I feel like I could murder a cheeseburger in cold blood right now. Wanna see if we can maybe yogi something to eat?"

"Uh-huh."

"You ever yogi food before?"

Bartleby shook his head.

"Me neither...should come up with some story, you know, so people will feel sorry for us."

"Or," Bartleby said, his mind warming to the idea, "if Chatter was here with Jane, we could let her off the leash and then when she wandered over and crashed a picnic, we could go get her and apologize and maybe they would see how hungry we were and give us burgers and ice cream."

"Right. Or I bet Hairbrained would—"

A lanky trio of teenage girls passed by. It was easy to overhear their conversation.

"Did you *see* them?"

"So dirty. He looks like a caveman with that beard."

"Smells like one too. I almost gagged."

"Little bitches," Fancy Pants muttered.

"Come on," Bartleby said, walking towards a large and festive gathering of folks. He dropped his pack just at the periphery of their area, and stared over with a dolefully pathetic hangdog expression on his face. While he was able to achieve the look without any great effort, it did him little good.

"They're ignoring us," Fancy Pants said, "like we're panhandlers."

Shuffling near to other picnics earned the same response—backs were turned, eyes were averted and faces went hard. Apparently, nobody was interested in sharing their weekend festivities with a couple of vagrant hikers.

"Excuse me," a woman with a pinched face called over to Bartleby.

"Here we go," he whispered.

"You're blocking our view," the woman said, her tone brusque and businesslike, "would you mind, I don't know, scooching over to the far side of those trees? Thanks so much..."

Fancy Pants took an aggressive step toward the lady, but Bartleby caught a hold of her pack and pulled her away to an empty picnic table near the park pavilion.

Bartleby hadn't known they were going to cross through Pen-Mar Park today, hadn't woken up looking forward to the prospect of bumming food from strangers, would've been quite content to stay in the woods. Though now, surrounded and assaulted by the smells and sights of so much abundance, it was a hammer blow of disappointment to be so close and still, for all intents and purposes, so far away.

From his seat, he watched a steady trickle of picnickers wander over and buy sodas at a pair of vending machines.

"I don't even like soda," he said, "and right now, I feel like I'd give a middle toe for one cold can."

Fancy Pants had her eyes closed, hat off and head down on the table top, "This sucks. We suck."

After a bit she followed those declarations with another, "Middle-class white people suck."

❦ ❦ ❦

Register: Antietam Shelter

6/20 LIGHT IS RIGHT!!! In the spirit of going "ultralight" I've hacked away the last bit of dead weight hanging on my neck. And Aesop got it wrong, the hare is definitely faster than the tortoise.   Hairbrained

❦

Fancy Pants flipped through the register. Bartleby lay nearby in the shade with his eyes closed.

"Did you see this entry from Hairbrained? Do you think he's talking about me? I think he's talking about me. I think he's calling me dead weight," Fancy said. "I think…"

Feeling an acute need to fill the uncomfortable silence, Bartleby offered, "Maybe he was talking about shipping his rain gear home."

"Do you really think that?"

"No."

"Me neither. I can't believe I dated him," she shuddered. "Did I tell you why we finally broke up? My friend Callie sent me a care package in Waynesboro and among other goodies, she includes four pot brownies. Which is absolutely crazy to put in the mail these days, but hey, it's not like I had a say in it, right?

"I didn't tell Hairbrained about the brownies. Figured it'd be a cool surprise down the trail, right? So we're somewhere in the Shenandoah and he talks me into getting him Twizzlers at one of those gas stations. I leave my pack with him and when we start hiking again, he's acting all strange. First I think it's a joke, but it's not. He's out of his gourd. Loopy-loo. Turns out he'd snuck into my pack and horked down two and a half brownies. Which pisses me off, and we start right in fighting. Becomes this four day running battle. He's slippery; real good at turning things inside out, and by the end, somehow I've become this awful person that ruined his life by poisoning him with pot brownies. Went on and on about how he might have to take a drug test as part of any job interviews after trail. Then he told me I was tainting him with all my wickedness, and that he couldn't hike with someone like that.

"Burgling brownies is bad enough, but then laying the blame on me, I mean, what a total buttplug, right?"

❧

6/22 Contrary to Hairbrained's recent entry, he isn't actually
going lightweight now. Since losing me as his personal
pack mule, he's stuck carrying all his own gear and food.
Something poor Bri-Bri hasn't done yet this whole trip!!!
Fancy Pants!

❧

Fancy Pants hadn't quite zipped the screen of her tent closed before tears filled her eyes. Now that she was alone, she buried her face in her sleeping bag and let the emotions run free.

Her legs ached. Her feet throbbed. She was tired of walking. Tired of drinking water by the gallon and being sweaty for days on end. Tired of the constant hunger. Tired of being surrounded by strangers and tired of being alone. Tired of being mad and sad and scared.

She hated Brian. She missed Brian. She couldn't believe he'd abandoned her and yet she was happy to be free of him. The idea of walking another hour with him was revolting. The idea of walking to Maine without him was horrifying. All by itself, the idea of walking to Maine (another thousand miles) was simply overwhelming. Despite how far she'd already come, she couldn't imagine actually reaching Katahdin. She couldn't imagine walking twenty-three miles tomorrow. She couldn't imagine walking another dozen steps. Not by herself. Not alone.

More than anything, Fancy wanted to quit. She wanted to go home. She wanted to take a year-long bath. She wanted to eat an endless supply of ice cream. She wanted to wake up in the morning and do anything else but walk all day long.

More than anything, Fancy wanted to keep on hiking. She wanted to finish trail. Prove to herself, to Brian, to her parents and the world at large that she wasn't a quitter. That she was strong enough and tough enough, that she had what it took to be a thru-hiker.

But she knew she couldn't. It was impossible. It was all so dauntingly long, too hard, too painful, too lonely. By the time her tears dried, she'd decided to hitch out at the next road crossing and head for home.

❧

Morning brought a warm sprinkling rain, but that didn't matter to Fancy. She had only another mile or two still to walk to PA-233.

"Seriously," Thunk said, "you gotta have a preference. Even if you don't."

"Why exactly?"

"It's a long trip still to Maine. We're killing time here."

"Okay. Go through it again."

"Hash browns are grated and fried up into patties almost. Home fries are thick cubes and cooked with onions and peppers."

"I don't know. Hash browns, I guess."

"Personally, I'm a huge home fries guy, but okay. What about french fries— waffle-cut, thick-cut or shoestring?"

"Thick cut?"

"Me too! Nice, Fancy."

After some time, Thunk started up again, "Maybe talking about food isn't a good idea. I'm here daydreaming about a fifty pound sack of spuds. Wanna play the animal game?"

"No thanks," Fancy said.

"Why not?"

"I don't like games."

"Why not?"

"Don't know." Except she did. Whenever Hairbrained beat her at something, he made her feel about an inch tall.

"It's fun."

"Uh-uh."

"Come on, I gotta get my mind off food."

"You really wanna beat me that bad?"

"Actually, I've never won. Only ever play with my sister and she mops the floor with me."

"Really?

"Oh yeah."

"Alright. How's it go?"

"Couldn't be easier. Pick a letter."

"M."

"Okay. Now we take turns naming animals that start with the letter M."

"And then what?"

"That's it. You lose if you can't come up with one or if you repeat an animal. Here, I'll start. Monkey."

"Mouse?"

"Good. Easy, right? Meerkat."

"Minx."

When Thunk ran out of M animals and conceded the victory, they'd hiked miles past PA-233 and started straight in on the letter N.

Sweet Jane was moving along with Mad Chatter in tow. She came up on a waist-high trail sign. It's yellow letters read:

MASON DIXON LINE

Chatter looped the dog's leash on the signpost and sprinkled ashes around the ground at the sign's base.

The old guy was wearing a gray wool kepis, a forward-canted, duck-billed confederate soldier cap. He hung it on the signpost and pulled a dark blue slouch hat out of his pack. It was one of those hats Union officers wore during the Civil War—looked to be a cross between a fedora and a cowboy hat. A golden braid looped the base of the hat's crown, and two short tassels lay flat on the hat's brim.

After satisfactorily settling the slouch hat on his head, Chatter and Jane started making their way northward again.

＊ ＊ ＊

Quarry Gap Shelter, a day's hike over the line into Pennsylvania. Dusk. Bartleby stirred a pot full of instant mashed potatoes. Once he'd made sure all the powdery granules were good and soaked, he slopped in a generous dollop of A1 sauce. Before screwing the cap back on, Bartleby slugged a mouthful straight from the bottle.

Thunk and Fancy Pants were giggling uncontrollably and otherwise having a grand time of making duck lips with the Pringles he was carrying. When they'd snorked away the last crumbs, they got around to talking about what they missed most from back in the world.

"Running water."

"Clean bathrooms."

"Microwaves."

"Air conditioning."

"Email."

"Netflix."

"Pillows."

"Big fluffy pillows," Thunk agreed. "How about you, B? What do you miss?"

Bartleby shrugged the question off.

"There's got to be some little luxuries you're pining for."

Bartleby shook his head.

"Come on. How about internet porn? Or listening to NPR on the morning commute? The box scores? It's the porn, right? Decent shoes at least—you gotta be missing a good pair of shoes right about now."

"I had all that. Don't miss it. Tell you the only *thing* I miss is Comfy Chair."

"Yeah? What's a Comfy Chair?"

"This lumpy old recliner. Was losing its stuffing and all rusted up inside. Screeched like a dying cat every time it reclined."

"Doesn't sound any good so far."

"Yeah, well...when things got bad at home, I stopped sleeping. Just laid in bed fretting and fussing all night long. Turned out Comfy

Chair was pretty much the only place I could sink down and totally tune out the shitstorms. Comfy Chair became my security blanket, my binky and my escape from reality."

Fancy cringed, "That doesn't seem healthy."

"Most days it was a struggle to get up and out of the chair. Sometimes I didn't. Spent whole days sitting and hiding from the world in Comfy Chair."

Bartleby might've gone on further about Comfy Chair or his life back at home, but just then Sweet Jane came trotting up the trail. When she spotted Bartleby she came bounding over and almost bowled him off the bench. The big girl was so excited she hopped and yipped and bucked like a bronco.

Mad Chatter came limping along soon thereafter.

The old guy looked worn thin and flat as an old bike tire. His red face was sweat-streaked and he seemed to be favoring his right side. Dried blood was visible from a cut under his knee.

"Heya," Chatter called, "there they are. Me and Jane were like to kill ourselves catching up."

After dropping his pack, Chatter weeble-wobbled his way to a seat next to Fancy Pants. He gave her a big beaming smile. "They call me Chatter."

"They call me Fancy."

"I like your cartwheel hat, Nancy."

"Thanks. Yours is cool too. Can I try it on?"

Chatter removed his hat with a flourish, "It would bring me great pleasure, young lady."

❦

From Quarry Gap, the plan was to pack up quick, bang out 14.6 miles and take an oh-so-brief lunch break before blasting out the final 3.7 into Pine Grove Furnace State Park. Once there, they planned to partake in the Half-Gallon Challenge.

The plan went to shit pretty much from the get-go.

Morning hadn't quite arrived yet, it was still yawning and waiting for coffee to brew. A heavy fog embraced the ground. It was quiet and calm and on account of the rain, not so terribly hot. For high-summer out in the wilds of Pennsylvania, the sleeping conditions were surprisingly decent. And then they weren't.

WHIP-POOR-WILL-WHIP-POOR-WILL

Quarry Gap Shelter consisted of two separate four-man sleeping structures. These were connected together by an overhanging roof, under which sat a picnic table.

Because of the wet weather, Chatter and Jane and Mudsucka had slept in one mini-shelter, while Bartleby, Thunk, Fancy Pants, Lemming and Grog squeezed into the other. It was uncomfortably crowded; Bartleby spent much of the night with Fancy's elbow in his back and Thunk's breath on his face.

WHIP-POOR-WILL-WHIP-POOR-WILL

Grog and Lemming were cuddled close against one wall. They arrived late, ignored everyone else and whispered loudly to each other. Apparently, he had risen above the rest of the harem and won her favor.

Now with morning just under the horizon, the sleepy silence was irrevocably splintered by the repetitious call of a whippoorwill.

WHIP-POOR-WILL-WHIP-POOR-WILL

The noise was piercingly shrill and incessant. There was no sleeping through it, or ignoring it, though at first, everyone tried. Bartleby lay there, counting individual whips. Fast as they came, he couldn't keep up.

WHIP-POOR-WILL-WHIP-POOR-WILL

Grog finally sat up, "Cut it out, Thunk."

"It's not me. *You* cut it out."

"Make it stop," Lemming whined.

WHIP-POOR-WILL-WHIP-POOR-WILL

Grog ventured to the shelter's edge. By then, everyone was sitting up, restively awake, attempting to make some sense of this sudden audible assault. Even with multiple headlamp beams illuminating the heavy fog, they couldn't make out much of anything.

WHIP-POOR-WILL-WHIP-POOR-WILL

Bartleby yawned, "I think it's a bird."

"Don't sound like any bird I ever heard," Grog said. He'd taken up a defensive stance with a hiking pole cocked back and ready for action.

WHIP-POOR-WILL-WHIP-POOR-WILL

"What kinda bird makes a noise like that?" Thunk wanted to know.

"You're seriously asking that?"

WHIP-POOR-WILL-WHIP-POOR-WILL

Grog whacked at the shelter wall with the hiking pole. When he stopped, so had the whippoorwill.

"Think I scared it away?"

WHIP-POOR-WILL-WHIP-POOR-WILL

❖

It was on account of the whippoorwill's harassing call that they started the hiking day grumpier than usual.

Chatter and Jane were already gone and Mudsucka was about to set off when Bartleby shucked himself free of his bag.

When asked about the whippoorwill, Mudsucka shook her head, "I didn't hear a thing. Doubt Chatter did either, or at least Jane didn't wake up."

❖

It was full-on hot as hell high–noon by the time Bartleby, Thunk and Fancy reached Toms Run Shelter.

Chatter was sitting in the shelter with his back to a wall and his hat pulled low over his eyes. Having found a shady spot, he and Jane had settled in for their usual siesta.

Thunk immediately wrinkled his nose, "Think that stink is the privy? I mean—it's terrible. Must be overflowing. This state park coming up probably has real toilets, right? Guess I can wait."

They dropped packs and sat around the picnic table.

"I'll take my food bag, B," Thunk said.

Bartleby dug it out of his pack and handed it over.

"Not too heavy, right?"

Bartleby shook his head, "For spotting me a half gallon of ice cream, I would've tried carrying your whole pack."

"Told you I'd buy you ice cream," Fancy cut in.

"I know and thanks, but it's better this way."

"I remember people talking about some squishy rich guy back at Neels Gap. He was already whipped and ready to quit after those first thirty miles, so he tried hiring a sherpa to carry his gear. He was a Brit, I think," Thunk concluded, as if maybe that explained things.

"How much?"

"Fifty a day, but he still musta went off trail—I never heard anything else about it."

"For fifty a day, I could carry another thirty-five pounds no problem."

"Wouldn't be much fun, I don't think."

"No, but neither is scrounging old food out of hiker boxes."

Thunk poured the last of some honey-roasted peanuts into his mouth. "Okay, let's get. This stink ain't going away. Not sure how the old guy's sleeping through it."

Bartleby choked down a final handful of raisins and chased them with a mouthful of white sugar before packing away both his and Thunk's food bags.

"Time to get some ice cream, Chatter."

When this failed to rouse the old man, Bartleby walked over. Jane whimpered and licked Bartleby's hand.

"Hey ya, girl," Bartleby rubbed Jane's nose. "Chatter?" He lifted the hat's blue brim.

There was a moment of shocked realization, but it was blessedly short. Up close, the truth was glaringly obvious.

Mad Chatter wasn't breathing.

He'd slipped off and away to a place where the packs weren't so heavy and the terrain was perfect and he could walk forever on younger, stronger legs.

Thunk appeared at Bartleby's shoulder, "What's the hold up? Gaaaa. Smells worse over here." He lowered his voice to a whisper, "Did the old guy shit himself?"

Bartleby mumbled, "The old guy's dead."

"Holy shit."

"Are you sure?" Fancy asked. "Maybe if we do CPR or something."

"He's gone," Bartleby said.

Fancy Pants fought back a sob, "What do you think it was? Heart attack?"

"Could've been cancer, I guess," Thunk said. "My aunt died from cancer."

"I think he probably just had nothing left," Bartleby offered.

"We gotta call somebody." Thunk powered up his phone. "Who do I call?"

"911?"

"What do I say?"

Despite the tears brimming in her eyes, Fancy quick flipped through her data book, "We crossed Woodrow Road a mile back. We can meet someone there, lead them in."

Jane looked from Chatter to Bartleby, confusion and concern wrinkling her brow.

"Just a shitty situation all around," Thunk said, scatological phrases seemed etched on the tip of his tongue, "I mean, it totally sucks for the old guy an all, but what about Sweet Jane? What happens to her now?"

Bartleby was processing the situation as fast as he could, but he hadn't quite gotten there yet.

"Should I go?" Fancy asked.

"Go with her, Thunk. I'll stay here with Jane."

"You sure? Could take a while."

"Yeah. We'll be fine."

Bartleby settled down against the wall opposite Chatter. Jane laid her big flat head in his lap. He sat stroking her velvety fur.

"So, what *is* going to happen to you, Jane?" he wondered aloud. "Far as I know, you're about all the family Chatter has. Guess the cops will take you off to the pound. Which, I can't imagine, is a good place for a full grown Dane, huh? I mean, sure, you're a great trail dog, but there's not exactly a lot of people shopping for a hundred pounds of used trail dog."

Jane sighed.

"And I like you fine, but I got less than ten dollars left to my name— still waiting to see if I can even take care of myself. How could I possibly care for you too? I mean, it's not like I got fancy maildrops waiting for me all the way up the line like Chatter does. Or…he did.

"See—right there. You're lucky you don't talk. Shifting from present tense to past tense is such an awkward part of death. It took me months to get it straight when my dad died. But this conversation is about you and your loss, not me and mine. I used to hate when people swooped in on me like that.

"So yeah, Chatter *did* have maildrops waiting for him, but I don't…."

Somewhere in the dark of Bartleby's mind, a match was struck. The flame sputtered, looked like it would die out, but somehow didn't. It grew stronger, burned brighter and did some small bit towards illuminating the darkness.

This new light shone plainly in his eyes.

"There I go again, Jane. Getting my tenses confused. It's not 'Chatter *had* maildrops' it's 'Chatter *has* maildrops.' Dead or alive, those maildrops are still waiting for him."

If Jane comprehended the distinction in Bartleby's words, it was difficult to tell from the tilt of her head.

Taking a breath to steady himself, Bartleby crawled over and settled Chatter's hat back onto his head. Without it, the old guy had looked shrunken and small and awkwardly naked. The simple act of replacing the hat seemed to somehow give Chatter back some of his quirky poise.

And while Thunk had focused on one smell, up close now, Bartleby was struck by another. Old Spice Original. It was cloyingly impossible to ignore; it caught in Bartleby's nose and tickled his throat like incense.

A suspicious shiny moisture brimmed in Bartleby's eyes as he started rifling through the old man's pack. Wasn't long before he produced a wallet and, more importantly, a photo ID. "You see this, Jane? This means that you and me, *we've* got maildrops waiting for *us.*"

Jane knew something was wrong, but not what exactly. She'd followed Bartleby over. As he rummaged for a wallet, she leaned in close and licked Chatter's cheek. When this failed to rouse him, she turned to Bartleby with this worried–wincing–soulfully–helpless–please–tell-me-what-to-do look.

It was a look Bartleby immediately recognized. He'd been wearing it for years now.

First there was one trickle and another, then the floodgates burst open.

Shiny snail trails tracked down his cheeks, seeped into his mustache, caught in the matted tangle of his beard. When Jane started licking his tears away, Bartleby reached over and pulled her close. He buried his face in her fur and wept for a very long time.

🍁

Register: Toms Run Shelter

6/24 Rest easy, Mad Chatter. You will be missed.
                              - Bumblebee + Sweet Jane the Greatest Dane

PART THREE:

THE WAY LIFE SHOULD BE

It took Coyote roughly 1,037.3 trail miles to hit his first honest-to-goodness, no-fooling, this-is-what-I've-been-talking-about trail magic. If anyone had bothered to ask him, he would have said it was worth the wait.

Happened in Maryland, just north of the footbridge over I-70. Coyote spotted two men lugging coolers in from a nearby parking lot. He would've kept hiking, but they waved him down.

"Thru-hiking?" the first guy asked. He had a reddish-purple birthmark on his face. The thing was bigger than a chicken's egg, smaller than a grapefruit and vaguely shaped like an angry amoeba. Turned out, his trail name was Rorschach.

"Trying," Coyote answered. His beard was still so splotchy bad and thin, one couldn't immediately assume he'd been out in the woods for the last twelve weeks.

The second guy smiled, "Thirsty?"

When Coyote nodded, the man opened a cooler, tossed Coyote a white/maroon beer can and took one for himself.

"Me and Lewd here," Rorschach started, "we thru-hiked in '06. Got four cases of Schlitz. Hope you aren't keeping to any kind of hard and fast schedule."

"Had planned to go another twelve today," Coyote shrugged, "but it sounds like that just got shot to shit, huh?"

"That's the spirit. Katahdin ain't going nowhere."

Coyote helped carry a portable grill, some old beach chairs and another cooler packed full of bratwurst, back up from the parking lot.

Rorschach lit the grill and set two dozen brats to cooking. Lewd passed around more beers.

"Got like a gross of these Sheboygan Specials flown in fresh from

Wisco. We're hoping there's a bunch more nobos coming along behind you."

Coyote rolled his eyes, "Oh, sure, lots and lots of nobos. Too bad they're all bobos. I fell behind my old crew way back in Virginia. Been trying to catch up ever since."

The spread was Machiavellian in its simplicity. Beers, brats and buns with a gallon-sized tub of spicy mustard on the side.

"Seriously, dude, take a load off. Stay a while."

They didn't have to ask twice. The muscles of Coyote's right calf felt like they'd already marched a hundred miles and it wasn't even noon yet. He cracked his second Schlitz and settled into a beach chair.

"So, how'd you come by the name Coyote?"

Wasn't much to it, just that grin of his really, but he puffed it up and spun a little story out. Seemed like the least he could do in exchange for the beer and food. When he was done, he turned the question back to them.

Rorschach gestured at the birthmark covering the better part of his face, "Mine's self-explanatory."

"How about you—Lewd is it?"

"Actually it's Lewwwwdite."

"Yeah?"

"Yeah," Lewd chuckled. "Remember Cable Gap Shelter? Back before the Smokies."

"Not really."

"Doesn't matter. You just need to know 2005 wasn't a good year for me business-wise. Come tax time, I was tits deep in wet shit. This slick dick at the IRS had climbed way far up my ass. Threatening letters, liens—he gave me the works. I really had no call starting a thru-hike in April, but I'd been planning and preparing for like two years. All the bullshit with the business just made me want to disappear even more. I got a lawyer involved and hired a couple of butt-crumb accountants. They all started dialoguing with those scabby IRS cunts and I headed for the hills.

"Left my pregnant wife home alone, holding the bag. For which, I know I'll be batting lead-off in hell. But at the time, what did I care? I was tromping through the wilds and sniffing daisies."

Lewd tossed an empty beer can into a garbage bag and started on a full one. "Course, I really didn't get away from anything. I'd turn it off at night and have a ton of messages each morning.

"And God bless my wife for sticking around, but the woman called a dozen times a day. No lie. She bitched about the latest from the lawyer, sobbed about morning sickness, hollered about me running off and leaving her. Bad news, good news, no news—it didn't matter, she couldn't not call.

"Meanwhile, all I'm doing is trying to keep on keepin' on, right? I was completely and utterly assholed and I didn't even know it until that day I took lunch at Cable Gap. I remember, I was sitting there with an old guy named Shepherd and this girl—"

"Beachsand," Rorschach said, "and the Speckled Shepherd."

"Beachsand, right. But spectral, not speckled. Beachsand and the Spectral Shepherd. Beachsand's telling about this hike she did in Spain. The Pilgrim's Way. Two months walking, drinking wine and slamming ham with random European dudes. What's not to like, right? Then my phone rings way deep in my pack. Piece of shit musta turned itself on. The Pilgrim's Way sounded cool and I didn't really want to go home, like ever, so I'm asking her about guide books. And the phone rings again. And again and again and again.

"Something like six calls in three or four minutes. Which you'd think was impossible, what with taking time for leaving messages, but all I know is by that last call, I'd gone all cold inside. Dug out my phone and set it on the bench. Beachsand's still going on about Spain, so I put my finger up, like, hold on just a minute chica, I don't want to miss a word of your story.

"Now, Spectral Shepherd carried this heavy bastard of a hickory stick. So I say, 'Hey, Shep, can I borrow your walking staff for a sec?' And I took it and swung for the bleachers. Only meant to, you know, give the phone one good crack, but that first whack was so satisfying,

I went at it like a madman. Spitting out curses and smacking the shellac right off the phone. It was bad; I came totally unplugged.

"When I stopped there were jagged bits of plastic, buttons and shards of screen scattered everywhere. Shep even had some caught in his beard. I remember Beachsand's eyes were wide as a blue whale's b-hole, but the old man, he was cooler than an ice cream truck. Blinked once and said, 'You must be one of them Luddites I been reading about.'

"'I don't know nothing about that,' I told him, 'just hate this fucking phone is all.'"

"'Welp, I guess that's pretty much a Luddite, son.'"

"By then, I'd recovered enough to be embarrassed as a kid with stains in his shorts and I start picking up pieces. Pack it in, pack it out, right? They both helped and we got as much as we could. Then Beachsand looked over and said, 'Lewwwwdite is more like it.' Which struck me as about the best trail name going, all things considered."

Never in her life had Flutterby considered eating an entire half gallon of ice cream in one sitting. She didn't even much like ice cream and now she had four big scoops to go.

"I think she's gonna do it, Skunks," Old Man Trouble said.

"I don't know. She ain't looking too good."

She didn't feel very good. Had pushed beyond brain freeze and well into body freeze territory. She was stuttering cold and bursting full; her bare arms and legs were goose-pimpled and shaking. Probably the first time since way back on Hawk Mountain her stomach couldn't keep up with what she was putting into it.

"I still got some room," Skunkers said. "Could help with that last bit, if you want."

The Half-Gallon Challenge. Another AT tradition; a rite of passage showcasing the hyper metabolisms of thru-hikers. Skunkers, Flutterby and Old Man Trouble sat on the shaded stoop outside of a little store in Pine Grove Furnace State Park. Trouble's beard had come in and covered over the liverspot on his chin. Generally, he looked well-used and rumpled, but in a comfortable way, like Saturday night's jeans on Sunday morning. Skunkers' hair mushroomed above a filthy headband. If he'd lost weight it wasn't immediately noticeable beneath all the trail grime and facial hair he'd picked up.

The men had both finished their own brick-blocks of ice cream. Skunkers in about seven minutes. He looked like maybe he was actually still hungry. There was, at least, an appropriately bloated-unsettled-sickly grimace spread across Trouble's face.

Flutterby sporked another helping in. Her teeth chattered, her hands shook and she really regretted going with dark chocolate. It was way too rich; felt like she'd never get the taste out of her mouth. Felt like her stomach was gonna burst. Felt like she'd gone and eaten an iceberg. She wondered why the hell she'd let Skunkers talk her into trying this ridiculous challenge.

Skunkers licked his spoon clean, "You don't gotta do this, Flubby."

She'd stopped talking a few minutes earlier, but she gave him a hard look.

"But you wanna do it, don't you? Okay, good. Now shake your head if you want me to work the spork for ya. Alright then missy, here we go. Watch the airplane coming in to the hangar...rrrrrrrrrr... loop de loop aaaand...touchdown.

"Now swallow it. You swishing it around your mouth don't help none. Come on. We got one super big scoop left. Think of it as a C-5 Galaxy. Ready? Okay, now open up extra wide."

❦ ❦ ❦

Register: Alec Kennedy Shelter

6/29 Bawdy: If you're still bumbling along back there, waddle
      faster. I'd prefer not to wait another five hundred miles
      before you catch up.   - Bartleby

6/29 Passed the halfway point today. Just another 2,500,000
      steps to go.   Thunk

6/29 With my short legs it's probably closer to 3 million.
                                                  Fancy Pants

❦ ❦ ❦

Bartleby stood waiting at the counter of the Boiling Springs post
office. His palms sweated and he couldn't quite catch his breath.
When the postal worker returned from the back room under a hefty
armload of packages, she dropped them on the counter and started
reading names off the ID's in her hand.

"Shannon Meggarty?"

Fancy Pants raised her hand, smiled. After quick-scanning Fancy's
driver's license, the woman handed both the ID and package over.

"Todd Smilch? Okay, here you go."

"Thank you, ma'am," Thunk said.

"Thorpe Ingleside? Thorpe?"

Bartleby didn't step up so much as Fancy Pants and Thunk faded
back, left him standing front and center. The mailwoman did a
double take on the photo ID, squinted, gave Bartleby a lazy once
over. "*You're* Thorpe Ingleside?"

"Yes, ma'am."

"Somebody who cared, might point out you don't look a bit like
your picture, *Thorpe*."

"It's...all the...fresh air," Bartleby sputtered. "I'm a—a new man."

"I'll say." She gave a little you–sir–are–entirely–full–of–shit–but–they–
just–cut–my–hours–for–the–third–time–this–year–and–I–don't–much–
care–anymore–who–picks–up–what–packages shake of her head. She
snapped the ID down on top of the maildrop and pushed both across
the counter. "Have a nice hike, Thorpe."

❦

Sitting on a bench outside, Bartleby's hands were still shaking. So much so, he let Thunk cut the maildrop open. It was as good as he had dared hope. The box was bursting with dog food and new socks, hand sanitizer, a squeezy roll of two-ply toilet paper and spare batteries, a bottle of Ibuprofen and an assortment of other pills.

And there was the food. A tub of almond butter, a dozen pita pockets, organic rice-noodle soup, dehydrated refried beans, candied pecans, a little glass jar of sun-dried tomatoes in oil, hand-rolled cheese tortellinis, two big baggies (one full of homemade jerky, the other red lentils), garlic powder, Werther's candies, an oversized pie slice of parmesan cheese and a soda bottle filled with that expensive whiskey he liked so much. There was even another hunk of that cave-aged cheddar they'd eaten back in Pearisburg.

Lying there at the bottom of the box was a white envelope with the message *Next stop: Port Clinton* scrawled across the outside and a single hundred dollar bill tucked inside.

"Super score," Thunk said. "Lemme try some of that I-Be-Dopin', will ya? Make sure it's the real deal and all."

Bartleby tossed the pill bottle to Thunk and began painstakingly working to open a can of dog food. Poohbah had been right, those little p-38 can openers barely weighed anything, but he'd neglected to mention how hard they were to use. A thick loop of slobber hung from the rubbery folds of Jane's lips by the time Bartleby finished cutting the top free. While she slurped down the can's sludgy contents, Bartleby leaned back and considered his hands. They were blistered and bruised and beat up pretty good.

Back a day earlier at Toms Run Shelter, a long while passed before Thunk and Fancy returned leading two paramedics and a state trooper. Long enough for Bartleby to etch:

R.I.P.
Mad Chatter
2011

into the shelter wall with the tip of a hiking pole.

The state trooper asked a few questions and otherwise made quiet small talk. The paramedics went through their procedures, bagged the body and strapped it to the stretcher. Which, in Bartleby's opinion, wasn't much more than a glorified body basket. When the paramedics finished, Bartleby and Thunk helped carry Chatter out. With the five men working together, Bartleby figured that physically speaking, it would be an easy task.

In this he was dead wrong.

Despite having Olympic-level cardio and Atlas strong legs, Bartleby's chest was a sunken hollow and his arms were chicken wings. They'd been fairly lame back in Georgia and had atrophied noticeably since. So much so, he couldn't help but think his body had begun prioritizing needs and filling them by looting and cannibalizing low priority muscle groups. He didn't actually know if the human body worked like that but it made sense. Wondered what muscles might be slated for recycling next.

Chatter didn't weigh much, but he was an awkward load over difficult footing. They never fully dropped the body, but that was only on account of one of the paramedics being built like a couple of Brinks trucks. During a rest break, Brinks explained that he'd only come to emergency medical services after injuring himself in a local mixed martial arts circuit fight.

It didn't help that Bartleby was carrying his backpack too. Thunk and Fancy had had the foresight to stash their packs back with the emergency vehicles before returning to the shelter, but Bartleby hadn't had an chance to do so and now wore it while struggling under his share of Chatter's body too. The whole of Bartleby's upper body burned with fatigue until it went blessedly numb. Fancy ushered Jane along and brought up the rear with Chatter's effects. It took the little band almost ninety minutes to cover a distance Bartleby had covered in twenty minutes earlier in the day.

By the time the trooper collected statements and contact information, it was nearing dusk. He offered to drop them at a local motel.

Bartleby felt so drained, so low, so back to the bottom, he didn't have it in him to object when Thunk and Fancy split the room's cost between themselves.

❦ ❦ ❦

Birch Run Shelter to Boiling Springs, Pennsylvania: 29.1 miles of the flattest and most monotonous hiking you could expect to see along the entire AT. Farmland stretched out in every direction—acres upon acres of corn, wheat, soybeans, sunflowers and who knew what else. It was hot as holy hell and so stifling humid, a seated body could perspire just thinking about standing up. Had to be a buck-oh-five in the shade and the trail didn't much stick to any shade.

Skunkers was up with the birds, hiking before dawn and full-on sweating just from packing his ruck.

Hydration was key when covering that kind of mileage in that kind of heat. Luckily, Skunkers had learned all about how to keep a body wet in Iraq. He filled his water bladder at every opportunity and kept the platypus hose plugged into his mouth like a baby's pacifier. He drank deeply while hot-footing over Pennsylvania's countryside and set his watch alarm to beep on the hour. At which time, thirsty feeling or no, he stopped and chugged a quart.

In this manner, Skunkers managed to keep himself in the black, water-wise. He wasn't flush, wasn't stopping to pee ever, but he wasn't drying out either. Of course, what goes in, must come out. He drank gallons of water and promptly sweated them out. Doesn't matter what they promise at the gear shops, no one has engineered a wicking fabric that could keep ahead of all that. He soaked through his shirt. He soaked through his booney hat. He soaked through his shorts and his socks. After a while, there was even moisture bubbling up through the stitched leather seams of his hiking boots.

He hiked shirtless until the sun started to cook his shoulders and back. After that, he wore his shirt and, for all the good it did, stopped and wrung it out every so often. After a few hours of repetitive motion in salty wet clothes, the friction started up. Just like most of the guys out there, Skunkers had lost weight, was still losing weight at an almost noticeable clip. But unlike most of the other guys, he was still strapping big, with bulging pecs, corded triceps and a set of quads that could have come straight off a pack animal. All that mass had a tendency to rub up against itself and chaff against wet fabric.

At best, it was a perpetual powder keg down there in the deep notch of his crotch, what with his junk and thick thighs vying for limited breathing room. Let a few layers of wet clothing work themselves up into the mix and the area began to feel suspiciously like the Iraqi Civil War: a three-way clusterfuck that everybody loses, with more blood and pain than seems necessary.

He pulled in for a break at Tagg Run Shelter. Shaggy Bob and Ella were already there, tucked into some shade. Sitting with his back to Ella, Skunkers pulled his shorts down to his knees and surveyed the damage. The last two miles had felt like a pair of sadistic lumberjacks were using the leg-hole hem of his jockey's as a crosscut saw, drawing it back and forth and cutting into all the meat and bone that kept his leg connected to his pelvis.

With a two-handed grip on his briefs, Skunkers ripped them off in one go, like Hulk Hogan used to do with his tank tops.

He called over his shoulder, "Anyone packing extra duct tape?"

Shaggy Bob handed him a roll. "Got some Neosporin too, if you need it. Duuuude—that's pretty bad."

Skunkers grunted and got to work. He rinsed the area clean, cleared away the scabbed and peeling skin, the dried blood and the invisible salt crystals. Smeared ointment over entire swaths of abraded skin. Then he wrapped everything with duct tape. Upper thighs, inner thighs, groin and scrotum. Strip after strip of silvery tape, layered on like a lobster's shell.

🍁

The AT skirted north along the edge of one last field, hooked a louie and headed into the setting sun for the final quarter mile. The land was so flat, Skunkers couldn't make out much of the town as he closed in on it. Crossing railroad tracks, he saw a small clearing with a port-o-john and a few tents. Didn't see any hikers so he walked over a little bridge, continued under tree cover for a hundred yards and came out in a dirt parking lot. There was a massive stone pyramid over on his right, but he didn't care enough to investigate further. Following the white blazes, he crossed a road to the shores of Children's Lake. This wasn't any bigger than many ponds Skunkers had swum in, but it was obviously a civic attraction, gaggled full of geese and ducks and kids plopping rocks into the shallows. A wide gravel path led him along the manicured lakeshore, took him past a white gazebo and stalled out at a single-story building clad in white clapboard. A sign explained that he'd reached the Mid-Atlantic Regional Office of the Appalachian Trail Conservancy. A pack of hikers were lazing around out front. At first glance Skunkers didn't recognize anyone. Instead of stopping to talk or make friends, he went straight for a hose laying on the ground and proceeded to splash water all over himself. Peeled off his shirt and shoes, wrung out hat and socks. He stuck the hose down his shorts, jostled everything around and rinsed off as best as he could.

❦

Thunk elbowed Bartleby, "Get a load of that guy."

Skunkers was standing there under the hose with just his shorts on and splashing himself cleanish. Rising welts and silvery swatches of tape were visible along his waistline where his pack belt had been rubbing. More tape circled his thighs. His armpits were rashy red and silver crosses of tape covered each nipple.

"Never pegged you for a religious man, Skunkers," Bartleby called over.

Thunk was less subtle, "Got you some nice pasties there, dude."

Flutterby slowed her pace to let Tommy Hawk, T-Ball and Slip-stream pull ahead. Tommy was in the middle of another crazy war story, they'd never even miss her. When they disappeared around a bend she stopped, looked back and listened for anyone coming along behind. Fast as they'd been walking, she didn't expect anyone to be close on their heels, but it didn't hurt to double-check.

Confident she was alone, Flutterby took three steps off trail and jammed her hiking poles into the ground. With her pack still on, she squatted awkwardly, held the crotch of her shorts to one side and let loose. She used the planted poles to pull herself upright when finished. Was hiking again in less than forty seconds.

This was a coup of sorts. After three months of trying, she'd finally mastered the coveted art of peeing with her pack on.

There was no true escape from the irrepressible hordes of buzzing black flies, swarming gnats and thirsty mosquitoes that occupied AT airspace. Every hiker had to develop their own method for avoiding the nasty buggers.

Thunk used DEET like it might somehow be good for him. He drenched himself every day and bought a new can whenever he hit town.

Fancy Pants went after them with a double hand slap, like a cymbalist at the Boston Pops.

Skunkers was quick enough, he could reach out and catch the big green-eyed horseflies in one hand. He enjoyed whipping them against any nearby hard objects. Whenever available, Coyote's head served nicely.

Flutterby used lemon-scented eucalyptus oil. It didn't work particularly well, but it smelled nice and she suffered quietly.

Insects had always been attracted to Bawdy. Consequently, he slapped at them with a reckless abandon that left his skin splotched with stinging red hand prints, smears of dried blood and bug carcasses. He tried wiping all this away, but it was tough keeping up with the carnage. There were a lot of bugs out there.

Coyote liked to let mosquitoes start up sucking. He'd take his time, calmly set up his shot and, when the moment was right, flick the little fuckers as far as he could. He liked to use Bawdy for a target.

Even when temps hit triple digits, Old Man Trouble wore pants, long sleeves and a head net around the shelters. This made him look like an old, puttering beekeeper.

In the beginning, Bartleby hardly registered the presence of bugs. Later, he felt them but largely let them be. Wasn't that he enjoyed being bitten so much as he enjoyed the realization that feeling their bites probably represented some small improvement in his wellbeing.

The rocks of Pennsylvania ranged from smaller than a golf ball to larger than a picnic basket. Some were half buried and immovable toe-stubbers, others shifted dangerously underfoot. They were universally sharp-edged and largely unavoidable. Or at least, bypassing any given one just meant stepping and stumbling over others.

The rocks of Pennsylvania provided a level of obstacle heretofore unseen on trail. Ruts and potholes threatened to snap ankles, piercing points stabbed into trail-sore feet and larger stones teetered unexpectedly. More than brute strength or stamina, hiking over these rocks required fine-motor control, balance and mental acuity. Each and every foot placement required blink-quick consideration and an exacting precision that was no less fatiguing than hiking up mountains all day long.

The rocks of Pennsylvania weren't simply physically demanding and mentally taxing. They were emotionally challenging as well.

After more than a thousand miles, thru-hikers had grown accustomed to moving along at certain rates of speed. Over rocks, those rates became unrealistic. For many, readjusting to this slower pace was an infuriating experience, much like driving a shiny new Corvette round and round a parking lot littered with speed bumps.

The trail loped along easily enough. The terrain was perfect for letting the stride out and covering ground; if not for the rocks, Skunkers could've done better than four miles an hour. Instead, he clenched his jaw, got in touch with his inner aggro and kept on just as fast as he could. Left rising dust and a string of curses in his wake.

Bartleby watched Skunkers widen the gap and eventually disappear up trail. He didn't pretend to try and match that road-rage fueled pace, was content to keep on slowly and calmly. Didn't feel any macho need to try and sprint through a rock field.

Besides, he wanted to take it easy on his new pair of trail sneakers. They weren't anything special, picked them up at a nearby Dick's Sporting Goods for seventy bucks, but hardscrabble rocks or no, the new shoes were a dream. Felt pounds lighter too without all that stupid duct tape weighing them down.

Just ahead, at the end of her leash, Jane jingled along. When he'd bought shoes, he also picked up a shiny new bell for her collar. He worried about her adjusting to his faster hiking pace, but so far that didn't seem to be a problem. And with four feet instead of two, she definitely had an easier time going over the rocks than Bartleby did.

❦ ❦ ❦

Register: Darlington Shelter

6/19   Rocks, rocks and more rocks.
       My poor feet are singing the
       Pennsylvania blues!

                              High-Ku

＊ ＊ ＊

When Bawdy caught up, Bartleby was sitting on a boulder, taking a break next to a trickling stream.

After doing a double-take, Bawdy chortled, "And lo, there before me appeared the peculiar aspect of the unaccountable Bartleby."

"Good to see you too, Bawds."

"What the shit?" Bawdy mock-protested. "You don't stop for nothing. I been chasing after your woebegone-ass for like seven hundred miles. Goddamn!" He flopped to the ground. "And don't tell me you're about to start off hiking now either."

Bartleby had been. He shrugged, cracked a smile, "How's trail treating you?"

"Anybody call you Banana Boy yet?"

"Uh-uh."

Bawdy gave Bartleby's shirt a long look, "That thing is really something."

Jane lay in the shallows, lapping water and cooling off. After a good shake, she went up close and took a sniff of Bawdy.

"I remember you," Bawdy said to her, "you like to eat butterflies." To Bartleby he said, "Heard something about you taking on a dependent."

"We're more like co-dependents."

Bawdy sucked on his water hose until it made a gurgling air noise that meant it was empty. With some effort, he roused himself and filled it in the stream. "Not exactly easy keeping tabs on you when you don't write nothing in the trail registers. Passed Bindle Stiff, he said you were close. I started sprinting, trying to catch up. So...you're still alive?"

Bartleby nodded.

"And you're still hiking?"

Another nod.

"And I guess you still aren't talking for shit?"

Big grin, "You lost weight. Look skinny."

"You too man. Shit—skinny feels good, doesn't it?"

Just then another northbound hiker came up and leaned against a tree to catch his breath.

"Bartleby, let me introduce my newest roll-dog, Rollin'. Rollin', this is my oldest roll-dog, Bartleby. But if you wanna start up calling him Banana Boy, I think we could make it stick."

Rollin' was a scrawny youth with smooth cheeks and crooked teeth. Had greasy black hair and glacier blue eyes. He was dirty in a rag-tag chimney sweep sort of way with earbuds stuck in his ears. Apparently he could hear over them because he shook his head with annoyance, "It's Roland. Not Rollin'."

"We've already discussed this, *Rollin'*," Bawdy admonished, "I'm not calling you Roland. You are not the last gunslinger, you are not of the line of Eld and Mt. Katahdin is not the Dark Tower. You are a self-deluded runaway—"

"I'm eighteen," Rollin' sulked.

"*Maybe* you'll turn sixteen by the time we reach Maine, but you haven't yet."

Rollin' huffed off hiking without another word.

"And I'm still waiting for you to finish reading the second half of *The Hunger Games*," Bawdy called after him.

Bartleby didn't know what to say to any of this, but before he could figure something, Bawdy started up.

"Insano, huh? It's like that Grateful Dead line, 'what a long, strange trip it's been', right? You got yourself a big dog, I'm brow-beating runaways for a girly YA novel and we're both looking like a couple of starvelings."

"What happened to all the others?"

"Let's see. Skunkers went racing ahead. He's trying to build up a cushion so he could stay a couple nights with his aunt and not fall too far behind. Flutterby's close—we could see her anytime. I think Pooh-bah's up ahead too, but good-bye to bad cheese, right? Far as I know, Old Man Trouble's still hiking, but I haven't seen him since Shenandoah. He stayed at one of those fancy lodges and we didn't. Pork Chop went off in Bland with a sprained ankle. Jersey George and Hungry Joe and a couple others went off in Waynesboro. The Wabash Cannonball dropped out in Pearisburg and Blodgett quit at Harpers."

"Anything on Lazy JoJo? Pony Express?"

"Don't know about Pony. Haven't seen him since, shit, maybe Atkins. JoJo's back a bit. Far as I know, she's still trucking along, pun intended. Did you hear about Coyote? Poor bastard got humperdinked." Bawdy hefted his pack, "You ready to roll, chief?"

Bartleby was, so they did.

"What's that mean, humperdinked?"

"Back before Shenandoah, there was this section hiker, going by Happy Humperdink. He was a squishy marshmallow who didn't know nothing from nothing. We first saw him slumped on the side of the trail next to this *huge* pack. Turned out he was carrying like fifteen days of food. The dope was out of water, out of steam and basically out of his depth in the shallow end. Just to be clear, this dude was a complete and utter bumblefuck. Right off, he started begging us for water, which sucked, because we both only had enough to get to the next spring, so like, what the fuck dude? We were still five miles from the shelter and Coyote, of all people, hooks Humperdink up with his last pint.

"Humpsy rinses his mouth out and splashes water on his face and neck before guzzling what's left.

"Short of carrying that sorry sack of stupid out to a road, that's about all we could do for him. So later, at the shelter, it's already dark by the time Humpsy comes limping in. But not so dark we can't see he's lost his pants. When I met him, I swear he had pants on, but now he's just wearing dirty boxers. Everyone's watching, cause no one can look away, right? It's like a crime scene or something. He spills his cooking water, can't start his stove. Spent, I'm not kidding, most of an hour down by the water source doing God knows what. Then he spreads all his gear out on the picnic table, looking for his toilet paper. When he hangs his food bag in the shelter, it drips tuna juice all over Wham-O. And being that Humpsy was the last person to arrive, the only shelter spots left were in the loft. In retrospect, one

of us should've gone up there and let him sleep on the floor but..."
Bawdy shrugged his shoulders.

"Skip to early morning. Humpsy has to pee. If he'd waited another twenty minutes there would've been light enough for him to see by, but he didn't so he couldn't and he started monkeying down in the dark anyway. It's like climbing from a top bunk, except instead of one person, there's eight people sleeping beneath you. He makes enough noise, I wake up to see his legs dangling down, probing for something to stand on. But of course there's nothing, because he's still got a foot and a half to go. Then his grip slips and he crashes to the floor.

"Humpsy goes down with a grunt and Coyote pops up with a surprised-as-shit yowl. The whole shelter comes awake. Poor Yote's rolling in pain, holding his leg and Humpsy keeps saying, 'The fat of the calf, I got him in the fat of his calf!'

"Guess he pinched Yote's calf muscle against the floor."

"Owwww," Bartleby winced at the thought.

"Come daylight, it looked like Coyote had a swimming floatie around his leg and a big, uuuugly puke-green bruise coming in. He barely made it to Buena Vista. Last we knew, he was holing up in a motel for a coupla days, giving things a chance to heal."

"Humperdinked, huh?"

"Big time."

Following a street one removed from the main drag, the AT moseyed through the poor, post-industrial town of Duncannon, Pennsylvania. The obviously unloved houses were cramped close and sagging with age. Rusty grills sat abandoned on front stoops and furniture lay forgotten or lost in weed-riddled lawns. Some houses were abandoned and others had metal bars fixed across their ground floor windows.

And rough and tumble as Duncannon looked, the town's much celebrated dive bar/seedy hotel, The Doyle, looked rougher and tumbled. Among thru-hiking circles, The Doyle enjoyed a reputation as a legendary watering hole where a week's old corpse had once been found swollen and rotting in an upstairs room. It was one of a very few trail-side establishments that grimy, stinking hikers could frequent without ever feeling underdressed or out of place.

Coyote added his pack to a line of packs outside The Doyle's front door. His was far and away smaller and, if the way he handled it meant anything, lighter than all the others. But light pack or no, Coyote had come twenty-seven miles since morning. His ankles ached, his busted up calf throbbed and his lips were chapped and flaky. When he removed his sunglasses, he was raccoon-eyed from a combination of sunburn and dirt.

The Doyle's bar was fronted by an assortment of mismatched stools. These were occupied by both thru-hikers and Duncannon's finest. It was hard to tell which group had been having a tougher time of it. Behind the bar, a cheery woman filled plastic cups from a tap. With the way she wore her cap backwards and hollered jovially at customers, she could've been a catcher for the local softball team.

Coyote caught her eye, "Got anything gonna make me forget how much my feet hurt?"

"Coming up, hon," the bartender winked and sloshed him out a shot of brown liquid with a beer back.

He gulped the shot, glugged half the beer and grinned for the first time in eight hours, "That's a good start."

❦

Some few beers and shots later, Coyote shared a table with Lazy JoJo and Pony Express. He was just finishing off a second cheesesteak sandwich. Had greasy smears on both cheeks and bits of sautéed mushroom dangling in his beard like fresh dingleberries.

Pony sipped a beer and wrote in his journal, though he seemed to be doing a lot more writing than sipping. JoJo, drinking Wild Turkey with a splash of coke, zoned out to the Merle Haggard selections she'd plugged into the jukebox.

"You guys wanna get a room here?"

JoJo nodded. Pony looked up long enough to say, "Sounds good."

With his hunger sated, Coyote's restless energy quickly returned. He got a gleam in his eyes when he spotted a pool table in the side room, "Hey—either a you schmoes shoot stick?"

"Sure," JoJo said, "I play a little."

❧

"Six four in the corner." JoJo settled her pool stick in the notch of her thumb and shifted her toothpick in her mouth. A gentle stroke sent the cue ball rolling into the six, which kissed the four into the corner pocket. Then she cracked the six into the side with enough draw to give herself a clean shot on the eight-ball.

Before taking the shot, JoJo took out her toothpick, chugged a full beer with more grace than seemed possible, burped with less and blew her exhalation in Coyote's direction. Then she sunk the eight.

Coyote looked ragged around the edges and worse for wear. Still and all, he had enough of his wits to know she'd beat him yet again.

"What's that now? Four in a row?"

"Five."

"Shit. That's it, I'm done and drunk."

"Was your stupid rule about drinking on the eight."

"I know," he peeled a hundo off the top of his wad and waved it at her. "This is yours. Unless you wanna arm wrestle for it."

It became a big to-do in no time at all. Thru-hikers and local barflies gathered round the contenders; Old Man Trouble was elected to referee. Smirking uncontrollably, Coyote joked and juked, ran his mouth and otherwise engaged the crowd. *Welcome to the Jungle* played on the jukebox and the motley crowd bristled with anticipation.

When Trouble said go and they got to it, JoJo slammed Coyote down in four seconds flat. He tried, strained for all he was worth, but in the end that turned out to be not so very much.

Losing didn't faze him in the least. Coyote held up two hundred dollar bills for all to see. "Okay, here you go, JoJo—unless...you wanna cut for it?" He'd produced a deck of cards from out of nowhere.

Onlookers "oohed" in appreciation of this new twist.

She shook her head, "I don't never play cards." Dug a quarter out of her pocket, "but I'll flip ya for it."

And that's how, the next day, JoJo walked out of Duncannon with four hundred dollars more than she walked in with.

❦ ❦ ❦

Register: Eagle's Nest Shelter

6/30 Poison snake tally: 3 copperheads, 1 water moc and today a rattler sunning on trail. Had to wait 10 minutes for it to slither off.   - Pony Express

❦ ❦ ❦

Chatter's tent was a simple pyramid-shaped design that took Bartleby a few tries to get the hang of setting up. It was roomy enough that Bartleby and Jane could sleep inside without touching. That wasn't how it generally went down, though. Jane turned out to be an inveterate snuggler.

Using a tent meant extra work both morning and night, as well as extra weight to carry all day long. Despite that, Bartleby found tent living a pleasant change of pace. Sleeping on the ground was quite a bit more comfortable than a shelter floor, and the additional privacy didn't hurt. Much like Chatter himself had been, the tent was an older model, but the sun-bleached fly still worked and the bug mesh kept the worst of the bloodsuckers at bay.

The only downside was Jane's breath. Big as she was, there was lots of it and it was bad. Probably no worse than any other dog, but Bartleby wasn't sleeping six inches from any other dog. When the weather was good, this wasn't too big a deal. On rainy nights though, when he zipped the tent's fly all the way closed, Jane's heavy breath enveloped the tent in short order. It was hot and sour and, like mustard gas, surprisingly persistent. Took a good strong gust of wind to make the tent halfway habitable again.

Skunkers was back on trail now and pushing big miles. He was maybe a day behind and he had every intention of fixing that right quick in a jiffy (a phrase his great aunt Tabitha often used). He planned on not taking any breaks until he caught up with either Flutterby or Bawdy. Preferably both. But he couldn't help himself when he got to the top of the Pinnacle. The elevation was only sixteen hundred feet, the climb not worth talking about. But the view, that really was something.

It wasn't exactly purple mountain majesties or even wilderness as far as the eye can see. Instead, it was an incredible bird's-eye view of the Lehigh Valley. It was county lanes and cornfields, small tidy homes and highways stretching out to forever. There was a life-size living map grandiosity to all of this, especially when Skunkers looked through his spyglass.

"Are you kidding, Skunks?" Hungry Joe wanted to know. "What is that thing?"

"My spyglass."

Three telescoping sections of shiny brass. The thing wasn't simply antique, it was ancient; had probably been put to work on a pirate ship way back when. To keep it safe, Skunkers stowed it in a velvety black pouch which he kept inside a matching brass box roughly the size of a big baked potato.

"Isn't that heavy?"

"Uh-huh."

Skunkers had a map of Pennsylvania out and open on his lap. He studied it before using the spyglass to locate those same landmarks in the rolling landscape before him.

From this rocky perch, Skunkers looked down on turkey buzzards riding the rising thermals. After taking a few pictures, he swapped out his wet socks for a pair of freshies and started hiking again, leaving Hungry Joe to shake his head in wonder.

The visit with his great aunt had been exactly what he needed. He hadn't seen her since before going into the army, but she didn't look or act much different than he remembered. Tabitha was still that seemingly contradictory mix of old school kooky and happy-go-lucky New Age. She wore a toe ring and red, white and blue island beads in her ivory hair (to celebrate the Fourth of July), but she also wore an apron and put lard in pretty much everything she cooked. Maybe she had a few more wrinkles but he didn't figure that mattered too much. When you get up into your eighties, who's actually counting anyway?

His mother had strong-armed him into making the visit, but Skunkers didn't mind. Tabitha lived less than twenty miles from trail, and he'd had no problem catching a hitch right to her door. When he arrived she already had multiple meals waiting. A garlic infused pot roast, corn fritters, chicken dumplings, her secret recipe pork chops and a high stack of pancakes. There was even a strawberry-rhubarb pie cooling on the sill.

Aside from keeping a near constant stream of food coming at him, Tabitha did Skunkers' laundry (added a cup of lemon juice that actually got most of the stink out), darned any socks needing it (most of them) and wanted to hear all about the AT, the army and anything else he had to say.

When he yanked all the duct tape from his body, the skin beneath was pocked with dozens of fingernail-sized infections. These angry red boils were filled with a seemingly endless supply of yellow pus. When Tabitha caught a glimpse of them, she wouldn't hear any excuses. Every few hours, she drew a steaming hot bath, tossed in Epsom salts, hand-ground oatmeal and her only grand-nephew. Skunkers stopped grumbling about it soon as Tabitha lifted the ban on eating in the tub. By the fourth bath, Skunkers' skin was ridiculously prune-wrinkled but the infected boils were greatly reduced and visibly on the mend.

For his part, Skunkers moved some furniture, changed six light bulbs, swept a hornet's nest off the porch awning, re-seated the badly leaning mailbox and ate himself sick for almost two days straight. The visit flew by so quickly, he hadn't even been able to finish off the pie. He carried the last piece in his hand as he left her house.

Back on trail now, he felt rested and nourished. Far as he could tell from the registers, Flutterby was about thirty-five miles ahead and Bawdy a bit further than that. It looked like Coyote still hadn't reappeared. Skunkers wondered if Slick was still hiking or if he'd quit with a broken calf back in Virginia. But he didn't worry about it, because worrying wasn't Skunkers strong suit. Instead, he mapped out a plan to catch up with Flutterby within a day or two of crossing into New Jersey. This plan of his was elegant in its simplicity. He would hike all day, every day until he caught up to Flutterby or his legs fell off.

Following this plan wasn't going to be easy or any sort of fun. Back in the army, his CO might've said it wasn't a 'good' plan, per se, but such as is was, it allowed Skunkers to accomplish what he wanted to accomplish (unless his legs actually did fall off first).

Either way, he was going to find out right quick in a jiffy.

Register: Bake Oven Knob Shelter

7/6 This place got me thinking about the Easy Bake Oven my sister used to have. I remember cooking up many sweet-ass sprinkle-topped cupcakes in that thing.   Big Bro Bawdy

Flutterby wasn't alone. There were people around. Tommy Hawk,

Slipstream and Jive Turkey, specifically. She'd seen Giggles, Rock Steady, Nickleback and that hump-happy German shepherd of his, Lancelot, just yesterday. According to the registers, it looked like Fast Eddie and the Crying Hawaiian weren't too very far ahead either. If not tonight in town, she'd likely see them some time tomorrow.

She wasn't alone, but she was lonely.

Skunkers was still behind, Coyote was probably off trail and Bawdy had somehow slipped ahead.

Her boys were all gone, scattered to the winds.

She'd met Tommy Hawk early on in Georgia; he was a nice enough guy; smart, polite and considerate. When he could, he looked out for Flutterby in a fatherly way she found simultaneously comforting and smothering.

Had he been ahead of her, she was sure he'd have waited for her where the AT crossed PA-873.

He wasn't ahead of her though, and consequently, he wasn't waiting to hitch into Palmerton with her from Lehigh Gap. He was probably a few miles back yet.

She might've waited around for Tommy to catch up, but for the sight of Blue Mountain rising up on the north side of 873. It was about as nuclear-wasteland ugly as mountainsides get. A rocky barren rabble, a scrabbly scree-slide of stone and little else. She remembered reading in her trail guide that Blue Mountain had once been the sight of a massive zinc mining operation and was now an equally massive superfund site.

Instead of waiting in such close proximity to what had to be one of the ugliest views along the entire Appalachian Trail, Flutterby stuck out a thumb. It wasn't thirty seconds before a bread truck pulled over for her. The driver was pear plump with pale, pale skin and lots of acne. He had a poof of white blonde hair up top and more dirt under his fingernails than Flutterby—and she hadn't seen running water in a full five days.

"You're gonna have to stand in back between the racks," he said. "If anyone sees you up front, I'll get canned. And they're just looking for a reason to can me."

"Oh, ah, well, maybe I'll just wait for another ride. Don't want to get you in trouble."

"It's fine. Climb on up. I can't not pick up a thru-hiker."

I *really* miss my boys, Flutterby thought as she climbed up and shimmied into the back aisle. She had to hold on tight as the truck jounced and bounced itself into the flow of traffic.

It took her about three seconds to decide the driver looked a little off. Another handful of seconds brought her to the conclusion that his "off-ness" was more in a bad-genetics-meets-something-in-the-water way than a serial-killer-gonna-sniff-your-old-sneakers kind of way. He was in his mid-twenties and familiar with the Jailhouse Hostel she was trying to get to.

"Stayed there myself," he said. "I thru-hiked two years ago."

"Seriously?"

"Yeah. Georgia to Maine in one hundred sixty-three days. They called me White Carrot. You know how when you get a bag of them baby-peeled carrots? Always seems to be one in there that's off-color and weird." He beamed goofily, "That pretty much sums me up: the weird one in the bunch."

To either side of Flutterby, the bread racks were packed with various rolls and loaves. She didn't realize at first, but her mouth had started watering.

"Smells good back here," she said.

He patted the jiggling fat of his stomach, "If you don't want to end up looking like me, you better be careful after you finish. Couldn't help myself. I kept right on eating everything in sight and with this job, the sky was the limit. Packed on forty pounds by Christmas. I'm heavier now than before hiking."

White Carrot drove Flutterby straight to the town hall parking lot. He pointed out the entrance to the basement hostel and left her standing there with two warm loaves under her arm.

🍁 🍁 🍁

"Am I being a baby, or were those last seven miles killer?"

Thunk lazed, shirtless and shoeless, in the shade of Kirkridge Shelter. "It's not you, Fancy. There was nothing fun about any of that."

She schlumped down nearby.

"It's like they say—PA ain't nothing but rocks and roots and rattlesnakes."

Fancy finished off whatever water she had left. After a minute or two, "Still six miles into Delaware Water Gap, right?"

"Six plus."

Fancy burped. "Time is it?"

"Two-thirty."

"Saturday, right?"

"Uh-huh. July 4th."

"Really? Wow. I didn't even know. Guess that means the PO is definitely closed. Can't get my maildrop until Monday. Really no reason to push on tonight. Everybody's ahead, should be nice and peaceful here."

Thunk nodded. The shelter wasn't anything special, but he'd happily stayed at worse. "Want company?"

🍁

The heat dropped down to a tolerable level and the bugs weren't too bad. It really was nice and peaceful right up until the Boy Scouts trooped in. Ten of the most rambunctious rotters to ever wear the yellow. They came bookended by two frazzled middle-aged men who looked like someone had sold them a bill of goods.

One of the scouts, using his walking stick as a stand-in for a Louisville Slugger, took batting practice on an associate's arm. This set off a riot of tears, name-calling, loogie-spitting and, when the scout masters intervened, the least sincere apologies Thunk had ever heard.

He'd planned to sleep in the shelter, but after this incident, Thunk promptly banished himself to the woods. There wasn't a whole lot of flat spots for tenting, but he managed to squeeze in between Fancy's tent and the trunk of a maple. They were a two dozen paces from the shelter, close enough to see the scouts, but far enough to muffle some of the clamor.

"We shoulda gone on the six miles," Fancy whispered.

Thunk nodded while sifting through his food, "Since we didn't, are you gonna help me eat my food down?"

"Nah. I'm fine."

"I know you're fine, but I got way too much. You like string cheese? Gorp? Look, I even got a Luna Bar, which would be perfect for you. I dare you to say no to gummy bears. And I'm not talking generic gummies either. These are straight-up, no-shitting, for-reals, Original Black Forest, because that's how I roll, Fancy P. I'm true-blue OBF."

Fancy Pants had started to smile back at Luna Bar, and by the end of Thunk's little speech, she was laughing and reaching for a handful of little grinning bears.

❧

Sometime after the scouts had eaten dinner, a general hue and cry went up. One of the scouts had discovered a rattlesnake. It was balled between the roots of a tree not more than ten feet behind the shelter. Thunk and Fancy broke their self-imposed banishment, went over and joined the troop in checking it out.

Hard to tell exactly, but stretched end to end, it was probably five feet long. The rattlesnake's skin was mottled over and hanging off in dry patches. There was a translucent film over its eyes. The snake didn't react, flinch or seem to breath, even as the scouts shook sticks, stomped the ground and spit at it.

Fancy grabbed one of the spitters by the ear, "Want me to spit in *your* face?"

This exchange momentarily balked the scouts and brought a tight smile to the scout master's face. Much as she wanted to stand and admire the snake, maybe take some pictures, Fancy couldn't tolerate the collected rabble. By the time she'd gotten into her tent, they were chanting, "Rat-tle! Rat-tle! Rat-tle!"

It was all the leaders could do to herd the kids back to the front of the shelter.

✢

"Handsome old man, wasn't he?" Fancy asked.

It was mostly dark. She and Thunk lay in their respective tents.

"How do you know it was male?"

"I don't really," Fancy admitted. "But what a gentleman, not rising to all that baiting, huh?"

"Another fifteen, twenty years and those kids will be running this country."

"That's a depressing thought to sleep on, Thunk."

Thunk could feel maple roots and other unidentified hard nubbins poking at him through his sleeping pad. These kept him awake well after Fancy's breathing shifted into a gentle sleeping rhythm.

He lay there listening to the boom and crackle of distant fireworks. Nearer by, he could still hear the scouts, and from the sound of it, they weren't leaving the snake alone. Sneaking over to it, daring each other to get close and generally distressing the molting reptile. The scout masters were barking at the boys, but to no avail. Thunk could see the idea of losing a scout to snakebite wasn't sitting real well. Keeping one eye on the boys, the two men peeled off and conferred amongst themselves. Thunk couldn't make out what they were saying, but watched as the older man talked and the younger nodded along. After coming to agreement, one man forcibly gathered the boys into the shelter. The other took up a walking stick and disappeared around to the back of the shelter. Thunk couldn't see what happened next, but he heard the unmistakable WHUMP-WHUMP-WHUMP of the stick being repeatedly brought down with force.

Thunk took it on himself to get Fancy quickly up and out in the morning. He made a point of never telling her what he'd witnessed.

Register: Kirkridge Shelter

7/9 There once was a coyote named Slick
Who didn't hike very quick
He fell far behind
But we didn't mind
Cuz he was a crusty b-hole!

Ballbustin' Bawdy

(Catch up, Yote, or suffer the stinging lash of
my razor wit!)

Bartleby picked up another maildrop at the Delaware Water Gap post office. In addition to the usual collection of fancy foods, whiskey and money, it contained a gray tweed flat cap. Remembering what Chatter had said about Thunk looking good in just such a cap, Bartleby gave it to him. Everyone agreed that Chatter had been right—when tilted rakishly forward, it set off Thunk's dark eyes nicely.

After tasting one sip of Chatter's whiskey, Skunkers promptly agreed to buy any more that came along. In exchange for the old man's baggie of assorted pills, Bawdy bought Bartleby dinner at the local diner. Bartleby didn't hold back. He chomped down a bacon cheeseburger with french fries, onion rings and a side of potato skins. Sweetened the meal with a hefty slice of cheesecake and a large chocolate shake.

Not being a big fan of Werther's candies himself, Bartleby gave them over to Mudsucka on the promise that she share them with Pony Express if ever he caught up.

When Bartleby crossed the state line into New Jersey, he actually had a little spending money in his pocket.

***

Extensive as it was, by the time Bawdy walked the length of Virginia, he'd run through and grown bored of his entire repertoire of known jingles, ditties and theme songs. So sometime after Harpers, he'd begun making up his own. These weren't masterworks of lyric or tune by any stretch of the imagination. Instead, they were occasionally entertaining and unapologetically vulgar.

Currently he was working out the kinks in a jaunty little ballad about what he'd do if ever he met the person responsible for all the pointless ups and downs (in hiking parlance these were known as PUDs) along the trail. This song of his was tentatively titled *Punishing Mr. PUD*.

And once Bawdy got going, he would keep at it for hours at a time, like a dog licking at himself.

Bartleby listened for a short while and then tuned out for a long time, but finally couldn't take it anymore.

"Bawdy," Bartleby called.

"What?"

"Did you stay at Ensign Cowall Shelter?"

"I don't know. Describe it. They've all blended together."

"Nothing special. Back in Maryland. Ten or twelve miles south of PA."

"Was it a bit of a rat trap?"

Bartleby nodded.

"Might've lunched there. Why?"

Pause.

"I got an erection there."

After another, longer pause Bawdy said, "You won an election?"

"Erection," Bartleby repeated. "You know—a stiffy." He stopped hiking, turned back and made an unmistakable gesture.

"The old leaning tower of penis, eh? Your toy soldier stood to attention? Sporting wood, raising the pole barn, pitching a—"

"What are you doing?"

"I thought we were coming up with funny names for hard-ons."

"No. I was telling you about my first erection in like forever."

"Oh," Bawdy said. "Huh." Then, "Mazel tov?"

"Been dying to tell someone."

Drip. Splash.

Coyote was squatting, catching individual drips of water as they fell off the rock. It was an excruciatingly slow way to fill up his water bottles, but there didn't seem to be much choice in the matter. A small puddle had collected beneath the rock, but it was scummed over with green-black algae.

Drip. Splash.

Old Man Trouble wandered down from the shelter.

"Gonna be a long wait, Trubs. This is taking forever."

"There's an easier way to do that," Trouble said. "Here, look."

Trouble plucked a leaf from a nearby rhododendron and set it higher up on the rock where, like an aqueduct, it caught and channeled the flowing water before it diffused across the rock face. It wasn't anything like turning on a kitchen faucet, but Coyote gave Trouble an appreciative nod when his bottle began filling more quickly.

Trouble dropped his filter into the algae-scummed puddle. After pumping his water bag full, he set off back to the shelter.

Coyote topped of his bottles and turned to leave. Ella passed him on her way down. "Do me a favor, Yote," she called, "don't let anyone come down here for a few minutes, okay? I gotta get this bra off, rinse it out a little."

Coyote saluted sharply, clicked his heels together and marched off.

Up at the shelter, he took a seat at the table next to Pony Express and gave JoJo a big wink, signaling he was up to something.

"You're into birds, right, Pony? Think I just saw a weird one down by the water."

"Really?"

"Yeah. It was like this big and had a, a beak."

"What color was it?"

"Really pale and splotchy red in spots."

"The bird or the bird's beak?"

"Yeah, and it made this funny noise."

"Like a cheep or chirp or what?"

"More of a squawk, really. But I don't know shit about birds—probably wasn't anything special."

"Well, I might as well check it out." Pony started off, came back, fumbled for his bird book. He set off again, came back again and fumbled for his camera, "You said it was right near the spring?"

"Yep," Coyote called after him, "and I want copies of any pictures."

Bawdy and Bartleby together again. The two of them sauntered along the AT like they owned the place. Or at least rented with an option to buy.

In particular, Bartleby stepped with a semblance of pep and cranked away miles like an organ grinder going through a playlist. If his face wasn't hidden behind the scratchy wool of new beard, it might've been possible to catch the occasional smile resting there like some elusive gnome napping under a mushroom cap.

Jane and Bawdy followed him past sporadic patches of purple flowers (violets, he guessed) and across a level span of wet rocks near the top of a minor up-jut. Officially, it might've been a hill, but it certainly wasn't a mountain. This rise was unnamed and unremarkable, save that the climb up had seemed unnecessarily sharp. It didn't even pretend to offer a view. Really, it wasn't so different from a speed bump. By Bartleby's best guess, the AT had gone over a thousand such humps already and this was only New Jersey. Probably another thousand to go before trail's end.

With his mind drifting off to consider how one might actually go about calculating the number of pointless humps still left to climb, Bartleby's right foot went out from under him. It slipped backwards just as he was beginning to transfer weight forward to his left foot. The weight of his body and that of his pack, temporarily unsupported, drove him down on one knee. By rights, his kneecap should've been hammered into the unforgiving granite. And it would have been, if not for the hiking poles. Over the last twelve hundred miles, he'd learned to react with an almost cat-like speed and assurance. He braced his arms and caught himself; stopped his fall an inch short of a shattered patella.

Bawdy, trailing a few yards back, waited while Bartleby regained his feet.

"If you didn't have those poles," Bawdy said, "that one would've hurt muy-muy. Might've ended your hike right there. Bartleby goes bye-bye with a busted kneecap."

Bartleby nodded and started up hiking again, "Would have been something to watch you carry me out."

"Bump that. I would've stuck around for emotional support. Sent Skunkers off to get help. I mean, if you squint enough, he sorta looks like Lassie."

"But isn't he back a day or two?"

"Maybe more. So what? I got food. And anyway, it's crazy lucky you got those poles from STD back at...was it Woody Gap?"

"I feel guilty whenever I think about it. Far as I know, the poor guy's half a day behind, hurrying to catch up and finally get these things back."

"Nah, that big baby's done and gone for good."

Just across the Delaware River bridge and officially into New Jersey, the trail started to rise. By the time Thunk reached Sunfish Pond, he was amazed. Already in its first five or six miles, New Jersey had surpassed his expectations. The rolling terrain displayed a savannah-like beauty, a serenity-scape of golden grasses interrupted by the occasional billowy green copse.

In the eyes of New Yorkers (even those raised upstate), New Jersey was *the* perpetual punch line. A cultural dead-zone, a social backwater, an industrialized wasteland with hypodermically-polluted shores. It was smokestacks and oil tanks and little else but a thoroughfare to points south.

Or, in more explicit terms, New Jersey was New York's green glowing, mutant-eyed kid brother best kept locked away in a dark closet.

New Jersey called itself "The Garden State" and Thunk had always assumed this was ironic, PR spin or a healthy dose of both. Now, as he inhaled piney rich air, he had to wonder.

Register: Brink Road Shelter

7/1 **The Jersey Devil**
     wanders through the pine barrens
     hunting for hikers.

                    High-Ku

Skunkers was trucking serious trail, hauling sixty-five pounds of who knew what on his back, and hurrying ahead with little complaint. Strong and steady and not slowing for much of anything, except to occasionally change out wet socks for dry.

Then he got a whiff of something. Something citrusy. Something warm and wonderful, in the way of flowering meadows.

This something was faint, but hanging unmistakably in the still air.

He tightened shoulder straps, hipbelt and any other fastenings he could reach on the fly. Once all the hatches were battened, his stride lengthened. Skunkers snugged his booney hat down and accelerated from a fast walk to a slow, ungainly jog.

He covered a mile before catching sight of her up the trail. She faded into the summer foliage almost immediately. If he'd been thinking about flagging, this spurred him to new speeds. Skunkers trotted along, his pack jerking and jumping wildly behind him.

He closed to fifty yards. Forty.

She was fully in view now.

Thirty.

Dashing this last bit, Skunkers sounded like a thundering buffalo.

Flutterby heard something, but only turned in time to see Skunkers walking casually behind her. He gave her a look of innocent surprise, "Oh hey, Flubsy—didn't even see you there."

❧ ❧ ❧

"You're not the only one. I loved him too, you know. Don't give me that look. I did—I do. I mean, that time when he bought us pizza? That, right there, was enough. Of course, I didn't know him like you did, but we still spent quality time together.

"Did you know he was eighty-three? Huh, did ya? So what were you thinking letting him come out here? Dragging him over mountains—that was some crazy bad math on your part.

"No, don't get mad, I'm not blaming you. He was doing exactly what he wanted. If there's a good way to go, that's gotta be it. But my point is that you miss him. And you're not alone in that—I miss him too.

"Also, it's important to mention that you could be rotting away in some dog pound. And I could be surviving on coffee creamers and ketchup packets. But we aren't, are we?

"What I'm trying to say is that I feel bad about taking the old guy's ID. And his tent and food and money. Feels like grave robbing. But I couldn't keep the both of us fed any other way. Wanted to say I'm sorry, if you don't approve. I've notice you haven't missed any meals, so probably you're okay with it."

Jane's only response to this confession was seven inches of slobbery wet tongue. With it she set to swabbing the deck as it were, mopping Bartleby down from cheek to chin.

"We're doing what we can. We're keepin' on keepin' on. With a little luck, maybe things'll work out. No promises—guess anyone can have a heart attack, right? Again with the look. No, that's not my plan, but I never planned on hiking the AT either.

"What's that—flappers, huh? So what, you're all done with this conversation then?"

Bartleby sat face to face with Jane hugged close to him. He gently bonked foreheads with her before letting her free to career off after butterflies.

❧ ❧ ❧

At Pochuck Mountain Shelter, V.A. Moose clumped over to Flutterby's hammock about as quietly as a guy named moose could be expected to move. He rumble-whispered, "You awake?"

She hadn't been. "What?"

"Another nightmare," was all V.A. Moose said before crunching back towards the shelter.

Flutterby found her Crocs, her headlamp and her way over to the shelter where Skunkers was tossing and moaning and sweating through his sleeping bag. It was just like old times—the moment she laid a hand on him, Skunkers noticeably quieted and calmed. He slipped back to a peaceful, snoring sleep shortly thereafter.

She'd done this dozens of times now. If she stayed touching him for about ten minutes, he would likely be good for the rest of the night. Unbeknownst to Skunkers, the gang had done some experimenting through Virginia. It turned out, it wasn't a gender thing. While physical contact from Coyote and Ella had no apparent effect on the nightmares, Bawdy's touch was calming, but not nearly as much so as Flutterby's. She couldn't imagine how her touch brought the big dope comfort, but she couldn't pretend it didn't bring her an inner satisfaction.

V.A. Moose shifted his feet over, made room for her at the foot of his pad. Which is where she woke in the morning.

Register: Wawayanda Shelter

7/14 Crappy shelter. Crappy .4 walk to water. Lucky for me, I just caught up to Bawdy and he's an equally crappy Scrabble player. Would've hated to go and get my own water. Considering I haven't lost in 15 games, it seems appropriate that I bingoed "dynasty."   Flubbers

Bawdy washed down the last bite of breakfast (three Hostess honey buns, their white icing just beginning to run in the morning sun) with a slug of warm Mt. Dew he'd bought back at the last mini-mart. He followed this with a wincing grimace of pain.

"What's the matter with you?" Flutterby asked.

He waved her off, "It's nothing, Nurse Flubby."

She was watching now, saw another, longer grimacing wince contort his features.

"Are you sick?"

Bawdy shook his head and slugged more Dew. "Uh-uh. It's just... euw that was a bad one...sometimes I get cramps. But they always go away...after a while."

"With the way you eat, I'm not surprised. All that refined sugar can cause muscle cramps."

"Sugar cramps, huh?" Bawdy sucked at the soda. "Sweet."

***

In New York, Pony Express slipped coming down the north face of Prospect Rock. He'd been distracted by a bird call and not watching his step. Ended up hyper-extending his right knee. He couldn't put weight on it without tack-sharp feedback sending tears to his eyes. Little choice but to plop his not-quite-but-certainly-on-its-way-to-being-bony ass down and wait. Luckily for him, Lazy JoJo and Coyote weren't very far behind. Between them, they carried his pack and emotionally supported his hobbling efforts forward. Emotional support wasn't either of their strong suits, but they tried their best.

They passed much of the time playing a final round of Dirty Birdy. A "game" invented back in Pennsylvania when Pony had been blathering on about birds and Coyote noted how many of the names sounded intriguingly illicit. This snowballed into Pony offering up actual bird names and Coyote or JoJo rejoining with a humorous (at least to them and all boys still stuck in their potty humor phase) pervification.

"American Woodcock," Pony offered.

To which Coyote promptly responded "Purple-headed Throbber."

"White-breasted Nuthatch."

"Saggy-breasted Nutsucker."

"Red-throated Loon."

"Deep-throated Knob Gobbler."

"Yellow-rumped Warbler."

"Lumpy-rumped Cornholer."

"Blue-eyed Cockatoo"

"Splooge-eyed Cocktease."

"Scissor-tailed Flycatcher."

"Beaver-stamped Felcher." This from Lazy Jojo.

Pony paused, "I don't even know what that is."

"I don't either and I've been to prison," Coyote mumbled under the snorting-guffaw of JoJo's laughter.

By the time they reached NY-17, his knee was puffed up to double its size. Conveniently, Pony's sister lived an hour and a half away. She'd been planning to bring the kids to meet him for a picnic up on Bear Mountain. When he called her from JoJo's phone, she answered and set right off. They waited with him until she arrived.

"Ice the hell out of it," Coyote said, "and I bet you'll be back out in no time."

Pony shook his head dejectedly and patted his swollen knee, "Nah, this duck is plucked."

All told, it took about four hours from foot slip to final extraction.

Once he was safely in his sister's car, yellow-blazing back to his life, Pony experienced a rapid series of emotions. In the course of the first few miles of asphalt, despondent grief became disappointment became frustration became resignation became a niggling sense of relief way down in his considerably diminished gut.

Register: Fingerboard Shelter

7/16 Need to make another trip back to Syracuse. My sugar
      momma (aka unemployment rep) wants to talk about how to
      "broaden the focus of my job search." Too bad for her
      I've been so busy cranking miles + humping mountains to
      bother mailing any resumes off.   Thunk

7/16 Before losing 35 pounds, I wouldn't have fit through the
      narrow rock formation known as the "Lemon Squeezer."
                                        —Bawdy-boy Slim

The summit of Bear Mountain was guarded by an impressive stone lookout tower offering a grand view of the Hudson River. At least Skunkers claimed it did. There were so many car and motorcycle tourists lingering around, Bartleby didn't want to go up and risk leaving Jane alone. Instead, he sat with her on a bare stone slope and watched a bluebird forage through the undergrowth for seeds and bugs or whatever else it deemed suitable for lunch.

Thunk and Bawdy rolled up shortly after Skunkers descended from the tower. "You guys really ought to go up and check out the view. It's pretty sweet."

Bawdy rolled his eyes, "You say that about every view."

"Don't be a hater, Bawds."

"I'm not a hater."

"Ya-huh."

"Nah-uh, dude, I'm just a lover with super high standards."

After losing most of twelve hundred feet in elevation over the next two miles, the trail led them through a heavily populated park. They passed between a glassy little lake and a massive lodge.

"Hotdog cart," Thunk called out like a sharp-eyed sailor on watch in a crow's nest. "Who wants? New York's Department of Labor is buying."

"Booya! I could definitely wolf down some barkers right now, bro."

Skunkers and Thunk peeled off and queued up at the cart.

"None for you?" Bawdy asked Bartleby.

"All these people…everywhere. It's…wow."

"Right? Let's go. I think the trail squirts through an actual zoo up ahead."

They kept moving, following the paved trail as it burrowed under the road and popped out by a municipal swimming pool.

"Jesus, this pool's bigger than that lake we just passed."

"It's like all of New York City decided to come swimming today."

"Uh-huh."

If there weren't actually thousands of people swimming, sunning and otherwise enjoying a scorching Saturday afternoon at the park and pool, it sure seemed like it. There were screaming children, big hairy bellies, gold chains and bulging tight bikinis for at least as far as Bawdy's bad eyes could see.

Bartleby and Jane stood gawping at the multitudes. When he

turned to say something to Bawdy, Bawdy wasn't there. He was kicking angrily at an ice cream vending machine.

"You got any singles, B? This biotch won't take mine."

"Doubt it."

"Can you at least look. I'd love me some Blue Bunny Brand ice cream sandwiches."

Bartleby dug through his wallet. "Here," he said, "I got two."

"Nice." Bawdy carefully fed them into the machine. The machine swallowed the bills with no complaint but failed to register them as a credit towards a purchase.

"Are you kidding me? This gerbil humping—" Bawdy kicked and jostled the machine to no avail. "Goddamn, can you believe this shit? Back in civilization for like thirty seconds and already I'm getting screwed over by the man."

Bawdy was still trying to recover his money when Skunkers and Thunk reappeared. Remnants of their hot dog feast were still visible in their beards.

"Come smack this thing for me will you, Skunks? It ate my money."

"It ate *my* money," Bartleby corrected.

While Skunkers took a turn beating the vending machine, Thunk quick scanned the pool area, "Is this the zoo?"

Bawdy snorted, "Weird as they all look to us, we've got to look worse. I'm wearing the same shirt and socks since Virginia, I haven't showered for a full week or shaved in three months."

"We don't look that bad," Skunkers said, giving Bawdy a once-over.

"This from the guy with mustard smeared in his eyebrows."

"Seriously?"

"Yeah, you're a mess, dude."

Bartleby gravitated to a sign near the entrance to the actual zoo.

"No dogs allowed," Bawdy read aloud. "That totally sucks."

"You want me to go and talk to someone?" Thunk offered. "You know, maybe they'd let you slide or...."

"No, we'll go back, loop around and catch the trail on the far side of all this."

"I'll come with," Skunkers offered. "Zoos make me sad."

The Trailside Zoo wasn't much more than a single asphalt thoroughfare passing by the occasional animal exhibit. As far as Thunk could tell, the animals were all local specimens. The family of porcupines asleep in their tree stand looked like huge, drying burdocks. The fox was hidden behind a rock, Thunk could only see a delicate black nose. Two coyotes restively paced the length of their cramped cage. Their coats were sleekly handsome and their movements graceful. The cement corral of the Bear's Den was bleakly spacious and looked to have been hosed clean recently. A few long-faced black bears sulked in the shade of a far corner, hardly moving except to swat at the occasional fly.

A sizeable crowd of city folk had gathered at the Bear's Den. They were patiently waiting for the bears to dance, rampage or otherwise provide entertainment.

It wasn't too long before one of the bears showed a little life. It got up, gave itself a good shake and yawned before ambling to center stage where it promptly squatted and shat. Deed done, the bear wasted no time returning to the cool comfort of the far shade.

"With my luck," Bawdy sighed, "these'll be the only bears I see on this trip."

"That sign says we're only a hundred and twenty feet above sea level," Thunk informed Bawdy.

"That's interesting-ish."

"Says this is the lowest point on the entire AT."

Bawdy nodded agreement, "We can always hope."

The suspension bridge spanning the Hudson River was a striking piece of engineering set amidst the lush topography of New York's Hudson valley. The bridge's support cables stretched to nearly half a mile and its two towers stood at least three hundred feet above the water. Skunkers and Bartleby had met up with Flutterby and the group of them were halfway across when, with almost no warning, two planes thundered close by overhead.

The low flying jets were blocky, short snouted and painted to match the desert camo scheme of Skunkers' hat.

"Booya, B-Boys!" Skunkers called after the departing jets.

When the planes passed out of sight, Flutterby looked at Skunkers questioningly.

"A-10 Thunderbolts. Except they're so ugly, most everybody calls them Warthogs. We called 'em B-Boys, short for Beastie Boys, cause they always came flying in so slow and low.

"Did you see that black nub sticking out the front? That's a seven barrel, 30mm cannon. Spins around like a Gatling gun, but like *way* bigger and faster. I saw one of them shred an old Ford Bronco once. Nuttin' left but the engine block and that looked like swiss cheese."

Register: Hemlock Springs Campsite

7/5 Mr. Zookeeper:
   Why not let the bears run free
   up on Bear Mountain?

                    High-Ku

Except for sporadic heat lightning and distant rumbles of thunder, it was dark and quiet when Lazy JoJo and Coyote arrived at the grounds of Graymore Friary. With their headlamps lighting the way, they followed blue blazes to a ball field where other tents were already set out for the night.

JoJo was footsore and tired as hell. By pushing themselves hard, she and Coyote had managed to crank out more than thirty miles in some of the most prickly, miserable humidity she'd ever experienced. She walked with her shoulders hunched and her arms propped out from her body like some muscle-bound beefcake from the Jersey Shore. Funny as it looked, she'd found this unnatural posture helped minimize the chafing inferno that was burning in her armpits.

Her legs felt weak and wobbly, like a couple of rubber chickens the Swedish chef had recently had his way with. Despite the generalized agony throbbing through her body, this last thought still made her chuckle. Back during Trail Days, Bawdy had play-acted the part of the Swedish Chef. The memory of him singing that crazy "umn bork! bork! bork!" song, tossing imaginary cooking utensils and reaching a squinty-eyed orgasm atop a bewildered muppet chicken (he'd enlisted Coyote as a stand in for the chicken) had been tickling her funny bone for hundreds of miles now.

"The book says the monks have an outdoor shower setup for hikers," Coyote stage whispered. "You wanna go first or should I?"

"You," she croaked. "I gotta sit for a bit."

These were the first words either of them had spoken since crossing Bear Mountain Bridge. Neither had had the interest or the energy necessary to maintain a running conversation.

JoJo killed her light and flumped to the ground. The dew-wet grass felt cool against her legs. It took some doing, but she wrestled her sweaty shirt off and sat there in a droopy sports bra, swiping her hands through the grass and wiping that moisture into her armpits.

Though, unfortunately, in JoJo's case, the term *armpit* wasn't technically accurate. When she lifted her arms overhead, raised mounds of flesh appeared in the spots where normal people (i.e. everyone else in the world) have sunken armpit hollows. It was just another unfortunate symptom of being big-boned and too massy. Despite losing inches off her waist, ass and legs, these arm mounds hadn't shrunk appreciably. In the course of her previous life driving truck, she hadn't been aware of this unusual condition, much less bothered by it. But now on the AT, where every day involved constant motion and the tiniest amounts of friction quickly led to physical discomfort, it was nothing short of a torment.

She couldn't see much in the dark, but she felt the raw abrasions well enough. Had been feeling them since that first week in Georgia. It was simply too much skin and sleeve fabric and hair and salty sweat all vying for room in too small a space. Hikers had suggested she try Gold Bond Triple Medicated Body Powder and Bodyglide anti-chaff cream. When these products didn't produce worthwhile results, JoJo tried keeping the works lubed up with globs of Vaseline. Any relief this provided was strictly temporary and came at the price of making a greasy mess of everything she owned. Eventually she gave up trying to manage away the symptoms of friction and focused on eliminating the motion responsible for the friction. And this meant walking along with her arms held out to the sides like the world's first thru-hiking ape.

When she finished cooling her salty, stinky, hairy mounds, JoJo produced an Almond Joy bar she'd bought from a vending machine back at Bear Mountain Zoo. Took one bite, lay her head back on her pack and listened to the sounds of Coyote's shower.

❦

JoJo woke sometime after dawn with a horrible crick in her neck, a square of bug netting draped over her face and a strange dog licking at the melted chocolate still clutched in her hand. Her teeth felt fuzzy and her mouth was Death Valley-dry.

The dog, an unkempt looking mutt, snarled when she pushed it away.

"Dogs can't eat chocolate," she grumbled.

When the mutt continued snarling, she gave a little you-get-what-you-deserve shrug and tossed the Almond Joy remnants, coconut meat and all, across the lawn. The dog snatched it up and trotted away into the woods without a backward glance.

Standing upright was a multi-stage ordeal as awkwardly prolonged and painful as one's first rectal exam. By the time she'd managed it, Coyote was peeking out from beneath his sleeping bag. He'd slept atop a picnic table under a nearby pavilion.

"Tried waking you, but no dice," he said. "So I gave you my bug mesh. Helped keep the suckers off your face, at least."

JoJo bent to retrieve the mesh square, missed and lurched unsteadily to one side.

Even bleary-eyed and out of sorts as she was, JoJo could see that the bare skin of her arms, shoulders, stomach and legs was pocked and swollen with red welts. She stumbled to the picnic table and removed her boots. Immediately set to rubbing the aching soles of her feet.

"I feel like roadside retread."

"Yeah, well," Coyote gestured to the hilltop looming steeply above them. Glimpses of crenelated stonework and gothic architecture were visible through the trees. "Unless you're gonna go up and ask the good friars to pray for your soul or your soles, you better take a quick shower, pork down last night's dinner and get ready to boogie. We got ground to pound."

🍁 🍁 🍁

The air at RPH Shelter was so thick and sticky that Bawdy had trouble sleeping. He lay in his sleeping bag, naked and sweating. With each shift of position his wet skin stuck to the synthetic material and felt clammy gross. Besides which, there was a rank foulness wafting up from the dankest depths of his bag he found difficult to ignore. It definitely would've made Coyote sick.

Despite the heat, Bawdy was sleeping in his bag because of the mosquitoes. His tarp was great in the rain and certainly light enough, but it really didn't offer much in the way of insect protection.

NNNNNNNNNNNNNNNN

Even with most of the night to think about it, he couldn't decide which he hated more—the whining drone of an inbound blood-sucker or that pregnant moment between when they landed and when they stuck him with their needle-nose.

NNNNNNNNNNNNNNNN

For every mosquito Bawdy killed, there was another waiting and willing to take its place.

NNNNNNNNNNNNNNNNN

"Welcome to Suck City," he grumbled. "Population: me."

His inflatable air mattress must've gotten punctured recently. It had a slowish leak, and unless he reinflated it every hour, he was essentially sleeping (or laying at least) directly on hard ground.

For lack of better options, Bawdy kept tossing, turning, slapping at bugs, swabbing sweat from his brow and occasionally taking a break from all that to huff and puff his mattress back to life. After which, it took a full five minutes for the dizzy headrush feeling to go away. He managed to steal a snatch or two of sleep, but nothing close to a real, rejuvenating rest. When the birds started doing their thing, he knew it was time to throw in the towel.

He got up and packed his gear as quickly and quietly as he could manage by headlamp. A headache was already thrumming behind his eyes when he set off hiking in the fuzzy dark of early morning.

🍁

In those first waking hours, Bawdy busted through what must've been a couple hundred cobwebs freshly strung across trail. It took him little time to decide that first-one-out-in-the-morning cobwebs sucked serious horsecock. He'd heard hikers complain about them, but being a late riser, had never experienced that particular unpleasantness himself. At a normal walking pace it was hard if not impossible to spot many of the invisible tangles. And even when he spotted gossamer filaments, avoiding them was no easy matter. As he was strapped to an unwieldy pack, limboing under or bushwhacking around weren't realistic options. He tried waving his hiking poles ahead of him, but that was only marginally successful and seriously impeded his walking pace. It seemed like there was really nothing for it but to put his head down and power through. Even so, cobwebs stuck to his arms and legs with a lingering creepy-crawly tickle. They found his mouth and eyes. Silky strands clung to his beard, his ears and the greasy hair of his head.

❧

Bawdy reached Morgan Stewart Shelter by midmorning. No one was there. He took a shaded seat at the table, set his notebook out and held his pen poised to write. After waiting like that for a full five minutes, he finally shook his head with disgust and scribbled a single line.

After slapping the notebook closed, he lay on the bench and shut his eyes. He only managed a catnap before waking in direct sunlight and drenched in sweat. Still no one around, so he pulled his gear together and started hiking again.

❧

When Bawdy saw Bartleby and Jane come strolling around a bend in the trail, his head was like to pop off. He stopped, closed his eyes, ground his teeth and waited for them to close the distance.

"Hey, Bawds. Got out early, huh?"

Bawdy opened his eyes and gave Bartleby a pathetic, pleading look, "Please don't tell me I'm southbounding."

Bartleby wore Chatter's latest. A navy blue baseball cap, the letters NY embroidered in white on the front. Beneath the hat, a crooked smile appeared on Bartleby's face.

"Nah," Bartleby shook his head, "I'm not going to tell you that. But I will suggest maybe you whip it around and start moving north."

❧

Bawdy was uncharacteristically quiet as he hiked in Bartleby's wake. On reaching Morgan Stewart Shelter (again), he kept right on going.

They passed another mile or so in silence.

"You ever hike south by mistake?"

"Uh-uh."

"Can't believe I did that."

"No big deal, really. Couple miles only."

"I know. Just sucks."

❦

It also sucked when the ruffed grouse came exploding out of the undergrowth, feathers all puffed up and wings going a hundred beats a second. The grouse wasn't a big bird, but it had a heavy body for its size and wasn't any kind of graceful flyer. Really fought for every inch of altitude. This one came straight at Bawdy—he could've reached out and touched it if he hadn't been so busy falling over backwards in surprise.

"Fa!!!!" Bawdy cried out as he went down. Then, with the bird safely away, "Christ! Did you *see* that?"

Bartleby reached out a hand and hauled Bawdy back to his feet. "Lost my glasses. See 'em? Thanks. Shit. What was that?! A turkey?"

"Didn't look like a turkey."

Bawdy held his hands out a good two and a half feet apart, "Thing was huge."

Bartleby put his hands about eight inches apart.

"Seriously?"

Bartleby nodded, "Pony would know exactly, but I'm gonna guess it was some kind of grouse."

"Grumpiest grouse ever. You gonna give me that at least?"

"That was one grumpy grouse."

"Grumpiest. Ever. Say it."

"Grumpiest grouse ever," Bartleby amiably conceded.

✤

"Is that what I think it is?"

"Uh-huh," Bartleby replied.

"Race you in."

The small, wooded lake looked about as inviting as one might imagine considering the stifling heat and humidity.

Bawdy dropped his pack on the rocky shore, peeled off his shirt and kicked his shoes free before Bartleby could even fish a snack out for Jane. Bawdy dove in and swam a few overhand strokes before turning to float on his back.

"How is it?"

Bawdy spit a stream of water straight up in the air. "A veritable wet dream."

Bartleby was pulling his socks down when Flutterby pulled up.

"Is that you, Flubby Pie?" Bawdy called. "Come on in, the water's great."

Flutterby wrinkled her nose like someone had just tried to hand her one of JoJo's mousetrap victims. "Didn't you see that sign about how they call this Nuclear Lake?"

"What? Shut up. Where's the Skunky One? I know he'll come swimming."

"He caught a hitch into Pawling for lunch. I can't remember, they've either got a deli or a diner or a drinking hole."

"That's like four days in a row he's gone in for town food."

Once Bartleby was barefoot, he gingerly stepped to the shoreline. Flutterby stopped him before he put a foot in the water. "I'm not kidding. The book says there was a plutonium accident here."

Bartleby might've still gone for a quick dunk, but then he watched Jane approach the water, take one little sniff and walk away. Since he'd been hiking around her, he couldn't remember a body of water Jane hadn't happily splashed through.

"I'm thinking you don't wanna be in that water, Bawds."

✤

The trail followed a series of raised bog bridges across a wide fen. To either side, tall marsh grasses swayed and bent under their own weight. It was late afternoon and already the peepers were singing their single note song. Just as suddenly as they had started, the marshlands ended at a commuter rail line. A little wooden platform with a blue bench and a sign overhead said Appalachian Trail in big station lettering.

"I remember reading about this," Bawdy said.

Bartleby looked up and down the tracks. "Where's it go? What state are we in?"

"New York still, I think. Let me check."

Bawdy reached for his data book. "What the hell? My pack's soaked."

When Bawdy emptied his pack, everything fell within the range of very damp to soaking wet. He got to his empty water bladder and held it up for inspection. Stuck his finger through the hole where hose used to meet bladder.

"Blew the bung right out of it."

"Musta been during that grumpy grouse attack."

"Good work, Columbo."

The bladder's drinking hose was still threaded through the hydration port on the body of his pack. Bawdy herky-jerked it free. Once it came fumbling loose, he hurled the plastic bladder to the ground. A growl-groan of tortured fury came boiling out of him. This was so primal and pained, Jane quick hid her head in Bartleby's armpit.

Bawdy took a running start and placekicked his empty pack. It launched with a creaking-clank, like some internal superstructure had snapped, and cleared the train tracks by a respectable margin. Because of all the topspin, it managed a couple cart-wheels before settling to a dusty stop with a muffled sigh.

Bawdy broke the strained silence that followed with a barely audible, "Sorry, man."

"There's still some sun, your bag will mostly dry out by tonight," Bartleby zipped Bawdy's sleeping bag open, laid it out to air on the back of the bench.

"It's not the bag. It needed a good douching anyway—smelled like a homeless shelter."

"Alright. Good."

"No—it's not alright. And it's not good. It's not anything but cataclysmically horrendous."

"Horrendous? What's horrendous?" Pause, "Who says that?"

"I do. I did anyway. Sorry, I see now that it was a little much."

"So?"

"So, I mean, what are we even *doing* out here?"

"You said we were staying at Wiley Shelter tonight—"

"Not right now." Bawdy waved his arms to indicate the trail, the surrounding woods, the world at large. "What am *I* doing out *here*? Walking two thousand miles? I'm just wasting time, hiding from life. Do you know why I came out here in the first place?"

Bawdy brandished his little black notebook. "I had this plan. Disappear into the peace and quiet of the great eastern woods and start writing *the* great American novel. Like Thoreau did, but you know, not like how he did, cause he didn't write novels or actually stay in the woods very much. Spent most of his time sneaking to town and boffing Emerson's wife.

"I was gonna write about the AT or maybe my sordid adventures in grad school. And a day hasn't gone by without me cracking this notebook open. Figure I could at least sketch out some character notes or maybe an outline, right?

"Here, I'm gonna read you the sum total of my collected wisdoms. Okay? Ready? 'You are nothing but a suck-ass grad student, a stuffed shirt, dot, dot, dot.'" Pause. "I couldn't even come up with a third alliterative insult for myself. I mean, how terrible is that?"

Bawdy flipped blank pages, "After beers in Harpers, I just wrote

'FRAUD'. And today's entry—'the dream is dead'.

"Old Man Trouble's always going on about how the trail provides. Like it's a mystical force giving hikers whatever they need most. Well—you got hiking poles, you got a dead guy's maildrops and now you're popping woodies like a fourteen year old. Don't get me wrong, I'm happy for you, B, but...what about me? So far all I got is a hunger I'd eat soggy shitsticks to fill, a looming case of radiation poisoning and a dripping wet pack."

With nothing but Bartleby's open-mouthed silence for answer, Bawdy higgledy-piggled his wet gear back into his pack and left drips dropping down in his wake as he trudged up the trail.

By the time northbound thru-hikers walked into New England, they had whittled away at their packs and possessions until only splinters and slivers remained. Except for maybe Skunkers, everyone had lightened their pack loads from those early days of wide-eyed wonder back in easy-rolling Georgia. By opting for less and lighter gear, thru-hikers commonly shaved ten, twenty or even thirty pounds of pack weight. Some few others, like Coyote, streamlined well beyond good sense.

It used to be, if the next resupply point was four days away, people carried five days of food. The prevailing attitude being "better safe than sorry." After playing pack mule for fourteen hundred miles, most hikers came around to a "light is right" mindset. Now those same people who carried five days of food in Georgia, only carried enough for three and a half days, intending for hunger to help drive them along at an appropriately brisk pace. Personal water requirements were dialed in so accurately, no one carried more than a few extra gulps beyond their expected needs. Gone were the plastic privy trowels, the compasses, spare clothes, leather bound journals, hairbrushes, deodorants and all extraneous electronics.

Which isn't to imply that everyone's load was identical. Far from it. While the majority of those still wending their way northward leaned towards minimalism and hauling only the barest of necessities, the definitions of the term "necessity" were as varied as the men and women hiking the trail.

Bawdy carried books. He couldn't help himself, especially once he got over his hang-up about ripping them apart. The middle section of this, the first half of that and the last six chapters of the other. He quickly read and traded them away to make space for new books. He was like a traveling library, a bookmobile (footmobile someone joked) lending, swapping and borrowing books all the way to Katahdin. Also, he carried one candle, so on the off chance of his headlamp breaking or the batteries dying, he'd still be able to read.

The cold, hard ground felt colder and harder since Old Man Trouble's last thru-hike. After a succession of sleepless nights, he picked up a second foam sleeping pad in Virginia. He'd been sleeping like the world's baldest princess ever since.

Fancy Pants didn't like being cold. Even during the hottest days in June and July, she carried a complete layer of fleece. Thermals, gloves, socks and a windproof hat that pulled down and covered not just her ears, but also the tip of her nose. She didn't need all of it every night, but no way was she taking chances.

Skunkers carried socks. At least seven pairs. They didn't all have partners, but such aesthetic issues rarely blipped his radar. He had super sweaty feet and sopping around in wet socks, day after day, wasn't an option. On the scorchingly driest days of the hike, he would stop and swap out for freshies as many as three times. If he wrung the wet pairs out good and hung them on his pack during the hiking day, they usually dried by morning.

Because she posted daily mixed-media updates to her blog, Ella carted a small production studio around with her. This included an ultrabook, a smartphone, a digital camcorder, a mini tripod and extra batteries, plus all the requisite plugs, dongles and adapters. She also hauled a portable solar charger that unfolded to the size of a cafeteria tray. Hung this on the back of her pack whenever the sun was shining.

Tommy Hawk carried a floral print Hawaiian shirt for wearing around camp at night. It was cottony cool and somehow never had a single wrinkle in it.

Flutterby kept an expired epipen way down in the bottom of her pack. Just in case. She wasn't particularly allergic to bee stings, but she'd once seen a patient get rushed into the emergency room, their face and lips inflated to monstrous proportions and their throat puffed shut. They were DOA and it had impressed her as a particularly unpleasant way to check out.

On top of all his own gear and food, Thunk made sure to carry little treats he could share with Fancy. He thought of it like his own personal MasterCard commercial. A bar of Hershey's Milk Chocolate: 1.55 ounces. A big box of Grape Nerds: 6 ounces. Ripe peaches: 2 pounds. The way her face lit up: Priceless.

Bartleby carried along his doubts and fears and a double helping of self-loathing. Strictly speaking, none of this emotional detritus weighed a single ounce. Still though, he would've gladly traded it for a sixty pound sack of quikrete.

❦ ❦ ❦

Register: Ten Mile River Shelter

7/20 Must be back on home turf. Can smell nutmeg in the air.
Bartleby

❦ ❦ ❦

It was a nice change of pace to find a decent grocery store in Kent, Connecticut. In addition to the usual resupply purchases, Bawdy bought a bunch of green grapes and two baguettes. Bartleby got a box of red wine. Fancy Pants picked up hunks of muenster and havarti cheese. They wandered to a cemetery near the middle of town, nestled in amongst the old headstones, took a load off trail-sore feet and had themselves a picnic. The threesome spent some time puzzling out the newest addition to Chatter's hat collection. It was woven straw, with upward pointing ends. Looked as much like a bird's nest as anything else.

Fancy pointed at Bartleby's shirt, "Like the hat your Chiquita Banana chica's wearing."

"Where are we again?" Bawdy asked.

"Connecticut."

"I got it," Bawdy clapped his hands. "It's a Huck Finn hat. Twain actually lived in Hartford when he wrote Huck Finn. And the Mississippi and the AT really aren't that different, you know, metaphorically speaking. I gotta give it up for your boy Chatter, B. He was good."

Fancy snatched the hat from Bawdy and popped it on, "How's it look? Too tomboyish?"

"Nope. Yours if you want it," Bartleby said.

With the mystery solved and the wine sucked away (literally—they drank directly from the spout) they were starting to make noise about pushing on.

Which is about when a police car rolled up. A single electronic chirp burped from the siren. Having spent the majority of his life living in Connecticut, and knowing well the state's reputation for puritanical uptightedness, Bartleby had been halfway expecting to get rousted for most of the afternoon.

What Bartleby hadn't expected was for Rollin', Flutterby and Skunkers to come spilling out of the police car's back seat like sprinkles from a hastily eaten donut.

Before accelerating away, the cop called over, "Don't you leave a mess behind."

There was a flurry of high-fives, a general outpouring of good humor and, when Skunkers got back from the package store, a thirty rack of Bud Lights to share around.

🍁

Counting Jane, seven of them merrily crammed into the cheapest motel room available. Flutterby showered first and Bawdy called next, but somehow Skunkers beat him into the bathroom.

Bawdy pounded the door with his fist. "I had next, Cheeseball!"

"Occupado."

"You better not butthole the soap, dude," Bawdy warned. "We all gotta use the same one."

Strategically, Fancy chose to shower last. In theory, this meant she could stay in as long as she wanted, but the tub's drain was so slow her shower was curtailed by the dirty water pooling around her shins. The water took most of the night to trickle away and left a grimy black ring in the tub. When she finished her shorter than expected shower, Fancy wrapped a towel around her head, one around her body and set to texting with Thunk. Just that day, he'd rented a car and high-tailed it home. He had a morning meeting with his unemployment rep and hoped to be back on trail by late evening.

Flutterby and Skunkers shared one bed, Bawdy and Bartleby the other. Bawdy and Flutterby set up the Scrabble board on the night-stand between them. The TV screen was snowy and the volume muted, but that didn't keep Skunkers from chugging beers and flipping back and forth between reruns of *In The Heat of the Night* and *Judging Amy*. After months of immersion in the calm and quiet of the natural world, he was utterly captivated.

Having drawn the short straws, Fancy and Rollin' were relegated to sleeping on the floor. Which didn't turn out to be so bad—they made nice little nests for themselves using all the spare sleeping gear. They were quite comfortable, so long as they could keep Jane from snuggling in on top of them.

After savagely walloping Bawdy yet again, Flutterby wandered out to a vending machine. She came back with a can of root beer.

Bartleby's breath caught in his chest when he laid eyes on it. Though neither of them actually liked the taste of it, he and Angie had always said A&W was their drink. Angie & Walter. He was overcome by a sudden ferromagnetic longing that struck with a spectacular inner violence. Bartleby's heart struggled against the bars of its thoracic prison, threatened to break free and escape eastward. It wanted to run home to Angie with or without the rest of him.

She was close too; no more than an hour's drive.

"Let me borrow a phone," Bartleby said.

Skunkers lobbed his across the room, "If you're calling for more pizza, I want in."

"Calling my wife."

"Don't do it, dude," Bawdy grabbed for the phone but missed. "Call her in the morning if you still want to. After four months of no contact, you do not wanna drunk dial her."

Fancy Pants came over to Bartleby's side of the bed. She sat next to him, gave him a doting smile and gently patted his arm. Then she twisted his nipple as hard as she could.

"Owwwww!"

This titty-twister provided ample distraction for her to swipe the phone out of Bartleby's hand. "Anyone gives him their phone, they're gonna get way worse. In fact, hand them all over to me. I'll sleep on them just to be safe."

❧

Bright cracks of light shone through the blinds. Doing his utmost not to wake anyone, Skunkers carefully tiptoed to the bathroom and gently closed the door. Once inside, he let go with a whiz that sounded like water pouring from a five gallon bucket and followed that with one of his infamous first-thing-in-the-morning farts. Except for the echo, it was indistinguishable from the trumpeting of a bull elephant.

Tired as they were, no one could even pretend to sleep through this.

With his morning ablutions completed, Skunkers checked on the cooler he'd improvised from a cardboard box and a garbage bag. "We got a problem," he said in a serious tone.

"Shut up, Skunkers," Bawdy growled.

"Seriously, Bawds. We got eleven floaters."

Skunkers tossed a beer to Bartleby and cracked one for himself, "We aren't in the business of leaving good men behind, are we?"

Under protest, Bawdy drank a beer. Fancy drank half of one and dumped the rest. Flutterby refused on the contention that she'd told him not to buy so many beers last night.

Bartleby didn't much care about the ethical conundrum of leaving undrunk beers behind v. drinking before 8am, but he did have a sharp hangover and a few beers couldn't help but help with that. Or at least postpone it. Also, Skunkers was so earnest, it seemed silly to do anything but give the kid a hand. They each drank two and packed the rest back to trail. After stumbling a few miles to where the trail paralleled the Housatonic River, they found a nice shady spot, watched the water go tumbling by and set to work on the stragglers.

After wading into the water up to her chest and drinking her fill, Jane flopped down nearby and fell asleep. She was having a leg-thumping doggie dream in short order.

"Why'd you wanna call your wife last night? I mean, didn't you catch somebody checking her oil?" As if this phrase wasn't quite graphic enough, Skunkers accompanied it with the universal finger-through-a-circle gesture.

"Nope."

"Really? That's what Coyote said."

"Which one is he again?"

"Little guy with the big greasy grin."

Bartleby nodded, he vaguely remembered, "No, Coyote had it wrong. I mean, I don't know what's going on now, but back then Angie didn't know what to do with me. I was a mess."

"Yeah? What about?"

"I don't know. Life and lots of other stupid stuff. None of it seems so big and bad out here, but...."

"So if Fancy lets you make that call—what do you say?"

"I don't know...I'm sorry, I love you and I'm in Kent, please come get me."

"You wanna go off trail?"

Bartleby drank deeply and thought about this, "Not really. I just...."

"Only been gone a few months."

"Lot longer than that since I've been home in any way that mattered."

"You still want it, you can use my phone."

"Nah. I guess the moment's passed. Best way home for me is to keep hiking."

Skunkers nodded sagely, finished off his beer, burped and cracked a new one.

"That the last one?"

"Yeah. Poor bastards never had a chance, huh?"

In the weeks since Hairbrained left her to hike her own hike, Fancy had come to appreciate many aspects of trail life (eating, talking and walking to name a few) that had previously felt unbearable. Chief among these was her nightly nesting ritual. Where before she'd had to fight for breathing room in a shared tent, now she could cozy in and stretch out however she pleased.

In the hurried division of gear that took place in Harpers, Hairbrained got "their" tent and left Fancy the squeaky water filter and the cooking pot he'd given her for Christmas. After deciding to continue northbounding, Fancy's first order of business was to buy a pricy little one-man (or in this case one-woman) shelter. She quickly grew to love the newfound privacy and comfort.

Out of the box, the tent had stunk of stale chemicals and plastic, but after a few nights that smell was replaced by an odorous funk of mud, mildew and sweaty socks. Fancy considered this new aroma an improvement, which was fortunate, as it grew stronger with each passing day.

After squeezing out what she hoped would be the last pee of the evening, Fancy crawled into the tent and zipped the screen door closed behind her. With the light from her headlamp illuminating the tent's farthest reaches, she set about killing any and all bugs unlucky enough to have followed her inside. This, generally, left the tent's bug mesh marred with fresh bloody black smears.

Next, she filled a fleece-lined stuff sack with every available stitch of clothing, all excess fabric and anything else on hand that was remotely soft. At one time or another she'd used her hiking shoes, toilet paper and even a sloshing water bladder to poof up her pillow. Such extreme measures wouldn't be necessary tonight though. With no rain in the forecast, Fancy opted to sleep on her tent's rain fly instead of under it.

Once fully squirmed into her sleeping bag, she found it necessary to jostle her sleeping pad over to avoid a particularly sharp root poking into her knee. Shifting one's pad while laying on it required manual dexterity, bodily coordination and the patience of Mother Nature herself. After shimmying the pad away from the offending root, Fancy found herself lying half in and half out of a rut. Additional bouts of shimmying introduced her to a raised mound, a steady decline dipping off to one side and a trio of pebbles before bringing her back around to that original sharp root.

After working herself into a relatively comfortable position (and yes, sleeping on the ground with any level of comfort generally required work), Fancy stowed her headlamp in the tent's gear pocket and lay back with nothing more than a silky cocoon separating her from the world.

Without realizing it, she sighed contentedly, snuggled her knees up to her chest and listened to distant snatches of shelter conversation until drifting off.

🍁 🍁 🍁

Riga Lean-to was situated up high on a bluff with a grand view of Connecticut woodlands. It was dark when Coyote got there, but the moon was almost full and already up, so he could just make out the forest in its textured monochrome magnificence. The shelter was empty save for a gracious Danish couple he'd never met before. Quiddler and Blue Cheese. They were, without a doubt, the two best looking people he'd ever seen coupled together. Both of them were tall blondes with creamy skin and sharp blue eyes. They spoke better English than he did and seemed genuinely happy for his company.

Started right in telling him about a spotted fawn they'd seen earlier that day.

Coyote was bored senseless before he got his shoes off.

He didn't want beautiful Danes or friendly Danes or any other kind of Danes. He didn't want to hear stories about a knock-kneed Bambi frozen with fear and he didn't want to look at a dozen Bambi pictures either. Coyote wanted cuttingly sharp remarks from Bawdy, casual brush-offs from Flutterby and all kinds of easy fun at Skunkers' expense. He wanted his old crew.

Towards that end, he was gaining on them. Pounding miles and covering serious distance each day. It couldn't be much longer now.

He woke later in the night to the distant baying of coyotes. As they howled and yowled and otherwise celebrated themselves under a high moon, he lay in the dark pining for his own pack.

❦ ❦ ❦

Register: Sage's Ravine Brook Campsite

7/24 IMO: Whoever left their crappy tent and camping gear strewn about this campsite should be strung up by their genitals and cornholed with a 4H blue-ribbon winning corncob! Teach 'em what 'pack it in, pack it out' is all about. These JACK-HOLES didn't just leave behind some garbage, they started a dump! Only YOU can help keep our shelters clean: death, dismemberment and ritual sodomy to all litterbugs!!!

—The Original Grand Poohbah

"Is it me," Bawdy wondered aloud, "or is Poohbah almost as big a tool as the 'jack-holes' that left this shit here? And I mean that figuratively. There's no way he's literally as *big* as whoever trashed this place."

"No," Flutterby said, "Mr. Huff-n-Puff's a surprisingly big tool. Back in Virginia, he spent an entire day talking at me about himself. I only stuck around him to see how long he could keep it up. He showed me, the dope was still going strong when I went to sleep."

"And how is him ranting and raving in the register going to solve—"

Bartleby cut in, "How far to the next town?"

"I don't know. Another ten-twelve miles."

Bartleby helped himself to the big serrated folding knife Skunkers kept clipped to a pack strap.

The abandoned tent was a three-man monstrosity complete with a vestibule big enough to fit a Weber Grill. It was storm battered, broken and deflated. Slimy pools of black water had collected amidst the swaths of slack material.

It wasn't just 12 pounds of tent that had been left behind either. There was a thirteen-inch cast iron skillet (an easy 6 lbs.), two pair of wet jean shorts (2-3 lbs. each) and an Igloo cooler with a broken handle. The cooler was filled with a variety of ruined canned goods (a particularly nasty 8 lbs.).

Bartleby shook the tent out like one might shake a beach blanket and sent water and debris flying in every direction. Then he began slicing it up.

"What are you doing, B?"

"Gonna carry this ugly sucker out of here."

"Seriously?" Bawdy was shocked by the idea. It went against the 'light is right' thru-hiking mindset. He looked from Skunkers to Flutterby and back to Bartleby. "Shit. Okay. Gimme half of that thing."

The next morning, when they arrived at the Appalachian Trail Conference's New England Regional Office in South Egremont, Massachusetts, Skunkers held the cooler in his arms and had the skillet lashed to his pack. Sections of tent body were visible on both Bawdy and Bartleby's packs. The broken tent poles stuck above Flutterby's pack like a bent antenna.

The office wasn't open yet, it was still too early, so they wrapped everything into a big wet bundle and left it on the front porch with a note.

❋ ❋ ❋

It was nearing dusk when Flutterby passed under a twining vine of honeysuckle. The smothering sweet smell caught at the back of her throat. She stood there breathing it in with her eyes closed until a furious twister of midges swept through and forced her to move on.

❋ ❋ ❋

Skunkers, Bartleby and Jane arrived at Mt. Wilcox South Shelter first. Rollin' was close on their heels. Flutterby came in ten minutes later and finally, some ways behind her, a very wet Bawdy slogged his way to the shelter. They huddled together for an impromptu respite from the surprisingly frightful weather. For the last few hours, the rain had alternated between torrential downpour and blinding monsoon. It showed no signs of letting up.

If one were going to wait out a rain squall in a shelter, Mt. Wilcox South was a good choice. The structure was relatively new and generously proportioned, with a high ceiling that extended out like an awning over a picnic table.

After sucking down a few quarts of water, a soupy hot lunch and half a roll of Necco wafers, Bawdy lay back and sighed contentedly.

If anything, the rain was drumming against the roof with increased intensity. Which was just fine, he'd rather come to enjoy spontaneous hiking breaks.

"Hey, Skunks," Bawdy cajoled, "tell us a story."

Skunkers was meticulously carving his trail name into the table's planking, "That's your department, Doc."

"Nah, I'm closed on account of weather. Come on—I wanna hear stories about jumping out of planes or some shit. You gotta have some good ones saved up."

"Uh-uh," Skunkers said, "I got nuttin'."

"How about something from back in your early days as a country mouse. A quaint anecdote from rural America. Or, or something from Iraq. A haunting tale of struggle and survival."

"I don't tell war stories."

"Fine, but you've gotta have some little gem tucked away."

To be fair, Skunkers didn't actually scratch his temple, but he might as well have. He sat there for a long moment, visibly thinking, sorting through his memories for one worth repeating. Nothing readily came to mind.

"Okay, then," Bawdy prompted, "how about telling us how you ended up hiking the AT."

"That's easy."

"Yeah?"

"Yeah, me and Monkey Bars McCook made this pact to thru-hike when we came back from Iraq."

"You got a friend called Monkey Bars? Goddamn," Bawdy crowed, "tell us more."

"He was this big, burly mother-freakie I met in Basic. Got me by a couple inches every which way. They had us doing this obstacle course and Private McCook was working across a section of climbing rungs and one a them broke off in his hand. Wasn't ten seconds before the drill sergeant started up calling him Monkey Bars."

"Great name."

"Turned out we got selected for Ranger Training together. Let me tell ya, that was some shit. They had us up for days at a time, marching all over Georgia. Live fire exercises, the whole works. Anybody see rangers trooping past Hawk Mountain Shelter?"

"I did," Flutterby said.

"Well, that was me and McCook a couple years earlier. We must've hiked over Hawk Mountain a dozen times, and each time there were thru-hikers chilling at the shelter, looking about as carefree and happy as we were exhausted and miserable. And then one time, Monkey Bars says, 'Danger Dick, you and me are gonna come back from Iraq and hike that Appalachian Trail.' And I was like, shit yeah, we are. So here I am."

"So what happened to your friend McCook? He bag out?"

"Nah. He never came back from Iraq."

Rain drummed down against the roof.

"Damn," Bawdy said, "I'm sorry man."

"No, it's okay. He married this Czech chick and opened a Thai restaurant in Prague."

❦ ❦ ❦

Register: Mt. Wilcox South Shelter

7/13 Buzzing by my head,
      the Massachusetts skeeter
      could be the state bird.

                    High-Ku

❦ ❦ ❦

Sensing the kill was close at hand, Coyote pushed on past dark. A big bright moon shone down, followed him through the woods like a policeman's flashlight. Sometime around midnight, he laid out his sleeping bag on the trail. From his wily grin all the way down to the far ends of his chicken-legs, every part of him ached or throbbed or

170

twinged or straight-up screamed for rest.

He woke up some time later to a high-pitched gibbering. The noise was so close and so ridiculously out of place that Coyote thought someone was pulling a prank.

"Hey—who's out there?"

No response. Coyote got his headlamp out and flashed it around. Didn't immediately see anything, so he followed the noise to a tree. And there, hugging the trunk just above eye-level was a porcupine. A big fluffy fellow with a shag of needles, hooked claw hands and prominent buck teeth.

"Hey, Porker," Coyote grumbled. He was too tired to appreciate this interlude on any meaningful level.

Porker ignored him, kept on with a sing-song jabber as it chewed tree bark.

"I'm trying to get some sleep here, so maybe you could stuff a sock in it?"

The porcupine didn't quiet down much, but Coyote had slept through worse.

When he woke before dawn, he was up and hiking again in less than three minutes; set off with a quick stride and a grim determination that today was the day he was catching the old crew. No more rolling solo, no more reading about their good times in the registers. Just one more hard push and he'd have them.

Upper Goose Pond Cabin was only a mile south of the footbridge spanning the Massachusetts Turnpike. The pond's water was deep and clean all the way out to a rocky islet. It seemed about the perfect spot for dirty thru-hikers to pass a hot afternoon and maybe wash off some of the accumulated stink and grime.

Bawdy had only been intending to lunch there, but after setting eyes on the place, he knew he was done hiking for the day. After a quick meal, Bawdy borrowed Thunk's sleeping pad and sloshed into the water. Amongst their other qualities, closed-cell foam sleeping pads float. Not well, but enough for Bawdy to swim out to where the sun was on the water and lay back with his eyes closed. Before long, Skunkers and Flutterby swam out and joined him.

"Didn't know you were packing a bikini, Flubsy."

"I'm not. Sports bra and undies."

A sickly canine yowling cut short this discussion of Flutterby's unmentionables.

OWWWW-OWWWW-OOOOWWWWWWWWWWWW

Skunkers looked to the shore, concern scribbled across his face, "Z'at Jane?"

OWWWW-OWWWW-OOOOWWWWWWWWWWWW

They couldn't quite see the shore well enough to tell, but then Jane started up barking.

"Bartleby's got Jane over by the cabin. That *noise* came from around the pond."

Skunkers wasn't listening, he was already paddling hard for shore.

OWWWW-OWWWW-OOOOWWWWWWWWWWWW

He got there about the same time Coyote loped out of the woods. Grinning wide as the Grand Canyon.

"Goddamn, Yote—you making that racket?"

"I don't know nothing about any racket, but I've been reduced to howling at the moon since you all abandoned me in Virginia."

Skunkers scooped Coyote up, pack and all, in a crushing hug. Lifted him clear off the ground.

"Hey, hey—you're soaking wet!"

"Got half a mind to toss you in."

Flutterby followed Skunkers' hug with one of her own. Bawdy gave Coyote knucks, a high-five and knucks again for good measure, "Thought we lost you for sure."

"Well, now I'm back with you suckers for good. You're gonna need the Orkin man to get rid a me."

Jane charged up and stuck her nose into Coyote's crotch. Bartleby, Thunk, Rollin' and Fancy weren't far behind.

"I know this dog, is that old crust here? I'm still pissed about—"

"He died in Pennsylvania," Bartleby said.

"Seriously? He was that Mad Chatter dude? I read about that in the registers."

Bawdy waved a hand at the others, "Yote, let me introduce Rollin' and Thunk and—"

Coyote put up a hand, "STOP. Don't bother, Bawds. Nothing personal, folks, but I'm choked full up to here on new faces. Enough is enough already. I mean, how many people are out here hiking this damn trail anyway? It's crazy. Doesn't anybody have a job?"

❧

Early evening. Hanging out on the front porch of Upper Goose Pond Cabin.

"So, I gotta ask, Yote," Skunkers said. "Where's your pack?"

"What'd'ya mean? It's right here."

"Where's the rest of it? That's only like half a pack."

"Got everything I need, see for yourself. But I wanna sift through all your shit."

"Beat it."

"It'll be fun. Like show and tell."

"Uh-uh."

"I've been dying to see what all is in there since Georgia. Come on. I'll buy drinks next bar we hit."

"How many drinks?"

"How many you want?

Skunkers twirled his finger around, "Enough for everybody. When we hit the Long Trail Inn. The book says there's an Irish pub there."

"Everybody who?"

"Everybody anybody. All us hikers."

Coyote grimaced. This was a terrible deal, but still, it was exactly the sort of ridiculousness that he'd been in such a hurry to catch up to.

"Alright, Skunkies—you got a deal."

✦

Skunkers never bothered poking through Coyote's rig. He wasn't the least bit curious and he knew the only thing he'd see was the absence of things. And what kind of looking was that?

"Why do you still have topo maps from the Smokies?"

"I liked the Smokies."

"Yeah, me too, but they were like twelve hundred miles ago."

Skunkers pulled more folded maps out of a side-pocket, "I like maps."

"PA? Virginia? You got like five pounds of paper here."

Coyote was going grab-bag style, blindly sticking his arm in and selecting items at random. As this was obviously going to be the evening's entertainment, the usual crowd had gathered round.

He pulled out a thick cotton hoody with RANGER spelled across the front in gold letters.

"Never seen you wear this."

"It's my pillow."

A single D cell battery, "What's this for?"

"Dunno, but it's a good battery. Couldn't just throw it away."

A well-used jar of Vaseline.

"That's for the friction," Skunkers explained. "I got lots of friction."

When it came out, Coyote passed the spyglass around.

Fancy looked through it, but couldn't see anything. "Does it work?"

"It's sorta fucked. Got a cracked lens or suttin'. If you jiggle it, sometimes you can unfuck it."

"This the same six pound, two-man tent you were carrying before?"

"Yep."

"But there's only one of you, right?"

A water pump. "You ever use this?"

"Once maybe, but pumping sucks. That's why I got the Aquamira."

"A family-size spray can of Brut deodorant?"

"For my feet. Helps with all the sweat."

"And what—did you swap out your Obama PEZ dispenser for Batman?"

"Batman's my backup. You know, just in case I lose Obama. Gotta have a backup."

"You don't need a dispenser to eat PEZ."

Now Skunkers shook his head like maybe Coyote was the loony bird.

"This your food bag? It's smaller than I would've guessed."

"That's my dinner bag. This one's lunch and there's another smaller one for breakfast."

"You're carrying *three* food bags? Gotta be like twenty-five pounds of food."

Just the idea of that was enough to put a contented glimmer in Skunkers' eyes.

"Look at this—I snuck this rock into your pack way back in Virginia. You never found it?"

"No, I think I did."

"So why's it still in your pack?"

"Thought it was kinda funny."

"A can of beer?"

"Oooo-yeah, a stowaway. Gimme that guy, I'll show him how we deal with stowaways."

Coyote was fishing deep now. He pulled out flattened beer cans, the packaging from various foods, a corkscrew, even a carved wooden figurine Skunkers had picked up in Hot Springs.

"Keep meaning to send that to my moms."

"You got all kinds a bric-a-brac in here, huh?"

"Yeah," Skunkers somehow admitted with a straight face, "I always been bric-a-brac-able."

Continuing with his investigations, Coyote pulled out a *Backpacker* magazine Skunkers had "borrowed" from the hostel back in Delaware Water Gap. A few yellow, crumpled McDonald's cheeseburger wrappers. Then his eyes went big. He quick looked at Skunkers' feet (Big Boy was wearing Crocs) and they went bigger.

"No way, hombre," Coyote said. "Please tell me you aren't still carrying that flip-flop."

Coyote pulled it out and, sure enough, it was a left-footed flip-flop, with eyes and a face markered on.

"Yeah, that's Flipper. Didn't seem right to get rid of him just cuz I lost his partner. Wasn't his fault, right? He's like Spalding from that Tom Hanks movie."

"Wilson," Bawdy corrected.

"Yeah-yeah," Skunkers agreed, "whatever."

❦ ❦ ❦

Register: October Mountain Shelter

7/27 Snapped my 300th varmint last night   —Lazy JoJo

❦ ❦ ❦

If not for the traffic circle, the paved parking lot and all the touristy types who had driven up to the summit, Mt. Greylock would've been an impressive place.

Skunkers sprawled on a bench, "That Bascom Lodge is something, huh?"

"It was a CCC project way back when. Built with all local materials."

"Those CCC'ers did nice work, huh?"

"Yeah, in a let's-ruin-yet-another-mountaintop-with-buildings-and-roads-so-stupid-lazy-people-can-get-up-there-too kind of way," Bawdy said. "Here he goes. Watch."

A hang glider launched off a nearby cliff edge. Dipped down out of sight. After a moment, the glider caught an updraft and soared vertical. The pilot hooked his feet in behind him and banked off into the blue.

"Sweet. Wanna check out the Veteran's War Memorial Tower?"

"You mean the thing that looks like a huge chess pawn?"

"It's a lighthouse tower or something. A beacon."

"It looks exactly like the missing pawn from the world's largest chess set, and symbolically speaking, I don't see how that's a nice comment on veterans."

"It doesn't look like a pawn."

Bartleby wandered over in time to watch the next hang glider take off.

"What's that tower look like to you, B?"

He squinted up, "Dunno. A big stone pawn?"

❦ ❦ ❦

Register: Wilbur Clearing Shelter

7/28 ***ATTENTION HIKERS***

If you are even remotely close behind, PLEASE consider getting the lead out, putting the petal down and burning some (vibram soled) rubber. Coyote Slick is buying drinks for any and every one that shows up thirsty at the Long Trail Inn. Ya don't know Coyote? It don't matter. Ya don't drink? Maybe it's time to start. Ya don't think you can catch up in time? That's why God gave you a thumb. Come by foot, by car or by camel—we don't care, so long as you come thirsty.

C' YA in 111.3 miles!!!   Skunkers

❦ ❦ ❦

"Fook."

"What, like how the Irish say it?"

"Yep."

"In England they say feck."

"Mudsucka."

"Cheeseball. I met her too."

"So? Shoulda said it first."

"Mothahumper." Bawdy fired this last with an easy rapidity that was nothing but discouraging to Coyote.

"I been saving those for three hundred miles now."

"You aren't gonna beat me."

Coyote grunted noncommittally.

"So what's the news from behind? Who's doing what?"

"Lazy JoJo's a lot stronger than she looks. And Pony Express is off trail. Blew out his knee pretty bad. Me and JoJo helped him get out to a road."

"That sucks."

"Yeah, but I don't think he was too broken up really. Did you hear Fast Eddie got bit by a rattler?"

"No way."

"Him and Goodtimes Charlie had this thing where they would pick up any snakes they came across. Not just the little ones but copperheads and stuff. I personally saw Charlie pick up a black that was at least six feet long. Thing looked like it coulda swallowed him whole."

"Sounds like Fast Eddie needs a new trail name. Something like, Not Really that Fast Eddie or maybe—"

"I think Donk would pretty much cover it. And let me say it's good to be back rolling with the crew. Nothing but duds and dummies back there."

"How are those new kicks?"

"They're ultralight. Each one weighs seven ounces. Which is about ten ounces less than your shit-kickers. Saving more than a pound on my feet alone. And they say a pound on the feet is equal to ten pounds on the back."

"They look flimsy."

"Oh, they're super flimsy. Can feel everything through these soles. Hurts like hell."

✤ ✤ ✤

Register: Congdon Shelter

7/29 Is anyone thinking we might be doing permanent damage to our legs? It's gotten so my knees never not hurt. Going uphill hurts. Going downhill hurts. Recently, going over level ground has begun to hurt. Pretty much, when I bend them, my knees hurt. Except, when I don't bend them, they still hurt.   —Busted Up Bawdy

✤ ✤ ✤

Lounging around outside the Bennington, Vermont post office.

"Now that, sir—that is one serious hat!" Skunkers exclaimed loud enough to turn heads. He snatched it out of Bartleby's grasp, "I wasn't a big fan of that last one. I mean, what have the pilgrims done for us lately, right? But this is a beaut. How's it look?" Skunkers walked to a window, inspected his reflection there. "What'd'ya call it?"

The hat was a tricorner special straight out of the revolutionary war. The wide brim's thick green felt was pinned up on either side to make a triangle shape. The edges of the brim were done over in gold brocade. Inside, a small tag had the words "Green Mtn. Boys" stitched into it.

Skunkers stuck it onto Bartleby's head, "Looks good, man."

Bartleby quick checked his reflection before tossing the hat back, "It's all you, man. I'm sticking with the Yankees cap."

"Stankees," Bawdy interjected.

"Seriously?" Skunkers asked. "But I can't wear it hiking. It'll get ruined."

"Mail it home, eat soup out of it—I don't care, it's yours."

"Sweet, dude. Thanks."

* * *

Vermont's Green Mountains were green. They were leafy green, dappled green, pine green, bottle green, rolling green and, of course, forest green. Except where cleared for ski runs, mountain summits were tree-covered; the bases flush and fertile with grassy meadows and farmer's fields. The AT itself was a great green tunnel; a secret, leafed over and hidden away for the summer. The world beneath this living roof was cast entirely in shades and shadows of green-gray.

Lazy JoJo didn't much care about the surrounding verdure and the foliage hanging overhead. She could take it or leave it. What she did care about was the sensation of burning and itching she was feeling down below. She had a five-alarm fire blazing up about as fierce as she'd ever felt. It was all she could do this past hour to not go after it with the spike-tip of her hiking pole.

Last night, she'd sailed past Bennington without giving it the consideration she now realized it deserved. At the time, the decision made sense. She'd recently taken on supplies in North Adams; had plenty of food for the forty miles to Manchester. She had momentum and little interest in seeing yet another trail town.

All the trail towns were nice, even the ones that weren't. In her mind, they all blended together. And nice or not, trail towns were all the same: bottomless sinkholes waiting to swallow weak-willed hikers. She hadn't gotten on trail with the intention of stopping at every town and watering hole along the way; she'd already seen more than her share of dusty, dying towns while driving truck.

Lazy JoJo wasn't a person who pursued creature comforts. It just wasn't her nature. Still, though, she'd reached a point now where she would've checked off a long list of dirty deeds for a hot shower and a supersized tube of Preparation H.

From JoJo's perspective, there was no question about it—Hell Hollow Brook was heaven sent. She had her pack off, her boots unlaced and what was left of her vastly reduced "wide-end" soaking in the clear, tumbling waters quick as you please.

Presently, Old Man Trouble came tromping along.

"Heya. How's the water?"

JoJo nodded. He knelt on the bank, dipped his face in and came up spluttering and gasping.

"It's freezing. You gotta be numb all the way to your neck."

JoJo just smiled.

❦ ❦ ❦

Sleepy-eyed and bedheaded, Bartleby set his morning tea to boil. As the chilly gusts were more than occasional, he hugged Jane tight, stuck his cold feet under her warm body and wrapped a sleeping bag around them both.

Goddard Shelter faced a southern valley. And while the rising sun was working on it, morning mist still lay heavy below. Bartleby waited and watched and imagined he could see it draining away, like soapy water from a tub.

❦ ❦ ❦

"So if dying alone at some crummy shelter in Pennsylvania isn't the worst way to go," Coyote wanted to know, "what is?"

"Gotta be friendly fire. That's just plain wrong."

"Uh-uh," Flutterby said, "lava. You're utterly and entirely dead and gone in like half a second. Not a trace left, like you never existed."

"Least it's quick," Bartleby said. "Gotta be more pleasant than getting burned at the stake. Takes a whole lot longer for the same result."

"Or like in a plane crash," Coyote said. "You got that minute or two between when the plane starts to drop and when it finally crashes. Nothing to do but tuck your head between your knees. Which is just the polite way for them to tell you to stick your head up your ass, right?"

"Since we've been out here," Bawdy offered, "I've come around to thinking starving's a bad way to go. Never mind a minute or two of knowing you're gonna die, hunger could take *weeks*. I don't think I've ever really been *hungry* before this trip. Now I know it's a flat-out, no fucking around, terrible feeling. Doubt I'll ever pass another street person without remembering how hunger feels.

"But if you wanna talk about the worst way to cash out—let me tell you about this guy I knew in school. Sammy was studying poetry with me, but he was actually a decent poet. Maybe even good. Had this witty, subversive, wounded outlook on the world that really came through in his verse. On top of which, he was a nice guy. You just had to talk to him for a few minutes to see that he genuinely cared about people. And not just certain people, but the whole ugly horde of us.

"Me and Sammy were teaching assistants. School was free and we got paid this birdseed stipend which barely covered rent, never mind living. To pay bills, I tutored on the side. Sammy invented Turtle Races—this wacky event he MC'd at a local pub on Wednesday nights. It came complete with real live turtles, a circular wooden stage and lots of ridiculous pageantry. He would call each race like the turtles were actually moving around a track at high speed. Could take five minutes for a turtle to win, and the whole time Sammy kept up a frenetic play-by-play. The turtles had numbers painted on their shells and ridiculous names like *Number Three: Little Molasses* and my personal favorite, *Number Ten: Drunken Asshole, The Worst Fucking Turtle in the World*.

"Fast forward to our last semester. He'd talked about going for a Ph.D., but instead he met a girl and fell in love. She wanted to get married, have a normal life. And her idea of a normal life did not include him being a broke-ass poet or a turtle race announcer. So she set to work and eventually convinced him to get a real job, quit the turtle gig and put his poetry on a cold backburner.

"Of course, an MFA in poetry doesn't qualify you for many jobs.

After a ridiculously long search, Sammy finally lands a gig with UPS. By then, it's August and hot as rats humping in a wool sock. He spends his first day of work going around with another driver, you know, learning the ropes. I guess the back of those trucks are pretty much metal saunas. After a couple hours hustling packages, poor ol' Sammy had himself a stroke and died.

"Poor bastard croaks the moment he gives up on his dreams. I mean, Jesus, he couldn't have gone the moment before he gave up on them? If that's not the worst way to clock out, I don't want to know what is."

❦ ❦ ❦

"You seeing them baby woodchucks, Slick?"

"Uh-huh."

"How many, three?"

"Four, I think. And they're groundhog pups."

Skunkers and Coyote sat in the open grassy area of a ski run. Overhead, a line of cable-hung ski lift chairs swayed in the breeze. The lift's upper turnstile was visible behind them and thirty yards downslope, four fuzzy balls of brown were scrimmaging in the high grass. Occasionally, one of these four fuzz balls would stand lookout on its hind legs and survey the world for danger. Invariably, the other three would romp over and tackle the fourth into a squirming pile.

"Woodchucks."

"Groundhogs."

"Bet you a box of popsicles that they're groundhogs. Next person to come through is the judge."

"Deal."

When Fancy Pants and Thunk came along, Coyote wasted no time recruiting her as the judge. "So…what do you think, Fancy?"

"I think they're adorable."

"Yeah, but what are they?"

"I don't know…maybe muskrats?"

"Again, the choices are woodchuck or groundhog."

"Could they be beavers?"

"Alright, Fancy, you're done," Coyote growled. "Woodchuck or groundhog, Thunk?"

"Groundhogs?"

Skunkers groaned and Coyote pumped his fist, "Winner, winner, chicken dinner!"

❦ ❦ ❦

Register: Spruce Peak Shelter

8/2 Far as I can tell, I haven't had a pimple since somewhere
in VA. Who would've guessed the secret to a healthy
complexion is showering once a week, sleeping in your own
sweaty-stink every night and using absolutely no product of
any kind?   "Un" Fancy P

❦ ❦ ❦

Seven of them bunched together waiting for a hitch back to trail on the road leading out of Manchester, Vermont. Skunkers, Bartleby, Jane, Coyote, Bawdy, Rollin' and Flutterby. It would've gone quicker if they'd broken up and hitched in smaller groups, but nobody wanted to hang back, so the whole motley crowd stood roadside with their thumbs out. Except Coyote. He sat on the guardrail and cut the sleeves off his hiking shirt. Liked that so much, he lopped a few inches off the torso as well. Made himself a tank top half-shirt and saved another half an ounce.

It was a big Ford Super Duty flatbed that eventually pulled over. With four hundred and fifty cubic inches of engine, the thing growled to a stop. Two big chrome exhaust pipes jutted up behind an extended crew cab. The backseat was occupied by a slobbery pack of dogs. The driver rolled down the passenger window, "Got room for one a y'all anyway."

Somehow Coyote reached the door before anyone else. As he was climbing in, Bartleby went around to the driver's side, "Think we could sit in back, mister?"

"Nothing back there. You'll fall right out."

"Not going that far."

"Hell," the driver shrugged, "I wouldn't, but go ahead." He patted the steering wheel, "I'll try and drive gentle."

Bartleby lifted Jane, plumped her down on the truck bed and scrambled up after. Everyone stared at him.

"You really riding back there?"

Bawdy squinted, "Gonna fly off on the first turn."

"So wait for another ride," Bartleby answered and Jane barked once for emphasis.

"Shit," Skunkers said, "he *might* make it." Laughing like a kid at the beginning of recess, he tossed his pack up and climbed aboard.

First Rollin', then Flutterby and lastly, after Coyote banged on the door panel and told him to move it already, Bawdy crabbed and crawled his way up onto the flatbed.

Five hikers and one dog pressed themselves tight to the back of the truck's cab. Everybody held on to each other, their backpacks and poor Jane, who's lack of dexterous digits was keenly felt. The road was a lot curvier, much longer and more steeply pitched than Bartleby remembered, but still, it was easily the best hitch so far. Coyote getting carsick, turning green and spitting-up a little afterwards, was just icing on the cake.

Peru Peak Shelter. The deepest dark of night.

"zortz-zortz-whuff-whiff...."

"rho-rho-rho-rho-rho-rho-rho-rho-rho—euwwww...."

"memememememememememememememe...."

"whuff-snort...whuff-snort...whuff-snort...."

"mmmmrmmmmrmmmmrmmmmrmmmmr...."

"gnort-pooooos...."

* * *

The rocky ledges on Baker Peak offered a wide western view. Skunkers couldn't help but stop, take out his map and set to comparing the ink and paper world with the real one.

"Here, look," Skunkers said to Bartleby. He handed over the spyglass. "See that? I think it's the Stratton Mountain fire tower. And out there, that looks like a stone quarry."

As Bartleby scanned with the spyglass, Skunkers scratched Jane's ears. When she came in close and licked at his face, he licked her right back.

Shaving cream clouds scuttled across the sky and sent fleeting shadows to darken the patchwork landscape below. From where Bartleby stood, he counted three white church steeples half-hidden behind low hills.

"And look out straight ahead to the west. You see that line of mountains? Those are the Adirondacks. Which means Lake Champlain's snugged down somewhere between here and there. Sweet, huh?"

* * *

Register: Greenwall Shelter

8/4 Spent the night here with 2 southbounders (Wild Oscar and Church Mouse) and one crotchety possum. We banged pots and waved poles and he finally went running off. For a while, I thought I was gonna have to light him up. —Rollin'

* * *

The AT crossed over Clarendon Gorge by way of a suspension bridge. Compared to what normally passed for bridges on the AT (backcountry carpentry and slick, rotting wood), it was really quite a sight. Metal girders and steel cables supported a sturdy plank walk-way sided in with chain-link fencing.

Beneath the bridge, a slow moving river wended its way over and through a number of pools.

"Swimming hole!" Skunkers whooped. "Think I can jump from here?"

Bawdy looked over the side and gauged the distance and water depth. "Doubt you'll survive, but I'm willing to risk it, Skunks."

"There's a path down over on the bank," Bartleby pointed. Being behind Skunkers as they were, Bartleby and Jane were able to passively herd him across, sort of mosey him along before he got his heart set on jumping. In the short time Bartleby had spent hiking around Skunkers, he'd seen the kid do enough stupid things—jumping off rocks, climbing trees and picking up a shoebox-sized snapping turtle—to know that diving thirty feet down into a three foot pool of water wasn't entirely beyond him.

The pools were shallow enough that the water was actually warm-ish. It felt good to cut through the dust and dirt, wash away the sweat and cool down. The way Skunkers was horsing around, swimming and splashing, it was like he was part river otter. After their initial dunks, Bawdy and Bartleby joined Jane in the shade. Coyote didn't get wet, he preferred instead to bask in direct sunlight like a scrawny, farmer-tanned, raccoon-eyed and badly-bearded lizard.

"You gotta come in, Yote. Best swimming hole yet."

"As cold as I was last night, I'm happy to sit here and suck up some heat."

"What are you talking about? It wasn't cold, I woke up sweating."

"Well, you got a jacket and a real sleeping bag. Alls I got is a six-ounce silk liner."

Bawdy rolled his eyes. He was clipping toenails with the scissor on his little knife.

"Had to get my weight down or I never woulda caught up. Hey— let me borrow that when you're done, Bawds."

"Where's yours?"

"Got rid of it in Harpers." Coyote pulled a razor blade out of his pack. It was less than half the size of a sugar packet. "This is like a fifth the weight of your knife."

"So cut your nails with that."

"I tried. Almost lost a pinky."

When he was done, Bawdy put his knife away.

"Hey, come on, Bawds."

"Beat it. No way am I humping over hill and dale with thirty-five pounds of pack just so you can carry fifteen pounds—"

"It's like ten pounds without food or water."

"—and borrow everything you need from me. Gotta hike your own hike, Slick."

"Now this is a sight," Flutterby called down from the bridge. "Y'all look like a Norman Rockwell painting. Could call it *Four Dopes and a Dog.*"

❦ ❦ ❦

"Skunkers," Bawdy bellowed through megaphoned hands, "you gotta hurry up!"

From the general direction of Clarendon Shelter's privy, a faint and garbled reply came wafting back. It sounded enough like "Occupado" for Bawdy to assume it still was. He hopped one leg to the other and gritted teeth. "Is it me, or does he take for-fucking-ever in the privy?"

"Go whiz behind a tree," Flutterby suggested.

"It's more of a whiz-bang, if you know what I mean." Then, "Skunkers!"

"Bet you he's reading," Coyote said.

"Uh-uh," Flutterby grimaced, "was an ugly mess in there and almost overflowing. Part of the seat was cracked off and that stupid door kept swinging shut—no light, no fresh air. Easily one of the worst privies so far. No way is anyone spending a second longer in that stink-hole than they have to."

"I'm telling ya—Bawdy created a monster."

Flutterby shook her head, "No way."

"Bet me," Coyote said. "One king-size Snickers says he's reading on the can."

"I don't have any Snickers."

"What do you have?"

"Pineapple rings and papaya spears."

"What's the matter with you? Never mind, I don't care. Just trade me your sleeping bag for a night."

"Even for you, Yote, that sounds pretty pervy."

"I dream about sleeping warm."

"And what do I get?"

"I don't know, if he's not reading, I'll carry your hammock all day tomorrow."

"Done. Deal."

"Skunkers!" Bawdy called again, his voice heavy with desperation.

"Well, shit," Coyote grinned, "let's go see."

The three of them slunk down the privy trail. The scene was much like Flutterby had depicted: the door was closed and the little building engulfed in a buzzing cloud of flies. So many and so loud, it reminded Coyote of remote controlled planes that people fly around empty fields. As he had the most at stake, Bawdy tried to hurry the whole process along, but Coyote wouldn't be rushed. He paused with his hand on the handle and let the moment draw out dramatically before flinging the door wide.

And there was Skunkers, hunkered on the broken seat, with his shorts at his ankles and a dog-eared copy of *Catch-22* open in his lap. The look on his face was one part surprise and two parts happy to see people.

"Oh, Skunkers…" a look of horrified awe spread across Flutterby's face, "how could you?"

❦

That night at Governor Clement Shelter, Flutterby was still

shaking her head when she traded her sleeping bag for Coyote's silk liner. He'd just started brushing his teeth, but somehow still managed a taunting smirk despite a mouthful of toothpaste.

"You're gonna be wishing you had more blubber on that tushy, Flubbers. It's gonna freeze right off."

"First of all," Flutterby slapped her flank, "there's *no* blubber on this tushy of mine. And secondly, do you have any idea how hard it is to take you seriously when you've got fresh pee stains on your shorts?"

❦

She tied up her hammock near enough to Skunkers' tent that he couldn't help but hear her shivering come the middle of the night.

"Flubby," he finally whispered.

"W-w-what?"

"Don't take this the wrong way...but you can come in here—"

She was already moving, working the zip on her hammock, before he could finish the sentence. Never did finish it. He'd spent ten minutes preparing a little speech about how he felt responsible and whatnot. Didn't matter. Didn't need it.

Flutterby climbed in and wormed under Skunkers' sleeping bag. Cozied in tight to him real quick in a jiffy.

She was already asleep and purring before he really knew what had happened.

❦

Since Coyote hadn't slept warm for over a week, he was happy to zip into Flutterby's mummy bag, turn on his side and sleep straight through to morning. When he woke (almost an hour later than usual) he wandered away from the shelter for a much needed whiz and returned via Flutterby's hammock, to check and see if she survived the night.

By how the hammock hung, Coyote could tell there wasn't anybody inside. He looked in through the netting of Skunkers' tent and saw the big dope's arm draped over Flutterby. She was spooned in tight and all but hidden beneath his bulk.

"You have got to be kidding," Coyote growled loud enough to wake them.

"Guess I didn't freeze my tushy off after all, Yote. Can ask Skunkers if you don't believe me."

"Yeah," Skunkers confirmed in a sleepy deadpan, "it's definitely in here."

Register: Cooper Lodge

8/5 Killer climb up Killington. Maybe some foreshadowing of what's in store for us in NH + ME. But right now I don't care because from here it's all downhill to the Long Trail Inn. Just gotta tuck my chin and roll.   —Bawds

P.S. I'm in the best shape of my life, was chugging along like a champ, and Rollin' caught up and blew past me in like three minutes flat. That's counting the time it took for the little fucker to stop and ask if I was having a heart attack....

Skunkers couldn't help himself. He pretty much jogged those last few miles down from the summits of Killington and Pico. He reached VT-4 well ahead of anyone else. There was no traffic coming in either direction, so he crossed over and, following the signage, walked a couple hundred yards uphill. There, situated just off the road near the crown of Sherburne Pass, was a long blocky building sided with rough-cut brown clapboard and capped with green metal roofing. The Long Trail Inn.

Bartleby, Bawdy, Rollin' and Jane got a room together. Coyote, Thunk, Squirtz and Skunkers shared another. Instead of squeezing in with the boys, Flutterby and Fancy splurged and got one by themselves. It had been months since either of them slept out of the company of snoring men.

❧

The evening's carouse started mid-afternoon. As promised, Coyote opened a tab, put a credit card down and told the barkeep to keep the Guinness flowing.

McGrath's Pub was equal parts cozy and rustic. The bar top was an eight-inch thick slab of tree trunk ripped lengthwise and poly'd to a gleaming sheen. The pub's back wall was cut into the living rock rising up behind the building. Similarly, natural stone benches ran along the far wall. With his long white apron and a bushy handle-bar mustache, the barkeep fit the part of Irish publican superbly.

Things started off slowly enough. There were still all the logistical issues of trail life to be dealt with. Clothes needed cleaning, mail-drops needed collecting, groceries needed securing, electronics needed charging, postcards needed mailing, emails needed writing, showers needed taking and tents, boots and bags needed airing. The group came and went, people stayed for a beer then ran off to resupply or change laundry or call home.

Except for Skunkers. He didn't much worry about anything but putting his next pint on Coyote's tab.

❧

Most everyone was off running errands. Skunkers and Coyote were playing cribbage and eating shepherd's pie. Or Skunkers was. It was fresh out of the kitchen, steaming hot and after burning his mouth once, Coyote waited for his to cool. Skunkers kept shoveling steaming forkful after steaming forkful.

"Aren't you burning your mouth?" Coyote asked.

"Uh-huh."

❧

Three men sidled in and took seats at the bar. They were so disheveled, so scrubby, so beat to hell looking they could only be thru-hikers.

After they ordered drinks, Skunkers waved the bartender over, "You can put them on our tab, too."

"What?" Coyote protested. "I don't gotta pay for every random person that comes in."

"The deal was *any* hikers," Skunkers said.

Coyote gave Skunkers a long squinty look and growled, "You're a bad man, Sergeant Skunkers."

Skunkers nodded agreeably and called to the trio, "Hey, excuse me—are y'all thru-hiking?"

One of the men nodded, "Started Katahdin on June 9th."

"Congrats. Your beers are on us. Seriously. All night long, so drink up." Skunkers grinned at Coyote, "Sorry, man, but hey, like it or not—southbounders are hikers too."

When their drinks came, the three men (Mocking Jay, Wooly Booger and Tiki Torch) moseyed over and started swapping stories.

❧

The band was almost done setting up when Flutterby joined the festivities. There'd been a bottleneck at the laundry machines, and she'd just gotten a load started after waiting for hours. With every single stitch of her clothing soaking in a rinse cycle, she appeared wearing only Bawdy's raincoat and a too short pair of thermal tights borrowed from Fancy.

By her second Guinness, Flutterby's tongue was fuzzy feeling and flapping free. "Have you lost weight?" she asked Fancy Pants.

"Not much. *Maybe* five pounds."

"Can you believe, I've actually put a few on?" She slapped a flank, "I mean, everything's leaned down and toned up. Which is great down below, but not so good up top. Every guy out here drops thirty, forty pounds and here I am, gaining weight. Can someone explain to me how that is even remotely fair?"

"It's not. *And* we still gotta deal with our monthly," Fancy commiserated. "Which isn't any fun out in the woods."

"Right? I got cramps and bloating and, oh yeah, I guess I'll quick hike twenty-seven miles in a hundred degree heat."

"And the boys get to pee standing up."

Flutterby's face lit up, "Actually, I can too now."

"Seriously?"

"Yep. And I'll tell you another thing—did you know that guys don't actually like to pee standing up?"

"What?" Fancy Pants and Bawdy said at the same time. This last nugget had caught his attention.

"That's crazy talk, Flubs."

"Uh-uh. My husband, he used to pee sitting down all the time. Said the whole standing to pee thing was only when there wasn't any choice. Don't look at me like that, Bawdy, I'm serious. He used to go in there for hours at a time. Played solitaire on the toilet tank."

Flutterby had said this loudly enough, most everyone heard her and went quiet.

"What?" she said.

"I don't really know what's going on over here, but did you just say your husband sat and played solitaire on the toilet tank?"

"My *ex*-husband."

"Well," Coyote was wide-eyed and horrified, "that's about the creepiest thing I've ever heard and I spent four years in the slammer." He gestured at the group, "Has any man here ever sat on a toilet when all he had to do was pee?"

Silence.

"Has anyone, man or woman, ever mounted a toilet facing back towards the tank?"

More silence.

"It's no wonder you two didn't work out—"

Flutterby stabbed Coyote with a sharp look, "How's that exactly?"

"Because he's a wackadoo, a couple cards short and half a bubble off plumb."

Here ensued the third and longest silence. This was broken by Flutterby as she lunged across the table and wrapped her arms around Coyote's neck. Her eyes glistened wetly, "That's gotta be one of the nicest things anyone's ever said to me."

🍁

After making a brief introduction, the band started playing Celtic folk music.

Sometime during the first set, two more sobos showed up. A man and a woman, both in their late twenties and both with dirty looking dreadlocks hanging down to their shoulders. Skunkers, happy to be playing the role of host for the evening, went right over and got them their first beers.

The man went by Al's Pants, the woman Nurples.

"Well, I can guess where Nurples came from, but Al's Pants, huh? How'd that one come about?"

"It's a funny story," Al's Pants said. He took a pull on his beer, started up talking again with foam in his mustache, "I'm actually named after Al's pants. We met this guy, Al, in Monson. He left his pants at the hostel and I've been wearing them ever since."

The pants were well-stained, missing the top button on the fly and had a badly sewn patch over one knee. The inseam of Al's pants (the pants) was too long for Al's Pants (the man) and as a result, the hems were worn and frazzled down to trail-ragged draggles.

Skunkers didn't think that was a very funny story at all, nor did he think much of the pants themselves, but he didn't say so. His role as host was to make people feel welcome and he was taking his duties seriously.

❦

In all the comings and goings, Bawdy managed to sneak Rollin' into the pub despite the kid being well underage. Rollin' sat sipping beers without saying much of anything to anyone.

For a moment, as Rollin' first took a seat, Bartleby thought he saw something orange tucked into Rollin's pant waist. Wondered what it could be, until Bawdy elbowed him, "I used to think *you* were quiet. The kid goes entire days without speaking a word."

Bartleby shrugged. Personally he didn't have any problem with a little silence. Figured the world would be a better place if people only talked when they had something worth saying.

❦

The southbounder, Tiki Torch, asked Bawdy if he'd gone to Trail Days.

"You bet'cha I was there. Take everything you've ever heard about Trail Days, and then double it. All the goddamned loony birds, greaseheads, rough riders, free spirits, and scruffy-ass hikers you'd ever want to see, spilled into the little town of Damascus with nothing much to do but drink and smoke and make noise. Rained the whole weekend, there was mud everywhere. By Saturday night, tent city was a bog. You couldn't stay clean to save your life. And back in the woods behind tent city, there were these tarped-off enclaves. So yeah, it was all mud and music, bonfires, drum circles, and every other kinda crazy you can imagine. You couldn't drag me back with a team of horses."

❦

The band had just finished a lively rendition of *Johnny Jump Up*, when Lazy JoJo, Old Man Trouble and Tommy Hawk staggered into the pub.

Old Man Trouble was smiling, but obviously exhausted. Tommy Hawk looked about ready to zip himself into a body bag.

Lazy JoJo draped an arm around Coyote's shoulders, "I been whipping these two slug-a-bugs like a pair of rented mules ever since we read that first note Skunkers wrote."

"What's she talking about 'notes', Skunkers?"

"We came twenty-miles over Killington today alone. Actually had to shake a stick at 'em back at Churchill Shelter, but here we are. Hope you ain't joking about buying the beers tonight."

Coyote was too busy glaring at Skunkers to do anything but nod.

JoJo gave him a one-armed squeeze, "I don't care what everybody says about you, Yote. You ain't all bad."

🍁

"Oh, come on, admit it," Old Man Trouble said to Skunkers, "you're everything a great hiker should be—young and strong and stupid."

Skunkers just nodded along, but it was easy to see this set him to beaming with pride.

🍁

"So, I meet this bloke," Mocking Jay said in his clipped British accent, "my first hour on trail. Introduces himself as The Pure Pilgrim. We hike up to the summit of Katahdin together, we take each other's picture and we go down to Birches Campground Shelter.

"All the while, this Pure Pilgrim is talking at me. At this point I've been in the U.S. for all of thirty hours, but after two cab rides, a bus trip and a hitch, I've begun to understand this is how all Americans behave. He goes on and on about how he's going to do the first pure AT thru-hike ever. And the way he explained it, a 'pure' hike meant avoiding everything that was man-made. No climbing ladders or going over stiles, no sleeping in shelters, no hitching rides into towns. Said he wasn't going to shower or stay under a roof the entire time. Back to basics. Nothing but him and the wilderness.

"That first night, he builds a dodgy little lean-to out of dead wood and cooks his dinner over hot coals. Doesn't even use the fire ring."

Bawdy cut in, "But unless he was going barefoot—"

"I know. When you break it down, it doesn't follow. Why were trainers okay, but a tent wasn't? As I understand it, trail crews made every step of the AT, so how is walking on any of it allowed?

"Come morning, everything's aces until we hit Abol Bridge. Do you know Abol Bridge? It spans the Penobscot River and in June, that's one serious river. And only after reaching the south side do I realize Pilgrim's back on the north bank, getting ready to swim.

"He stuffed his pack and gear into a big black garbage bag and starts side-stroking his way across with the garbage bag bobbing along behind. There must've been a small hole in the bag, because it rode lower and lower until Pilgrim gets about halfway and the bag disappears entirely. He's still got a hold of it, but it's going to pull him down. So he lets go, and the bag with all his gear in it sinks away, never to be seen again."

"Holy frijoles."

"And that's it. By the time Pilgrim reached the south bank, he's coughing, shivering and wearing nothing but knickers. I helped him up to the road and gave him a shirt. He flags down the next car to come by, and poof, in no more than a quarter hour, The Pure Pilgrim is bleeding done and gone. Silly sod went AWOL at Abol."

❦

"So," Bawdy asked Lazy JoJo, "what exactly is your problem with shelter mice?"

"What'd'ya mean?"

"I mean, you've killed hundreds now. Why do you hate them?"

"I don't hate 'em. I love 'em."

"You love them?"

"Sure. I love them mieces to pieces."

❧

"Here," Thunk said. "Have a bite."

He'd ordered a bacon cheeseburger. Had only taken one bite when he noticed Fancy Pants was watching him, or more accurately, his meal, with predatory interest. She couldn't take her eyes off his big, fat juicy burger.

"Thanks, no, I just—"

"Come on, I can't finish it myself," he lied. Held the sandwich out to her, "Seriously, have a little nibble. You'd be doing me a favor."

❧

Despite having to pay the bill at night's end, Coyote was enjoying himself. From his spot at the bar, he took in the unruly mob of hikers. It was cool that Lazy JoJo had made such an effort to show up. Her having to flog Trubs and that skunk-cursing Tommy Hawk along with a switch was even better. For one raw moment, Coyote was sure he'd gotten himself into a heap of trouble with Flutterby, talking about her freak-job of an ex-husband, but even that turned out unexpectedly well. Best of all, his calf didn't bother him much despite all his hurrying to catch up.

He had to admit it was good to stretch his legs and breathe fresh air. Of the last seven years, he'd spent the first four in prison and the next three living in a casino. Nothing about his life was normal, or how he'd expected it to go, but finally he was feeling healthy and mixing with good people instead of the usual lowlifes and reprobates.

Maybe things were finally starting to turn arou—

Coyote didn't quite finish that thought before he was tackle-hugged from behind. He barely kept his footing. When he looked up, Ella's freckled face was only an inch away.

"Wha—" he said as she pressed a big wet kiss on his lips.

"Told you I'd see you again," she smirked. "Me, V.A. Moose, Giggles and Slipstream hitched from Manchester."

Before he could do anything, she was kissing at him again.

🍁

Bawdy rubbed at his eyes, "I guess I'm drunker than I thought, because it looks like Coyote's over there making out with Ella."

"I don't know who Ella is," Bartleby said, "but he's definitely sucking face with some redheaded chick. You know that girl?"

"That's Ella; aka Frecklebutt or Ginger Nut or simply, The Worst. We heard she went off trail with shin splints back in Virginia."

Lazy JoJo leaned in, "He didn't tell you about all the *recuperating* those two did back in Buena Vista? When I went through, they hadn't left the motel room for five days straight."

"For real?"

"Sure. They got this love/hate thing going. She stayed an extra day in Harpers and he lit out like a greased weasel. I hiked with him until I took a zero in Connecticut."

🍁

Flutterby was feeling no pain by the time the pub lights came on. Somewhere about her fourth beer, she'd stopped caring that she was wearing little more than an oversized raincoat. In fact, she found it clammy and uncomfortable, kept unzipping the front to let some air in. If it weren't for Fancy Pants hovering close, playing chaperone and keeping both eyes on the mischievously rising hem, Flutterby would've been tossed for indecent exposure hours earlier.

As the crowd drifted out of the bar and off to bed, Flutterby hooked arms with Skunkers.

"I'm in absolutely no shape to come find you and put out nightmares tonight, Mr. Skunkers."

This candid mention of nightmares brought a blush to Skunkers' face. He actually looked around to check if anyone was listening, "Shouldn't be a problem, usually don't get 'em when I drink."

"All the same, we should be prepared. Isn't that one of your army mottos?"

"Boy Scouts, I think."

Flutterby was hanging on Skunkers arm; she might've pulled him over if he wasn't so big. At the door to her room, she turned and looked up.

"Promise you like women."

"I like women."

"And sex? I'm not a nympho-chick or anything, will probably say no to it about as much as anyone else, but I like sex. During, before, after. Do you like it?"

"Didn't have a lot of it in the army, but sure, sex is good."

"You promise? I'm serious. Say it."

Skunkers looked down at Flutterby, held up the three fingered Boy Scout salute, "I like sex plenty. Scout's honor."

"Can you do something for me? Can you quick go to your room and get a sock? All my clothes are still in the laundry."

"What'd'ya need with a sock?"

"We gotta put it on the doorknob."

Stereotypically, the South has a reputation for being more open and welcoming than the North. The term *southern hospitality* speaks directly to this regional inclination. On the AT, this translates in a number of ways.

Southerners generally look on thru-hikers with a certain wide-eyed wonder. Up north this is, again generally, a wary-eyed watchfulness.

Down south, hikers can be confident someone will shuttle them to and from trail. It may be a crusty, toothless drunk in stained overalls who keeps forgetting he already offered to share the bottle of bourbon sitting between his legs; a red-necked yahoo with a bible on the dash and a shotgun in the rack; or a family of eight (not counting their hungry coon hound) in a boat-sized Chevy Caprice station wagon that came off the line two decades earlier. Hitchhiking through the north is less an adventure and more a tedious, drawn out affair. Northerners seem to have less time for giving rides and more objections to letting grubby hikers stink up their cars.

Big time trail magic—the random on-trail BBQ's and hiker feeds; the trail angels who drive sixty miles out of their way to bring a hiker to a bus station or a gear shop; the locals who open their homes to hikers needing respite from the rigors of trail life—is disproportionately a southern thing. Oddly generous moments of humanity are what the south does best. Conversely, the north is known for its mountain ranges and a certain romantic expectation of solitude.

"Soooo?"

"So what?"

"So come on," Coyote said. "Let's hear it."

"Don't know what you're talking about."

"I'm not stupid. I know where you slept last night. And don't think it doesn't gall me to think about how I've been your unwitting ally these last few nights."

"I wouldn't doubt that it doesn't," Skunkers said vaguely.

"I feel sick as a dying dog right now, I'm dehydrated and you just watched me puke up a stinking pile of Guinness-foamed bile. Seems the least you could do is gimme a few details, something to help me through the day. I mean, does that ass of hers feel as nice as it looks?"

Skunkers looked to Bawdy for support.

"Sorry, Skunks, but I've felt she was extremely callipygous since back on Springer."

"Yeah? What's that mean?"

"Means she's got a great kabooty and at the risk of being crass, I wanna hear all about it too."

"You can both get stuffed. Nothing happened."

"Would you tell us if it did?"

"Nope," Skunkers huffed. Then he picked up his pace.

"Come on, I'll tell you about me and Frecklebutt. She's this hoochie-coochie hellcat—"

Skunkers kept hiking hard until he couldn't hear them booing anymore.

Register: The Lookout Cabin

7/24 Looking down from above
I can see how Vermont was
quilted together.

High-Ku

8/6 Puked before I left the Long Trail Inn, and again two miles
into the hike. Have taken nearly a dozen Guinness-colored
beer shits. My b-hole is blazing, my a-hole is aching and my
poor little taint feels like shaved beef.   —Bawds

P.S. Despite feeling absolutely crapulent, I still noticed High-
Ku cheesed an extra syllable into his first line.

P.P.S. Also invented a new portmanteau today: kabooty = booty,
caboose and kaboom!

8/6 Thanks Slick. If you wanna go through my pack again, I
heard about this cool pub in Hanover.   Skunkers

8/6 Have a headache and still feel queasy, but I got to watch both Coyote and Bawdy puke on trail, so yeah...I'd say it was officially another fine day on the AT. Also, I'm thinking that maybe Bawdy's trail name could've been "Aching A-Hole". Besides being accurate on a number of levels, it's got a nice "ring" to it.   —Flutterby

8/6 Who thought hiking 17+ miles today was a good idea?
                                        Fancy Pants

8/6 I feel worse than a spunkless punk in a funk. Thunk

8/6 All you bloodsuckers earned every second of your hangovers. Believe me, I feel just as bad if not worse AND I footed the bill!   Coyote "Suckerfish" Slick

🍁 🍁 🍁

"Can't stop thinking about that burger we ate," Fancy Pants admitted.

"Good, right?"

Thunk and Fancy had just reached the crest of Thistle Hill.

"Yeah, but the idea of it makes my stomach flip. I've been a vegetarian since I was like ten years old. And now, out of nowhere, I'm a carnivore again. Wham, bam—have some ham."

"Don't worry about it. Our bodies are going crazy, we're literally starving. Doesn't matter how much we eat, we aren't getting enough calories to keep up with what we're burning every day. Surprised there aren't stories about hikers turning cannibal in the Hundred-Mile Wilderness."

"Isn't carn about the ugliest prefix going? *Carn*ivore, *carn*al, *carn*age...."

"*Carn*ation, *carn*ival, *carn*auba wax. But if it helps, don't think of yourself as a carnivore, think of yourself as an opportunivore."

"Opportunivore? Opportunivore. That does sound better, doesn't it?"

"Wanna sit? I'm still feeling washed out."

There wasn't any view to talk about, or even comfortable places to sit, but being out from under Vermont's ubiquitous tree cover and into direct sunlight was enough reason for a break. The sun was almost overhead and the sky was unremorsefully blue. Fancy laid back in the grass with her eyes closed. Thunk lobbed the occasional gummy bear to her (but only reds and oranges—her favorites) and gobbled peanut M&Ms.

When Lazy JoJo trooped up, she made a few remarks on the awesome weather and the lame view and kept hiking. A little while later, Old Man Trouble came along.

He stopped, scratched his head and finally said, "Without trying to micromanage or otherwise infringe on your inherent right to hike your own hike—I gotta ask if you kids know you're sitting in a patch of poison sumac?"

Thunk thought this was a joke. He didn't get it exactly, but he chuckled gamely, "Good one, Trubs."

"Seriously. You might want to stand up now."

Lounging in lawn chairs outside of the Village Shop in West Hartford, Vermont.

Coyote had his wad of cash in hand, "So what's the tally, Skunks?"

Since Upper Goose Pond, they'd been stopping to skip stones at every body of water the trail passed. Coyote was quickly improving, but so far he'd lost far more than he'd won.

"You owe me six candy bars, three pops, a box of popsicles and a big bottle of Old English. I owe you two candy bars and two pops."

"First of all, I don't owe you the Old English yet. That's best of thirteen."

"And so far, I got six and you got none. So you can stick a fork in that one. It's done."

"Whatever. So right now I owe you four candy bars, one pop and the popsicles, right?"

"No. You owe me six candy bars—"

"Yeah, I know, but the two you owe me can come off the ones I owe you."

"Uh-uh."

"What'd'ya mean 'uh-uh'?"

"You owe me six candy bars and I owe you two candy bars."

"Which equals out to me owing you *four* candy bars."

Skunkers shook his head. "*Uh-uh*, Slick. I won three pops and I want three pops. I lost two pops and so I'm gonna buy you two pops."

"But that's...I mean, it doesn't...you ..."

"Hey, don't go getting mad at me just cause you skim rocks worse than my great aunt Tabitha."

"I'm not complaining about losing, I'm trying to pay up."

"So get me six candy bars and I'll get you two."

Coyote looked to Bartleby for help, "Can you talk some sense into this dope?"

Flutterby's patience snapped before Bartleby could weigh in, "Can you two idiots not bicker for five minutes? I swear this must be what it's like to have kids. You're giving me a migraine."

This outburst stopped Coyote and Skunkers cold. They looked at Flutterby, then each other and back to Flutterby for a long moment.

And then they started up again.

"I just don't understand—"

"You owe me six candy bars—"

Thunk hiked ahead with Old Man Trouble and left Fancy on her own. Within a few hours, her legs and arms were splotched over with red welts. An hour after that, pus filled bubbles rose up out of the welts. Her hands swelled, her armpits burned. She'd had poison ivy before, but this was a higher level of itchy, poisonous pain. There was no calamine lotion, there was no escape to a cooling bath filled with Aveeno soothing skin products, there was no relief to be had. Instead, what there was, was dirt and sweat and friction, all of which greatly exacerbated her symptoms. Also, there was the inevitable spreading of the rash to the parts of her body that hadn't initially been exposed.

Before realizing that Old Man Trouble hadn't been joking, that she'd actually contracted poison sumac, Fancy had rubbed at her eyes, scratched her face, eaten food with her hands and gone to the bathroom.

Now Fancy wanted to cry. Fancy wanted to scream. Fancy wanted to scratch the skin off her body. Over the course of the day, she did all three, but none of them helped much.

The only thing that did help was to keep hiking. Much as it hurt, at least it kept her mind off all the bubbling and burning that was going on.

She couldn't hike forever though and finally stopped for the night at Happy Hill Shelter. It had stone walls and the styling of a Swiss chalet. From where she'd stayed the previous night (The Lookout Cabin), she'd already come almost twenty-five miles. Back in the flat Mid-Atlantic states, that kind of distance wasn't anything much, the norm, just another nine to five day at the office. Vermont wasn't the top of the world, wasn't all crags and notches, didn't zigzag back and forth from sea level to tree level, but it certainly wasn't a fast hiking flat state.

Hanover, New Hampshire was only another six miles further north, but twenty-five was all Fancy had in her. She doubted anyone she knew was still behind or would be overnighting at Happy Hill. As she dropped her pack, she grimaced. The idea of spending her first night alone in the woods wasn't appealing, but it was already dusk and she needed to stop.

"I'm betting you want to stay here tonight," Thunk said.

Fancy started. She hadn't noticed him, sitting back in the shadowy part of the shelter's interior.

"I want to spend the night laying in a hot tub, or maybe on pack ice. Really whatever helps the—" instead of finishing this thought, Fancy set to scratching maniacally at her legs. Blood and pus already oozed from sores she'd opened with vigorous scratching.

Thunk came out into the waning light. He hadn't gotten hit as badly as Fancy Pants but he certainly wasn't sumac free.

"Before the hike, I worried about what all could happen out here," she said. "Rapists and bears, the Blair Witch. Today is so much worse than anything I imagined."

"Here," Thunk held out three pills. "The white and pinks are antihistamines. They should help with the swelling. I got the other one from Bawdy. Some kinda pain pill. Should help."

She swallowed the pills dry, "I'd drink motor oil if I thought it would help."

❧

A high, girlish shriek was followed closely by a celebratory whoop. Both had come from Fancy. One moment she was quietly leafing through the register and then she was raising an uproar and beaming from ear to ear. With all the swelling, this contorted her face grotesquely. "Did you see the note Hairbrained left in here?"

"Who's Hairbrained?"

"You know—the guy I started trail with."

"His trail name was Hairbrained? I'm sorry, but that's lame."

"He thought it was *soooo* clever because his real name is Brian."

"What's clever about that?"

"Brian, brain. He switched the A and the I."

"Thinking it's actually clever makes it worse—"

"I know! But it doesn't matter, you know why?"

"Why?"

"Because that lame-named, calorie-stealing, brownie-burgling puddle of pond scum went off trail. Says in here, poor Bri-Bri found a tick embedded in his armpit a couple days back. He pulled the tick out, but it was too late. He's got a bull's eye ring around the bite. And you know what that means."

"What?"

"Bri-Bri got himself a single serving of Lyme Disease. He ran home to the smothering embrace of his fat-ass mama.

"Mister-I'm-bigger-so-I-need-to-eat-more-food-than-you-but-also-since-I-weigh-more-than-you-you-should-carry-more-gear-cuz-I'm-carrying-all-the-extra-weight-of-my-own-body sweet talks me into hiking the Appalachian Trail with him because he's afraid to come out here by himself, eats all of *our* food and treats me like moldy dick-cheese right up until he gets the nerve to hike his own hike at which point he casts me aside like a candy bar wrapper at Harpers. Can you believe I dated that guy?"

"No?"

"And the wonderful, beautiful, magnificent irony of it is, I started this nightly ritual of checking each other for ticks. He hated it, which I never understood. I mean, he was supposed to run his hands over my naked body. Don't men usually spend a lot of time and energy convincing women to let them do that? He always acted like it was a punishment."

Fancy closed the register. Tossed it down. Started up whooping and hooting and jumping around in a celebratory dance. Ended up with her arms around Thunk's neck. Hard to tell which one of them was more surprised. Before he could react, she quick kissed him on the lips.

"You know what today is?"

"What?"

"The best day ever!"

If not precisely the geographic center, The Green was certainly the emotional center of Hanover, New Hampshire. It was a wide, squarish space, easily the size of two football fields, crisscrossed with walking paths and bordered by trees and benches.

Wham-O, Skunkers, Squirtz and Thunk were playing Ultimate Frisbee with a four-man squad of southbounders. Whopping the unholy-hell out the sobos might be a more accurate depiction of the proceedings. Wham-O had the frisbee skills one might expect of a hiker who had carried a frisbee all the way from Georgia. Skunkers wasn't particularly skillful, but he was like a golden retriever out there—running, jumping and otherwise chasing down every disc that came within twenty yards. And having come more than eighteen hundred miles, Squirtz and Thunk were conditioned to nigh-Herculean levels. From the first toss, the relatively soft southbounders (BaoBOB, Johnny Chuck, Rock Steady and the long-armed Megilah) never had a chance.

Jane watched on with keen interest. She'd already slipped free once and stolen off with the disc. With Jane's leash wrapped around his leg, Bartleby sat and looked through another of Chatter's maildrops. Flutterby and Fancy lay sunning nearby. While still prominent, much of Fancy's rashy redness had at least been covered over in white lotion.

Bawdy wore a black wool Bavarian hat that could have only come from Mad Chatter. The hat had a short pointy brim that turned up in the back and a little red feather on one side. It looked like something an old German man would wear with lederhosen while trekking in the Alps. Bawdy was watching the game and pretending to listen while Coyote showed off his most recent gear purchases: a new sleeping bag and an insulated jacket.

"—and both of them are 1200-fill down."

"No such thing as 1200-fill down, Yote."

"The guy at the shop said it was newest thing. This sleeping bag weighs seventeen ounces and it's rated down to twenty degrees. Even with the hood, the jacket weighs less than ten ounces."

"What'd they cost ya?"

"Doesn't matter, no sales tax in New Hampshire. I saved seven percent right off the top."

"How much?"

"Jacket was four hundo and the bag was like seven."

"You dropped a grand on gear?"

"Eleven hundredish."

"But we've only got another four hundred miles to go."

"Well...the guy said he thought the 1200-fill down was hypoallergenic so I shouldn't have any problems. You know—with my allergies."

This last line earned Bawdy's undivided attention. He looked over, "You just bought a thousand dollars' worth of down gear and you're allergic to down?"

"Yeah, but I'm officially uber ultra lightweight now."

"Know what else?"

"What?"

"You're officially an uber ultra idiot."

Register: Velvet Rocks Shelter

8/11 New Hampshire: Where the men live free and die old.
Trouble

Looking out from Holt's Ledge, Skunkers watched the hawks circling and soaring overhead.

"Peregrine falcons," Bawdy corrected.

"You don't know."

Bawdy jerked a thumb towards the trail, "I know what I read on that big sign back there."

"Bartleby?"

"His eyes are closed. I think he's asleep."

"I'm not asleep."

"They peregrines?"

"Don't know, don't care, but the sign said this is a protected peregrine nesting ground."

"Huh."

Bawdy watched a larger than life peregrine shadow flicker and glide across the bare rock ledges, "Beautiful."

"Which one?"

"A shadow, it's gone now."

"We got half a dozen endangered falcons circling overhead and you're watching shadows?" Skunkers snorted, "That's so you, dude."

Before Bawdy could reply Coyote came trotting along.

His sunglasses were suspiciously absent, he was freshly shaven and the hair on his head was buzzed down to nubble. The newly exposed skin on his scalp and face glowed cadaver white. This wasn't exactly a good look for Coyote (or anyone really), but it would get better once the sun put some color on that too-bright skin.

Skunkers hooted, "What bet you lose this time, Slick?"

"No bet. The glasses were dead weight and my beard looked like a lazy rat's nest."

"And your head?"

"Borrowed electric clippers from one of the boys at the frat house. Once I finished off the beard, I just kept going," Coyote vaguely gestured at his nether regions, "after my head, I even did my pits and stuff."

"Before this? I told you," Coyote said, "I was playing poker."

"You didn't tell me. It's why I'm asking."

"Well, I was playing poker."

"What, like full-time?"

"More than. Sorta lived at one of them Indian casinos for a while."

"What's 'sorta lived' mean?" Bawdy asked.

"It means sometimes I slept in hotel rooms, sometimes I slept in a broken down van I bought off this dude. But really, I didn't sleep much. Mostly just played poker."

"That sounds wild."

"Guess so. After a week or two, it seemed pretty normal."

"How long did you live like that?"

"I got out of the clink in December of '07. So, a little more than three years."

"You seriously went to prison?"

"Uh-huh," Coyote shrugged off the thought. "Minimum security— not so bad, really. I embezzled the shit out of some money."

"How much?"

"Lots," Coyote smirked. "It worked out nice. Fresh out of school I landed this cherry gig as an energy trader for one of the big firms. It didn't take long to break it down and see how the firm's partners and their hot shot friends were exploiting loopholes and insider knowledge to make a killing. Before I knew it, I was in there with both hands siphoning off stolen monies."

"From who?"

"My bosses and their Washington connections. And I'm talking *big* fish. Politicians and other people whose names you would recognize. The bunch a dummies didn't even notice 'til I started getting sloppy."

"Robber barons? You were robbing the robber barons? Like Robin Hood or something, right?"

"Guess maybe, but I didn't give none of it to the poor or anything lame like that. Secreted it all away in cash and gold and off shore accounts. Since I was stealing stolen funds, the Feds didn't ever sniff out half of it. They recovered just enough to make themselves feel good and put me away for a little while. And considering how much gold has gone up the last few years, I totally rolled a yahtzee."

"That's...uh...."

"Cool, right?"

"Crazy might be a better word."

There was a big blowdown across the trail. Coyote stopped, tried to figure his way around it, "Financially I could coast once I got out, which was good because I can't imagine who'd hire me. We played a lot of poker in the can, you know, back when it was hot. And believe me, white collar criminals are about as mean and greedy a bunch as you'll ever meet. Was like shark week in there, or like trying to outfox a whole frickin' box of foxes. Those guys were smart and ballsy and loved winning almost as much as they loved risk."

"It's skulk," Bawdy corrected, "a skulk of foxes."

"After that, it wasn't nothing to sit down with all the soft, civilian donkeys at the casino. Taking candy from dead babies."

"So what are you doing out here?"

"Yeah, well—turns out, I've got a bit of a gambling problem."

"Like you're addicted?"

"More like I was bleeding out on the tables. The first couple years things were all aces. I ran good and easily outplayed the suckers. When the economy tanked, all the action dried up. Any gamblers with money left went broke real quick. Everybody else stopped gambling and started waiting for perfect hands. The game changed overnight, became cautious and careful and about as boring as you talking about books. Wasn't exactly a good fit for my particular skill set. I spent the last year spewing cash and chips all over the felt. Had to take a break, clear my head, you know? Reboot the system."

"Zowie. High stakes?"

Coyote nodded, "I tell ya, you've never lived 'til you've called off four gee on some suckerfish who shoved with only one card to come. I put him on a semi-bluff and sure enough, if he's *lucky*, there's only three cards left in the deck that can help the stupid donk. I got a ninety something percent chance at an eleven thousand dollar pot. Just had to fade three jacks. No whammy, no whammy—WHAMMY!"

Coyote emphasized that last whammy by smacking a fist into an open palm.

"Jack a Hearts."

"Seriously? What'd ya do?"

"You mean after puking in the men's room? I ordered up some hiking gear."

Register: Hexacuba Shelter

8/14 We've humped across smoky mountains, raced over blue mountains and wandered thru green mountains. The Skunk Man says: It's about time to climb some white mountains!

"How much longer now ya think?"

"I don't know, Bawdy," Coyote said, "probably a couple hundred yards less than the last time you asked me.

"More than a mile?"

"Have we crossed over a paved road yet?"

"I don't know. Guess not."

"Then, yeah, we got more than a mile to go."

"My feet are killing me and I got a dehydration headache banging away." He slipped into a spot-on sputtering impression of Speed Buggy, "Sput-sput-running-sput-on-fumes-sput-sput-here."

Coyote, Rollin', Bartleby, Jane and Bawdy single filed their way into the Jeffers Brook Shelter area. The structure was big and could obviously house a lot of people. Though, currently, it housed just one.

Bawdy shucked his pack with a certain relieved finality. Bartleby and Rollin' followed suit.

"Just beat the rain, eh? Y'all can call me Roach Belly."

Roach Belly looked like he'd been born under an old rug. Greasy hair hung below an equally greasy cap. He wore stained jeans, a rat-holed sweater and two unlaced black boots. There were enough teeth missing from one side of his mouth that his lips pucker-pursed and gave him a crooked, Popeye clench.

If he wasn't old enough to have survived a stretch in Vietnam, he was close. The stained fingers of his left hand held a hand rolled cigarette. His right hand never strayed far from the knife at his belt.

Roach Belly carried a metal ammo can over and sat close enough so he could feed the fire without having to get up.

"Got a good cooking fire going, if you wanna put a pot on before the rain picks up."

It was just starting to spit.

After pulling out his baggie of garbage, Bawdy sifted out a few paper scraps and tossed them into the fire.

"Is that trash?" Roach Belly gruffed, "Usually I go ballistic when people put trash in my cooking fire." The knife made an appearance somewhere in the middle of that sentence. The blade was curved and brightly worn. He pointed it at Bawdy as a sort of visual aid.

"It wasn't plastic or anything," Bawdy backpedaled, "just paper."

Roach Belly chewed on his lip, gave Bawdy a thousand yard stare. Jane's whine filled the ensuing silence.

"So, ah," Coyote coughed, "which way you hiking, Roach Belly?"

The hand holding the cigarette waved vaguely eastward, "South."

"So what's the terrain like ahead."

Roach Belly shifted his glare to Coyote, "Some ups, some downs; lots of elevation changes." After waiting to see if anyone would challenge his words, Roach Belly starting scraping the knife blade against a whetstone.

At first glance, Bartleby thought the shelter was strewn with garbage. Only after a second look did he realize this "garbage" was actually Roach Belly's possessions. Two raggedy tarps hung from the rafters to make a poor man's privacy screen. On the far side of these, a scatter of plastic bags bulged full of clothes and army surplus gear. Also in evidence: a cracked styrofoam cooler, a gallon jug of water and an external frame pack that looked like it had made the trip there and back again a couple dozen times over.

Bawdy flipped through his data book and gestured for Rollin' to check the register.

"Looks like Skunks and Flubby went ahead to Beaver Brook," Rollin' said.

"Seven more miles, most of which is a kickass climb up and over Mt. Moosilauke. It's officially the first mountain in the Whites."

With Bawdy's indiscretions against his cook fire at least momentarily forgotten, Roach Belly rapped a knuckle against his ammo can seat, "Hey, any a ya need poopy paper?"

Silence.

"Well, you need any, I got plenty."

The rain picked up as Rollin', Coyote, Bawdy and Bartleby shared a long look. Bawdy let out an exasperated moan and shook his head. One by one, they reharnessed packs and started hiking again.

❧

The trees gradually shrunk as Rollin' climbed upwards. At the mountain's base, they had been full-sized—towering spruces and what have you. As he gained elevation, eighty footers became thirty footers became twelve footers. Six foot dwarves became four foot midgets became thigh-high minis as the mountain rose up to and continued past a glass ceiling, an invisible line that the trees themselves seemed unwilling or unable to cross.

Rollin' stopped and sat on a fallen tree trunk. He waited for Bawdy and the rest in what looked to be the last bit of protection they could expect until the other side of the summit. Even so, the blustery wind drove stinging pellets of rain against his bare skin.

As the rain gained momentum, Rollin' removed his omnipresent earbuds. Zipped them and the connected ipod safely away into a dry plastic baggie and a deep inner pocket. He was listening to an audio recording of *Wizard and Glass*, book four of Stephen King's Dark Tower series. He'd read the entire series a handful of times already and this was his third time listening to it since setting off from Georgia. With the rain coming on stronger, he worried about ruining the ipod and losing his place.

Despite wearing a rain jacket, Rollin' was shivering by the time Coyote caught up. Another few minutes passed before Bartleby and Jane appeared around the last bend in the trail. By which time, Rollin's teeth were tat-tat-tatting uncontrollably and Coyote was doing jumping jacks to keep his blood circulating.

After digging into his pack, Bartleby offered whiskey around.

Coyote took a long pull, grimaced and passed it to Rollin' who waved it off.

"A little bit'll help warm ya, kid," Coyote said.

Rollin' looked to Bartleby. Bartleby nodded, "Go ahead, no telling how far back Bawdy is."

Rollin' took a swig from which he came up gasping and coughing. Coyote slapped him on the back. "Burns all the way down, right? Here, gimme another suck on that."

When Bawdy showed, he looked sulky and trail worn, "Who put the antifreeze, sput, sput, in my carburetor? Sput-sput. Yuuuuck."

When this didn't get any reaction, he took the bottle and drank down a good glug. Turned to Coyote, "Why aren't you wearing rain gear?"

"Got some I can borrow?"

"You're an idgit."

"Yeah? Well, then what'd'ya call your new BFF back at the shelter?"

"That guy was a stone-cold freakazoid."

"Hiking south my ass," Coyote said. "You know he's not leaving that shelter 'til the staties come and drag him away."

Bawdy slugged the last of the whiskey. "We need to keep moving, people. If I stop now, I'm never getting going again."

With the last wind-bent bush well behind them, the mountain's upper reaches were comprised of lichen splotched rocks and the occasional stone stacked cairn. A headwind swept rain into their faces at a nearly horizontal pitch while heavy clouds ghosted across the bleak moonscape. From tree line, the remaining incline was relatively gentle and no more than a mile's distance to the jumble of boulders that comprised Moosilauke's crest.

On reaching the summit sign, Rollin' spun around. He couldn't see more than twenty yards in any direction, "Supposed to be good views from up here."

"View schmew," Coyote barked. "I'm choked full of good views. Wouldn't give a wet broccoli burp for another one."

❧

Beaver Brook Shelter was two miles past Moosilauke's summit, tucked safely below the montane shrubs and scratchy low krummholz of the timberline. Flutterby and Skunkers were already bedded down when the boys arrived. They ornamented the shelter rafters with their wet clothes, cooked and otherwise settled in for the evening.

While dinner simmered, Coyote replayed the run-in with Roach Belly for Skunkers.

"I didn't even see him pull that knife out," Bartleby said.

"Me neither," Bawdy admitted. "One minute I was burning paper scraps and the next I was looking down a knife blade. I mean, for a second there, it looked like I was gonna have to give him a Chi-town beatdown."

"I had your back, Bawds," Coyote said. He flashed his little sliver of razor blade in a sweeping Zorro Z.

Skunkers laughed, "What the hell you gonna do with that thing?"

"Are you kidding? I may look all cute and cuddly—"

"No you don't," Flutterby assured him.

"—but I got some bite to me. This one time, I shived a basketball."

"What? Why?"

"It was this dude's favorite ball. He was disrespectin'."

Coyote kept on despite the riot of laughter, "Besides, I saw Bartleby circling round, ready to grab Roach Belly if he made a move.

Even Jane was set to rip his leg off."

Bartleby shook his head. "I didn't move an inch—couldn't even think to let go of my hiking poles."

"So Bawdy was shitting himself, Bartleby statued up, Jane probably wanted to sniff the dude's crotch and, even if Coyote was thinking about pulling his mini-blade, it was way down in his pack. That leaves you, Rollin'. What were you gonna do if shit went bad?"

"Easy," Rollin' said. A stubby orange revolver-type gun materialized in his hand, "Was gonna light him up."

"Holy—" Coyote sputtered.

"What the fuck is that thing?" Bawdy shrieked.

Rollin' twirled the gun once around his finger, reversed it and handed it over to Skunkers. "Careful, it's loaded."

With all of Skunkers' firearm experience, it took him no time to open the breach-loader and remove the single cartridge.

"You're carrying a gun? How long—"

"It's a signal gun, Bawds," Skunkers explained. "Fires flares, like for boaters and stuff."

"I don't care if it's a glue gun. Why are you packing heat?" Bawdy demanded.

Rollin' shrugged.

"These are 12-gauge flares, right?" Skunkers sighted down the barrel, "Can you actually hit anything with this?"

Rollin' shrugged again.

Bawdy shook his head, "This is all part of your gunslinger delusion, isn't it?"

"What kinda range?" Skunkers wanted to know.

"Shoots a hundred yards easy," Rollin' said. "No accuracy outside of fifteen, though."

"Sweet."

"Not sweet. This is crazy. You're underage, you can't just be packing a flare gun around." Bawdy put his hand out, "Give it over, Rollin'."

"Uh-uh."

"You're not *the* gunslinger. You aren't even *a* gunslinger. I've been saying that since Virginia and you aren't hearing me, so now I'm gonna prove it to you. You get one shot. You hit that metal sign over on the side of the privy, you keep the gun and I'll even start calling you Roland. You miss and I'm taking the gun away."

"Hike your own hike, Bawds," Coyote suggested. "Give the kid a break."

"That's like thirty yards," Skunkers said. "Nobody could mak—"

Even as Skunkers was saying that the shot was too difficult, Rollin' snapped the breach closed, thumbed the hammer back and fired. At most, all this took him half a second.

A brilliant pink sparkle swooshed from the gun's barrel. Despite wind and rain, the sparkle flew true, splashed against the metal sign and blossomed like a bouquet of bright phosphorus flowers.

Register: Beaver Brook Shelter

7/29 Up above tree line
     there is no place for hikers
     to poop in the woods.

               High-Ku

From Mt. Moosilauke the AT followed the course of a tumbling waterfall down into Kinsman Notch. It was only a mile and a half down to NH 112, but it was slippery and steep and painfully slow going.

"So right now," Skunkers asked, "how many Soft Taco Supremes could you eat?"

"Like from Taco Bell? Dude, I bet I haven't had Taco Bell in five years."

From the rear of the line, Coyote called, "I'll take that bet."

"You're sick, Yote. You need help."

"Says you. I'd snarf a couple chalupas—"

"Uh-uh, Slick," Skunkers said. "Just Soft Taco Supremes. How many, Bawds?"

"Remind me—what's in them?"

"Got this little soft tortilla shell, some rat meat, wilted lettuce, orange shreds of cheese, whitish cubes of tomato and a squeeze of sour cream. They slide down super easy."

"I don't know. Twelve?"

"I couldn't hear," Coyote called, "how many did he say?"

"Twelve," Bartleby relayed back.

"Well, shit. If he can keep twelve down, I could go fifteen no problem. Eighteen probably even. How about you, Flubby Pie?"

"Pass. Yo no como Taco Bell."

"Twenty-four," Bartleby said with conviction.

Skunkers gestured eastward, "Over there, some of the bigger bases had all kinds of fast food for us, and this one time, I choked down thirty-one of 'em."

Except for Flutterby's gasp of disgust, this was met with stunned silence.

"On a bet?"

"On a bet. Got food poisoning or suttin' too. Spent three days shitting and puking in the infirmary."

"Did you at least win the bet."

"Depends how ya look at it."

"What'd he say, Bawds?"

"Sorta," Skunkers repeated.

"Yeah—how's that? Who sorta wins a bet?"

"A bunch of us bet to see who could eat more. Me and this guy Chub were the last men standing. Officially, Chub won—stuffed down thirty-four and one third soft tacos."

"Zoinks."

"Then you lost."

"Yeah, but while I was laid up, Bode's HumVee got *fucked up* by an

IED. The turret gunner lost most of his head."

"Yeah? And who's Bode?"

"The guy I usually rode turret for."

"Wowzers," Bawdy said. Then, "You know, I bet Taco Bell would pay you to be a spokesman, go around, tell that story to all the health food nuts who say Taco Bell isn't good for you. You'd be like that Jared guy from Subway, only you wouldn't be a goofy-ass pussball."

"He's running marathons now," Flutterby said.

"He ran *one* and it took that fish-lipped fucker almost six hours. I mean, shit, we're running the equivalent of a marathon every single day out here. Skunks could do most of twenty-six miles carrying a pack over mountains in the same time Jared ran it on pavement."

"Personally, I still think you're a goofy-ass pussball, Skunks," Coyote called, "but either way, the guys at the casino are gonna love that story."

"Thought you were done with all that poker stuff," Bawdy said.

"Done *losing*. Came out here to get my head straight. Soon as we summit, it's game on, baby. I'm gonna saddle up and ride the donkey!"

❦ ❦ ❦

From down in the nook of Kinsman Notch, the AT scrabbled its way up to Kinsman Ridge. From the summit of Mt. Wolf, the trail dipped into a saddle before ascending South Kinsman Mountain and loping across to North Kinsman. Red spruces gave way to balsam firs, which in turn gave way to stunted black spruces and finally a spongy heath of lichens and moss lapping at the stony shore of South Kinsman's peak.

"I don't know where exactly," Bartleby said, "but I think The Old Man in the Mountain used to be around here somewhere."

"Yeah, who's that?" Skunkers asked.

"Are you kidding?" Coyote scoffed. "You been talking about seeing the Whites since I met you, and you never heard of the Old Man in the Mountain?"

"He some famous caretaker dude at one of the huts?"

Bartleby opened his mouth to explain, but Coyote beat him to it, "No, ya dope, he was this crazy old yodeler guy. Carried one of them long Swiss horns around and sung from all the mountaintops. The locals said you could hear him for miles and miles."

"Seriously? We gonna meet him?"

"You can't. Well, not really. He's dead. But they say his ghost still haunts these hills. When it's real quiet you can hear him blowing on his horn."

"Sweet." Skunkers pulled toilet paper from his pack. "Gonna go lighten my load, but remind me to tell Flubs that one, okay, Yote?"

"You got it, pal o' mine."

"You gonna tell him the truth?" Bartleby asked once Skunkers had disappeared off trail.

"What truth? That before it broke off, the Old Man in the Mountain was just a massive rock formation vaguely shaped like a face?"

"Uh-huh."

"Nah. The truth's just...not as much fun."

"Come on, girl, you can do it."

If Jane's look said anything at all, it said she couldn't do it.

Bartleby stood at the top of a crude log ladder. Glancing upwards, Jane put a foot on the bottom rung and then quick pulled it back like the wood was hot. She whimpered and settled her rump down at the ladder's base.

Things pretty much continued along in this fashion until Skunkers showed up.

"The ladder's too steep for her?"

"Yeah," Bartleby said, "I don't know, maybe you could cajole her along from behind or grab her leash and we could...."

Without thinking twice, Skunkers chucked his poles up to Bartleby. He patted Jane's head once and quick scooped her into his arms. He did this so fluidly and fast, he had her cradled against his chest before she could protest.

Sensing things were well out of her control, Jane simply rested her chin on Skunkers' shoulder and hoped for the best. Meanwhile, with his pack still on and a hundred pounds of scared dog in his arms, Skunkers walked up the round ladder rungs as if it were nothing more than a short flight of stairs.

❦ ❦ ❦

The bunkroom of a hostel in Lincoln, New Hampshire.

Old Man Trouble scurried here and there, looked under the bare mattress and re-checked his stowed gear.

Bawdy clipped a final buckle and hoisted his pack. "We're the last ones out, Trubs. You coming or what?"

"Feels like I'm forgetting something."

"Got food?"

"Uh-huh."

"Sleeping bag? Tent poles? Puffy jacket?"

"Yep, yep and yep."

"Toilet paper? Water? Fuel?"

Trouble nodded and shrugged, "Guess I'm getting dotty is all."

"Facts o' life, Trubs. Now, let's make like a rock and roll."

❦

It didn't take long to score a hitch back to trail. Nestled between the crotch of Franconia Notch and the west end of the Kancamagus Highway, Lincoln was inhabited by plenty of outdoorsy folks who were happy to help a couple of thru-hikers resume their journey.

Trouble sat in the bed of a pickup truck with the wind plucking at the sparse horseshoe of hair ringing his shiny dome. For the life of him, he couldn't shake the nagging feeling that he'd forgotten something.

Bawdy leaned close, yelled to be heard over the wind, "Got your phone?"

Trouble grimaced. His phone, that must be it. He'd talked to his wife last night. Couldn't remember exactly what he did with it once they'd hung up, but now he was sure he'd misplaced it.

He half-heartedly searched the top pocket of his pack. Was pleasantly surprised to find the phone right where it was supposed to be.

He gave Bawdy a thumbs up and circled a finger round his temple, like maybe he was losing his mind.

Somewhere along the saddle between Liberty and Lincoln Mountains, a rocky outlook offered southwestern views of Moosilauke and the Kinsman ridgeline. The climb up out of the notch was, in Bawdy's words "a hairy ballbuster," so any and all rest spots were welcome. The low morning sun lit every crag and cranny of the distant granite slopes.

Trouble dug out string cheese and a few eggs while Bawdy vacuumed a pecan roll before setting to work on a bag of Chex-mix.

"Sunnova—" Old Man Trouble growled. He looked at Bawdy, shook his head and started to laugh. Something wet and yolky dripped through his fingers. "*Now* I remember. Forgot to boil up my eggs."

After scaling Mt. Liberty, the AT skipped to Little Haystack to Lincoln to Lafayette to Garfield to the north spur of South Twin and finally up and over Mt. Guyot in a dizzying succession of desolate heights.

These were the White Mountains in all their rugged glory. Much of this stretch of trail was above tree line. The views were stunning and sharp, breathtakingly wide and, in many cases, the hard-earned payoff for the last 1,800 miles of hiking.

When Skunkers reached Mt. Lafayette's peak, there wasn't one cloud in the sky. Not a single wisp of white all the way to the horizon and that seemed to be about half a world away. He stood on the highest point of rock, slowly turning and taking in the panoramic view. It felt like he could see all of New England. He kept turning and looking, turning and looking with a silly bemused gape stretched across his face.

❧

Bawdy was gasping and sweating like an old porn star when he reached Lafayette's summit. After dropping his pack, he stumbled to a seat near Flutterby and Fancy Pants. "Remember how we thought all those climbs down south were killer? Up into the Smokies, Roan, the Humps? Looking back now, I realize they were nothing but a warm-up."

Fancy nodded, "That was some climb up Liberty, huh?"

When he'd sufficiently caught his breath, Bawdy jerked a thumb at Skunkers, "What's Big Boy doing?"

"No idea," Flutterby said. "Been standing up there since before I got here."

"He's still got his pack on."

She just shrugged and kept eating a peanut butter, jelly and cream cheese wrap.

"Hey, Skunkers—you alright, man?"

"Don't you worry, Bawds, I got overwatch."

"What's he talking about overwatch?"

"It's some military term," Thunk said.

"He looks like that Christ the Redeemer statue, you know, overlooking Rio," Bawdy said.

Thunk fiddled with Skunkers' spyglass, turning and twisting it until finally he put it down, "For the life of me, I cannot get this stupid thing unfucked."

"Where's Yote? He go ahead already?"

"Down to Greenleaf Hut."

Bawdy's eyes went big, "Seriously? Isn't that like…off trail?"

"Uh-huh." Flutterby explained, "There were a coupla cute day hikers up here, asking all kinds of stupid questions about thru-hiking. He chatted them up for a while and followed them down to Greenleaf for lunch."

"He went chasing off trail after some baby fresh nugs, huh?"

"So we've been talking about putting together a calendar, Bawdy," Fancy said. "The Wandering Men and Women of the Appalachian Trail. What'd'ya think?"

"Lame. And I'm not posing naked, if that's what you're asking."

"That's not what I'm asking."

"I would," Flutterby said.

"Seriously?"

"Yeah, why not? Not an ounce of fat on me. No cellulite, no extra bumps or lumps, nothing here but me. Doubt I'll ever look this good again in my life."

"Yeah," Fancy said, "but you know what guys do with naked pictures of women. You don't want thousands of random men doing that with your picture do you?"

"God bless 'em. Have at."

"In that case," Bawdy conceded, "I think an AT calendar's a great idea. Where do I get one?"

❧ ❧ ❧

An old abandoned concrete foundation clung to the summit of Mt. Garfield. It had probably been the square base for a lookout tower decades earlier. To get out of the persistent and chilly wind, Bartleby and Jane hunkered low against the foundation's leeward side.

They drank water, shared jerky, listened to the windy silence and watched a glider plane perform silent acrobatics overhead. With a slender body and delicate wings, it was the praying mantis of airplanes; couldn't have looked more fragile if it had been made with toothpicks and notebook paper. Bartleby watched and cringed, half-expecting the glider to come snapping apart at the joints as it stepped through loop de loops, stall turns and barrel rolls. It was still coasting on drafts and riding the wind long after he and Jane bucked up and moved on.

❦ ❦ ❦

"Definitely Drake's Cakes. Definitely. I practically grew up on Drake's."

"Bump that, Big Boy. Hostess rocks. Drake's got nothing that compares to the Twinkie, the Snowball or even them iced Honey Buns."

"You're forgetting about Devil Dogs, Slick."

"Hostess—"

"Listen up you two knobs," Bawdy cut in. "First off, Hostess and Drake's are sister brands put out by the same parent company. They're not competitors, they're coworkers. Secondly, have either of you ever had a Tastykake Krumpet? Nobody, and I mean *nobody,* bakes a cake as tasty as a Tastykake."

❦ ❦ ❦

Tenting on the Saco River, just a few hundred feet south of Webster Cliffs and the beginning of the Presidential Plateau.

Under the leafy boughs of silver maples, Bartleby shambled down to the river, waded in up to his knees and sunk down. He sat with the cool river water tumbling over him; soaking his aching legs, his throbbing feet and his stiff knees. Jane watched him from the sandy bank. He held himself anchored with one hand and floated in the shallows; zoned out, dazed off and lost track of life for a while.

"Mind if I join you?" Flutterby's call snapped him back to the here and now.

When he waved her ahead, she plopped to a seat nearby.

"Rrrrrrr. Colder than it looks," she said. "Not interrupting any deep thoughts, am I?"

"I don't know," Bartleby said, "everything seems to be...moving faster now. Maybe it's just me, but those first few weeks back in Georgia went by in slow motion. Thinking back, I can remember every water break, every day hiker, every little climb and a couple thousand weird little moments. But I can't remember the shelter where we woke up this morning. Not its name or even what it looked like. The mountaintops and trail towns, the hitches, the hikers—it's all blurred together into one fuzzy lump."

"It does seem like Coyote caught back up only a day or two ago, but that had to be almost two weeks now, right?"

"Longer. Three and a half, I bet."

Flutterby thought it over, "Yeah, I guess so. Huh. Now that I'm thinking about it, that first month of trail did seem like a whole year. And Virginia felt like another whole year."

"That was a *big* state."

"And now the miles and views, the conversations and dinners are all flying by."

"Faster and faster, right?"

"Maybe we've grown numb to the day to day. It's all become old hat. Like before we couldn't see the forest for the trees and now we can't see the trees for the forest."

"The trees for the forest," Bartleby mused, "yeah, I like that."

Unprecedented cardiovascular conditioning or no, the climb up Mt. Webster was brutal. A nearly twenty-eight hundred foot elevation gain in just over three miles. On top of which, Bawdy kept psyching himself out, thinking the next rise was the end of the road and the top of the world. At each crest, he was disappointed to see there was more ground yet to be gained. False summits had a way of quickly sinking one's spirit.

Upon (finally) reaching the (real) summit of Mt. Webster, Bawdy took a sitting, pack-on break. He must've been going too slow, as everyone had already moved on towards Mt. Jackson. He was the last of the bunch, the rest of them were faster and earlier and somewhere up ahead. More often than not, Bawdy was stuck playing the role of group caboose, and he'd come to understand that the tail end of things sucked.

❧ ❧ ❧

Register: Mizpah Spring Hut

8/16   Overheard a couple of day hikers talking back on Mt. Webster. They were trying to decide who from history they would have lunch with if given the chance. I'm thinking cheesesteaks with Hannibal (the general, not the cannibal)....   Tommy Hawk

8/16   A cup o' camel piss w/ Osama bin Laden (just to rub it in).
                                             Skunks

8/16   Crumpets and tea with Billy "the Bard" Shakespeare.
                                             —Bawdy

8/16   Andre the Giant. "Anybody want a peanut?"   Bartleby

8/16   Hardtack with John Muir.   Old Man Trouble

8/16   I'd pop a couple cans of PBR with Lynyrd Skynyrd.   JoJo

❧ ❧ ❧

The Presidential Range of the White Mountains had it all. Plenty of knee-high montane shrubbery and sloping sedge-rush meadows in their varied browns, reds and greens to go around. Vast blue views tempered by the occasional bout of romantically dangerous weather. Windswept heaths, stony scree inclines, more old dead white guys and photo opportunities than you could shake a big stick at, and that wholesome feeling of accomplishment that comes from looking down on the world from a high peak. Also, the Presidentials had somehow achieved the appearance of remote wilderness while still having an auto road leading straight to a summit-top gift shop, like a pulmonary vein delivering oxygenated blood directly to the heart. It was, without a doubt, the pièce de résistance, the cream of the crop *and* the mac daddy of all the mountain ranges found along the length of the Appalachian Trail.

Unfortunately, the Presidential Range also happened to be a logistical nightmare for thru-hikers. On the AT, the hiking distance from Crawford Notch to Pinkham Notch was twenty-seven miles. Much of this mileage consisted of sharp rock footing and leg numbing climbs; nearly all of it was situated above tree line and regularly subjected to what's been billed as the world's worst weather (highest surface wind speed recorded by man: a whopping 231 miles per hour).

Sanctioned tent platforms were rare, sharply limited in capacity and overseen by caretakers who merrily turned overflow campers away. The Appalachian Mountain Club operated a network of mountain huts which offered rudimentary lodging to anyone who could afford it. Bunk space in the huts was plentiful, but grandly expensive. For $114, a single person purchased the rights to rudimentary bathrooms, a group dinner and gender segregated bunk rooms filled with thin mattresses and bunkmates unaccustomed to rustic sleeping conditions. Worse still was the social component of hutting—being subjected to whiny kids (particularly when their hand-held devices ran out of juice), miserable moms and dopey-ass dads, all of whom looked at thru-hikers like they were zoo exhibits.

And sleeping out of bounds wasn't a much better option. This entailed bedding down on sharp rocks and endangered lichen, no reliable water access and potential exposure to unpredictably harsh weather. It was also against the rules.

"So what do you say, Bawds? I'm thinking we might be able to stealth camp just over the other side of that ridge."

"It'll really suck if somebody rousts us in the middle of the night."

"Well, even if we wanted to pay to stay in a hut, which I can't afford, I doubt they allow dogs so I've got no choice anyway."

"Humph. What about water?"

"I filled up at that last spring. Carrying more than I need."

"Me too, actually," Coyote offered. He shrugged, "I'm in."

Bartleby led Jane off trail and across the tip-tilted landscape with Coyote following close behind.

"What about Skunkers?" Bawdy called. "Shouldn't we wait for him and Flubby?"

When nobody answered, Bawdy glanced furtively around. As soon as he was convinced there was no one in sight, he hurried after.

They'd gone a couple hundred feet down off the ridge and over a stony outcrop before finding a likely little spot down out of view. It wasn't exactly comfortable, spacious or even flat, but it was certainly free and somewhat protected from the steady crosswind.

Just after dusk, a tall man suddenly appeared above them on the ridge. He quick ducked down behind a rock and put a finger to his lips, indicating everyone should be quiet. Then he passed long, silent minutes peering back from where he'd just come.

"Ha!" the newcomer said before dropping his pack, folding gangly limbs and taking a seat. "Hey, folks. I'm MEGA Mike."

MEGA Mike was tall enough to have played center for a Division I college team; he was also a southbounder who'd been chased off by some manner of authority figure. "Ranger, ridgerunner, concerned citizen—I don't know what exactly, but Deputy Douchbag stood there watching while I packed up my shit. I set off in a huff and he followed behind, like maybe he was gonna escort me to the next hut or something. So I started power hiking, built up a lead and slipped off trail. Sucker flew right by.

"I mean, I don't know about you folks, but I pay taxes. And as a non-profit, the AMC sure as shit doesn't, so why do they get to have a mountaintop monopoly? Who made them the bosses of the AT? They say we can't sleep out anywhere above all tree line because of the fragile ecosystem, but at the same time, they plop down these huge buildings and traffic thousands of city slicker slobs across the Whites all summer long? Is it me, or does something stink in Denmark?

"You folks nobos? Mind if I camp with?"

"Uh, yeah, you're welcome to squeeze in," Bartleby offered.

In no time at all, MEGA Mike had his bottom three-quarters stuffed away into a bivy sack. His upper quarter: shoulders, arms and head, stuck well out of the opening.

"That doesn't look comfortable," Bawdy observed. "And don't you get wet when it rains?"

"No, look," MEGA popped an umbrella open and settled it over his head. "Works better than you'd think."

Bawdy nodded, "It would have to."

MEGA tore into a sandwich a day hiker had given him a few huts back. It was thick with sliced ham, provolone cheese, sprouts, cucumbers, onions and dripping red tomatoes.

Jane sidled up close and pensively licked her lips until MEGA asked, "Is it okay if I let her lick the sandwich foil clean?"

After Bartleby nodded yes, the boys watched him eat the last bite with jealousy roiling in their stomachs.

"I am literally sitting here drooling," Bawdy admitted.

"Don't be. The texture was okay, but you know how it is out here. Pretty much tasted like Purell."

Fancy Pants and Thunk reached Lake of the Clouds Hut early on a Monday evening. The hut was half occupied with civilian tenderfoots, whiny greenhorns and a few straggling weekenders.

They hadn't even gotten their packs off before one of the hut staff approached them, "Thru-hikers, right?"

"Uh-huh."

"If you wanna do work-for-stay, we can feed you a little something and put you up for the night in the attic."

The dinner wasn't much to talk about, barley soup and crusty bread, but since Thunk hadn't been banking on a free meal, it was perfect. Though, in his whole life, he might not have washed as many dishes as he did that night. And he still didn't clean out all the packed grit from under his fingernails. It was getting on towards the end of the season and the hut workers were fed up with the unending parade of blister-footed yuppies with entitlement issues. This was all they talked about in the kitchen during the after-dinner clean up.

The attic was jammed full of boxes and supersized canned goods. The only space for sleeping was the narrow pathway snaking between the stacked foodstuffs. Thunk didn't care; he and Fancy Pants lay with their heads no more than a foot apart. It wasn't long before he heard her breathing shift to that gentle sleeping rhythm that he'd come to love.

Mt. Washington was still twelve hundred feet above Lake of the Clouds Hut. Just a mile and a half scree stroll up to the roof of New England. Old Man Trouble scowl-sneered as he passed by a side trail that led to a parking lot, weather station, post office and visitor center. He'd seen all that stuff before and it did nothing but set his blood boiling. It was unconscionable; an industrial blemish, an ugly scar dead-smack in the center of one of the most beautiful spots in all of America.

A hundred steps down the far side, Bartleby and Jane were sitting trailside, taking a rest.

"She doing okay?" Old Man Trouble asked. "All these rocks are beating the meat off *my* feet and I'm wearing inch-thick boot soles."

"Better than me, probably. Quite a view, huh?"

"You mean except for the auto road and that Cog Railway catastrophe?"

"Is that what that is?"

"What it is, is horrible. A genuine, twentieth century travesty."

Trouble spit to one side. "Every time I see one of those 'This Car Climbed Mt. Washington' bumper-stickers—"

Trouble's rant was cut short by the shrill blast of a train whistle.

"Oh-ho, does this trail ever provide, or what? Come on, Bartleby, we gotta get closer."

After pulling Bartleby to his feet, Old Man Trouble hurried down the trail.

A train chugged into sight. A green locomotive pushed a single, cyan blue passenger car up the steep, rocky slope. Both were runty; less than half the size of traditional rail cars.

"They've switched over to biodiesel engines," Trouble called over his shoulder, "like that somehow makes it all better. Still trespassing, still disturbing the fragile eco-system. Still futzing up the crown of New England. The only upside is that now the engineers don't have any coal to throw at us."

The train belched smoke and closed fast. Trouble jumped, waved his arms and yelled "Death to the Cog Railroad!" and other similar disparagements.

Uncharacteristic as Trouble's antics were, Jane looked to Bartleby for some explanation. He shrugged and started yelling and waving too. After a moment, Jane joined in, though her barks weren't directed at the oncoming train so much as the two men.

The train tooted hello and kept climbing. It passed so close, Bartleby could see the curious faces of individual passengers peering at the raving madmen with the confused dog.

"So, we got their attention. Now what, Trubs?"

Trouble stopped and gave Bartleby a breathless grin, "Now we show those candy-asses what a couple of hard-asses look like."

With that, he worked the buckle on his shorts, bent over and flashed the train passengers a full moon.

❧ ❧ ❧

Way up in the Presidentials and still above timberline. A rocky ridgewalk with sedge-rush meadows sloping off to either side. The wide sky was close and clustered with scuttering white clouds.

Old Man Trouble hiked along, leaning into a blustery crosswind.

A particularly strong gust knocked him sideways. He stumbled to a seat on a boulder and sighed as his pack cover sailed off into the wild blue yonder, tumbling away on the wind.

The last few miles into Pinkham Notch were relatively easy compared to the terrain of the previous days. Even Bawdy couldn't find much to complain about.

When the buildings of the Pinkham Notch visitor complex came into view an excited buzz swelled through the ranks.

"Time check, Skunks."

"Oh seven three eight."

"Alright people," Bawdy called, "the book says the breakfast buffet closes at eight-thirty. If we're gonna put a hurting on it, we gotta spread out and find it ASAP."

Carter Notch Hut was a low stone building situated next to a pond way down in the shadowy crook between Wildcat Mountain and Carter Dome. Shortly after arriving, Bartleby removed Jane's leash and saddlebags. Soon as he did, she made a breakneck dash for the water. Her momentum carried her in over her head and she paddled in a big lazy circle, all the while yipping and barking until the hut caretaker came out to see what all the noise was about.

"Don't worry," Bartleby said, "I know we can't stay here. Okay for her to be swimming?"

The caretaker was young and athletic except for a solid round belly. By way of an answer, he produced a stick from somewhere and tossed it out for Jane to fetch. "Be sure to check him for leeches."

"Her name's Jane."

"Jane the Great Dane?"

"Sweet Jane the Greatest Dane.."

"Gotta be the best trail name I've heard all season. You're thru-hiking, right?"

"Uh-huh."

"I nobo'd in '08. Went by Judah Buddha Belly."

"I'm Bartleby."

"Bet it wasn't easy coming over the Presidentials with her, huh? Did you have to stealth camp?"

"Every night. "

"Yeah, I know how that is. We're off the beaten path here, don't get the crowds like they do at the other huts, so you two are welcome to hunker down in one of the bunk rooms."

"Seriously?"

"Oh yeah."

Register: Carter Notch Hut

8/4 Dark granite, bright heights
      notches, huts, dead presidents.
      Hiking New Hampshire.

                              High-Ku

The climb up from Carter Notch was exhaustively sharp, but at least it gave a good view of the impressively massive stone boulders and scree field known as the Ramparts. When they reached the top of Carter Dome, Flutterby and Skunkers paused for a break. There weren't any good rocks to lean against, so they sat back-to-back and leaned against each other. It wasn't the most comfortable setup, but one learned to make do on trail.

"I don't really care, Flubby, but I'm thinking you stink," Skunkers said.

"Like normal hiking stink or like super-special bad stink?"

"I mean, I've smelled worse. Burning flesh and stuff, but yeah, pretty bad."

"But today is new sock day. I've got nice clean socks on."

"Didn't say it was your feet that stunk."

"We got what—another fourteen miles into Gorham? Can you put up with my stink until then?"

"I could put up with your stink for the next fifty years. Was just making conversation."

Gorham, New Hampshire. Another quiet little town, skewered through by a long, busy main street. After leaving Jane with Skunkers back at the hostel (it was a toss-up who was actually keeping an eye on who), Bartleby walked to the post office. He picked up a waiting maildrop there, sat on a bench outside and sifted through the newest goodies.

Coyote wandered past on some errand or another, "You score another hat?"

The hat was dark leather and lined with luxurious gray fur.

"Elmer Fudd special, huh?"

"Think it's called a trapper hat. And yeah, this one actually looks functional."

"Gonna keep you toasty in the Wilderness. Heard there was a Mickey D's down the road. Last one 'til Katahdin. Come on—I'm buying all the nuggets you can eat."

They each polished off a twenty-piece in no time.

"You know, my kids always order nuggets," Bartleby mumbled through a mouthful. "Usually when they can't finish, I bat clean up, but I've never had more than one or two at a time."

"Good, right?"

"Uh-huh."

"I'm thinking we run it right back."

"Ask for more sauces," Bartleby suggested. "They like to skimp on the sauces."

The second twenty-piece went down, but not nearly as quickly. Coyote's face was flushed by the time he stuffed the fortieth lump of breaded, unidentifiable chicken(ish) parts into his mouth. He chewed on it for a minute or two before swallowing. There was a pained look in his eyes, like maybe this hadn't been one of his better ideas.

Meanwhile, Bartleby dipped his last nugget deep into a barbecue sauce container. He did his best to scrape up the last little bits of flavor stuck way down in the corners.

"We'd be crazy to do it again, right? I mean—sixty nuggets?"

"I don't know." Bartleby shrugged, "Probably another twenty doesn't kill either of us."

"Really? You think?"

"Willing to find out."

❦

Nugget fifty-seven was cold and shaped like a Christmas stocking. It went down rough.

"Only three more," Bartleby said. He'd polished off his sixtieth minutes earlier.

"I'm done. It's too much. I'm gonna blow."

"You're not gonna blow. Stuff those last three in quick and we'll head back. The walk will feel good."

"You know you're full," Coyote groaned, "when you can feel the nuggets right up here in your throat." He looked bloated and miserable, was breathing deeply through his mouth. "I can't do it."

"You can do it."

"I don't wanna do it. I'm not doing it."

"Alright, so don't do it."

"I'm not."

"I bet you couldn't do it, even if you wanted to."

Despite his condition, a little spark flashed in Coyote's eyes.

"Bet what?"

"What?"

"What would you bet that I couldn't eat three more nuggets?"

"Betting? Who said anything about betting?"

"You did."

Bartleby thought back, "Yep—guess I did."

"So what'll you bet?"

"I don't know. You eat three more *without* blowing and I'll carry your tent through the Wilderness."

"Got rid of it."

"You got a sleeping bag now, right? I'll carry that."

"And my jacket?"

"Okay," Bartleby nodded, "but no puking. Not even a little bit."

Coyote pushed the fifty-eighth into his mouth. He chewed and chewed and chewed until it was little more than gristly puree and sucked most of it down. He was audibly moaning when he started nibbling at the fifty-ninth nugget.

And then something went wrong. Instead of continuing its descent, nugget fifty-eight started to rise. And it brought friends. Coyote dashed out the door, knocked the top off a garbage can and blew into it.

Bartleby watched him go, then leaned over and poached the last nugget.

❦

"You better now?"

"Uhhhh...."

"Hey, I'm gonna get a milkshake for the walk back. You want? My treat."

❦

Coyote shambled along main street, one hand holding his distended stomach. Next to him, Bartleby slurped noisily at a supersized chocolate shake.

A tiny car honked as it drove past. Thunk was driving. From the passenger seat, Fancy Pants waved and called out, "Don't go too fast!"

Bartleby waved, yelled, "Hurry back!"

After they'd disappeared, Coyote said, "Where'd they get a car?"

"Rental. He's got another meeting with his unemployment person. It's gonna be a few days, so Fancy went with him, instead of getting too far ahead."

"That's nice," Coyote said.

"Yeah. They're good together."

"I meant about him collecting unemployment. Wish I thought of that one."

🍁 🍁 🍁

The ground around Gentian Pond Shelter was spongy wet and largely inhospitable to tenters. Bartleby looked for a long time before settling on a muddy spot surrounded by clumps of Jurassic-sized ferns.

He'd barely sat down to cook before Jane had her head resting in his lap. All the climbing through the Whites had taken a heavy toll on her. Recently, her movements had been noticeably slower and stiffer. So much so, that Bartleby'd given her a thorough going over up near Madison Hut and again in Gorham, but hadn't found anything obviously wrong. Hopefully it was nothing more than the general trail fatigue they were all feeling. He let her rest like that for a good while, gently stroking her neck and listening to the twangy

242

thrumming of a nearby band of bullfrogs.

The sign was bolted to a tree. It was painted blue with white lettering:

WELCOME TO
MAINE
THE WAY LIFE SHOULD BE

Flutterby took a picture of Bawdy posing by it.

"Our last state. Almost done now, huh?"

"Just another two hundred eighty miles."

"*Only* two eighty. Funny how that doesn't seem like anything at all."

Come Maine, beards had grown to be a point of pride amongst the menfolk. It was the first time many had ever let things grow unhindered. The bigger, the bushier, the more crazily robust, the better.

Skunkers looked like a Viking; his face was all but hidden behind a huge blonde bush. Beyond his white teeth, it was impossible to make out any facial features below his blue eyes. There was a bristly growth jutting from his bottom lip that he'd begun to refer to as a "supper scoop." It curved outward and often met his meals before his mouth did.

Bartleby's beard was darker, but not much tamer. Bawdy, Thunk and Old Man Trouble had each grown perfectly decent facial fuzz (black, sandy and white respectively). Young as he was, Roland's looked more like an eight o'clock shadow than a full beard, but it had come in uniformly at least.

Some hikers (Shaggy Bob and Frizzly Adams for example) had

started trail with thriving beards already in place. These had continued to blossom until they'd become the very stuff of legend.

At the other end of the spectrum, before he shaved it off, Coyote's beard was, without a doubt, the runt of that year's thru-hiking litter. To call what had been lingering on his face a beard was a disparagement to beards the world over. It had been little more than an unfortunate combination of seedy bare splotches and sickly long black follicles with a scraggly billy goat bush sprouting under his chin.

Register: Carlo Col Shelter

8/27 Last few days have been a crazy whirlwind. Finally back on trail and trying to do some serious catching up. Somehow we drove seven hours, resupplied, returned a rental car AND hiked sixteen miles today. Way past dark now and time to rest my sleepy head.   Fancy

8/27 Had a great time hanging with the fabulous Fancy Pants. Unemployment update: my rep actually suggested I shave off the beard AND take a shower if I was serious about finding a job. Note: I showered three times (!) before the meeting. Guess it's sad but true: Thunk Stunk.

"Lemme ask you something, Skunks. What's that mean exactly?"
"What?"
"What you just said. 'Fucked if it ain't.' And sometimes you say 'fucked if it is.' For the life of me, I can't tell if being 'fucked' is a good thing or a bad thing."
"Shit, Bawds," Skunkers winked, "I'm fucked if I know."

✤ ✤ ✤

Bartleby sat at the top of a steep, stony ledge. The slope wasn't quite a cliff, but awful close. He was boiling up noodles for an after-dinner snack. Behind him lay a rough circle of tents.

Close by, Bawdy had his black notebook out and open. Roland was lying on his pad reading the first half of *Catch-22*. Next to him, Skunkers was half reading *The Long Walk* and half tossing sticks to Jane. Flutterby and Coyote played a round of Spit. This involved frantically flipping cards, slapping them down with a certain infectious hysteria and, mostly on Flutterby's part, plenty of squealing laughter. When their game was done, Coyote wandered over and took a seat between Bawdy and Bartleby.

"Writing anything good, Bawds?"

Bawdy shook his head and, after another moment, gently closed the notebook. "Not a good goddamned thing."

When the sun touched the horizon, the group congregated at the ledge and watched it silently slip away. It was a beautiful sunset, complete with soft shades of pink, purple and orange.

"I'm always surprised at how fast it goes down at the end," Flutterby sighed.

As the gloaming sky darkened, everyone drifted off and settled in for the night. Bartleby drank down the last bits of soupy noodles before getting to his feet.

"You coming?" he asked Bawdy.

Bawdy stood, took a final look at the notebook in his hand and hucked it over the precipice with a whole body heave. It went spinning off into the abyss, flapping and fluttering and finally dropping like a dead duck.

When the notebook vanished out of sight, Bawdy shrugged at Bartleby.

"Sorry about the littering, but I really needed a big symbolic gesture. You know, for closure."

"That's it?"

"Yeah. Shit. Guess I've always known I wasn't a writer, just needed a good kick in the pants to set me straight. I've got some contacts in publishing, probably time to start peppering them with resumes. That doesn't work, I can always teach. Believe you me—I teach a mean English Comp."

❦

Come the morning, Bartleby took his time packing up. Most of the crew had already moved out. Only Bawdy was still left, and he was buckling his hipbelt.

"You coming, B?"

"Getting a slow start. Go ahead, I'll catch up."

"You gonna pull another disappearing act?"

"Nah. I'm stuck like old gum."

Soon as Bawdy was out of sight, Bartleby's pace picked up measurably. When he finished stowing his gear, he left his pack, took his poles and set off down the slope.

Sweet Jane looked from Bartleby to the trail along which everyone else had already disappeared and whuffed questioningly. She didn't know much, but she knew Bartleby wasn't going the right direction.

"Come on and don't worry," Bartleby called to her, "we're going that way. We just gotta do something first."

❦

"The hell happened to you?"

"What?"

"What what?" Bawdy snorted, "You're all ripped to shit. Got blood dripping down your leg, claw marks across your eye. Looks like you got stuffed in a bag with a couple of alley cats."

Bartleby shrugged and proceeded to eat slices of dried apple dipped in cream cheese. He couldn't see his own face, but his left leg was an obvious oozing mess; there were enough bloody welts and criss-crossed cuts to suggest the alley cats had played out a few games of tic-tac-toe on his skin.

"Seriously, B—you tore your shirt even. What happened?"

"Pit stop."

"Pit stop? I'm not buying it."

"Shit stop then."

"The middle of a briar patch?"

"Hey, it's like Squirtz says, 'you never know where you gotta go'."

Mahoosuc Notch was famously jutted full of jumbo rocks, tight spots and craggy crawlways. It was a mile-long obstacle course, a boulder strewn gorge through which hikers climbed, clambered and squeezed over, under and between car-sized stones. Many considered it to be the longest mile of the whole AT.

Skunkers had himself a hell of good time going through. Jane just had a hell of a time.

Coyote didn't mind all the squirming and scrambling but he did freak out about the slugs.

They were pretty much everywhere.

"I mean look at them all—they're everywhere!"

Many of these slugs were a burnt shade of orange and the rest a rusty brown color that really wasn't too terribly different from the orange. Universally, these slugs had two waggling eye stalks up front and an unfortunate textural resemblance to living snot. As they were propelled along by a single fleshy foot, their progress was almost imperceptibly slow.

Apparently, Maine had experienced an unusually wet spring and summer and the wild slug populations had ballooned up accordingly.

"These fuckers are truly disgusto," Coyote continued. After finding three slugs attached to his pack, he'd taken an impromptu break to both remove and condemn them. "And look, they left this nasty slime trail on my gear."

"I hate how they're always climbing and sliming up the walls of our tent," Flutterby said.

Bartleby was resting back on his pack, staring up at the sky. "Slug slime is like two-thousand times more slippery than anything science has been able to produce."

"So?"

"So nothing."

Coyote flicked the final hitchhiking slug from his pack. It happened to land near Jane. She gave it a short sniff before eating it.

"Dude, your dog's eating slugs."

"So?"

"So nothing, except now she's probably gonna get sick or die or something."

"She's eaten way worse. Besides, people eat slugs all over the world."

"How do you know? You ever eat one?"

"Uh-uh, but I saw it on the nature channel once."

"I'll give you a hundred bucks if you eat one right now."

"No thanks."

"Well, will you give me a hundo to eat one?"

"Beat it, Slick. I don't even have a hundred."

❦ ❦ ❦

Register: Speck Pond Campsite

8/12 Pure luxury is:
      peeing into a bottle
      on a rainy night.

                        High-Ku

❦ ❦ ❦

Bawdy huffed his way to the spur trail for Old Spec Mountain just as Skunkers and Flutterby were coming down from the summit.

"Is the summit really point-three off trail?"

Flutterby nodded, "At least that."

"Jesus," Bawdy grated. "All this climbing and still no summit view. Gotta keep on climbing off trail for that. I mean, why make us climb any of the mountain if we aren't gonna go over the stupid summit?"

"I don't know, but there's a fire tower up there."

"Yeah? Good view? Worth the effort?"

"You should go up. It's totally broke-dick."

"Why would I go up if it sucked?"

"Dude, it didn't suck. It was awesome."

"You said it was broke-dick."

Skunkers nodded, "It was."

Bawdy's confusion didn't clear up until Flutterby interpreted. "I think he means the view from the fire tower was *like* a broke-dick. You know," she giggled, "unbeatable."

❦ ❦ ❦

Register: Baldpate Lean-to

8/26 Have had Bon Jovi's "Shot Through The Heart" stuck in my head for the last two days. No one can save me, the damage is done.   —Bawdy

Baldpate Mountain looked about like its name sounded: a bare basalt dome, ringed round with short, scratchy conifers. The route down the northern slope followed a tedious series of washed out chutes of rock and root. These were tricky slick and steep. When Bawdy slid onto his ass for the third time, Skunkers whistled, "This'd be hairy scary in the rain, huh?"

"It's hairy scary now," Bawdy groused, "I'm like to bust a knee."

"We got suttin' like five more into Andover?"

"Yeah," Coyote said. "So what's the plan—get in there nice and early for a nearo?"

"Nearo-schmearo. I'm thinking we push through, get there tonight and take a full zero tomorrow," Bawdy called back.

"Could be our last chance for a beero," Skunkers suggested hopefully.

"You say that every town."

"Just in case. You never know."

❦ ❦ ❦

The Andover Guest House was the cleanest, airiest place Flutterby had stayed since leaving home. Brocaded white curtains hung over the windows and the well-used furniture was also obviously well loved, a first in her experience with AT hostels. The place felt less like a hostel and more like a cozy B&B, but somehow still managed to charge reasonable hiker rates. There were both private rooms (in which she and Skunkers had enjoyed the hell out of last night's unexpected privacy) and a communal bunkroom where everyone else was staying.

Looking out from the hostel's second story front porch, Flutterby could see all the goings on around town. Across the street at the Citgo, two camo-clad hunters leaned against their pickup, drinking beers and talking with Skunkers. Snatches of the conversation—a discussion of the relative merits of hunting with the .223 Remington cartridge versus the .308 Winchester—came floating up to her. The truck's bed was filled with the oddly deflated looking carcass of a black bear. A patch of something dark, oil or blood, slowly soaked into the gravel beneath the open tailgate.

A small boy in an oversized t-shirt rode a bike up and down the street. Like his shirt, the bike was much too big for his frame. He could barely reach his feet to the pedals, and Flutterby suspected he smacked his little nuts on the crossbar each time he dismounted. Which could explain why he'd been doing big lazy circles up and down Main Street for hours now without stopping. Even from a distance she could see that the rear tire of his bike badly needed air. Down the street some, out front of the diner/ice cream shop/liquor store/convenience mart, Bawdy scrutinized his new food purchases. And beyond him, Lazy JoJo walked Sweet Jane around the town green.

Every once in a while a car or a mud splattered ATV cruised through town. There weren't any traffic lights, but no one seemed in any hurry. And already, after lounging away the afternoon on the porch, Flutterby recognized many of these drivers and vehicles as they went about their business.

Tucked up high in the roof eaves overhead, a series of elaborate wheel-shaped webs were visible. A flesh-colored orb weaver spider (or so Bartleby had identified them) sat at the center of each web, waiting for supper to appear like Archie Bunker in his armchair after a hard day at the docks. The boys had all picked webs and bet which would catch more flies. Before dinner, the action had been hot and heavy with a fly getting trapped every few minutes, but nothing much since.

Skunkers and Flutterby had jointly cooked dinner for the group. A huge vat of pad thai noodles in peanut sauce. Mainly because the ingredients were limited to what they could get across the street, it hadn't come out very well. It was, in Flutterby's epicurean opinion, overcooked and under flavored. Nobody complained though, and there weren't any leftovers.

And now with her good deed done, Flutterby sat relaxing in a high-backed rocking chair, letting the meal digest, listening to evening's cricket song and watching over this idle corner of the world. Nearby, and lost in his thoughts, Bartleby occupied another chair.

When they finished doing the dishes, Old Man Trouble and Coyote joined them on the porch.

Coyote dropped into a chair, "You guys still hungry? Want some dessert?"

When Bartleby and Flutterby both nodded, he called down to

Bawdy, "Hey, pick up dessert, will ya? My treat."

"Like what?"

"Something chocolaty," Flutterby yelled.

Bawdy gave a thumbs up and disappeared back into the store.

Finished with their beers, the hunters climbed into their pickup and drove slowly away.

"That bear's huge, huh?"

"Serious rug," Bartleby said.

"Gross," Flutterby sneered.

"I know," he agreed, "but still, I'm sorta happy it isn't out there in the woods waiting for us."

When a black fly buzzed close to Coyote, he swatted wildly at it and somehow batted it into a web. After a few moments' struggle, the fly was trapped for good.

"Did you see that? Unbelievable," Coyote grumbled. Then he called down, "You got another one, Skunks."

Skunkers booya'd but didn't look up. He had flagged the boy on the bike over and was filling the kid's tires from the gas station air pump.

Trouble stood for a long bit watching the spiders work their webs. Finally, he reached into the cooler for a beer, cracked it and took a sip. "I don't wanna hear any more pining or whining about living the good life. This is it, people. Right here and right now, this is as good as life gets."

The morning sky was clear when Bawdy set off from Bemis Mt. Lean-to. It took a mile or two for his legs to warm up. He still had breakfast crumbs loitering in his beard and already he was hungry. But otherwise, life was good. Extremely dirty and weird, but indisputably good. With something like another two hundred forty miles to go to Katahdin, he was almost ninety percent there. On top of which, the desolate gloominess that was Maine's character, suited him well. There was a Tolkienesque quality to the wilds of Maine; a mossy, moody, muddy, sluggy, buggy bogginess that spoke to Bawdy's soul in words and ways those boring Mid-Atlantic states couldn't conceive.

Bawdy was good. The hike was good. Life was good.

When he reached Beamis Stream it was swollen full with rain water; every drop of which was hurrying along with a mindless determination not so unlike early morning commuters on Chicago's El train.

Looking left and right, Bawdy saw no obvious way to cross; no stepping stones, no tree trunks, no rope bridges or swinging vines for that matter. He considered scouting up and down the bank to see if any easy crossing point presented itself, but decided this was a waste of time. Currently the Beamis was a good twenty-five feet wide, probably a third again beyond its usual width. He couldn't tell exactly, but it didn't look to be much more than knee deep.

Seeing no other options, Bawdy removed his footwear. He knotted laces together and stuffed socks safely away before wrapping the laces securely around his left hand. Not wanting to hold both hiking poles in one hand, he javelined one across the water to the far bank and entered the water barefoot.

Many years later in a memoir, Bawdy would describe the experience as "ball-shriveling cold." The round river stones were moss covered and slick as fresh snot beneath his feet. He shuffled out five feet from shore before hitting the edge of the real current. Which was when he realized this crossing wasn't any kind of good idea. At the very least, he should've waited for company. He also realized it was way too late to try and turn around and return to the safety of the south bank.

Bawdy took his time, carefully placed and set each foot before transferring any weight to it. He used his remaining hiking pole like Tiny Tim Crachit used a crutch. The water was up to his knee, mid-thigh and then the tip of his johnson. The current started to pull at him, tug at him, suck at him. When Bawdy reached the middle of the stream, the flow was so persistent, so ruthlessly determined, his planted hiking pole was literally shaking. It gave off a metallic keening noise. Strong as they were, even his legs started to tremble from the effort of fighting the flow.

Somewhere in there, his foot slipped out from under him. He stumbled forward in an effort to catch himself, but the water had other plans.

In an instant he was down and underwater. Pack and all. Everything but his shoes still valiantly held aloft in his left hand. If ever there was an Olympic event called "the flop & plop" this performance would've made Bawdy a frontrunner for gold.

As it was, he came up spitting and spluttering. When he regained his footing (a minor miracle) he floated/fought his way to the north bank.

After recovering from the shock of this sudden dowsing and catching his breath, Bawdy couldn't help laughing at himself, "At least the silly city mouse kept his shoes dry."

Luckily, the sandy bank faced the morning sun. He laid out the contents of his pack to dry. Wrung out whatever needed it and hung everything out on low branches. This was nothing more than a minor setback, a funny story to tell back home. With a little luck, he'd be dried off and moving again in an hour, two tops.

Except, September can be a finicky time of year in Maine.

Dark clouds Bawdy hadn't even realized were in the sky, swooped in and blocked out the sun. It was raining before he could finish gathering his gear. So much rain came on so suddenly, the individual drops looked like solid streams of water pouring down.

Fast as Bawdy covered the next four miles to Sabbath Day Pond Lean-to, it didn't matter. His shoes were soaked through when he got there.

❦ ❦ ❦

Rangeley, Maine possessed a quaintly rugged charm or maybe a conservative quiet properness. In a good way, the place felt like it was stuck back in 1942 or thereabouts. The persistent wind coming off Rangeley Lake helped to sweep the fresh asphalt fumes up and away. A second shift road crew was repaving ME-4 through the center of town.

Bartleby lounged in one of the wooden Adirondack chairs lining The Rangeley Inn and Motor Lodge's wide front porch. After borrowing stationary from the front desk, he was writing yet another letter to his wife. He hadn't decided if he'd mail this one, but considering he hadn't mailed any of the last hundred, the odds weren't good.

Skunkers settled into a seat nearby and started petting Jane. He had a paper bag full of oversized Foster's beer cans and drank a long gulp from one of these.

"So you're pretty much fucked up, right, B?"

Bartleby stopped writing mid-word and looked over.

"No offense or nuttin', but I mean—isn't that why you started hiking in the first place? That's pretty much what you said back in Connecticut, isn't it?"

"Yeah," Bartleby nodded, "I guess so."

Skunkers chewed this over, took another pull on the beer and scratched at Jane's ears.

"And what—now you're magically all better?"

It was Bartleby's turn to think. After a while he reached over, helped himself to a beer. He took a swig and cleared his throat.

"Honestly, I don't really know. I feel different, but no...I guess I don't think I am all better yet, not exactly."

"Huh."

"Before I didn't...couldn't care much either way, but now, now I very much want to be better."

"Figure that's enough?"

"Seems like it should be, doesn't it?"

Skunkers nodded.

"You wondering if your PTSD is gonna go away?"

A blush slow bloomed up Skunkers' neck and disappeared into the scraggle of his beard.

"I might be fucked up, Skunks, but I'm not a complete dope. What's that Trubs is always calling you? Young and strong and stupid? Well, you keep right on being young and strong and stupid."

"Yeah?"

"You do that, and there ain't much gonna slow you down for long."

❦ ❦ ❦

Coyote, Bartleby and Jane waited for a hitch back to trail. Even in old-time Rangeley, cars willing to stop and pick up a couple of stinking hitchhikers and a big dog were few and far between. To pass time, Coyote sifted through his gear, making final adjustments.

"Dude, get your smile on. Nobody's gonna stop if you don't show some pearly whites. Stand up and put your shoulders back. What kind of operation are we running here?"

"Lots of advice from a guy sitting on the guardrail."

A pickup slowed, looked like it might stop, but continued puttering past.

"Fuckers," Coyote grumbled.

"Their truck bed was filled up with crap. We never woulda fit."

"*I* woulda fit fine."

There was a long pause in both passing traffic and conversation. Coyote lobbed rocks at a tree across the road, "Hey—you're from Connecticut, too, right?"

"Uh-huh."

"Follow the Huskies?"

"A little. I went to UConn."

"Knew this dude, put a thousand on them to win it all in the *preseason*," Coyote whistled, "he cleaned up. You ever go down to the casinos?"

"Once, back when they opened. Not really my scene."

"Hey, gimme a twenty. I need a twenty."

Bartleby looked suspiciously at Coyote, but still reached for his wallet and pulled out a twenty.

"Yeah, gimme that thing," Coyote plucked the twenty away.

"I can't really afford—"

Coyote handed back a wadded crumple of dirty money, "Here, trade ya."

The crumple included two fives, fourteen singles, five quarters, three nickels, two dimes and seven pennies. A grand total of $25.67.

"What's all this?"

"You just made five dollars and sixty-seven cents and I probably just shaved off another ounce. No reason for me to carry all that to Monson, right?"

Bartleby shook his head, "You really are sick."

Coyote just grinned.

Register: Piazza Rock Lean-to

9/1 Happy birthday to my first + best trail nemesis, STD aka
      Windy Indy aka Stray Dog. Wherever he may be.
                                              Bawdy

9/1 And thanks for the hiking poles. –Bartleby

From where she was resting on top of Saddleback Mountain, Flutterby could just barely make out Jane and Bartleby as they worked across the saddle and up the southern face of The Horn. Even with her camera zoomed in tight, they didn't look like much more than black ants, but she thought it might still be a decent shot.

Flat tenting spots were few and far between up on the rock strewn summitscape of Lone Mountain. The best of these were filled with either Bartleby's tent, Skunkers' tent or Bawdy's tarp. Coyote slept out under the wide universe of stars.

They decided to camp up there to catch the sunset. It was colder and windier up high, but the evening sky was clear and cloudless. Seemed like a fine night to sleep out, to bear witness to one of their few remaining sunsets on trail.

Nobody saw the clouds come rolling in. It was late and dark and everyone but Coyote was tucked away safe under cover. Shortly after the stars and the moon slipped away, the first specks of rain pattered down.

Between the hard rock mattress, the warmth-sapping wind and all the allergic sneezing, Coyote had hardly slept. Operating on the premise that the worst sleep was better than none at all, he dug deeper into his sleeping bag, hoping this was nothing more than heavy dew. He did his best to ignore the spitting rain, but the random pits and pats joined together and formed a demoralizingly steady pitter-patter. He sat up and scanned the sky. When he didn't find any solace there, he cast about for his headlamp.

"What time is it, Skunks?" Coyote didn't worry about waking Skunkers up. Everyone woke whenever the weather turned bad.

"Oh two hundred."

"Fuck a fat duck," Coyote barked. It was way too early to start up hiking. But without a tent of his own to hide in, he didn't have many other options. Only three other tents there with him on the summit; Flutterby was in with Skunkers, Bawdy's tarp was barely big enough to keep him dry and Bartleby and Jane were in their pyramid.

Coyote gathered up his gear, dragged it towards Bartleby's tent. He unzipped the door and started haphazardly stuffing things inside.

Jane was awake and alert, Bartleby less so, "Whuz' happening?"

"Starting to rain, I'm coming in with you two bedbugs."

Sometime back when he was young, Coyote learned it was always better to push himself into places than wait for an invitation. He shoved the last of his gear through the tent flap before Bartleby could mount any objections.

"Yote, toss my pack over, will ya," Bawdy called.

"Hand me my shorts and Flubby's socks hanging in the tree," Skunkers said. "And can you tuck our shoes under the fly?"

Coyote dashed around, tossing and handing and tucking. When he finished, the wind and rain were starting to get serious.

"You need anything while I'm out here, B? Want your pack? These your shoes?"

"Yeah. Bring it all in, I guess."

Mad Chatter's tent swallowed up Coyote and his minimal belongings without much difficulty. It took some shifting and organizing, but they made room for him to lay out his sleeping pad and get settled with his feet resting on his pack.

Jane looked dubiously from Bartleby to Coyote and back to Bartleby before squirming over to lay alongside Bartleby's body. She put all four feet, and her corresponding trail worn toenails, onto Coyote's sleeping bag.

"Dude, you actually let her sleep next to you?"

Bartleby was lying back-to-back with Jane, "Don't got a seven hundred dollar sleeping bag to keep me warm. I'd be freezing without her."

Coyote sneezed.

"Moron," Bartleby mumbled sleepily. It was only a few seconds before he started snoring.

Fearful that her nails would puncture the fragile lining of his sleeping bag, Coyote spent the next hours shifting Jane's feet away and listening to the weather.

❦

The crack of lightning sounded close. Felt close. Was close.

An angry boom of thunder followed.

"Five seconds," Skunkers called out. "Getting closer."

The wind was howling, the thunder less individually distinct rumbles than one long steady rumble fluctuating in intensity. The lightning was frequent and sharp and about as scary as anything they'd experienced on trail so far.

Because he hadn't been able to drive stakes into the rocky ground, Bartleby had instead opted to anchor the tent with melon-sized stones. Under normal circumstances, these were a fine substitute, though they weren't standing up to the current onslaught of heavy weather well. Already one corner of the tent fly was snapping in the wind like a locker room full of wet towels. Wind and wet both were coming in under the fly, but Coyote was still warmer and dryer than he would've been.

"Barometer's dropping faster than a hajji with a rifle."

"Do you know what that means?" Bartleby whispered.

Coyote shrugged.

Jane whimpered.

GGGGRRRRCRACKATHOOMGGGGRRRR

The lightning was so bright, Coyote saw it through his eyelids.

"We don't get off this mountaintop," Skunkers called, "we're gonna get fried. My tent poles are shaking like a hajji without a rifle."

Bartleby grimaced.

"What? I'm not going out there," Coyote yipped. "Bawdy, what do you think? Bawdy!"

"I can hear him snoring," Bartleby said.

"No way is he snoring." Coyote listened, "Alright, he's snoring." Coyote yelled to the other tent, "Skunks, Bawdy's asleep and I don't want to go out in this shit. What time is it?"

"Oh-four-hundred-thirty. Be light soonish. We all got metal tent poles, and there isn't any tree cover up here. Gotta get lower."

"Bawdy!" Coyote yelled loud as he could, but the storm drowned him out. "Bawdy you droopy boob, wake up!"

A sleepy, "What?"

"Skunks says the barometer's dropping and we gotta get off this mountain."

Bawdy's groan carried on the wind, "G.I. Joe must be so happy he has that stupid watch right now. Where are we supposed to go?"

"Yeah, Skunks," Coyote called, "where we going?"

Skunkers busted out his data book, took a minute to figure a plan, "Spalding Mountain Lean-to. It's less than three miles."

"Spalding Mountain Lean-to," Coyote relayed to Bawdy. "Like three miles."

Nothing but silence from Bawdy's tarp.

"He's snoring again," Bartleby said.

"Bawdy. Bawdy! BAWDY!"

"What?"

"We're going to Spalding Mountain Lean-to."

"It might pass."

"He says it might pass, Skunkers."

"And he *might* be the smartest man in the world, but I doubt it. Flubby and I are packing up and getting the flock off of this summit. You chumps do whatever you want. I don't see you at Spalding Mountain, I'm coming back up here tomorrow and getting myself a seven hundred dollar sleeping bag."

Coyote looked at Bartleby, "What'd'ya think?"

Bartleby sat up, shrugged. "I think I didn't walk all the way from Georgia just to get struck by lightning on some no-name mountain two hundred miles short of Katahdin."

"So does that mean we go out in this or stay here?"

"I guess we gotta get wet."

It was the fastest pack up ever. Two minutes from wearing a sleeping bag to wearing a backpack.

By the time Bartleby finished securing Jane's panniers, Skunkers and Flutterby were already gone. Coyote stowed the last of his gear. Bawdy, having stalled for forty seconds, was still ramming items hurry-scurry into his pack.

Standing there waiting for Bawdy in just a t-shirt and shorts, Coyote started shivering.

"Take Jane and get hiking," Bartleby told him. "I'll help Bawds.

We'll be right behind."

Coyote headed off with Jane in tow. Normally she wouldn't have gone with him, but the booming thunder was so frightening and close, she would have willingly followed a stranger off the mountain.

❧

The hiking wasn't pleasant. Slickrock footing, watery runoff and stiff winds catching at backpacks like they were jib sails, made for a precarious descent off of Lone Mountain. The rain was sharp and cold as steel. This, on top of the looming darkness and the occasionally blinding brightness of lightning, made for the worst visibility conditions possible. From all around came the eerie moans and ominous creaking protests of large branches and small trees bending madly before the wind.

A stray gust caught at Bartleby's Yankee cap and swept it away into the darkness before he could reach a hand up.

"Good riddance," Bawdy called.

"Nicest ball cap I ever owned."

"Sorry man, but I'm a Cubs fan."

With the hat gone, Bartleby felt more vulnerable than ever. For the remaining distance to the shelter, he inadvertently slouched low and kept his head ducked, as if that might somehow ward off any stray bolts of lightning.

In a general sense, Spalding Mountain Lean-to was a fine shelter. It was plenty roomy with a roof that didn't look to be leaking. There was even translucent sections of corrugated roofing that acted as a poor man's skylight. A very nice touch, but only when the sun was shining.

Specifically though, the wind had driven rain into the shelter's mouth. More than half the floor was wet and getting wetter. Inside, Old Man Trouble and Lazy JoJo were struggling to hold a tarp over themselves. This was only a marginally successful deterrent to the encroaching storm.

On the whole, the shelter was better than nothing, probably more than that for two people. But for seven hikers and a dog, it wasn't close to ideal.

Everyone crowded under the roof, dripping wet and wondering if they could make do for the remainder of the night.

Skunkers was looking at the data book and a map, "What do you think, Trubs?"

The single earbud of Old Man Trouble's palm-sized weather radio was plugged into his ear. "This is all part of that hurricane coming up the coast."

"Hurricane? First I'm hearing about any hurricane," Coyote snorted.

"Just a little one," Old Man Trouble winked. "They kept saying it wouldn't reach the interior until this morning. Figured I could make Stratton before the heavy stuff started coming down. Now I don't know. Lemme look at the book."

Flutterby eyed the shelter space. "I guess we could make this work. We're going to be sitting in each other's laps, but we'll be warm at least."

"Hot damn," Old Man Trouble crowed. Then to Skunkers he said, "Gimme that map, son. Yes sir, looksee here. We're only three miles south of Sugarloaf Mountain."

"So?"

"Don't hold me to this, but I seem to recall a warming hut up there."

"Yeah?"

"Yeah. A great big place with windows all around. Nothing too fancy, but it's all closed in. Or was anyway. Could be the perfect spot to wait this out."

"We gonna be able to get in?"

Trouble shrugged, "Generally, warming huts are left open year round so hikers won't have to break in. Of course, Spalding Mountain is between us and Sugarloaf. We gotta go up and over a four thousand feet peak which is gonna be every type of unpleasant."

❦ ❦ ❦

❦ ❦ ❦

Bartleby had thought he'd been happy to see the shelter back on Spalding Mountain. When the warming hut on Sugarloaf Mountain came into view, he broke into a goofy big smile of relief. He'd spent the last mile mentally preparing himself for the worst—he fully expected the hut to be inaccessibly locked, burned down, somewhere else entirely or simply a figment of Old Man Trouble's imagination.

But indeed, the warming hut existed. It was ugly as an ass pimple from the outside, maybe a little uglier on the inside, but it wasn't locked, it wasn't wet and it wasn't windy.

Essentially, what it was, was an empty space, a single huge room with a fireplace hearth in the middle and rattling windows lining the outer walls. On a clear day, it was easy to imagine the view being spectacular. Currently, he couldn't see much more than heavy rain, wind bent evergreens and close, gray clouds.

There was little in the way of furniture beyond a single picnic table and a few old, broken chairs. By the look of the place, it hadn't been used for much of anything official in years.

Old Man Trouble looked around, "Home sweet home, eh? Not quite nine AM and we're in safe for the day. Once again, the Trail has provided for one and all. Who could still doubt the mysterious purposes of an all-wise providence?"

Throughout the morning, the storm continued to strengthen. Though, once everyone had time to eat a hot breakfast, slip into warm clothes and hang out their wet gear, this was of little concern.

✤

It took them well into the afternoon, but Coyote and Skunkers eventually got so they couldn't stand to play another game of cribbage. Bawdy finished reading *A Day in the Life of Ivan Ivanovich* and didn't have another book on hand (that he hadn't read), so he consented to play some euchre. Old Man Trouble, Bawdy and Skunkers all knew how to play, Coyote learned on the fly. It was a simple Midwestern game played with a short deck and, good as he was with cards, he caught on and was winning in no time.

✤

A one-for-all-and-all-for-one attitude permeated the day. Skunkers and Bartleby went outside with Bawdy's tarp and used it to catch enough rainwater to fill everyone's water bottles. Flutterby had plenty of denatured alcohol fuel and shared it out to anyone who needed extra. JoJo enjoyed working her stove, so she boiled up pot of tea after hot pot of tea. English, Irish, Prince of Wales—it didn't matter so long as someone would drink it.

Old Man Trouble peeled and sliced all of his raw garlic. He offered it around as an afternoon snack. Bored as they were, everyone tried some. After the garlic, Skunkers passed one of Chatter's whiskey bottles around. Even Bawdy got into the spirit of giving. He poured all of Chatter's pills onto the table.

"Seriously, take some. Be sure and try one of these green guys—they give you a kinda frizzled, floating-above-the-clouds feeling. The white/pinks too, but they're more like floating *in* the clouds. And the blues get me giggling like two school girls. Love the blues. But not the light blues. They'll make ya itch. Nothing harsh, it's like a gentle, tingly oxy itch, but I swear I can't tell if they actually do anything else. Watch out for the white/yellows, they'll make you groggy/foggy in about five minutes. Great for going to sleep, but…."

"Mmmmm," Skunkers said. "Gimme one a each."

After popping pills, Coyote emptied out his food bag. The pickings were painfully slim. Two mismatched ramen, a child's handful of cashews and a rat-sized nibble of cheddar.

"That all the food you got left, Slick? That totally sucks," Skunkers consoled. There couldn't have been more genuine sympathy in his voice if he was giving condolences on a stage-four cancer diagnosis. Then he proceeded to empty all three of his food bags into one steeped heap of edibles. A foil packet of Pop-Tarts went skidding off the table. He had easily enough food to feed an average human for a week.

"It's only another nine miles into town, we would've been there already today if not for this weather," Coyote grumped, "why in the name of Ray Jardine are you carrying all that?"

"Don't be a hater, just cuz you don't got no Pop-Tarts." Skunkers stacked like items together, noodle bricks on noodle bricks, condiments, snack bars and cans of meat towered atop each other. He hummed happily to himself as he plotted out what he was going to have for late lunch, early supper, dinner, second supper and his bedtime snack.

Bawdy read the label on a tin of chicken, "Says this contains 100% mechanically separated chicken."

"Sweet."

"What the fuck does that mean exactly? Separated how? From what?"

"I think mechanically separated meat is just another way of saying 'pink slime'," Flutterby sneered.

Skunkers didn't care, might not have even heard. He was too busy singing the 'Gotta keep 'em separated' line from Offspring's song *Come Out and Play*.

It was quickly obvious that Skunkers was carrying more food than everyone else combined. Half a dozen pairs of hungry eyes watched as he arranged his store of dry goods.

It took him a bit, with the whiskey and pills working their magic, but when he finished, Skunkers looked up and beamed around, "I will now consider any offers."

"Seriously?

"Bartleby," Skunkers continued, "you still carrying Q-tips? Got enough for everyone?"

"Yep."

"What would you take for them?"

"I'd give them up for free."

Skunkers tossed him a mac and cheese.

"Bawdy, you got any books I might like?"

"First half of *The Sea Runners*. Great little adventure story. Flubby's reading the second part now."

"Will you take a ramen and two Twinkies for it? Good. Flubsy, you take anything and everything that catches your eye—I haven't slept so well since before going overseas. Here, Trubs, have the rest of these wasabi peas for knowing about this awesome place. You want anything else, consider it in exchange for a little after-dinner harmonica music. JoJo, I would happily part with some M&Ms if you could see your way to starting a fire. Probably enough scrap wood and busted furniture to warm us up for a couple hours anyway. If you need it, my deodorant spray works better than lighter fluid. Don't wanna leave Jane out now, do we? You think she'd like the rest of this mozzarella cheese, Bartleby? It's not too melty."

Jane barked her affirmation before Bartleby could say anything.

Skunkers looked around, "Now is that everyone?"

Coyote sat with his eyes down. He didn't dare look over.

"Hey Slick, almost forgot about ya. You're sitting so quiet when usually you're laughing and calling me The Big Bumpkin, Hillbilly Hayseed and help me out, what's the other one?"

"Sergeant Skunkers?"

"Not that one."

"Ranger Rick?"

"No, I think it was 'Bubba Boob the Country Rube.' Which, I gotta admit, does have a certain ring to it. So if you want a little something to eat, all you gotta do is repeat after the Big Bumpkin. Sound good?"

Coyote grumbled something that sounded like "this sucks" under his breath.

"What's that?"

"Sounds good."

"Okay, here we go. A light pack is a lazy pack. Go ahead, you can do it."

"A light pack is a lazy pack."

"And a heavy pack..."

"And a heavy pack..."

"Is a happy pack."

"Is a happy pack."

And with that, the heady smell of white gas, kerosene and denatured alcohol filled the warming hut as everyone set to cooking up their Skunkers' Special.

❦

After dinner, they dragged the picnic table close to the fire. Bawdy sat on one end of the bench seat, the whiskey bottle clutched in his hands. Next to him, Flutterby leaned back with her eyes closed. Lazy JoJo twisted a Q-tip in her ear, took it out, inspected it, grimaced and stuck it back in for a second go-round. When she was good and done with it, had used both ends to her satisfaction, she flicked it into the fire. On the bench's far end, Old Man Trouble played a slow, somber tune on his harmonica.

Sitting to one side, Coyote quickly scanned and slowly fed the pages of an old *Jugs* magazine into the fire. Opposite him, a barefoot Skunkers was arranging everyone's wet socks and shoes in front of the fire— laying them out, turning them over and generally facilitating the drying process. Bartleby sat nearby with Jane's head rested on his thigh.

When Old Man Trouble stopped playing, a contemplative silence filled the void.

Bawdy took a small sip before handing the whiskey back to Skunkers, "Here, Skunks, take this away before I finish it on you."

Skunkers looked over, "It's alright, Bawds, I got another one." Reaching into his pack, he produced a second plastic bottle full of whiskey. "See?"

Coyote snorted, Bawdy gaped and everyone laughed pretty good.

"You know, when I was napping earlier," Bartleby said, "I dreamed I sat down and ate a whole whoopie pie."

"What's whoopie pie?" Coyote asked.

"No clue. I saw somewhere it's the official dessert of Maine, but I've never actually seen one."

"So what'd they look like in your dream?"

"Was like this big, with this perfect crust and cinnamon crumbs and—"

"Sorry to burst your bubble," Old Man Trouble cut in, "but they're not anything like a real pie. Look like those flying saucer ice cream sandwiches that Carvel makes and they taste like a Devil Dog, a chocolate cupcake and a Ring Ding mixed together."

"You had me at Devil Dog, Trubs. I'd mug a troop of girl scouts for a couple of whoopie pies."

"You seriously still hungry, Skunks? You've guttled four meals since lunch."

"You think it's easy keeping this figure? Shit," Skunkers took a long pull before passing the bottle. "So it's only eight o'clock—what's next?"

A long minute passed. Outside, hurricane winds battered against the hut.

Finally, Bawdy said, "That's the big question, isn't it? We're all sitting here wondering what's next, right?"

A heavy silence spread out and filled the warming hut.

"I'm not wondering," Old Man Trouble offered. "I live in New Hampshire. My wife's gonna be waiting for me at Katahdin Stream

Campground. She'll put on a post-summit hiker feed and then she'll bring me home and make me spend the next four months playing with the grandkids."

Flutterby shrugged, "I don't know exactly where or when, but I'll be getting back into nursing sometime soon. Just gotta make sure I don't marry another toilet-tank loving asexual doctor."

"I'm starting school," Skunkers said. "Down in Tennessee. So I'm not wondering as much as worrying. Never been one for schoolwork or teachers, but I guess I didn't used to like books either. I'm never gonna be a doctor, but I can promise all y'all I'll never sit down backwards to pee."

Skunkers kept staring into the fire, avoided looking at Flutterby when he said this. Which was too bad, he missed the little smile that crept across her face.

"And if school doesn't work out, I'm gonna seriously consider another hike. I don't know, the PCT or maybe the Colorado Trail."

A quiet moment passed as everyone processed the idea of another long hike.

"Well," Lazy JoJo grumbled, "guess we'll have to see where the road takes me." She followed this by flicking a soppy splinter of toothpick into the fire. "Driving truck's gotten pretty old and home ain't nothing special. Might be I stay in Maine for a bit and see how it fits."

"Going back to the world is gonna be weird," Bawdy admitted. "We've been out here, what, five months now? Feels like a lifetime. In a good way. I mean, I'm beat to six shades of shit, but I've never felt better. Bet I lost fifty pounds. They say the transition back to "the real world" isn't easy and I believe it. Everything's so simple out here. Get some food, walk all day, sleep all night and keep on following blazes until you need more food.

"I'm gonna try to get a gig in publishing and if nothing comes through, I'll go back to teaching. Gonna be mad at myself if I spackle all the weight back on." Pause. "On a side note, I've been thinking about giving stand-up a shot."

"Like stand-up comedy?"

"Yeah, it's probably a crazy idea, but it seems like all the comedians play down to the masses. I could be the "smart" comedian, right? Play to the intellectual types, talk about grad school, teaching dopey, disinterested kids and being overlorded by self-important professors. I don't know...theoretically, hilarity ensues."

Coyote tossed the last pages of magazine onto the fire. They swooshed up brightly, "My situation's particularly strange. I don't have a home. Haven't had anything close to one in a long time. Not sure I even know how to start that process. Or where I'd possibly want to do something like that."

"Maybe you and Frecklebutt can figure it out together," Bawdy suggested.

Any answer Coyote might've had was drowned out by a chorus of groans.

As the paper burned away, the fire died down dark and low.

"I'm wondering and worrying both," Bartleby admitted. "Don't know what happens after Katahdin. My wife told me not to come home unless I finished the hike, but she didn't say what happens after that. I'm heading to Connecticut, but I don't have any idea what's waiting for me. Maybe nothing. Maybe everything. Scary to think about it, so mostly I'm not."

Just then the warming hut's door blew open. Eight heads snapped around as Roland appeared from out of the darkness. He was hang-dog wet but smiling; happy to see people and the fire both.

"Rough out there," was all he said as he shed wet gear and clothes and leaned in sizzling close to the fire.

"You just hiked through the best part of a hurricane in the dark," Old Man Trouble told him.

"Crazy kid," Bawdy snorted. "Hey, we were just going around, saying what our plans are for, you know, after. You got anything planned?"

"What? Climbing the dark tower isn't enough?"

"Well, yeah, just in case you're still with us after that."

"Guess I'll go pay a visit to the Red King."

"What's that mean exactly?" Skunkers asked.

"Gonna look up Stephen King. He's a big time Maine guy. Shouldn't be too hard to find."

❦ ❦ ❦

Stratton, Maine was little more than a way station. Pretty much, it consisted of a diner, a combination hardware/grocery store and a motel called the White Wolf Inn. Presumably the White Wolf Inn's name came from the wolf-shaped plywood cutouts arranged along its rooftop, but nobody bothered asking.

Stratton was both woodsy and remote enough, it was tough telling the hikers from the natives.

After a quick resupply, a dry night indoors and a heaping helping of whoopie pie as an after-breakfast dessert from the diner, Bartleby and Jane caught an early hitch back out to trail. They were the first of their group to get up into the Bigelow Mountains. Despite not knowing what was waiting for him in Connecticut, Bartleby was antsy and anxious; after one hundred and sixty some days in the woods, he was feeling the pull to get home and find out.

Everyone caught up by the time the trail tumbled out of the Bigelow Range and Flagstaff Lake came into view.

The lake's long, stony shore was too beautiful to pass up. There wasn't a house, a boat or a sign of human habitation anywhere in sight. Skunkers and Coyote jabbered and jawed at each other, skipped rocks and bet cans of Moxie soda on the outcome. Roland and Bartleby wandered the shoreline, collecting driftwood for a campfire. Flutterby scratched Jane's belly while waiting for Bawdy to play his turn at Scrabble.

Summer was good and done. Autumn could be seen in the coloring of the leaves, felt in the evening's chill, heard in the loon's willowy cry.

❦

Long after the fire died away, Bartleby lay in his sleeping bag. The fur ruff on his cap kept out the creeping chill. The night's sky was brilliant with individual stars and a mesmerizing green glimmer furled and unfurled across the northern horizon.

"Anybody awake?" Skunkers whispered.

"Yep," Bartleby said. "You watching that green glow up there?"

"Fucked if I'm not. Is that them northern lights?"

"Uh-huh. Aurora Borealis."

"Sweet."

❦ ❦ ❦

Skunkers was already knee-deep when Bartleby reached the southern bank of the Kennebec River. He carried his sleeping pad under his arm, like a flimsy-ass kickboard.

Where the AT crossed it, the Kennebec was seventy, maybe seventy-five yards wide. Deep and swollen with the recent rains, the river was cold and fast and about as uninviting as any they'd seen so far.

"Tell him he's gonna die, Bartleby," Flutterby enjoined.

"You're gonna die, Skunks."

"I'm not gonna die. Just wanna see."

Skunkers had removed his watch and given it to Flutterby for safekeeping. She checked the time, "It's almost quarter to one. The ferry guy comes back at two o'clock."

"I know—I'm the one told you that. No big deal, just wanna see." After smiling big, Skunkers turned, dove atop his pad and started kicking furiously.

Bartleby took a seat next to Flutterby.

"You know, sometimes he acts so stupid I could scream."

"He a good swimmer at least?"

"Probably. I don't kn—"

Skunkers made it twenty-five yards across before his sleeping pad/ kickboard flipped out from under him. He sunk into the drink for a long moment, popped up sputtering and laughing a ways downstream. Fast as the current had moved him, it was moving his sleeping pad faster. He raced after, lunging and stroking and kicking for all he was worth. Took him most of a hundred yards before he corralled it and came wading back to shore.

Laughing like a ten year old, "See, I didn't die, Flubby Pie."

"You're a dope."

"Yeah, but I'm *your* dope."

Turned out, the Ferry Man was a guy with a red canoe. He shook his head when Skunkers told him how'd he'd tried swimming across.

"You could've died. There's a hydro station upstream. Never know when they're gonna open the floodgates."

It took some convincing, but Bartleby got Jane settled into the boat. He sat up front and paddled for all he was worth. By the time they reached the far bank, he couldn't feel his arms.

They waited on the bank as the Ferry Man went back for Skunkers and Flutterby.

There was some negotiating going on, Bartleby couldn't tell exactly, but it looked like Skunkers refused to take the front seat. He sat in the belly of the canoe and let Flutterby have the front.

They were two-thirds of the way across when Skunkers stood up, put his hand on his hip and pointed purposefully toward the distant shore. With his tricorner hat snugged onto his head, he gave a fair impression of Washington crossing the Delaware. As the canoe cleaved the Kennebec's waters, he started up speechifying, "Four score and seven years ago—"

"Flying high. Like from the radio edit of that song. *You're Beautiful,* I think."

"Yeah, by James Blunt. That's a good one, Yote. How about folk?"

"You're coming back with 'folk'?"

"Flight of the Concords first album was called *Folk the World Tour*. But if you don't like that one, how about...fooling. As in, I'm not *fooling* around with you anymore. Could keep spitting out f-bomb euphemisms—freaking, frosted, funked—all day long."

Register: Moxie Ball Lean-to

9/5 Walking today, I could totally smell autumn in the air. But I couldn't figure what it smelled like exactly. Wood smoke and dead leaves? Flubby

9/5 Drying hay? Bawds

9/5 Somehow smells warm and cold at the same time. Bartleby

9/5 First time I've been outside during Fall in eight years. Definitely doesn't smell like prison or a poker room. —Suckerfish Slick

9/5 Sunshine + cider. Skunky

Monson, Maine. The second to last stop on the Appalachian Express and famous for being the southern gateway to the Hundred-Mile Wilderness.

Bawdy lay on the little front lawn of Shaw's Boarding House and Hostel, rubbing his bloated belly. Breakfast had been an all you can eat bonanza of french toast and now, two hours later, he was just getting so he could comfortably breathe again.

He passed time studying his data book, calculating how many days of food he would need to carry into the Wilderness, "Just another hundred seventeen-point-eight miles to go."

Coyote shook his head, "Let's go ahead and call it one eighteen."

"Thanks, but I'll stick with a hundred seventeen-point-eight. Don't wanna walk any more than I have to. Seriously, once I touch that summit sign, I'm not taking another step. Gonna use Flutterby's hammock as a stretcher and have Skunkers and Bartleby carry me out."

"Even for you, Bawds, that's surprisingly lazy."

"That's not lazy, that's self-preservation. Look at me, I'm wasting away." He pinched at his waist. "Never in my life have I not had love handles. I swear the doctor used 'em to pull me out of the womb. Do you see any now?"

"Nope."

"You're goddamn right you don't—there's nothing left but skin and bone. I'm not careful, I'm gonna disappear entirely."

Coyote looked to Flutterby for support, "You wanna chime in here, Flubby?"

"Stop being such a lame-ass pussyfooter, Bawdy," she said.

Bawdy bridled, "You're calling *me* a pussyfooter?"

"What else should I call someone who pussyfooted all the way to Monson?"

"Never!" he cried. "Not once have I ever pussyfooted!"

Flutterby snorted, "With your aching knees and your sore feet and your sugar cramps, you're the very definition of a pussyfoot. The crown prince of pussyfooting. It's about time for you to finally man up."

"Yeah? Why's that?"

"For starters, I mailed my hammock home from Gorham, so there won't be any stretcher rides for you off Katahdin."

"Well, that sucks for me but I'm not being a pussyfoot. My knees hurt, my ankles feel broke and I all but walked my feet flat. Seriously, not one extra step. I don't care what you say, I'm swearing off walking for an entire month when I get done. Not getting off the couch for nothing. Gonna read, surf the web and watch bad TV until my eyes bleed." He shot Flutterby and Coyote a final defiant look. Then he nodded up the road, "Looks like the Skunky One and Banana

Boy got some beers."

Skunkers handed cans around, "Ladies and gentlemen, please join me in raising a drink to commemorate what is, in all likelihood, almost definitely going to be our very last beero together here on the AT."

The Hundred-Mile Wilderness. Considered by most anyone that knows anything to be the wildest, woolliest section of the whole Appalachian Trail. Except for a few overgrown logging roads and remote lakeside cabins, the AT didn't cross over or come close to any civilization from Monson all the way to Abol Bridge, one hundred miles to the north.

As last pushes went, it was a doozy. Up to this point, thru-hikers had been able to get off trail and resupply as often as they wanted. Doing so wasn't always ideal or easy, but it was always possible. Not so in the Wilderness. And with the coming change in season, the weather was growing increasingly harsh. Snow in September wasn't unheard of in central Maine. With most of a week's worth of food and newly reacquired colder-weather gear, thru-hikers generally set off from Monson carrying their heaviest packs since Georgia.

Register: Leeman Brook Lean-to

8/23 No roads, no escape.
      The Hundred-Mile Wilderness.
      Katahdin or bust!

                    High-Ku

9/8   Hey Roland: You want company stalking Stevie King? I'll
      wait for you at Katahdin Stream Campground if we don't
      see you before then.   Bawdy

"Gotta be the biggest one on the whole AT," Skunkers yelled.

Bartleby could barely hear him over the thunder of falling water.

Way back south of Springer Mountain, Bartleby remembered Amicalola Falls as a series of little unimpressive drops strung together like so many bulbs on a string of Christmas lights. Individually, none of the falls were particularly impressive, but as a whole they combined to make for a grand seven hundred foot spectacle.

Little Wilson Falls wasn't anything like Amicalola. It was big and brash; a splashing, roaring exhibition of raw power in a single forty foot drop. It seemed that thousands of gallons of water went thundering over Little Wilson Falls every second. Already, the stultifying noise of it had gotten into Bartleby's brain, made thinking all but impossible. Which turned out to be an unexpected respite from all his wondering and worrying.

Somewhere in the Wilderness. A hard hour's hike short of stopping for the night at Long Pond Stream Lean-to.

"Had a pizza dream last night," Bawdy said. "You know, Chicago-style deep dish all slopped up with sausage, peppers, mushrooms and seven different cheeses. I've had the taste in my mouth all day. Oh man, I tell ya, I could suck down a few slices right now."

"I've been thinking about my great aunt's pot roast since the Whites," Skunkers admitted. "Bubbly moist and stuffed with cloves of garlic. And she does these little roast vegetables on the side—mmmmmmmmm—the potatoes and onions are crusty brown on the outside and mushy soft inside. I would...I don't know what I *wouldn't* do for a steaming hot plateful right about now."

"Okay, Skunks, you really wanna play this game?" Bartleby called back from the front of the line. "Because my wife makes this lasagna that would make tears of joy dribble down your dirty cheeks. If we stumbled onto a pan of the stuff at the shelter, you would literally cry for an hour after eating it."

"That don't really mean nuttin' anymore," Skunkers said, "I might cry if we found half a box of moldy prunes."

"There was this restaurant back at the casino, an old school diner called The Slop Shop. I used to go in there sometimes after long poker sessions. Flirt with the waitresses, read the paper, have something to eat and unwind a bit."

"So?"

"They served up one serious slice of meat loaf. Two inches thick easy. Had olives baked into it and this tangy-sweet brown crust." Coyote shuddered, "Man, I used to love me that meat loaf."

"Used to?"

"Yeah. This one time, I was going on about how good it was, how I could eat it every day for the rest of my life. And this guy, Bad Ronnie, a real lowlife, I guess he got tired hearing about it. Propped me I couldn't eat nothing but that meat loaf for two months."

"Propped?"

"Proposition bet. You know, like, I got a proposition for ya. He offered me two thousand dollars if I could go a full eight weeks eating only the Meat Loaf Special Platter."

"What was on the platter?"

"Like I said, there was this big honking slice of meat, a plop of lumpy mashed potatoes under a scoop of gravy and a sprig of parsley on the side."

"Sounds sweet."

"Or at least not *too* bad," Bartleby said.

"It was terrible. I mean, I loved it for the first week. Definitely could've done it once a day for the two months. Longer even. But that wasn't the bet. I didn't even have to eat, but whenever I did, it was meat loaf and potatoes or nothing at all.

"Halfway through the second week, I was all plugged up. I mean, the stuff went down like bricks and mortar. Kept burping up that tangy brown sugar/mustardy taste. I'd brush fifteen times a day, but I still couldn't get it out of my mouth.

"Probably only ate two or three times that whole third week. Towards the end, I thought I was getting scurvy. Wanted to take a multi-vitamin, but Bad Ronnie said they counted as food. Got so I was asking for extra, extra, extra parsley, you know, trying to keep greens in my diet."

"Did you do it? Did you win the bet?"

"I lost twelve pounds and my skin turned meatloafy gray. That last week, I puked a coupla times, but, yeah, I won the bet."

"Nice work, Yote," Skunkers said. "What'd you do with the money?"

"Never got it. Bad Ronnie went broke; lost his whole wad playing Pai Gow Poker upstairs in the Asian Invasion. Last time I saw him was the day before our bet was up. He was slumming, playing low limits with a short stack and looked worse than me. I should've known something was up."

The sun hadn't quite gone all the way down and already a huge orange moon had tiptoed over the horizon. A big fat pumpkin floating close in the evening sky.

"Would you get a look at that thing? Zowie."

Flutterby gazed up, "Big and bright, huh?"

"And orange," Skunkers said.

"Harvest moon," Bartleby confirmed.

"Yeah? Wonder what makes it so big."

"Not actually any bigger or brighter or oranger," Bartleby explained, "just looks that way. Happens when any celestial bodies appear low on our horizon. Something about how white light gets scattered away by atmospheric particulates and more red light than usual passes through to our eyes."

Nobody would've batted an eye if Bawdy had spewed forth such an unexpectedly informative answer. Also, nobody would've listened. But

Bartleby coming out with something like this was a bit of a shock.

"Look at the big brain on Bartleby," Bawdy whooped.

"You shitting us?" Coyote asked.

Bartleby shrugged, "For a while there, I was gonna be a science teacher."

"Big science guy," Coyote chirped.

"Huge," Bawdy agreed. "Shit, if we weren't all but done hiking, I'd change your trail name to BSG. Turns out, you're nothing like the real Bartleby anyway."

The mountains of the Barren-Chairback Range weren't particularly big or high (the highest, Barren Mountain, reached an elevation of only 2,660 ft) but having to cross over all five peaks in less than fifteen miles made them feel twice their actual size.

A line of hikers slowly moved towards the humped rock summit of Third Mountain.

These hikers were sunburned, with wind-blasted cheeks, dry flints of skin flaking off their ears and shoulders, grime-filled wrinkles and dirt collecting in just about every seam imaginable.

They were lean and toned and toughened. And more than just muscles, a certain confidence and strength of character was obvious and visible in their smiles, their eyes and the way they kept moving upwards and onwards.

Their clothes were ragged, stained and hanging loose.

Skunkers went first, his camouflage booney hat barely containing the mane of blonde exploding beneath it. He'd lost weight, but not anything as drastic as some of the others. His backpack was still large, but a few extra pounds wasn't going to slow him down. After surviving two combat tours in Iraq, there really wasn't much that would.

Flutterby wore the fan-favorite Blueberry Hills, though the much-loved sports bra didn't have quite the same bounce as it once had. She didn't think to look, but the band of white skin on her ring finger was gone; had entirely tanned over and disappeared. With it went the last trace of a marriage best forgotten.

Next came Coyote loping along with a hungry grin and his pack bobbing lightly in his wake. He looked young and clean with no beard and only a buzz of hair. Cold or hungry or allergic, he didn't care, just so long as he was playing to win.

Bartleby's Chiquita shirt was still ridiculous, but it had lost its hard-edged banana coloring. Had faded to a softer, mellower yellow. He still wore the shorts he'd bought at Neels Gap. They were ripped and shredded, and a few sizes too big now, but still wearable. It was difficult to read much of anything in his face, but Bartleby's step had a certain spring, a buoyancy that hadn't been there on Springer.

Jane came close on his heels. If she still grieved for Mad Chatter, it wasn't obvious. She had Bartleby now and that seemed to be enough. Every so often she turned back, looked to see that Bawdy was still bringing up the rear.

Which, of course, he was. The pointed Bavarian hat cocked on his brow, a shoulder length mullet sweeping along behind him like Dracula's cape, his glasses streaked with sweat, his face flushed with effort. And light as it had been, he was happy to have rid himself of the burden of his little black notebook.

🍁 🍁 🍁

"Woe," Bawdy moaned for the hundredth time. "Woe is me."

This seemed to be more for attention and comedic effect than because something was actually, imminently wrong with him. Though, so far, no one was laughing.

"Shut your yap, and go to sleep, Bawds."

"Woe. Woe is me. I'm too hungry to be tired."

"Well, I'm too tired to be hungry, so unless you want me to stuff your woe-hole full of a knuckle sandwich," Skunkers offered, "you'd better check your volume. I was almost out."

Most everyone was snuggled in for the night. Only Old Man

Trouble was still out and about, swatting away bugs and watching for his water to boil. In the meanwhile, he drank occasional slugs of whiskey straight through the netting of his head net.

"Ohhhh, woe."

Flutterby sat up, "Okay, Bawdy, what exactly is wrong now?"

"What isn't wrong? I got yellow bruises lingering on both hip bones and my neck's all kinked up like a thirty-six year old Slinky. And I tell ya," Bawdy banged a fist against the shelter floor, "I'm not gonna miss these hard wooden floors one bit."

"Well, I'm not gonna miss peeing in the middle of the night," Flutterby confessed. "It's dark, it's cold, you're trying to slip into camp shoes without stepping on anyone, then you're tripping on rocks and trees and worrying about getting eaten by a bear. It's a nightmare."

"Anyone else feel that breeze in the privy this morning?" Coyote chimed in from his corner of the shelter. "Whistling right up from underneath, nipping something awful. My boys are used to stewing in a sweat lodge, which is no preparation for wind tunnel toilets. I'm talking chilly willy the penguin."

Old Man Trouble laughed, "It'll be most of six months now wearing these same stinky clothes. And believe me, there's no saving them. From shoes to shirt, you just gotta burn it all when you get home."

"Looking forward to wearing cotton again."

"And changing clothes whenever you want," Flutterby added. "Sweats, jeans, skirts, tops, fresh underwear, comfy jammies. None of this wearing something for a week straight."

"And hungry as I am, I'm done with camp food," Coyote grumbled. "Tired of eating pasta with a spoon, tired of being locked into menu choices I made five days ago. I'm *tired* of cooking. Before Springer, it'd been more than seven years since I'd cooked for myself."

Skunkers raised himself onto an elbow, "I'm tired of sweaty cheese," he proclaimed. "It'll be nice to live out of a fridge again and have options. And I'm really tired of this beard. I swear it's got rotting bits of food, and who knows what else, caught in it. Sometimes, when the wind's in my face, I catch a whiff of something that smells, I don't know, like fresh monkey butt."

"They do hold a certain odor," Bartleby agreed from the depths of his tent, "but I don't mind that nearly as much as putting on wet socks in the morning."

A collective groan of agreement circled through the chill evening air.

"Wet shoes."

"Wet clothes."

"Sleeping in a wet bag."

"Setting up a wet tent."

"And never mind having hot water for a daily shower, it'd be nice to have any running water at all," Bartleby continued. "I'm tired of walking out of the way for water sources. Tired of filling up from mud puddles and I'm sick of my drinking water tasting like an over-chlorinated swimming pool."

Flutterby nodded agreement, "And I'm not gonna miss drinking from a plastic hose."

"Plastic anything," Bawdy agree. "Gimme some nice glassware, right?"

Register: Carl A. Newhall Lean-to

9/10   Slipped off a bog bridge today. When Yote and Skunkers hauled me out, my shoe got mudsuckered off. If Skunkers hadn't stuck his arm into the mud hole and rescued it, I'd be one-shoeing it up to the top of K.   —Flutterby

Bartleby couldn't help but think about the white blazes he'd been

284

following now for as long back as he cared to remember. It was surprising how much they helped to simplify things and imbue him with a sense of purpose and direction. There was no worrying about where to go, you just kept on walking until you saw the next splotch of paint. And then the one after that. Trail hadn't been easy, but it had been obvious and straightforward. And for him, that had almost made it easy. He worried that life back home wasn't going to be so blazingly obvious, so linear, so point-to-point. He knew it wasn't going to be.

He hoped it didn't matter.

Jane saw it first and froze mid-step, her nose working furiously.

When Bartleby stopped, Bawdy bumped into him, "What the—"

"Shhhh."

Forty yards off trail, downhill and half-hidden behind two trees.

A moose.

"Goddamn," Bawdy whispered. Recently, Bartleby had been lax about leashing Jane during the hiking day. Now he reached down, got a firm grip on her collar.

Even from that distance and the downward angle, the moose looked big. Clydesdale-big but with thinner, longer legs. Its massive antler spread came complete with hanging strands of moss.

The moose must've sensed something, because after a moment's pause, it snorted and set off at a trot, crashing away through the undergrowth.

They watched until they couldn't hear it anymore. At which point, Jane gave Bartleby a look which plainly asked: Just what the hell was that thing?

From up on Whitecap Mountain, Bartleby got his first view of

Katahdin. If he'd had a data book he'd have known he was still seventy-two-point-eight miles away. Of course, he didn't have a data book and he hadn't been expecting it or even looking for Katahdin, but there it was all the same.

The mountain certainly looked formidable, but different than he'd expected. From this distance, it wasn't so much a single distinct and dramatically sharp peak, but instead a raised ridgeline, a massive plateau rising above the horizon.

"See that, Jane? No, not the dragonfly. Follow my finger. Look. Out there. See? That's where we're going. That's Mt. Katahdin."

The forest floor was carpeted over in leaf-fall and Bartleby couldn't have said exactly when this had happened. It seemed like one day everything had been dark green or just hinting at the coming change in season. And then, suddenly, the trail was buried beneath a brilliant litter of leaves. Somehow, despite being out in the woods night and day, he'd blinked and missed the seasonal transitional.

The day was still and crisply bright. What remained of the over-head canopy was visibly thinned. Despite the lack of any breeze, leaves kept letting go their grip on life and spiraling down to join the growing, golden ranks of the fallen.

Beautiful as this all was, Bartleby kept his head down and his eyes focused ahead. The leaves were ankle-deep and treacherously slick underfoot. The usual trail hazards of rock and root were completely obscured. He kicked up a leafy scatter with each crunching step.

As he came around a bend, Bartleby flinched back.

Trailside and tucked partially behind a rock, a silver-haired woman sat working at a tangle of yarn with knitting needles.

"Sorry," she said. "I didn't mean to startle you."

Jane raised an eyebrow, looked from Bartleby to the woman and back again. Then she sat her rump down and sighed, as if to say, "It wasn't me that had been startled."

The woman's legs were splotched with bruises. These exhibited the full spectrum of rainbow coloring. Both her pack and her clothes possessed that grubby-cum-soiled air of insouciance specific only to thru-hikers and late-stage crack addicts.

"I'm thinking," Bartleby said, "that you must be The Knitty Biddy."

Knitty's eyes lit up, "That's me."

"I'm Bartleby."

"Hello, Bartleby."

"Hi. And this is my hiking partner, Jane."

"Well, isn't that a lovely bell, Jane. I guess I should introduce my little friend, though I'm afraid I don't know his name."

To clear up Bartleby's confusion, Knitty gestured to her leg where a bright green inchworm crawled the length of her shin.

"Just after I sat down, this little soul came rappelling down on a gossamer string. And now he can't quite figure where to go next."

Bartleby squatted down. He and Jane peered in close.

The inchworm humped its way down Knitty's leg. At the first touch of sock, the worm balked, turned and started humping its way upward.

"Same thing happens when he reaches the hem of my shorts."

As soon as it became clear to Jane that no food was forthcoming, she yawned wide, rested her head on her paws and dozed off.

As Bartleby took a seat, he caught a quick whiff of Knitty. She smelled sweetly of time and improbability.

"Been here long?"

"Least an hour now."

"I could brush him off real gentle."

Knitty shook her head, "I don't mind waiting. Sooner or later, he'll figure things out. And besides, who are we to tell him where to go?"

❦ ❦ ❦

There were two unfamiliar faces in residence at Cooper Brook Falls Lean-to when Skunkers and Bawdy arrived. Knitty Biddy and a beaver-faced man at the mean end of middle-age.

"You can call me C4," the man said.

"What—like the explosive?"

C4 rattled a blue and yellow travel-sized game of Connect Four at them, "I used to play with the village kids back in Mozambique during my days with the Peace Corps. My wife gave me this as a gift when I left for a southbound thru-hike in '05 and I still haven't lost a game."

Despite having just hiked eighteen miles over rugged terrain with a heavier than usual pack, Bawdy whooped spiritedly at C4's opening salvo.

"We've got ourselves a winner, ladies and gentlemen," Bawdy announced, "That's gotta take the cake—Peace Corps Volunteer Effect right off the charts. And by a Peace Corps volunteer no less. Fucking brilliant."

Bawdy turned to the woman, held out his hand, "Sorry for the outburst, ma'am. I'm Bawdy."

"Yes," Knitty Biddy agreed, "you are."

Register: Cooper Brook Falls Lean-to

9/11   Under 60 to go! Good thing too, because I am strung out
       and about done in. Feels like I've spent the last 5 months
       chasing after the roadrunner.   Meep-meep, Coyote

"Don't wanna talk about it," Skunkers said.

"It'll help."

"What'd'you know?"

"I know stuff. I'm a nurse."

"ER work's got nothing to do with what's in my head."

"Stop being a baby and answer the question: are they different or always the same?"

Skunkers huffed, "Always the same," through clenched teeth.

"Can you describe it?" When he didn't answer immediately, she was wise enough to wait him out.

Most of a mile later, they reached a stony outcrop. Skunkers stopped and blew out a long breath. "Okay," he said, his voice unusually quiet, "I'm in the desert. The sun is blinding bright overhead. I'm stuck down in the trough between sand dunes. Got no water, no radio, no nuttin' but two good feet. So I start climbing. But it isn't a real dune. I mean, it's sandy an all, so it looks like a dune, but it's *huge*. Big as a mountain. Bigger even. Steep enough, I'm pretty much climbing on all fours. The sand is loose and shifty. For every six steps I take, I lose two or three back in slippage. My feet are sweating, my hands are burning raw in the sand, my legs and back are exhausted from the effort. I don't know if it takes hours, days, maybe years, but finally I get there. I get to the top. And you know what I see?"

A pause, "Nuttin'. There ain't fuckin' nuttin' to see 'cept more dunes and more sand going out past the horizon in every direction.

"Can't see nuttin', can't smell nuttin' and there's no wind, so I can't hear nuttin' but all the quiet and my own breath. I stand up there, turning round and round, trying to see suttin' and catch my breath, but I can't. And I'm not still winded from the climb—I can't catch my breath cuz I'm scared. Not scared I'm gonna die in the desert, not scared of being alone out there or that someone's coming for me. You know what's got me so scared I can't breathe? The fact that I got no earthly idea where I am. I'm not just lost or missing or a coupla klicks off target. No, I'm gone, I'm disappeared, I'm off the whole fucking map.

"The nightmare stops when you're around cuz my sleeping brain recognizes you—your smell, your touch, your whatever—and reminds the confused parts of my mind exactly where I am."

❦ ❦ ❦

It was almost ten o'clock and all quiet at Hurd Brook Lean-to.

By quarter after, two headlamp beams came bobbing out of the darkness. After one last ditch, balls to the wall, twenty-nine-point-seven mile effort from Potaywadjo Lean-to, Thunk and Fancy Pants had caught up with Bartleby.

They were equal parts ecstatic and exhausted.

"Whazzat?" Bartleby mumbled. He'd been fast asleep in the shelter for two hours already, would've kept on sleeping but for someone shaking his foot.

Fancy Pants was laughing and wouldn't let go his big toe, wouldn't stop until Bartleby sat up and acknowledged her. When he finally did, she surprised him with a tight hug that crushed the straw brim of her hat between them.

Jane stood and stepped on Coyote to lick at Thunk's face.

"No way were we letting you summit without us," Fancy Pants scowled happily at him.

Bartleby was all packed, but before starting off, he went over to where Thunk and Fancy Pants had pitched camp. Their tents were facing each other and kissing close.

"You two alive?"

Thunk snored. Fancy managed a drowsy grunt.

"Bawdy says it's like eleven miles to Daicey Pond. Wanna meet there for a late lunch?"

Jane stopped and waited while Bartleby ducked under a low hanging branch.

"—Adria and Johnny. I know—I'm not a huge fan of it either, but it was my father's name and he'd recently died, so we had to go with it. Adria's gonna turn seven in another month, and Johnny turned four back in May. Don't start with that look, I know that look. You think I wanted to miss his birthday?

"Anyway, he's a mess. Leaves food on the floor, all over his face, his clothes. You're going to love him; it'll be like an all-you-can-lick buffet. He'll probably only come up to here on you, so you won't have any problem getting at him with that tongue of yours.

"Now Adria, she might try and dress you up a little. Jewelry, hats and whatnot. And you'll just have to play along. I mean, that's what I'm going to have to do and I don't see why we shouldn't suffer through together. Most days, their grandfather, Bud, comes and takes them for a bit. He's another good old guy, you two should hit it right off.

"Then there's my wife. Honestly, I'm not sure how Angie's gonna feel about you at first. I mean, she'll come to love you, that's a given, but the initial welcome might be a little chilly. I can personally guarantee it won't be chillier than the reception she gives me, so don't let it get you down.

"And don't kid yourself. It's not going to be easy fitting ourselves into their lives. It's going to take a lot of time and effort. But after walking twenty-two hundred miles across fourteen states, I'm guessing we both know something about time and effort."

As northbounders crossed over Abol Bridge, they took pictures of Katahdin in the near distance and otherwise marveled at how little trail was still left ahead of them, how close they were to the end of their journey. But not Bawdy. He peered over the bridge rail, got a good look down at the rushing waters of the Penobscot River. Remembering Mocking Jay's "AWOL at Abol" story, Bawdy shook his head at the idea of trying to swim across with a sinking backpack in tow.

Since dogs weren't welcome in Baxter State Park, Bartleby had had to make arrangements in Monson with a woman who offered kenneling services. And, as promised, the dog lady was waiting in the parking lot of a general store on the far side of the bridge when he, Bawdy and Jane arrived. Jane was so dog-tired, so ready to be done walking through the woods, she didn't hesitate when invited into the back seat of the woman's car. She climbed in and settled herself with what could've been interpreted as a relieved sigh. The dog biscuits waiting for her on the seat sealed the deal.

"Just for the night," Bartleby explained through the open window. Jane stuck her head out and barked, as if to say, "Take your time, have fun and don't worry about me, I'll happily sleep in this backseat for the next week."

The silhouette of Jane's large head, ears a-flapping in the wind, was the last thing Bartleby saw as the Subaru vanished around a corner.

"She'll be fine, Mopesy," Bawdy said. "Listen, don't be getting all glassy-eyed. Come on," he gestured at the store, "I'll buy you a breakfast sandwich or something."

❦ ❦ ❦

There wasn't any wind when Bartleby reached Daicey Pond Campground. The pond was so still, it was possible to see a reflected view of Katahdin on its shiny surface. The colors in the reflection were surprisingly sharp and more vibrant than the actual view itself.

Bartleby crossed to a picnic table, peeled his shirt off and sprawled across a bench to wait for Thunk and Fancy Pants to catch up.

As he lay there, a single goose passed overhead, forlornly *hrrrr-huuuunking* its way southward. He imagined flapping his way down to southern New England. Figured it couldn't be all that difficult to find his home from the air—at least if he hit Long Island Sound he'd know he'd gone too far.

Over these last five and a half months, Katahdin had gone from a far-flung pipe dream to a concrete abstract to an inevitable reality. As the miles had ticked down, Bartleby spent more and more time thinking about home and how he'd get there (hoped he had scrimped away enough for a bus ticket from Bangor). About what he might say to Angie and the kids in that first moment he arrived (nothing worthwhile had come to mind) and what he'd do when he got there.

Any and everything to keep from losing the forward momentum he'd gathered. First priority would be to drag Comfy Chair out into the backyard and set that soul-trap burning.

In Monson, he'd gone out of his way to get on the internet. With sweating palms and shaky fingers, Bartleby searched the obituary section of his hometown paper. He didn't think he could handle learning that kind of news at the threshold of his front door. Thankfully though, he found nothing to indicate his family wasn't still alive and well.

His reverie was broken by the whirring of a camera lens. When he opened his eyes, Fancy Pants was standing a few feet away, zooming in for a close up.

"Here, come look."

Except for the baggy shorts, there was nothing that Bartleby recognized about the man in the picture.

Not the defined calves or the smile loitering behind the unfamiliar scruff of beard. Not the deeply tanned limbs or the gleaming white torso. Certainly not the rib tips showing beneath his concave chest or the taut sheath of muscle wrapped around his abdomen. Not the sunburned nose and forehead nor the unruly tangle of cowlicks and curls up top.

The straight posture, the clear eyes, the months of wild hair growth and the vibrant aura—all of it made him feel like he was looking at someone else entirely.

❦ ❦ ❦

Mornings were coming noticeably later now. It was actually still dark-dark when Skunkers' alarm went off at 5:30 am.

Few words were exchanged as people packed their gear for the last time.

❦

Register: Birches Lean-to

9/15   Hip-hop, hip-hip-hop, hip-hip-hop, hooray!   Bawdy

9/15   One and done. Over and out. Best time ever. Skunkers

9/15   Happy to be done, but I'm sure gonna miss having my boys
       around.   Flutterby

9/15   Coyote Slick says, "A quick climb up K and then I'm back to
       riding the donkey. Suckers ain't gonna know what hit 'em."

9/15   Hope to be back in ten for another go round.
                              —Old Man Trouble

9/15   Now I really gotta start job hunting. Boooo!
                                        Thunk

9/15   Ha-ha, Hairbrained!   Fancy Pants

9/15   Who woulda guessed?   Bartleby + Jane

❦

Instead of staying at Birches Lean-to with the other thru-hikers, Old Man Trouble had booked a campsite in Katahdin Stream Campground proper. When the crew came trooping past, Mrs. Trouble, was just starting to cook thick strips of bacon over a feisty campfire. She waved up at the gray sky, "It's doesn't look too good now, but I hope it cooperates and you get a view. Either way, I'll have a couple dozen BLTs waiting when you come back down."

Except for the barest necessities, they left their gear (a wild jumble of dirty, worn stuff sacks and sleeping pads) with Mrs. Trouble. Old Man Trouble gave his wife a quick kiss before leading the group: Coyote, Skunkers, Flutterby, Fancy Pants, Thunk, Bartleby and

Bawdy along the final segment of the Appalachian Trail.

❧

The summit of Katahdin loomed five miles north of Katahdin Steam Campground and more than a mile above sea level. Under a canopy of black spruce, speckled alder and paper birch trees, the AT paralleled Katahdin Stream back toward its source. At Katahdin Stream Falls, the trail crossed over a rough log bridge and left the waterway behind. It was here that the climb began in earnest.

As the sound of falling water faded away, it was replaced by the sound of heavy breathing. Hundreds of steep stone steps led them upward. At the back of the line, Bartleby and Bawdy were sucking some serious wind. They would occasionally pause to catch their breath, and once he had, Bawdy used it to curse out the trail's precipitousness. As their way grew increasingly sharp, so did his language.

The trail became so steep that hiking poles actually became more hindrance than help. There were more than a few spots whose navigation required both hands free. After his poles got tangled between his legs for the third time, Bartleby collapsed them and lashed them to his pack.

Upon reaching tree line, "What the *fuuuuck*?" was all Bawdy could say. This next section, Hunt Spur, was most of a mile of rising rock with all the trajectory of a painter's ladder reaching to a high eave. Here the AT was less like a hiking trail and more like something you needed the stamina and surefootedness of a mountain goat to scale. The trail passed over and between massive boulders with the help of the occasional well-placed iron rung or handhold. Up and up and up they scrabbled, scrambled and slipped over granite ledges, stone risers and precipitous clifflets. As Bartleby struggled to navigate one particularly tricky bit of foot-over-hand hiking, he couldn't help but be grateful Jane was missing this.

Somewhere in there, the AT latched onto an increasingly distinct ridgeline. It followed this ridge through the top half of the Spur, and eventually, out into an area known as Tableland. Here the trail reverted back to actual, recognizable hiking path and proceeded along at a much more gentle rise. Fragile alpine tundra and loose slabs of rock dominated the barren landscape. Down below, the dark woods and stony mountains of Maine stretched to the horizon.

Skunkers pointed westward, "Looks like we might actually get a view."

The morning's cloud cover wasn't as thick or as close as it had seemed earlier and a persistent wind out of the west was slowly sweeping away the gray and leaving an icy blue sky in its place.

The cloud cover broke for good near Thoreau Spring, a mile short of the end. There were clouds overhead and then there weren't. With the angled brilliance of the morning sun, it was easy to see that Fall had beat them to the summit. To either side of the trail, a spongy carpet of fuzzy mosses, ghostly lichens and short stemmed grasses had taken on various autumnal tones.

The crew was surprisingly quiet during this ascent. Gone was the usual witless banter, the entertainingly inane stories (about the poker feud Coyote had going with James Woods back at the casino), the personal histories (how Thunk used to drive the ball-buggy at a driving range), the in-depth discussions of undeserving pop-culture minutia (the names and occupations of all the Smurfs) and the futilely foolish arguments (who was more badass: He-Man, Lion-O or Thundarr the Barbarian).

It was as if each of the hikers was alone, lost in their own thoughts and anxieties around the future and the happenings of the last five months. They were individually shrouded in an almost spiritual solemnity, like brown-robed monks hunched under vows of silence.

And then without realizing how close he was, Bartleby looked up and could make out the summit sign. It was only a couple hundred feet further. He and Bawdy reached it together; they were the last to arrive.

Thick posts angled together to make two inverted vees holding a wide wooden plaque. The aged wood was gouged up from long years of exposure to the elements. All along the way north, they'd seen hundreds of summits photos on the walls of hostels but now they were seeing the sign for real. For themselves. Bartleby ran his finger over the routed lettering:

KATAHDIN
NORTHERN TERMINUS OF THE
APPALACHIAN TRAIL

And there, the becalmed quietude burst like a balloon. Apprehensions about what came next dissipated amongst the euphoria of the moment. They'd done it. This crew of oddballs and misfits that had come together over the last months had actually done it. They'd thru-hiked the Appalachian Trail. Each one of them had walked 2,181 miles from Springer Mountain, Georgia.

Fancy Pants whooped and danced a funny little jig. Coyote gave his now trademark howl. Skunkers booya'ed and produced a bottle of champagne.

Which set Coyote to yelping, "I don't even wanna guess how many miles you been carrying that, do I Skunk?"

"Or how many states neither, Slick."

After popping the cork off into the stratosphere, Skunkers passed the bottle around. There were hugs and high-fives, an album's worth of pictures and a few tears.

Coyote caught Bawdy's attention, grinned big and said, "Fragged."

Bawdy had a bunch more stored up and ready to go. Would've been easy-as-pie to fire a few of them back, but instead he laughed and let Coyote have the win.

After the group poses, Bartleby sat off by himself, his sweat steaming and his skin dimpling in the chill wind. Bawdy wandered over and slapped him on the back, "Welcome to Endsville, bro. Population: us." When Bartleby gave him a little smile, Bawdy followed with, "And let me just say, that's some wife you got yourself, B."

The smile disappeared with the elusive speed of a flushed rabbit.

"What? Why do you say that?"

"Well, I don't really know anything about marriage and I've never set eyes on your Angie, but I mean, look at you now, dude. Remember when you showed up at the shelter back on Springer?"

"Like a zombie, right?"

"You made zombies look good. And now, now you're walking and talking like a real live person. I mean, you aren't gonna win any prizes for congeniality, but shit, you're definitely back in the land of the living. And all because that wife of yours manned-up and kicked your lame ass all the way down to Amicalola."

"Yeah?"

"Yeah. And you know what else?"

"What?"

"It's all downhill from here."

Bartleby nodded, but he wasn't so sure. He imagined these last months had been little more than a warm-up. Like prying a stubborn lid off an old paint can. Only after working the lid free could you actually get to work.

But that was okay, because he felt ready to work. Ready to enjoy the good stuff and face down the bad stuff. Ready to be a father, a husband and a human being again. Now, finally, he felt ready for life with all of its endlessly unknowable everything.

THE END

EPILOGUE

Minus the beard and wearing civilian clothes (baggy jeans, sneakers and a hoodie), Bartleby is barely recognizable as he peruses the aisles of a small grocery store. He tosses various items into a grocery cart—frozen corn, canned cranberry sauce, Yukon potatoes and a big turkey. At the checkout counter, he bags his own groceries. Instead of packing the food into plastic shopping bags, he stuffs everything into his pack.

"Mister," the checkout girl says, "that looks pretty heavy."

Just outside the store, leashed to a bench, Jane waits for him. He unlatches her leash. A random old man sitting nearby says, "Got yourself a good dog there."

"She's a *great* dog," Bartleby corrects him. "And it's looking like my wife's gonna let me keep her."

As Bartleby and Jane walk along the main street of a picturesque New England town, Thanksgiving decorations are visible in shop windows. A steady stream of cars pass, as does the occasional snow flurry. The sky overhead is a cold gray.

All but pulling on her leash now, Jane heads for home. Bartleby has to tug her back at a crosswalk.

"We got one more thing to do," he explains.

They cross the street and stop outside the town post office. He produces a manila envelope from his pack. It is addressed to someone in Chicago named Jack.

Bartleby pulls a little black notebook from his pocket and pens a quick note inside the front cover:

Bawdy,

Hope the readjustment period hasn't been too rough. Mostly, I am always hungry and my knees still ache. Looking for work. Guess you probably are too.

Angie doesn't know what to make of me, but I think we're okay. Or at least, I'm okay. WE weren't the problem. She loves me being skinny again. Jane is a big hit with the kids. She herds them around just like she used to with Chatter.

Found that little notebook of yours. Can't help but think you might still need it someday. Happy Holidays.

Your friends,
B + J

Bartleby puts the book on the ground and helps Jane stamp her footprint at the bottom.

❧

With their chores complete, Bartleby and Jane hustle across a large parking lot. Fast as he walks, Jane pulls on the leash, urging him forward. He checks his watch, grimaces and increases the pace. The pack bounces around on his back, the various cans and glass containers within clanking and sloshing excitedly. Jane leads him through a residential neighborhood. The houses aren't big or fancy; some are cute, most are simply well-maintained.

Man and dog cross through an empty lot, the back corner of a neighbor's yard and finally, into their own. Out front, a yellow school bus is just rolling to a stop.

Bartleby stoops to let Jane off the leash. Barking now, she tears away and ahead. He follows as fast as he can. Shucks his pack in the yard, near an ugly burnt husk; little more than a blackened metal frame and sprung coils—likely the charred remains of a recliner chair.

The bus starts to accelerate away without having let off any children when Jane gallops around the side of the house.

The bus jerks to a stop, but still the doors don't accordion open. Even when Jane whuffs at them, as if to say, "Open sesame."

Bartleby hobbles along on stiff knees, red-faced and sweating. When he reaches the front yard, his hand is up, waving to the bus driver.

"I'm here," he calls. "It's okay, I'm here."

Made in the USA
Middletown, DE
07 July 2022

68756617R00184